continued . . .

"If you loved Jennifer Weiner's *Fly Away Home* for its wise and witty look at the lives of people grappling with personal setbacks . . . then try *Ten Beach Road* . . . [a] warm, wry novel."
—*St. Petersburg Times*

"A lovely story that recognizes the power of the female spirit, while being fun, emotional, and a little romantic."
—*Fresh Fiction*

"Fun . . . heartwarming . . . [This] dynamic, fast-paced story is a loving tribute to friendship and the power of the female spirit."
—*Las Vegas Review-Journal*

"A near perfect summertime read . . . Beautiful setting and lovable characters . . . Full of: laughter, heartache, secrets, loyalty, and courage."
—*Night Owl Reviews*

"Funny, heartbreaking, romantic, and so much more . . . This story about recovery and restoration on so many levels is just delightful!"
—*The Best Reviews*

"Wax keeps the plot twists coming . . . Great escape reading, perfect for the beach."
—*Library Journal*

MAGNOLIA WEDNESDAYS

"Wax, the author of *The Accidental Bestseller*, writes with breezy wit and keen insight into family relations."
—*The Atlanta Journal-Constitution*

"An honest, realistic story of family, love, and priorities, with genuine characters."
—*Booklist*

"Bittersweet . . . Vivien's an easy protagonist to love; she's plucky, resourceful, and witty."
—*Publishers Weekly*

"Atlanta-based novelist Wendy Wax spins yet another captivating tale of life and love in this wonderfully entertaining book."

—*Southern Seasons Magazine*

THE ACCIDENTAL BESTSELLER

"It's a definite must for any beach bag this summer . . . Wax does a fantastic job giving readers an insight into the cutthroat world of New York publishing, and the story provides inspiration to budding novelists." —*Sacramento Book Review*

"A wise and witty foray into the hearts of four amazing women and the publishing world they inhabit. This is a beautiful book about loyalty, courage, and pursuing your dreams with a little help from your friends. I loved this book!" —Karen White

"A warm, triumphant tale of female friendship and the lessons learned when life doesn't turn out as planned . . . Sure to appeal."

—*Library Journal*

"A terrific story brimming with wit, warmth, and good humor. I loved it!" —Jane Porter, author of *The Good Daughter*

"A wry, revealing tell-all about friendship and surviving the world of publishing."

—Haywood Smith, *New York Times* bestselling author

"Entertaining . . . Provides a lot of insight into the book business, collected, no doubt, from Wax's own experiences."

—*St. Petersburg Times*

OCEAN BEACH

WENDY WAX

JOVE BOOKS, NEW YORK

THE BERKLEY PUBLISHING GROUP
Published by the Penguin Group
Penguin Group (USA) Inc.
375 Hudson Street, New York, New York 10014, USA

USA | Canada | UK | Ireland | Australia | New Zealand | India | South Africa | China

Penguin Books Ltd., Registered Offices: 80 Strand, London WC2R 0RL, England
For more information about the Penguin Group, visit penguin.com.

OCEAN BEACH

A Jove Book / published by arrangement with the author

Jove Books are published by The Berkley Publishing Group.
JOVE® is a registered trademark of Penguin Group (USA) Inc.
The "J" design is a trademark of Penguin Group (USA) Inc.

For information, address: The Berkley Publishing Group,
a division of Penguin Group (USA) Inc.,
375 Hudson Street, New York, New York 10014.

ISBN: 978-0-515-15428-3

PUBLISHING HISTORY
Berkley trade paperback edition / July 2012
Jove mass-market edition / July 2013

PRINTED IN THE UNITED STATES OF AMERICA

10 9 8 7 6 5 4 3 2 1

Cover design by Rita Frangie.
Cover photo by George Shelley Productions / Getty Images.
Text design by Kristin del Rosario.

This is a work of fiction. Names, characters, places, and incidents either are the product
of the author's imagination or are used fictitiously, and any resemblance to actual persons,
living or dead, business establishments, events, or locales is entirely coincidental.
The publisher does not have any control over and does not assume any responsibility for
author or third-party websites or their content.

ALWAYS LEARNING   **PEARSON**

This book is dedicated to Zena Adler
with love and gratitude.

You are missed.

ACKNOWLEDGMENTS

No book springs completely from the imagination. There are always so many things to learn and understand before, during, and after the writing has begun. Although the Internet is a great tool, for me there's nothing as satisfying as talking to people willing to share their knowledge and expertise.

This time out I'd like to thank Jeff Donelly, Public Historian, Miami Design Preservation League, for that first phone conversation and for pointing me in the right direction as I considered where on South Beach my story should be set.

Thank you, too, to Sharon Hartley, author and tour guide, for that first personal tour, and to Amanda Bush at the MDPL for funneling me to the right people.

Eternal gratitude goes to Lori Bakkum and Nate Miller of Retro Home Miami, who shared their knowledge and passion for the area, got me into some incredible homes, and answered every question I threw their way, sometimes more than once. Thanks also go to Julien Bergier of DN'A Design & Architecture. I knew as soon as we drove up to the Lenox house that I'd found The Millicent. Who knew that a day that began with a seagull treating me like its personal port-a-let could turn out so well?

A special thank you to Karen Kendall and Don Moser for

helping me experience the location more fully. I'm still smiling about our adventures, but my lips are sealed. "What happens in South Beach stays in South Beach."

Thanks to Tito Vargas and Rob Griffin for sharing their knowledge of construction, and to Rebecca Ritchie, interior designer extraordinaire, for her contributions to the look and feel of The Millicent.

Thanks are also owed to Sergeant Andres Varela, Special Victims Bureau, Miami-Dade Police Department, Debra Weierman of the FBI, as well as to the ever knowledgeable and always generous members of crimescenewriters.

Any and all mistakes are my own.

My thanks also go to charitable donors Lisa Hogan and Pamela Gentry, who won the right to lend their names to characters in this book. I'm not sure why such generous people tend to end up as such unpleasant characters—I can't seem to help it. Just ask Tonja Kay.

As always, I'm greatly indebted to authors Karen White and Susan Crandall for their friendship and insights. And for always taking my calls. (I think.)

Thanks also go to my agent, Stephanie Kip Rostan, for being the calm voice of reason and for always having—or finding—an answer.

Prologue

Millie couldn't bear to see her husband cry. He really didn't have the face for it. Or the experience. When you made your living making other people laugh, tears weren't a part of your repertoire. In all the time she'd known him, she'd only seen Max cry once. And that had been more than fifty years ago.

She, on the other hand, had become an expert at tears. But she'd also become an expert at hiding them.

"You're too old to cry," she said. "And I've got better things to do than lie here letting you drip tears all over me."

He smiled, as she'd intended. "What? You've got some-where else you have to be?" He used the beleaguered tone he'd played to the hilt onstage. The one that said, *See what I have to put up with?*

She reached up to wipe a tear from his weathered cheek and her eyes closed briefly. Who knew how heavy eyelids could be? "Yes, I do. I'm just waiting for that tunnel of light you hear about. Then I'm out of here." She tried for a sassy tone, but even moving her lips took effort. "I'll finally have the spotlight to myself for once."

Max smiled again. It was the smile she'd always thought of as his megawatter. A heart could break from that smile.

"You've always been the star, Millie," Max said. "Always. I was just the lucky guy who got to stand next to you." He swallowed thickly. "I don't want to be here without you."

The weight of good-bye hung over them. She cupped his face in her hand, ready to go. Except for one thing.

"Promise me you'll look for him one more time, Max," she said. "It's easier to find people now. Like on TV. That woman was missing for thirty years."

She stared into his eyes, using the last of her strength to will him to do what he'd refused even to talk about for so long. "Promise."

Finally he nodded. "I will, Millie." He took the hand that had fallen to her side and gave it a squeeze just like he had the first—and every—time they'd stepped onto a stage together.

"And get the house fixed up," she said. "He'll never recognize it the way it is now. I want you to get it ready. You know, for when he comes home."

She held on to his hand as long as she could, treasuring its warmth and comfort. Wanting to take it with her. "Do you promise, Max?"

A tear ran down his cheek. She watched it fall. Felt it land on their clasped hands.

"I promise."

Chapter One

Never let them see you sweat.

Nicole Grant, former dating guru and A-list matchmaker, knew it was a bad sign when the philosophy you were living by came from a deodorant commercial. As words of wisdom went, they were nowhere near as lofty as "Nothing succeeds like success" or quite as motivational as "If at first you don't succeed, try, try again." But as she stood in the archway of Bitsy Baynard's Palm Beach dining room struggling not to wipe her damp palms down the sides of the vintage Valentino cocktail dress, those words were pretty much all she had.

No one in that room knew, or would ever know, that she'd spent a good chunk of her remaining cash on a salon cut and color, or that her makeup had been applied for free at a Saks Fifth Avenue cosmetics counter after she'd made a show of cursing the airlines and pretending abject horror at arriving in Palm Beach without a cosmetics case.

She squared her shoulders and made her way through

the formal dining room to her seat, thanking the goddess of the gene pool that at forty-six she still had an air of command, a graceful neck, and her trademark cheekbones. A lifelong running habit and a recent, if unwelcome, bout of physical labor had prevented her once-speedy metabolism from sputtering to a stop.

Bitsy's table had been set for twenty. As she'd promised, her guest list had been culled from the appallingly short list of Palm Beach residents who had *not* lost money to Nicole's brother, Malcolm Dyer, who had recently checked into a medium-security prison for the criminally greedy.

Bitsy had assured her that none of the guests would bring up Malcolm's Ponzi scheme, which had bankrupted Nicole as completely as it had its hundreds of victims. But as they took their seats Nicole could feel their eyes on her like motorists unable to drive by a car wreck without slowing down to take a look.

Nicole raised her chin and welcomed their glances; every one of them was a potential client or a possible referral source. She smiled her thanks to Bitsy when she saw the seat that she'd been assigned. It was next to Helen Maryn, a divorcée whose first husband had left her for a well-known jockey and whose second had fled to a Tibetan monastery to find himself, a search so consuming that he'd still been looking three years later when Helen had found and divorced him.

Helen Maryn's face was round and pink and she bore an unfortunate resemblance to Miss Piggy. But while her physical attributes appeared skimpy, her net worth did not.

"So are you like the Millionaire Matchmaker?" Helen asked when the first course had been cleared away.

"Yes," Nicole replied with a friendly smile. "But without the four-letter words and the funky-haired staff."

Or the money and fame. All of which her brother had stolen.

"Nicole brought Bertrand and me together," Bitsy said helpfully with a smile for her husband, who had proved to be far more than a worthwhile investment. "She has a lot of high-profile marriages on her résumé. But she's very discreet."

Nicole threw Bitsy a smile of affection and gratitude. Bitsy and Bertrand's match had been one of Nicole's most satisfying achievements. Of the hundreds of wealthy and celebrity clients she'd found mates for, only Bitsy had not rolled up her welcome mat once Nicole's relationship to Malcolm Dyer had become public.

A fine bead of perspiration broke out on Nicole's upper lip and she reminded herself yet again that she was not to blame for Malcolm's crime. She was *not* her grown brother's keeper. The federal government had claimed that job.

She maintained her smile as the trout à la russe was served, and willed herself to enjoy it. She didn't foresee a meal prepared by a Cordon Bleu chef anywhere in her near future; there was no way she was going to waste it.

"And she's part of a new television show on Lifetime," Bitsy continued. "A home renovation program. She and her costars redid Bella Flora, a great Mediterranean Revival home that they own over on the west coast of Florida. And now they're going to do a place down on South Beach in Miami." She turned to Nicole. "What's the show called, Nikki?"

"Do Over." Which was what she was hoping the show

would turn into. "The pilot airs July first," Nicole added, seeing no need to mention that this opportunity would involve another backbreaking summer sweating over a house under the unrelenting eye of a video camera. Or that this time she and Madeline Singer and Avery Lawford would be laboring on a house that didn't belong to them and that they hadn't seen so much as a picture of.

Nicole reached for her wineglass. "If the pilot does well, the Miami episodes will air next spring."

If it didn't, sweating in front of others would be the least of her problems.

Across the table an eagle-eyed woman followed their conversation. Leaning forward, she offered up what might have been a smile if plastic surgery had left her any control of her facial muscles. "It must be impossible to find clients now," she said. "I mean, your company doesn't really exist anymore, does it?" Her tone should have been accompanied by a raised eyebrow, but this method of emphasis was no longer available to her. Both of her eyebrows arched upward in a perpetual state of surprise.

"*I* am Heart, Incorporated," Nicole said, raising one eyebrow, just to demonstrate that she could. "I've closed the New York and L.A. offices, but they're only addresses. I still offer the same services and set the highest possible standards in safeguarding my clients." She widened both eyes subtly just to make the woman jealous. "And I still guarantee results."

After all, she'd found an appropriately ripe young woman for the Greek grocery tycoon, Darios T., and delivered a laundry list of attributes from leg length to brain size for others. She'd learned over the years that marriage could be founded on many things as long as the risk–reward ratio appeared equally beneficial.

Nicole kept the conversation with Helen Maryn going over dessert and afterward in the grand salon, a wonderful room lined with floor-to-ceiling windows that overlooked the estate's beautifully manicured grounds. But even without the frozen-faced woman's inept smirk, she could tell that she'd lost her.

"I'd be happy to meet with you tomorrow before I drive down to Miami," Nicole said to Helen, careful to keep the desperation out of her voice. "We could have a late lunch and discuss what you're looking for." Even if she had to use her emergency credit card to pay for the meal, it would be worth it to collect a retainer and land a high-profile client. All she needed was one to build from.

Helen's eyes slid away. The woman with the frozen face nodded and lifted half a lip.

Keeping her own smile in place, Nicole pulled a card from her evening bag and handed it to Helen. For the rest of the evening she pretended that she didn't have a care or a debt in the world and that her matchmaking days were not over.

"She wiggled off the hook, didn't she?" Bitsy asked when she'd closed the massive wood door behind the last of her guests.

Nicole nodded and managed an unconcerned shrug. "I appreciate the evening. The meal was wonderful." She hugged Bitsy. "I won't forget your efforts on my behalf."

In the plush guest suite Nicole stepped out of the gray silk dress and hung it carefully on a padded hanger. In the gilt and mirrored bathroom she twisted her hair up in a clip, eyed the spa robe that hung on the back of the door, and opened the expensive jar of bubble bath that sat beside the claw-foot tub. She turned on the tap, and when the tub was full, she lowered herself into the steaming-hot water and sighed at its buoyant loveliness.

With her eyes closed and her body cocooned in the fragrant warmth, Nicole pushed back her worries, determined to enjoy this last night of luxury. She had no idea what she and Madeline and Avery would find in Miami. Or what conditions they'd be living in. Tomorrow would be soon enough to face those realities; all of their futures hinged on an uncertain television career and the sale of Bella Flora in the worst real estate market since the Great Depression.

Burrowing deeper into the warm water, Nicole reached for the waiting loofah. Tomorrow she'd meet up with the women who'd so unexpectedly become her friends. Together they'd do their best to make *Do Over* a success.

But until they knew they had a hit show and the rewards that that entailed, she couldn't afford to give up on rebuilding Heart, Incorporated. Even in today's economy Miami was rife with celebrities and high-net-worth individuals.

If she was lucky, she might find someone who'd never heard of her felonious brother. Someone who didn't read or speak English. Or who had been able to afford a ride on a Soyuz spacecraft and had just returned to earth.

...

"To us!" Steve Singer's tone was jubilant as he raised his wineglass to Madeline and smiled across the cloth-draped table of Bacchanalia, one of Atlanta's finest restaurants. "To twenty-six years as man and wife."

Madeline clinked her glass to his and took a long sip. The flickering candlelight turned his gray eyes a metallic shade of silver and cast shadows across the planes and angles of his still-handsome face. If she squinted just right, she could almost see Steve as he'd been when they'd first met twenty-seven years ago. Then he'd been tall and trimly built, his manner reassuringly calm and certain. For a moment Madeline could almost feel the too-rapid tattoo of her heart in her chest each time she saw him. And the delicious ache in her jaw that had come from hours of nonstop talk and laughter.

Today, they had crossed the great marital divide; she had now been married to Steve Singer longer than she'd been single. Madeline smiled and raised her glass for another clink. "Happy anniversary," she said. "To us!"

Steve watched her face as they drained their wineglasses and Maddie pressed play on their joint highlight reel to search for a specifically fabulous memory to drink to.

She realized just how many great moments there'd been as she fast-forwarded through the years in her mind. She paused over the births of their children Kyra and Andrew, and all of the special moments that had filled her twenty-plus years as a stay-at-home mom. Freeze-frames of Steve's achievements in the financial world followed along with the best of their family holidays and vacations.

Not that long ago she would have put their reel up against anyone's. Maybe even nominated it for Best Movie and Screenplay. So much of their marital movie deserved applause.

But the last year and a half had been brutal. It had reframed an entire lifetime of memories.

Maddie drank the rest of her wine while the waiter combed the last offending crumbs from the tablecloth and retreated with a bow, promising to return shortly with coffee and dessert.

She tried the squinting thing again but couldn't block

out the image of Steve lying on the couch after he'd lost his job, their savings, and, finally, his backbone.

Somehow they'd survived the nuclear blast that blew their lives apart. In many ways they still looked the same. All of their limbs remained intact. But inside, Maddie knew, their guts had been rearranged. She was afraid that crucial pieces might be missing.

Eyeing her empty wineglass, she almost smiled as the line "Other than that, Mrs. Lincoln, how did you like the play?" ran through her head.

"Mad? Maddie?"

Madeline blinked and dragged her gaze back to Steve. She looked directly into his eyes, which were the color of a stormy sky with clouds of what she recognized as hurt.

"I'm sorry," she said. "What did you say?"

"I said, I have a job now. You don't have to go to Miami and work like a slave on that house." His tone was eminently rational. "The television series is a crapshoot—nothing may even come of it—and for such a big network they're not even offering a living wage."

This much was true. But if Madeline had learned anything during their personal nuclear meltdown, it was that it was better to act than be acted upon. If she hadn't spent last summer in St. Petersburg with Avery and Nicole trying to bring the dilapidated Bella Flora back to life, they wouldn't even have that potential asset. And she wouldn't have this opportunity to do a television series with her daughter and the strangers who had become Madeline's friends.

"*Do Over* is a big break for all of us and especially for Kyra," Madeline said. "It was her documentation of our work at Bella Flora that made it happen and she deserves to reap whatever rewards come out of it." She shook her head, still amazed at how completely their daughter, now a far too young single mother, had turned her life around.

Steve reached for her hand. "Then let Kyra go. She'll shoot the video, Avery will run the construction, Avery's mother can handle the interior design. Nicole will do whatever it is she does." He smiled winningly. "I know how you like to mother everyone—and you're really great at it—but they'll survive without you."

Madeline stilled. "So you don't think I add value?"

"I didn't say that."

No, he hadn't. Not exactly. But that was the thing about being married longer than you'd been single. You no longer needed an interpreter for what had been left unsaid. She drew her hand back.

Not that long ago, when Andrew had left for college and their nest had first emptied, she'd dreamed of her own craft room and long periods of doing nothing, but she wasn't that person anymore. Now all that nothingness just looked like . . . not quite enough.

"We're married," Steve said. "I love you and I want you here with me. Where you belong."

"I love you too," she said. She did not need to replay their reel again to know that. "That's not what this is about. I can't just let Kyra go down to Miami and handle what could be the project of her life while she takes care of our six-month-old grandson by herself."

Nor did she want to.

The chocolate mousse and coffees arrived. Steve stirred cream and sugar into his coffee and took an exploratory bite of the dessert.

"I thought you were okay with this," Maddie said. He

had helped her pack the minivan for the drive down tomorrow and hadn't said a word.

"They're not paying you enough for this to make sense," Steve continued, turning on the earnest charm that normally served him so well. "I have an income now, and I'm starting to build clientele again. If Bella Flora sells, we can erase pretty much all of our debt."

He put down his spoon and reached for her hand once more. It was beginning to feel like the prize in a tug-of-war. "You've done enough, Maddie. I'm sorry you've had to do so much. But I know the worst is behind us. Or it will be if you let it."

There it was. The subtext to everything that had and hadn't been said. The thing they tiptoed so carefully around. Steve wanted to pretend that he hadn't broken rank and run when their foxhole had been shelled. He hadn't forgiven her for taking on the enemy, not really. And despite all the months of trying, she hadn't completely forgiven him for forcing her to do it.

Maddie watched her husband eat the mousse and sip his coffee, but could no longer imagine swallowing either.

"I'm sorry," she said as gently as she could. "But I've signed a contract with the network and I've given my word to Avery and Nicole. I know Kyra is counting on my help with the baby. But I am counting on you coming down to visit often."

Because she knew that it would hurt him, she was careful not to give away how much she was looking forward to working on this project with her friends and her daughter. And that she hoped that *Do Over* would be exactly that for all of them.

Chapter Two

Long before she went to college to study architecture, Avery Lawford was painfully aware that her exterior and her interior did not match. Like a multimillion-dollar Manhattan co-op filled with IKEA furniture or a Frank Lloyd Wright built around a Country French kitchen, her form just didn't fit her function.

The problem began with her height, which was too short to command respect, and was compounded by china-doll features, an oversize bust, and the kind of blue-eyed blondness that caused complete strangers to deduct IQ points and to speak to her slowly. Using really small words.

Avery was thirty-six, and despite her education and three years on HGTV, her struggle to be taken seriously continued. Even the successful—if desperate—double renovation of Bella Flora, the 1920s Mediterranean Revival–style mansion in front of which she now stood—had failed to garner respect.

Bella Flora had no such problem. The house sat in the

afternoon sun like a massive wedding cake fresh from the bakery box. Pale pink walls with white icing trim framed banks of arched windows. Bell towers topped a multi-angled barrel-tile roof and jutted up into the cloudless sky. Her massive façade stood in beautiful contrast to the deep blue-green of the Gulf of Mexico and the bay it bled into.

Avery's satisfied gaze skimmed from the house to the shiny new "For Sale" sign that dangled over the low garden wall. She knew and loved every inch of Bella Flora, had touched almost every part of the grande dame with her own hands.

A truck pulled up to the curb and Chase Hardin, the contractor who'd been a part of both renovations—before and after Hurricane Charlene had damaged so much of the tiny beach community of Pass-a-Grille—and become their partner in the process, joined her.

"I know," he said. "We all need for her to sell, but it's hard to think of someone else living in her."

He smiled, which was a far cry from the way he'd looked at her when they'd first been forced to work together. Then he'd treated her like the Vanna White of the do-it-yourself set instead of the professional she was, and fought her for control of the job. Now his smile caused a jumble of reactions, all of them complicated. "But then I'm not expecting anything to happen all that quickly," he said. "Even without the economy, summer is the absolute worst time to sell expensive Florida real estate."

It wasn't the best time to renovate it either. But none of them could turn down the opportunity that *Do Over* presented.

The worry she'd been tamping down reared its nasty little head. Part of the reason for their success in bringing

Bella Flora back to life lay in the fact that walking away had not been an option. Renovating an unknown house for television could be a dicey thing, and she knew firsthand what could happen when there was a network to answer to.

Avery's gaze moved to her car, which sat on the bricked driveway. The Mini Cooper's convertible top was down. Suitcases and baggage, almost none of it hers, teetered on the backseat and spilled between the front seats.

High heels tapped their way down the brick drive and she looked up to see Deirdre Morgan, Avery's former mother, interior designer to the stars, and unwelcome hitchhiker walking toward them with a large overnight case in her arms.

At sixty-one, Deirdre looked a decade younger. Her makeup was expertly applied and her blond bob had been wrapped in a designer scarf that would no doubt blow artfully behind her as they made their way south. Her chest, like the one she'd bequeathed to Avery, was too large for her frame, but the pale blue silk blouse that she'd tucked into white linen pants was cut for camouflage and her jeweled high-heeled sandals made her almost tall enough to counterbalance the weight.

She looked, Avery thought in irritation, as if she were planning to board a cruise ship, not shoehorn herself into an overstuffed compact for a bugs-in-the-teeth drive across Florida's Alligator Alley.

A whiff of Deirdre's gardenia perfume assaulted Avery's nose and once again Avery wondered why Deirdre had really come back into her life and how long she planned to stay.

"It should be a pretty drive down to Miami," Chase said conversationally.

This might have been true if Avery had been making

the trip down to South Beach without Deirdre and her possessions. And if the network hadn't gotten all wonky, refusing to tell them so much as the address of the house they'd be working on until they got to town.

She watched Deirdre contemplate the car and the makeup case, but made no move to help her figure it out. Avery was already half afraid the trunk would pop open on the highway and shoot Deirdre's possessions into the Everglades like a geyser spewing oil.

"Don't even think about it," she said to Deirdre. "I had to sit on that trunk to get it closed. The only way you're bringing that case is if you intend to hold it on your lap all the way to Miami." Avery removed her sunglasses long enough to stare into a pair of blue eyes the exact same shade as her own. Looking at a far more polished version of herself at every turn was incredibly annoying.

"Fine." Deirdre set the case on the passenger seat and placed her oversize hobo bag on the floor then looked Avery up and down, taking in the ancient halter top, frayed jean cutoffs, and fuchsia flip-flops. "As soon as you change, we can get going."

There was a strangled laugh from Chase, but the man was smart enough to remain silent.

"I'm not getting dressed up to sit in a car for five hours," Avery said. "Kyra promised no filming until tomorrow morning. But just to be clear, I'm not planning to try to protect a manicure or mince around in high heels while I sand floors and paint walls either."

"I know, dear," Deirdre said. "But we don't really know what we'll find when we arrive. Wouldn't it be best to have your game face on?"

"This *is* my game face," Avery said through gritted teeth. "And if it's not working for you, I can drop you off at a car rental place on my way out of town."

"No need," Deirdre replied. Which Avery assumed meant "no money." Like all of them, Deirdre was strapped. Her years as a big-name Hollywood designer, a career for which she'd ditched Avery and her father, had just made her more adept than the rest of them with smoke and mirrors. "I'll be right back." She turned and headed back into the house.

"She's giving us a chance for a private good-bye," Chase said, reaching for Avery and slipping his arms around her waist. His kiss was long and thorough. The power of it still surprised her. "I wish I knew how soon I'll be able to get down."

Avery sighed and looked up, way up, into his eyes. A widower with two teenage sons, Chase was running what had once been their fathers' construction business in a cratered construction climate while dealing with his father's failing health. She still wasn't sure how they'd gone from adversaries to lovers, but she was hyperaware of the daunting load he carried, and did not intend to add to it. "Don't worry about it," she said. "You'll come when you can come."

He let this go by and changed the subject with another kiss. "You can make it in under five hours and there's no sign of rain."

"If I see so much as a raindrop, I'm going to start ditching Deirdre's things on the side of the road so that I can put the top up."

"Are you sure you'll be okay?" Chase asked. "I'm kind of afraid I'm going to see a story in the morning paper about a woman's remains found along Alligator Alley."

"Well, if the remains are sitting on top of a stack of designer luggage, you'll know they're Deirdre's."

He smiled again and ran a hand through his short dark hair. "She's trying, you know." They stepped apart as Deirdre reappeared.

"Maybe." But with Deirdre there was inevitably an angle. Something self-serving that you only discovered when it was too late to protect yourself. Avery wasn't sure what she dreaded more, dealing with Deirdre or the network.

He pulled an envelope from his pocket and handed it to her. "The power of attorney with you listed as my legally designated representative is in here along with a copy of my contractor's license."

"Thanks."

"You can call me anytime," he said. "You know, to consult."

"Don't hold your breath," she replied. She'd grown up on her father's construction sites and she was, after all, a trained architect.

"I could put together a list of potential subs through people I know down there. And I thought we could do a conference call once a week. I know you—"

Avery put a finger to his lips to stop him. While she needed the POA to pull permits and satisfy the municipality, she didn't need Chase Hardin or anyone else to get her through this renovation. She raised her chin and silently dared him to argue, but inside she could feel the flutter of nerves. *Do Over* was more than a renovation project—way more. It was a lifeline for all of them. There could be no screwups.

She gave him a last kiss and Deirdre gave him a hug. They both watched him climb back into his truck and drive off, only wedging themselves into the Mini Cooper when Chase's taillights had disappeared from view.

She didn't speak to Deirdre as they left Pass-a-Grille and turned onto the Pinellas Bayway. Nor did she waste a thought on how uncomfortable Deirdre must be with the travel case on her lap and the purse balanced between her feet. She drove onto the Sunshine Skyway Bridge, which soared high above Tampa Bay, lost in her thoughts. All of those thoughts were unsettling.

She and her mostly merry band were headed to an alien city where they would be expected to renovate a house they'd never seen for an owner they knew nothing about. And they had to keep things interesting enough while they did it to convince the network that *Do Over* deserved to exist.

Avery's hands tightened on the wheel. She knew the sinking sensation in her stomach had nothing to do with the dizzying height of the bridge, but everything to do with fear of the fall.

• • •

It was almost 7:30 P.M. by the time they reached the MacArthur Causeway, which would deposit them on Miami's South Beach. Avery's bare skin was sunburned. Her hair, which had already blown to smithereens hours ago, was heavy with dirt and barely moved in the warm salt-tinged breeze coming off Biscayne Bay. The sun was at half-mast as they caught their first glimpses of the docked cruise ships in the Port of Miami, then watched Palm, Hibiscus, and Star Islands whiz by.

"Nervous?" Deirdre asked.

"No, of course not," Avery lied. They were at the corner of Fifth and Ocean Drive, facing the palm-tree-studded beach that bounded the Atlantic Ocean. It was time to call in for the address of the house they'd be renovating. In a matter of minutes, all her vague fears and worries could be put to rest. Or prove far worse than she'd imagined.

She felt Deirdre's eyes on her. "The call can wait a couple of minutes," Deirdre said. "Take a left. We deserve at least a drive-by of the Art Deco District."

A text "dinged" in but Avery was already turning. She wouldn't have been surprised to hear a celestial choir kick in as she spotted the first of the historic district's famously restored hotels. She held her breath, drinking in the tropical Art Deco façades and details, many of which echoed the themes and shapes of ships at sea. She drove as slowly as she could past the Park Central, the Beacon, the Colony, the Clevelander, the Carlyle. For ten fabulous blocks she pushed both the worry and the anticipation aside.

At a red light, she glanced down at the texts that had continued to ding in.

We're here. Where r u? Like the sender, Nicole Grant's text was direct and to the point.

Madeline Singer, whose thumbs and her iPhone often seemed at odds, had sent one that read, *Ee rhrwre. Bit te plce is . . . 'awh7gfplndy'*

Kyra's text arrived next. It sucked the air from Avery's lungs.

"What?" Deirdre asked. "What is it?"

Avery held her phone out so that Deirdre could see. *Were you expecting film crew today?*

"Shit," Deirdre said.

"No kidding," Avery said. She'd planned to have the weekend to get settled in and come up with some sort of plan.

Camera is on us, not house!!! Avery felt a flutter of panic at the exclamation points at the end of Kyra's next text.

Another text from Maddie arrived and Avery had a flash of Madeline, Kyra, and Nicole standing next to one another, fingers flying. It was an image that might have made her smile if not for the unexpected film crew and the near clarity of Maddie's message. It read, *Uree pup!*

Chapter Three

Meridian Avenue was tree-lined and well maintained with a mishmash of single-family homes and small apartment and condo buildings that ranged from spectacularly restored to "please pull me down." Lush tropical plants and flowers spilled over wrought-iron gates and rose junglelike above stucco walls. New plantings dotted the islands of fresh dirt between the sidewalk and the curb, and the streetlights were sleek and black and looked newly installed.

Number 301 took up most of one corner of Meridian and Third and was bounded by a shoulder-high wrought-iron gate that was only marginally taller than much of the grass inside it. A section of gate stood open, and Avery pulled across the sidewalk and onto the concrete strip driveway next to Nicole's Jag and beside Madeline's minivan.

She and Deirdre climbed out of the car, staring up at the imposing two-story structure. "They couldn't have picked a house that was more 'you,'" Deirdre observed as they both took in the house's streamlined design and whimsical nautical accents.

This was true, but Avery had no idea what, if anything, it signified. The house had magnificent bones, but its gouged plaster walls and the hodgepodge of window types and paint colors attested to long years of neglect.

Avery craned her neck in search of the others, but the grounds were a Florida fantasy run amok, overgrown and unkempt. Not sure they could actually make it through the yard without a native guide and pith helmets, they walked back out the gate and down the sidewalk to the front of the house, where they found Madeline, Kyra, and Nicole trying to ignore the two-man film crew and the camera and microphone currently aimed right at them.

The cameraman was tall with shaggy sun-streaked blond hair. The audio guy had a dark beard and a teddy-bear face. He was considerably shorter and stockier than the camera guy, with a thatch of dark hair that barely reached the video camera that sat on his partner's well-developed shoulder. They both looked to be somewhere in their twenties.

The camera and boom microphone swung toward Avery and Deirdre as they drew closer. Avery could practically feel the video camera's boxy lens zooming in for its close-up. She tried to imagine what it was focusing on; the jiggle of her breasts in the unfortunate halter top or the expanse of skin bared by the even more unfortunate Daisy Dukes.

"I don't want to hear anything that sounds like 'I told you so,'" she muttered to Deirdre out of the side of her mouth.

"I wouldn't dream of it," Deirdre replied. "Even though this is exactly what I was trying to protect you from."

"And no performing for the camera," Avery added. As soon as there was a camera within a five-mile radius, Deirdre had a tendency to flip the on switch.

"Who me?" Deirdre asked innocently, but her smile had already spread attractively across her face and she'd tilted her chin at an angle designed to camouflage neck sag.

The women hugged stiffly, all of them aware of their unexpected audience. Nicole looked the most together in one of her vintage sundresses, her deep red hair swirling around her slim shoulders. Maddie looked exhausted, the eleven-plus-hour drive from Atlanta with Kyra and her baby written all over her.

Kyra had fared better, but then when you were twenty-four, long hours were not as formidable an enemy. Her long dark hair had been pulled back in a ponytail, and she neither wore, nor needed, makeup. Her tall, lean frame had grown curvier with motherhood and she held the baby easily in her arms, his head of dark curly hair resting on her shoulder, a thumb slipped into his bow-shaped mouth. At six months, he was already a dead ringer for his famous father.

Kyra made the introductions, her lips tight with suppressed anger, her free hand on the video camera that dangled at her side. "This is Troy," she said nodding curtly to the tall, blond, broad-shouldered young man whose chiseled features could have easily put him in front of the camera rather than behind it. "That's Anthony on audio."

Anthony nodded. His eyes were dark and crinkly and his smile was far readier than the cameraman's.

Kyra reached out and pushed the camera lens aside. "I was told someone might be sent down later this week to start picking up some extra video," she said. "I don't understand what you're doing here now."

"I would think that's kind of obvious," the cameraman replied, swinging the camera back into position.

"I shot all the footage at Bella Flora," Kyra said. "And it was my YouTube posts of the renovation that led to the whole series idea." She resettled the baby on her hip.

The cameraman shrugged, but he didn't lower his camera.

"We weren't expecting a crew," Kyra said again. "And we don't need one."

"Noted," Troy said. "Now, I'd appreciate it if you'd shift slightly to your left so I can get a better shot of the baby."

Kyra's gray eyes flashed with fury. "No," she said, shifting her weight so that he couldn't shoot around her. "Dustin's not pertinent to the project. As far as I'm concerned, he's off-limits."

Troy's finger moved on the zoom, but his movements were subtle and Avery couldn't tell whether he was zooming in to try to frame a shot of the baby or out to include all of them.

Unease snaked up Avery's spine. She knew just how little a network could care about what its talent thought or felt. "Look," she said. "We realize we need to document the experience here, but we have Kyra and none of us signed on for constant surveillance." Even as she said this she realized she shouldn't have been surprised that a network that would force them to choose a renovation project sight unseen would want to record their initial reactions. "We're here to do a renovation, not a reality show."

Kyra reached out again and pushed the camera lens away. "That's right," she said as the rest of them nodded their agreement. "And my son is off-limits."

"Sorry," Troy said, his tone making it clear he wasn't.

"There is no 'off-limits' that I'm aware of. We're here twenty-four/seven and we shoot what we see."

Without discussion, Avery, Nicole, Deirdre, and Madeline stepped closer to Kyra to form a protective circle around Dustin. They were still huddled in the waning light, unsure how to end the standoff, when the front door creaked open.

The camera, the microphone, and all of their gazes swung toward the figure that stepped out of it.

. . .

The man who posed in front of the two-story circular entryway was short and old with close-cropped white hair, a tanned face, and a wide, welcoming smile that could be seen even from the sidewalk. He wore white pants with a white shirt and navy blazer that hung on him as if they'd been borrowed from a larger man; possibly Captain Stubing on *The Love Boat*.

The man came down the curved front steps and walked slowly toward them, the grasses and plant life so tall in spots that he looked as if he were wading through a tropical cornfield. Although his movements appeared purposeful, the closer he came the clearer it became just how carefully he was moving. So carefully that if he'd been racing a snail, the snail would have already lapped him.

Everything about him discouraged the offering of assistance and so they stayed where they were and waited for him to reach them. The red tally light of the camera remained on.

As he drew near, his features came into focus. His weathered face was anchored by a slightly oversize, but distinguished nose and a pair of intelligent brown eyes that were shaded by caterpillar eyebrows the same white as his hair. His hands were gnarled and covered with age spots. One of them held an unlit cigar. He'd tucked a captain's hat beneath one arm.

Coming to a stop in front of them, he plopped the hat onto his head and looked directly into the camera. Opening his arms wide, he boomed, "I'm Max Golden. Welcome to The Millicent!"

They watched him, too surprised to speak.

He lowered his arms and fiddled with the cigar.

"You want me to try it again?" he asked the cameraman. "I can do it with or without the cigar. Or maybe I should take off the hat since it'll be dark pretty soon?"

Troy gave an almost imperceptible nod. Anthony repositioned the microphone. "Yes, sir," he said crisply. "We're still rolling."

Max Golden revved his smile back up to full throttle, opened his arms wide once more, and said, "Welcome to The Millicent! I'm your host, Max Golden!"

"Got it," Troy said.

"That's a keeper," Anthony agreed.

"Good," Max Golden said, lowering his arms. "Because even now that the sun's gone down, I'm really shvitzing in this jacket." He pulled a handkerchief from his pocket and began to mop his forehead. Sweat glistened in the hollows of his cheeks and on his upper lip.

Avery stepped toward Max Golden. He was about her height and she stared him directly in the eye, which was a nice change from the usual cricked-neck conversation. "I'm Avery Lawford. I'll be coordinating your 'do-over.'"

His grip was surprisingly strong. As she introduced the others, Max shook each person's hand, making a special show of pumping Dustin's tiny appendage up and down until the baby broke into a gummy smile. "I was about his age when I first started in vaudeville," Max said. "I was more of a prop than a performer, of course, but I did learn to suck my thumb on cue."

"A useful talent, I'm sure." Nicole's tone was just the wee-est bit dry.

"Yes," Max said jovially. "Although it doesn't come in as handy now as it did then."

Dustin couldn't seem to take his eyes off the cigar Max waved around as he spoke. Kyra handed the baby to Madeline and lifted her video camera to her shoulder. The rest of them stayed close, doing their best to shield Dustin from the network camera.

"I haven't been around this many beautiful women since the last time we played Vegas," Max said. "This is a perk I wasn't expecting."

"You are going to be a little outnumbered," Avery agreed. "Are you sure you have room for all of us?"

Mentally, she was already putting Deirdre at the head of the list of things to move to another location. Maybe they could talk the network into arranging for the camera crew to join her.

"Oh, there's plenty of room," Max said in a hearty tone with a glimpse toward the camera. "But it's not in the best shape. We had to turn the upstairs into apartments back in the sixties. It was mostly just Millie and me for the last five or six years. And then . . . well . . . my wife passed away a little over a year ago just after the last tenants moved out of the pool house. I'm not much of a housekeeper. Or gardener." That was his only acknowledgment of the chest-high grass and junglelike overgrowth. "And I'm not too handy either."

"Well, that's why we're here, isn't it?" Deirdre said, stepping forward and taking Max by one arm. Nicole took the other.

"That's right," Nicole said as they began to move toward the front steps at a slightly accelerated pace, although Avery wasn't certain if Deirdre and Nicole allowed Max's feet to touch the ground.

Dustin let out a whimper and burrowed his head beneath his grandmother's chin.

Max glanced at the baby and then at Maddie, who was stifling a yawn. "It's getting a bit late," he said gallantly. "Why don't I show you to your rooms now and leave the tour for tomorrow morning."

Relieved, they agreed and Max changed direction, leading them back toward the garage and across garden pavers choked with weeds and tilted at unintended angles. Nicole and Deirdre tightened their hold on Max's arms and Avery offered up a small prayer that he'd make it wherever he was taking them without falling and breaking his neck.

"I absolutely love The Millicent's nautical elements," Avery said, looking up at the cruise-liner-inspired observation tower that topped the two-story entrance and the run of porthole windows. Double smokestacks rose majestically above the flat roof and into the darkening sky.

"We honeymooned on the SS *Franklin*," Max said. "We were the onboard entertainment even though it was Millie's first time onstage. When I saw this house for sale a couple years later, I knew we had to have it."

"It reminds me of the *Titanic*," Nicole said under her

breath. "Post-iceberg. Assuming it had mowed down a flock of flamingos first."

"There is a somewhat unfortunate pairing of pinks and greens," Deirdre said in quiet agreement. "And the walls are a mess," she added, motioning to the chunks of wall that littered the ground.

But Avery didn't care how many pieces of stucco the house had shed or how many colors it had been painted. With its sharp straightaways and sinuous curves, it was one of the most glorious examples of Streamline Moderne architecture she'd ever seen.

"The Millicent has weathered a lot of storms," Max admitted. "I'm pretty sure I told the network that it would take a good bit of work to get her back in shape." He fiddled with his cigar.

Avery and Maddie exchanged glances. "Where are you taking us?" Maddie asked as they passed the driveway and rounded the garage.

"Your rooms are upstairs and you can't get there from inside anymore," Max said. "At first we rented the upstairs bedrooms to other performers, people that we knew. But when we started renting to strangers, we walled off the first and second floors. The stairs are around back."

Like The Millicent's exterior, the backyard had once been wonderful. Two staircases designed to look like ship gangplanks led up to large decks rimmed with ship-style railings. One deck had a triangular "bow" that pointed east; the other was shaped like the stern.

The pool was cracked and filthy. A one-story cube of a building sat near it, barely visible through the hedge that surrounded it. "That's the pool house," Max said. "It was the first space we rented out." In a far corner of the yard, several citrus trees sagged against the wrought-iron fence.

Everyone was tired and they were far too aware of the Lifetime crew recording every word to engage in chitchat. Kyra had her video camera out, too. The lenses moved so constantly that Avery had no idea what they were actually shooting. She tried to keep the worry off her face as she absorbed the extent of The Millicent's damage and noted the ancient wall air conditioners, whose back ends protruded from the house like blemishes on a teenager's face. Surely the inside had been better maintained.

"Is there any central heat or air?" Maddie asked.

"No," Max said. "But a lot of the wall units still work." He said this with a certain amount of pride.

"South Florida Art Deco homes were built to make the most of cross breezes," Avery pointed out, though she wasn't sure whom she was trying to reassure. "And the walls are thick, though probably not as thick as Bella Flora's." Avery turned to Max, who had slung his jacket over one shoulder and was once again mopping at his brow. "I'm assuming the house was built around 1938 or '39. Do you have any idea who designed it?"

"Henry Hohauser," he said without hesitation. "We bought it from the people he built it for."

"It's a Hohauser?" Deirdre said, perking up. "That should up the price significantly when it's ready to go on the market."

An odd look passed over Max Golden's face. Once again he fiddled with the unlit cigar.

Dustin began to cry in Maddie's arms. He reached out toward his mother, who was filming the others staring at the house and talking. The film crew filmed her filming them.

Following behind Max, who now clung to the wobbly handrails, they started upward. Avery sent up a small prayer that the interior of The Millicent would be in better shape than the stairs that now swayed and shuddered beneath their feet.

Chapter Four

Inside, the air was thick with trapped humidity and smelled of too little air-conditioning and the underuse of cleaning products.

There were three bedrooms, each with a small kitchenette. The two bedrooms on the west side of the house shared a Jack-and-Jill bath.

"Do you mind if I open a window?" Nicole asked in the third bedroom. Her face had taken on a greenish tinge.

Avery had been doing her best to breathe only through one nostril. Which was no easy task when you were also trying not to hyperventilate.

"Here, let me." Max shuffled over to a block of casement windows. The first handle he grasped came off in his hand. He couldn't budge the second. Avery could barely keep herself from rushing over to help him when he put all of his weight into the third. All of them relaxed slightly when he managed to crank that window open a few inches.

Max turned on the room's wall air conditioner, which made noise as if it were on. Nothing stirred.

The baby started fussing in earnest. Avery had a bad feeling that her face looked as horrified as the others' and, of course, she was wearing ridiculously short shorts and what was now a sweat-stained halter top.

Max, too, was drooping, his earlier banter and stage persona long gone as he led them out to the eastern deck, where they stared out over the bow in the direction of the night-shrouded Atlantic.

"This would be a great place to watch the sunrise," Madeline said. "The ocean's only a few blocks away."

Avery winced at the suggestion. She was not now, and never intended to be, a morning person.

"I have to agree that sunset toasts seem a lot more civilized," Deirdre said, referring to their ritual at Bella Flora. "And I don't think I could bear watching Avery eat Cheez Doodles that early in the morning. It was bad enough at sundown."

Madeline and Nicole laughed.

"There's never a bad time for Cheez Doodles," Avery scoffed. "I'm pretty sure it says so right on the bag."

Max mopped at his forehead. His cheeks seemed even more sunken.

Cradled in his grandmother's arms, Dustin whimpered and yawned. His eyelashes brushed his cheeks.

"I think we've done enough for today," Avery said. "Let's divvy up the rooms and get a good night's sleep." As tired as she was, she knew she'd be spending most of the night openeyed and praying that the bottom of the house was in better shape than the top. She did not want to see it for the first time with the Lifetime crew documenting her reactions.

"What time do you want to get started tomorrow, Kyra?" she asked, intentionally ignoring Troy and Anthony. "Nine or nine-thirty?" She emphasized the latter, which would give her more time for a quiet walk-through and a chance to rough out a schedule, and was relieved when Kyra chose nine-thirty.

"Does that work for you, Max?" Madeline asked.

"Perfect," Max said, the relief etched clearly on his face. "I'll see you in the morning, kiddos. There should be clean sheets in all of the bedrooms." He tilted his captain's hat in their general direction and headed toward the gangplank staircase.

The women looked at one another, and Avery knew she wasn't the only one who would have liked to help him down the stairs; just as she knew he would have rejected such an offer.

Dustin let out a serious wail and reached for his mother. Kyra set down her camera and reached for her son. "That's a wrap," she said as she held the baby against her, his back to the network camera.

"But . . ." Troy began, his camera still raised atop his shoulder.

"I said, we're done," Kyra repeated in much the same tone that an officer might command an underling to "stand down." She continued to stare at him until he finally lowered his camera. "We'll pick up again tomorrow morning at nine-thirty if you want to come back then."

"We have instructions to stay here and be available to shoot twenty-four/seven," Troy said, shoving a hand through his hair. "I assumed we'd be assigned rooms on-site."

"I don't see how," Kyra said. "It looks like most of us are going to have to double up as it is."

Troy crossed his arms in front of his chest. "We're not leaving," he said.

Maddie fisted her hands at her sides, ready to spring to Kyra's aid. Avery, Nicole, and Deirdre faced Troy and Anthony. If this had been a movie, the opening strains of "I Am Woman, Hear Me Roar" would have begun to swell in the background.

"We're not going to argue about this right now," Avery said. "We'll call the network once we're settled in and make sure we're all clear on who shoots what."

"And where they're supposed to stay," Troy added.

"In the meantime, you two can have the pool house," Avery said, gesturing vaguely toward the hedge-covered concrete cube outside. "If you hurry, you'll beat Max to the front door and you can ask if there's a key."

"But we don't have any idea if it's habitable," Anthony pointed out.

"I didn't even see a door," Troy added, clearly irritated.

"Not our problem," Kyra said.

"We've done uninhabitable," Nicole said. "There's no such thing. It's just mind over matter."

"And you can always go to a hotel if you don't think you can hack it," Kyra added sweetly.

Troy and Kyra stared each other down for a few long seconds. Troy folded first, signaling to Anthony and grabbing their gear. Dustin cried and rubbed his eyes.

"I need to get Dustin's things out of the van. Then I need to feed him. We're way past his bedtime," Kyra said.

Sweat trickled down Avery's back. All of them looked like something the cat dragged in. She sincerely hoped there was running water.

"Would you mind if we take this room?" Kyra asked as they moved inside. "The attached sunroom will give us a little more space to set up Dustin's portable crib and you won't have to live with a diaper pail in your bathroom."

"Works for me," Avery said. "Are you all right with that?"

Deirdre and Nicole nodded. The three of them walked across the landing, which was lit by what little moonlight managed to penetrate the rectangle of filthy glass block and its neighboring porthole window.

"I think Avery and I should room together," Deirdre said. "Since we're going to have to share a double bed, it seems to make sense to divide by family."

"As far as I'm concerned, you and I aren't all that related," Avery said.

"Well, I don't have any plans to visit my sole remaining family member anytime soon," Nicole said. "I'm not a big fan of bars on the windows." Her tone was dry.

Avery remained silent, unable to actually choose Deirdre as a roommate.

Deirdre's lips pursed. "Fine. I'm going to take the back bedroom. If you don't want to share a room with me, maybe Max will let you sleep downstairs. Or you could bunk with the crew."

"Fine." Avery raised an eyebrow. "But if you snore I won't be responsible for my actions."

Deirdre shot her an eyebrow in return. "I don't snore."

"Yes, you do." They'd shared a room at Bella Flora briefly. And slept in the same bathroom when Hurricane Charlene had come calling.

They sighed.

"Oh my God." Nicole laughed. "You two are like mirror images of each other. It's downright Darwinian."

Avery gave her an eye roll and winced when she noticed Deirdre doing the same.

"All right," Avery said, careful not to purse her lips in the same way that Deirdre was doing. "I'm going to go down and get my things." She was almost looking forward to watching Deirdre carry all her luggage up the gangplank on her own.

She followed Nicole down the back stairs and around the house to the drive, pulling the warm night air into her lungs. Extracting her single suitcase from the trunk, she stared up at The Millicent's sinuous curves and soaring walls, bathed now in forgiving moonlight. This house deserved a second chance and so did they. It would be up to her to see them through this project unscathed.

· · ·

Nicole opened her eyes slowly, taking in the strange surroundings and trying to make sense of them. She'd woken often during the night, the first time to the sound of Dustin crying, which had taken her a while to process, and later in need of the bathroom, an urge she'd resisted as long as possible before feeling her way across the room and into a pink-tiled extravaganza.

Now early morning sunlight suffused the flimsy curtains and sneaked in through the gaps between and beneath them, illuminating the scars on the wood floor and the thick layer of dust that covered pretty much everything.

The dark wood nightstand and matching headboard had rounded corners and linear grooves cut at right angles. The lamp, fashioned from a totem of chrome and wood geometric shapes, had probably once been über-modern. Possibly around the time man began to walk upright.

Nicole turned onto her back with a groan and stretched to smooth out the kinks. The double mattress was both lumpy and deeply grooved and she really didn't want to think about how many others might have slept on it. Instead she focused on the fact that the sheets she'd found in the room's small cedar closet had appeared clean and at least this mattress, however lumpy, sat inside a bed frame and on top of a box spring. Unlike her mattress last summer at Bella Flora, which had sat firmly on the floor under a window with no covering at all.

With the exception of the irregular chug of the air-conditioning unit, the house was quiet around her. A lone bird chirped somewhere in the backyard and she heard what sounded like a garbage truck a few streets away. Removing her phone from its charger, she checked the time: seven A.M. Too late to go back to sleep. Definitely too early to deal with this house or her housemates if she could avoid it.

Promising herself coffee later, Nicole pulled on running shorts and a sports bra and T-shirt and laced up her running shoes. In the bathroom she twisted her hair into a clip and applied what she thought of as "basic armor"—enough makeup to banish the dark circles, even out her skin tone, and camouflage the wrinkles that screamed out for attention she could no longer afford to give them.

Treading softly, she walked past Avery and Deirdre's room, out the back door, and down the stairs to the backyard, where she stretched for a few minutes, keeping her eye on the tiny pool house for any sign of life or flash of a camera lens. Satisfied that she was not on camera for the moment, Nicole walked around the garage and through the gate to the sidewalk, breathing in the warm salt-tinged air.

At the corner she launched the GPS on her phone and began to jog east toward the ocean. She crossed Washington, which was dotted with offices and small retail shops, and then Collins, which offered more of the same. On Ocean Drive, she jogged through a small but well-appointed park and followed a concrete path that led through the dunes and onto the beach.

The sun had barely breached the Atlantic and hovered close to the water casting the first rays of the new day sparkling across it. This beach was a much deeper affair than last summer's Pass-a-Grille beach, just as the Atlantic Ocean was a completely different animal than the Gulf of Mexico.

Her morning jogs around Bella Flora had been accompanied by the caw of seagulls and the gentle wash of the waves on sand. Here the roar of the ocean was pronounced and the wave action more strenuous. Even the early morning beachgoers moved at a faster clip than they had on Pass-a-Grille, perhaps because here it was all about the sunrise and the start of the day. On the west coast of Florida there was a tendency to linger over the sunsets that closed out the day so spectacularly.

Her thoughts flitted at random as she turned north, jogging slowly and getting her bearings. A few blocks up she spotted the outlines of the pastel-colored Art Deco hotels and sidewalk cafés that had made South Beach famous. There would be nightlife here and the kinds of restaurants and shopping that had not existed on Pass-a-Grille, not that Nikki had the wherewithal to enjoy those things.

Another jogger passed her and she picked up her pace,

breathing in the salt air with each step, expelling it with the next. As she ran, she studied her new surroundings, scanning from the hotels down across the dunes and palm trees, over the boardwalk, past the walkers and joggers that now dotted the beach, and then out to the Atlantic. A truly funky lifeguard stand shaped like a 1930s version of a rocket ship painted flamingo pink and canary yellow rose out of the sand in front of her. Nicole slowed for a more thorough look.

"It's something, isn't it?" The deep voice startled her, and she stumbled as she recognized it. "There's a long string of them stretching up the beach." A strong hand reached out to steady her and she turned to see Special Agent Joe Giraldi falling into step beside her just as he'd done on Pass-a-Grille beach when he was trying to use her to hunt down her brother. As he'd done then, he'd removed his T-shirt and tucked it into the waist of his running shorts. Which made it hard to ignore the broad shoulders and lightly muscled chest that triangled to narrow hips. Nicole looked up to his face, noting the strong nose and chin. The thick black hair. The fine brown eyes that missed nothing and gave away even less were hidden behind the Maui Jim's.

"Aren't you a little out of your jurisdiction?" she asked.

"Actually, no." His lips curved into a smile. He was breathing easily and, unlike Nikki, seemed to be expending very little effort. "I'm attached to the Miami Bureau now."

"So you're not here to follow or harass me?" she asked.

"I don't recall ever intentionally 'harassing' you," he said. "I believe I was actually doing my job. Following every lead in the pursuit of a fleeing felon."

"Well, you caught your felon," she observed.

"*You* caught my felon," he corrected quietly.

She frowned at the truth of it, not wanting to remember. It wasn't even eight o'clock in the morning and the day was already heading downhill.

Nikki turned her eyes forward and tried to ignore him. Women stilled as they passed, practically going on point like hunting dogs, their hungry eyes aimed at Giraldi. A woman whose chest had settled somewhere around her waist stopped to watch him pass. So did an octogenarian with a Geiger counter.

"I hear you're doing another house here," Giraldi said. "That you all ended up with a television series."

"There's just a pilot right now. We're shooting a series of programs here that are slated to run next spring." Nikki kept her eyes averted. "What did they do, put out an FBI bulletin?"

"Nope," he replied. "*People* magazine. 'Ponzi Victims Become TV Stars.' I read it in line at the grocery store."

"I hope you bought that copy," she said primly. "Stealing is a slippery slope. One minute you're speed-reading a magazine article in the checkout line, the next you're—"

"—stealing three hundred million dollars and bankrupting the sister who raised you?" he finished.

That took care of the smile. "You know, sometimes I go a whole five minutes without thinking about that," she said. Without discussion, she turned and headed back the way she'd come, hoping he'd continue on his way. But the man was used to tailing people and didn't miss a step.

"So, what *are* you doing here, Agent Giraldi?" she finally asked. "I only have one felon in the family and he's already in jail." The sand wasn't hard-packed enough to run easily on and she was starting to feel winded, though she tried not to show it. She did, however, make a mental note to try the boardwalk next time. "I thought I was no longer a 'person of interest' to the FBI."

Two young women strolled by, long-limbed and gorgeous. Both of them were practically topless and perked right up, which was saying quite a lot, at the sight of Giraldi.

She had no idea whether Giraldi took note behind the sunglasses; he certainly couldn't have missed the display or their obvious interest. But he didn't rubberneck or comment. The only heavy breathing was coming from her.

"Oh, you're a person of interest all right," he said, so softly she almost missed it. "At least to me."

They ran in silence for a while as she tried to absorb what he'd said. The sun continued to rise over the Atlantic, growing brighter and warmer as it glinted off the turquoise ocean and painted the sky a clear, bright blue.

Nicole picked up her pace despite the ache of protest in her calf muscles. Sweat trickled down her back while Giraldi's impressive golden-brown chest barely glistened. Spotting the lifeguard stand where he'd joined her, Nikki fought the urge to slow to a walk.

"I haven't even seen Malcolm since he went to jail," she said, careful not to gasp for air. "And the only bank account I knew anything about was the one up in the Panhandle, which I already reported."

"I know," he said, giving nothing away.

"So, what is it you want?" she asked, coming to an abrupt halt, partly from irritation and partly because she was too winded to talk and run at the same time.

Giraldi removed his sunglasses and looked down at her, compelling her to look at him. "What I want is the same thing I wanted last summer but couldn't ask for without creating a conflict of interest." He smiled and this time there was nothing impassive about it or him. His fine brown eyes glinted with humor. "What I want, Nicole Grant, is you."

Chapter Five

Deirdre Morgan stared down into her daughter's sleeping face, treating herself to the view of it wiped clean of the anger, resentment, and hurt that were normally aimed at her when Avery was awake.

When she'd looked her fill, Deirdre leaned close so that her face was only inches away from Avery's and said, "Rise and shine!" She rocked back slightly, anticipating the eruption.

"Jesus!" Avery jerked awake, her eyes flying open. "You're going to give me a heart attack!"

Avery looked in vain toward the awkward kitchenette in the corner for something resembling a coffeemaker. "I had my alarm set. And I don't remember asking for a wake-up call."

"Sorry," Deirdre said. "But I figured you'd want to get up to do a walk-through downstairs before Troy and Anthony show up."

Avery's tone turned suspicious. "What makes you think that?"

Deirdre shrugged and stated the obvious. "Because that's exactly what I would do."

Avery reached out and pushed Deirdre back far enough to slide out of bed. "Yeah, well. Kyra wants to shoot the downstairs without them around. And I need to figure out how to put this poor house back together again."

"I forgot how grumpy you are when you wake up," Deirdre replied. "Do you want me to go out and get you a cup of coffee?"

"I'm not grumpy!" Avery bit out. "I'm just tired from listening to you snore in my ear all night."

And most likely from clinging to her side of the too small bed all night. Several times Deirdre had worried that Avery might actually get so close to the edge that she'd fall off.

"I am not grumpy," Avery said a little less grumpily. "And I don't need you trying to act all mother-y all of a sudden. It's a little late for that."

It was more than a little late. Deirdre had been trying to make up for her choice of career over her family for years, but it seemed that her attempts had been so unwelcome and, possibly, inept that Avery had simply stopped noticing.

Deirdre turned and walked toward the closet. "I thought I might join you. I'd like to get some photos and take notes on the decor." Keeping her back turned and her tone casual, she said, "I'm assuming you've asked Chase to consult on crew and a construction schedule."

There was a pause. In the murky reflection of the armoire mirror she saw Avery's cheeks go red.

"He's swamped," Avery said flatly. "And it's not like I can't handle this on my own."

She stomped into the bathroom and there was the sound of water splashing in the sink. When she came back into the bedroom, she'd swiped on mascara and lipstick and tamed the worst of a fairly virulent case of bed head. She rummaged through her suitcase and pulled on a pair of modest khaki shorts and a baggy blue T-shirt, which was safer than yesterday's outfit but not at all flattering. Deirdre had left her room in both the closet and the armoire, but Avery had so far made no move to claim it. Perhaps she was afraid that allowing their clothes to touch might be construed as an acknowledgment of an actual relationship.

There was a rap on the bedroom door. When Avery pulled it open, Kyra stepped into the room. Dustin had been strapped in a carrier and hung in front of her, face forward. His mouth was open in a gummy smile. Deirdre felt the oddest tug in her chest.

"They didn't have slings or papooses or any of that when you were born," Deirdre said to Avery, remembering how alien and frightening motherhood had seemed at the time.

"Would you have packed me in one and taken me with you when you ran away from us if they had?" Avery asked, the words flying out of her mouth like bullets. The words hurt far less than the ancient hurt that had propelled them.

"You were thirteen when I left," Deirdre said. "I doubt they make them that large." The room swam briefly and she was horrified to realize that tears were a real possibility. "And I don't know how many times I can explain and apologize."

"You're right," Avery said. "It's pointless. You can stop now."

Kyra's sympathetic look was almost as tear inducing as

Avery's rejection. The girl handed Avery a mug of still-steaming coffee. "Drink this," she said. "All of it."

Avery did as instructed. But Deirdre was watching her daughter's face, and although she could see that the warm jolt of caffeine was welcome, it didn't erase the old hurts or assuage the current anger. And it didn't turn Deirdre into the mother she had never been.

• • •

Outside in the morning light, The Millicent looked far better and far worse than Avery had expected. As she stood on the front stoop face-to-face with the heavy wooden door set in the circular two-story entry, she could see every fabulous detail from the chrome anchor doorknob in the center of the door to the etchings on the glass transom above it and the hand-carved bas-relief of fanciful sea creatures that surrounded it.

Unfortunately, she could also see the dire shape they were in. If it hadn't been for all the jostling and what was supposed to pass for whispering, she imagined she might have been able to hear the house's silent scream for help.

"I don't feel good about going inside without Max's permission," Maddie said for what might have been the fourth or fifth time.

"That's assuming we can get in," Deirdre said. "Too bad we didn't think to ask for a key."

"Shhh," Kyra said over Dustin's head as she filmed what was supposed to be a stealth reconnaissance, but that had somehow turned into a group field trip. "We don't want to wake up Max. Or Frick and Frack."

"Maybe it's not locked," Deirdre said as Avery began to feel around for a hidden key.

Avery ignored her as she upended an ancient flowerpot then shooed everyone off the front step so that she could look underneath the welcome mat.

"I really think that if Max wanted us to have access, he would have given us a key," Maddie said.

Avery looked under a rock and moved a loose brick. When she still came up empty-handed, she asked Kyra to go up on tiptoe to feel around above the door, but all she dislodged was dirt and bits of spiderweb.

Glad she'd come prepared, Avery pulled out a nail file she'd pinched from Deirdre's makeup bag and bent down to try to fit it in the lock.

"Hey," Deirdre said, "is that mine?"

"We can't break into the house!" Maddie said, shocked.

"Shhh." Avery tried to quiet them. "We're not breaking in. We live here and Max is expecting us."

"In an hour," Maddie pointed out. "What if he's walking around naked or something?"

There was a group wince at the thought.

"Maybe you should try the doorknob," Deirdre said quietly, her gaze still on her nail file.

"Or what if he hears us and the fright gives him a heart attack?" Maddie asked, offering yet another worst-case scenario.

"He's ninety," Deirdre pointed out. "I doubt his hearing is that good."

Avery sighed as she tried to insert the tip of the file at the right angle. "We're going to see and probably touch every inch of this house, I don't think a walk-through is going to violate anything. We don't have time to debate this."

"Avery, I really think you should try the knob," Deirdre said again.

"Don't be ridiculous," Avery said, jiggling the file in an effort to jimmy the lock. "That's . . ." Her voice trailed off as the file snapped in half.

With a sigh, Deirdre reached around Avery, grasped the bottom curve of the anchor, and gave it a gentle twist. The door creaked open.

Great. Avery handed Deirdre both halves of her nail file.

"I'm still not sure we should do this," Maddie said, following them in.

No shushing was required. They fell silent as they stood together in the circular entry, their gazes drawn upward.

The high domed ceiling was ringed in triple bands of concrete. An umbrella-shaped chandelier with shimmering panels of sculpted glass hung from its center and a Moroccan tile floor radiated outward. Straight ahead an oak-risered staircase angled gently upward, its rounded stepped wall open to a high-ceilinged rectangular living room that stretched to their right.

They moved left into the dining room, another long rectangle with a high ceiling banded in concrete. Avery felt a burst of adrenaline as she took in the expanse of glass block cut into the front wall and the matched set of casement windows that would flood the room with natural light once they were repaired and cleaned.

"That porthole mirror is great," Deirdre said, following Avery's gaze before moving toward a bird's-eye-maple and mahogany dining room suite. "I'm pretty sure this is Ruhlmann." Deirdre's hand practically caressed a stair-stepped chair back; her voice pulsed with pleasure as she uttered the well-known Deco-era designer's name.

Deirdre's flushed face and tone of excitement drew Avery back to the hours they'd spent together in antique shops.

Despite years of trying, she'd never been able to completely block the fact that her love of the clean-lined Deco style had been discovered at the side of the mother who'd abandoned her.

Deirdre led the way into the kitchen, which was large and roomy, with a corner banquette that overlooked the driveway and a curvy run of cabinets that would have looked right at home in a private railcar or the hold of a ship.

"I don't think this kitchen has been touched since the day it was installed," Deirdre said.

"It all looks original all right," Avery said, taking in the plain white cabinets and the chipped tile countertops. The built-in oven, cooktop, and vent hood were turquoise. The refrigerator was wide, boxy, and white.

Avery ran a hand over a lightly singed cabinet above the stove. "There's been some sort of fire here. And the tile work is pretty beat up."

"I can't wait to get my hands on this kitchen," Deirdre said happily. "We'll need to talk about whether to restore to original or renovate."

"That will depend on preservation codes and whether Max is planning to live in The Millicent or put it on the market," Avery said, her tone sharp with the sudden need to wipe the too-happy smile off Deirdre's face.

"The man is ninety," Deirdre pointed out for the second time that morning. "And obviously not up to the task of maintaining this house. He has to be thinking about selling."

She and Avery stared at each other.

"Well, fortunately that decision's not up to us," Madeline said in her best mother voice as she peeked inside a walk-in pantry and a laundry/mud room. A half bath opened to the pool.

They whispered and shushed their way back through the foyer to the living room. With their backs to the fireplace, they studied the baby grand piano that dominated the circular sunroom. Like the dining room set, it was made of bird's-eye maple and banded in mahogany and brass. Its raised split lid gave it the look of an airplane poised for flight.

There was a noise from behind the closed door to what had to be the master bedroom. They looked at each other. The thud that followed sent Maddie moving toward the bedroom door. "Mr. Golden, are you okay?"

There was no answer and no further sound.

"Mr. Golden?" Maddie called again.

"He probably didn't hear you," Avery said, but her voice wavered uncertainly.

They all moved toward the door.

"Did anybody bring their cell phone?" Maddie asked as she knocked again. "He could be lying there unable to get up."

Deirdre pulled out her cell phone while Madeline knocked more loudly and raised her voice. "Mr. Golden? Mr.—"

The door swung open.

Max stood in the doorway. He was neatly shaven and his hair was slicked into place. He wore a blue velvet smoking jacket belted at the waist. A silk paisley cravat was knotted at his neck. The unlit cigar was clutched between two fingers as he opened his arms wide. "Good morning, beautiful ladies," he boomed. "I trust you all slept well."

Kyra moved closer. Dustin waved his feet and hands at Max; his toothless smile lit up his face.

"And good morning to you, young man," Max said to

the baby with a courtly bow. "I see you've got the best seat in the house."

From the room behind Max, the Lifetime cameraman's voice rang out. "That's perfect, Max. Just like we rehearsed it. That's most definitely a take."

. . .

"Come in, come in," Max said, motioning with the unlit cigar. "Welcome to the inner sanctum." He stepped back to allow them to enter the large sun-filled space.

The bedroom was the largest they'd seen in the house. It had a parquet floor, two closets, and a short hallway that led to a bathroom. But it was the room itself, or rather the room's decor, that grabbed the eye and refused to let go. Two out of three bedroom walls were covered in a black-and-white-striped silk that had faded and yellowed over time. A turquoise silk chaise and a ladies' dressing table in the same vibrant shade anchored one end of the room. The other had been turned into a sitting area that was dominated by a black leather recliner that had molded itself to Max Golden's posterior and that faced a tabletop television. The walls covered in framed black-and-white photos. Maddie tried but wasn't able to make out their subject matter from where she stood.

Troy and Anthony stood next to their equipment, which had been set up across from the recliner and was currently aimed toward the bedroom door and them.

"I thought we agreed on a nine-thirty start," Kyra said to Troy.

"Me too," the cameraman said. He made a show of consulting his watch. "But it's only eight-thirty now. Yet here you are."

Madeline could actually feel Kyra wrestling for control. Dustin must have felt it, too, because he'd stopped waving his arms at Max and was craning his neck to look up at his mother. Avery and Deirdre stood next to each other, together but separate, watching the interchange with interest.

As always, Maddie wanted to step in and mediate, as she'd done when Kyra was a child, but Kyra was no longer a ten-year-old fighting with her younger brother. Or even the twenty-three-year-old who'd fallen in love with a movie star on her first feature film and come home pregnant and unemployed. Maddie held herself back. Ready, but back.

Kyra's shoulders rose then fell as if she'd drawn in a breath and expelled it. Maddie hoped Kyra was counting to ten, or higher if necessary.

Maddie drew a breath, too, then slowly let it out and was relieved when Kyra said, "It looks like we both have to work on our time management skills." Her tone turned less conciliatory. "I'm looking forward to talking with the network so that we can clarify who's shooting what, when."

Kyra unhooked Dustin from the harness, handed him to Maddie, then raised her camera to her shoulder. "In the meantime, maybe Max can tell us about his personal space. Assuming that hasn't already happened."

"No, we just shot his welcome." The cameraman didn't add that what he'd really wanted was their reaction, but then he didn't have to.

"I love to see young people so intense about their work," Max said with a wave of his cigar that drew all of their attention back to him. "I haven't worked in years," he said. "I finished out my comedy career playing lobbies full of retirees. And now I've got two cameras pointed my way."

He shook his head as if in wonder, then shot Dustin a wink. "If Millie were here, we could do one of our routines. It never was the same without her."

"I bet you two were fabulous," Kyra said, moving toward Max. "Will you show me some of the photos on the wall?"

"Of course," Max said, opening his arms wide.

"If it's okay with you, Max, I'm going to scope out the bathroom and make a few notes," Avery said. "And I think Deirdre wants to get photos of the bedroom suite. It looks custom made."

"I believe so." The old man smiled. "Millie loved nice things. She had an interior designer friend who used to practically live here."

Without further discussion, Kyra began to pan her camera across the photos while Madeline held her grandson close, trying her best to keep him out of camera range. Kyra's camera froze mid-move. "Oh my gosh," Kyra said. "Is that Frank Sinatra?" The camera panned to the next photo. "And Jackie Gleason?"

"Why, yes, of course," Max said, somehow managing to play to both cameras. Deirdre stopped shooting photos of the furniture and came over to stand next to Madeline. They all strained forward to see.

"Millie and I made regular guest appearances on *The Honeymooners*. And we opened for Frank at the Fontainebleau a couple of times." He beamed at them.

Madeline could hardly believe what she was seeing. There were photos of Sammy Davis Jr., Dean Martin, and Jerry Lewis standing next to an impossibly fresh-faced Max and a small blond woman, who had to be Millie. In another picture Max and Millie stood with Desi Arnaz and Lucille Ball, arms entwined, smiles lighting all four faces.

"Desi went to high school here on Miami Beach, though nobody was that wild about him. Lucy and Millie went to the same hairdresser," Max explained. "And they played canasta occasionally."

"So you actually knew all these celebrities?" Kyra asked as she continued to shoot.

"Of course," Max said. "Miami Beach isn't all that big. Back then it was even smaller in lots of ways." He adjusted the belt of his smoking jacket and his smile slipped a bit. "We weren't as big, but we were in the same business." He shrugged as if it were no big deal. "There are old films of a lot of those years somewhere. If I can find my projector and screen, we can pop some popcorn and have a movie night."

"We're in," Kyra and Maddie said while Avery, Nicole, and Deirdre chorused their agreement. Dustin kicked his feet happily behind their protective barrier. The Lifetime crew filmed on.

Chapter Six

Kyra stood in the grocery-store checkout line. She'd already helped her mother unload a bulging cart full of cleaning supplies and now waited impatiently for the checker to finish scanning their items and for the bag boy to pack them up.

Dustin was hanging in his canvas carrier, his head tucked beneath her chin. With her free hand she scrolled down her iPhone, but although it had been almost four days since Kyra had started trying to reach her, there were no unread messages or missed calls from Lisa Hogan at Lifetime. It was starting to become apparent that the lack of response was not an accident.

As she waited she scanned the rack of celebrity gossip magazines. Her irritation kicked up a notch as she studied the airbrushed photos of the already beautiful people. Beneath the photos were superficial articles designed to make celebrities seem like real people with regular problems. Which was absolutely ridiculous. Kyra knew from her embarrassingly short career in the movie business that by the time a celebrity made the cover of any one of these magazines, any semblance of their original selves had already been surgically removed.

She and Dustin had appeared on the cover of *People* and in the pages of other less stellar rags, but *her* photos had not been touched up in the slightest. They'd appeared under nasty headlines like YOUNG FILM ASSISTANT TRIES TO BREAK UP HEARTTHROB'S MARRIAGE and later DANIEL DERANIAN "LOVE CHILD" PATERNITY QUESTIONED. She needed no reminders that the famous and outwardly beautiful rarely looked as attractive when their true emotions and motivations were displayed.

Kyra shifted Dustin slightly in the canvas carrier and tickled one of his feet before burying her face in his soft dark curls. He was the one good thing that had come out of her brush with celebrity. *Do Over* was her chance to build something for herself and her child; she couldn't let anyone—not a cocky cameraman or a nonresponsive network executive—compromise that opportunity.

In the parking lot she buckled Dustin into his car seat and helped her mother store the bags in the back of the minivan. "Can you give me just a minute?" she asked Maddie. "I'm going to try Lisa Hogan again. I can't take this standoff with Troy Matthews. I'm tired of trying to hide Dustin from him."

"Go ahead." Maddie leaned over to rub noses with her grandson. "We'll be right here. Won't we, big guy?"

"Thanks, Mom."

Kyra walked around the corner of the building wishing that Karen Crandall, the development director who had originally offered them the show, was still at the network.

Although they'd only spoken with Lisa Hogan a few times, it had become increasingly clear that her vision for *Do Over* had little in common with her predecessor's.

In a shady spot beneath a palm tree, Kyra dialed Hogan's phone number. She was preparing yet another firm but succinct message, when the network head answered the phone.

"Hello?"

"Yes," Lisa Hogan replied.

Kyra felt a brief burst of nerves and shoved it away. This show was too important to all of them to jeopardize, but she was not going to spend a whole summer being screwed with.

"Hi, Lisa. This is Kyra Singer. Down in Miami."

"Oh," Hogan said. "I thought this was . . . Never mind. Hold on just a minute."

"No!" Kyra practically shouted. "No, don't hang up or put me on hold. I've been trying to reach you most of the week. There's a problem down here."

"Oh?"

Well, at least she'd gotten the woman's attention. Though not necessarily in a good way. Still, if she didn't speak, she'd have no one to blame but herself.

"Yes," Kyra hurried on. "It's your camera guy, Troy. He's shooting without my permission. We weren't expecting and we don't need a crew here. I thought you were happy with what we did at Bella Flora. Isn't that why we're here in Miami to . . ." She paused to regroup. She needed to stay direct and on target. "I understood we were shooting a show about renovating a really great home, but this is a—"

"Reality show," Lisa Hogan finished for her. "I know. Lock a bunch of disparate people up in a stressful situation with a camera rolling and watch what happens. It's genius. And relatively inexpensive."

"But—"

"Reality shows are huge right now, Kyra, and so is home renovation," the network head said. "*Do Over* is a win-win as far as we're concerned."

"But . . ." Kyra's stomach was churning from a particularly awful combination of horror and humiliation. How had she let this happen?

"Is there something else?" Hogan asked. "Because I've got someone waiting on the other line."

"I can shoot what we need," Kyra said. "We don't need the crew. I don't want—"

"The crew stays." Hogan's tone was crisp and firm.

"Then I need them to answer to me." Kyra was scrambling now, looking for a way out. If she couldn't be calm and collected, she'd have to settle for firm. "I can't have them just shooting whatever they want whenever they feel like it. They'll disrupt everything. No one will be able to relax long enough to focus on the work."

"That's a no," Hogan said. "Troy and Anthony are network employees, so we really can't have them answering to a freelancer. And especially not to a freelance talent."

"I'm not talent," Kyra said. "I'm a videographer and I understood that I was the show's producer."

"Sorry," Hogan said, though it was clear she wasn't. "I didn't see that anywhere in the notes Karen Crandall left me or the contract you all signed. Troy and Anthony have their instructions and Troy will be feeding footage to my office on a regular schedule."

Kyra took a deep breath and thought, briefly, about

counting, but she knew she'd be in the thousands before she cooled down. Lisa Hogan would have already hung up.

At the moment she was zero for two. It was time to focus on the most important part of the conversation.

"My son can't be a part of that footage," Kyra said. "I don't want him on camera." She stared out over the parking lot.

There was a silence. And then: "You're joking, right?"

Kyra didn't answer. Partly because she couldn't.

"Well, I'm afraid that belongs in the land of 'not gonna happen,'" Hogan said. "Your child is Daniel Deranian's son." She said the last words slowly and with relish. "That alone will have people tuning in. I assumed you realized that was one of the reasons you were offered this show." She no longer seemed in a big hurry to hang up. In fact, Kyra was getting the uncomfortable feeling that Lisa Hogan was enjoying herself.

"There have to be some camera-free zones," Kyra continued. "I'll shoot them myself so that footage exists, but your guys will have to acknowledge that certain places and times will be off-limits."

"No," Lisa Hogan said blithely. "That's not going to work out either."

Kyra's stomach stopped churning. The anger was back and there was far too much of it even to feel her stomach, let alone what might be taking place inside it.

"The upstairs bedrooms and baths are off-limits," Kyra said clearly. "And we get sunset toasts to ourselves." She named the tradition her mother had started in the grimmest days at Bella Flora, when they'd each had to come up with at least one good thing that had happened that day.

"Oh no," Hogan said. "I don't think so."

Kyra closed her eyes. The phone turned slippery in her sweaty palm as she prayed that the others would never find out about the gamble she was about to take with their futures.

"We get those camera-free zones and times," Kyra said on held breath, hoping that twenty-four was, in fact, too young to stroke out. "Or we walk."

. . .

By the end of their first week, The Millicent's rolled-up-and-forgotten-bathing-suit smell had been banished, replaced by the potent scent of eau de Pine-Sol. Cobwebs had been ripped out of corners, floors had been swept and mopped multiple times, vinegar and water had been used on every reachable window and piece of glass. Every stick of furniture had been polished.

It would be a stretch to say that the house gleamed or shone, but the improvement was noticeable. Avery drew in a great gulp of air and was delighted to discover that it was now safe to breathe through both nostrils.

Needing some time and space to herself, Avery left the house on foot, and with no clear destination in mind, she headed south. As she walked she drew in deep breaths of warm salt air along with the tropical foliage and the mix of residential and commercial structures that drew her eye. Within minutes she found herself at South Pointe Park, which lay beyond a towering condominium building and turned out to be a pedestrian-friendly mixture of green space and waterfront promenade that ran along Government Cut, a man-made channel designed to provide a direct route from the Atlantic to Miami's seaport. Fisher Island lay stranded across it.

She strolled past Smith & Wollensky's with its outside bar and bayside tables. Keeping the Government Cut on her right, she followed the walkway to the very tip of a long narrow jetty. There she stood, wrapped in a current of warm air, gazing out over the turquoise expanse of the Atlantic Ocean. To her left lay the very beginning of Miami Beach, which seemed to stretch into infinity.

Her cell phone rang and she answered it.

"Avery?" Chase Hardin's voice sounded warm and loud in her ear. "Are you there, Van?" Avery wondered how he managed to turn the very nickname that had so incensed her into an endearment.

"Yes." She turned her back to the wind to block the noise and stared out over the ocean and the beach that bounded it.

"I kept thinking I might hear from you."

"I'm sorry," she said, and she was. But she was far too intent on proving herself to give even the appearance of asking for help. "It's just been nonstop here."

There was a pause in which he waited for her to go into specifics. When she didn't, he said, "So, tell me about the house."

"The house is great," she said. "It's Art Deco Streamline—a perfect example of it. With incredible lines and insanely fantastic nautical accents. And it's a frickin' Henry Hohauser." She let that sink in. "Built in 1939."

"Seriously?" Chase asked.

"Completely," Avery replied. "I mean, I couldn't have found a house I'd want to work on this much if I'd had the whole world to choose from." She paused, thinking. "Which kind of worries me. I mean, why did they pick a house this perfect for me in particular?"

Chase laughed. "Count on you to look for the tarnished part of that silver lining. Maybe they just happened to find a great house that they knew you could make better."

She wanted to believe it was as simple as that, but nothing about this project felt anywhere near that simple. "I don't think that's it," she said, filling him in on the network camera crew and the whole reality-TV nature of the shoot.

"So there's not much that has to be done?" he asked.

"I didn't say that." It felt good to talk to someone who understood. Maybe too good. She knew that Chase's love of and appreciation for a well-designed home rivaled her own. She wanted to share the house with him. What she didn't want was unsolicited advice.

"The Millicent is a mess," she said. "There was a kitchen fire that was never dealt with, the floors are a nightmare, the upstairs has been carved up into apartments—someone stuck a really awkward wall at the head of the stairs. And, of course, everything's been horribly neglected."

Avery watched a cruise ship angle its way into the channel. Close up, it looked immense; the people lining its railings were tiny in comparison.

"What about the electrical?" he asked.

"Completely insufficient," Avery said. "It's all knob and tube and pretty much anything you plug in blows a fuse. We can't put in air-conditioning or do much of anything else until that's taken care of."

"I think I know a guy down in Davie that—"

"Thanks, but I'm all set," she said quickly. "I've got an electrician scheduled to put in a breaker box and rewire. Everything will have to be brought up to code."

The ship cruised past and she studied its wake, white and frothing.

"And the plumbing?" he said. "I once worked with a—"

"I've got a plumber," she said. "He's scheduled to come in after the electrician."

"I'm assuming there's a flat roof." Chase tried again.

"Yes," she said. "And it needs an overhaul. And I'm still looking for a good plaster-and-tile guy—there's a ton of both in this house and it's going to take skilled artisans with a delicate touch."

"How about En—"

"I've got Enrico Dante's number." She named the roofer who'd brought a number of talented family members in to work on Bella Flora. "I know his grandfather worked in Palm Beach for Mizner back in the day, and I've got my fingers crossed that at least a few Dantes migrated south."

Avery made her way off the jetty and followed the promenade, heading back the way she'd come. The cruise ship had passed out of sight like it had never been. Seagulls swooped and cawed over the water.

"If you'd like I could . . ." Chase began.

It seemed she'd been too subtle. "I appreciate that you want to help. But I don't need it, Chase."

There was a beat of silence followed by the creak of what she knew was the old office chair that his father had once sat in.

"It's my license and my reputation on the line," Chase said, clearly stung. "As far as the state of Florida is concerned, I'm responsible for everything that happens on that job. And I don't think either of us should forget that."

Avery stiffened at his tone but kept her voice even. "I'm not likely to forget it," she said. "But the last thing I want is for the network to think that I need someone male to help me figure out what to do. In ten seconds flat I'll be Vanna again and you'll be the big buff construction guy."

There was another pause and Avery knew her rejection of his help was not going down easy. She girded herself for battle. With Chase, you never knew for sure. She let out a sigh of relief when he said, "So you think I'm buff, huh?"

"Completely," she said.

"Well, I guess that's something," he replied. And then added a grudging, "You do seem to have things under control."

"The biggest issue is the budget," she said, wanting to offer something.

"It always is," Chase agreed.

"Right. But usually that's because there *is* no money," Avery said. "This time I think it's intentional. The network wants us desperate. I mean, what's a reality-TV show without stress and conflict?" She was going to have to find some way around the money thing. She was not going to turn The Millicent into "Do Over on a Dime."

"Reality shows need sex, too," he said. "Lots of it." His voice brightened. "I could definitely help with that." There was a pause. "Assuming that's not too intrusive of me."

Relieved that he seemed to have regained his sense of humor, Avery laughed. "That would be a little easier if we were actually in the same place at the same time. And I weren't sharing a bed with Deirdre."

"It may take me a little longer than I'd like, Van. But I'll be there . . ." There was a beat of silence and then: "I'm having a hard time picturing you and Deirdre duking it out over mattress space," Chase finally said. "And frankly I'd really prefer you were sharing that bed with me." A smile had stolen into his voice and she could picture it lighting up his face.

Avery felt her own face go hot. She was a lot more eager to share a bed with him than she should be. But she was not about to get all mushy and moony about Chase Hardin. Not until she'd proved herself here. After that she could figure out where, if anywhere, she might fit into his overfull life.

His tone turned teasing. "Maybe you should see what you can do about getting Deirdre out of your bedroom before I get down there. I'm a pretty open-minded guy, but there are a few things I'm going to want to 'discuss' when I get there that are definitely going to require some privacy."

"As long as it's not construction advice, you're welcome to 'discuss' away." Avery smiled and hung up, his chuckle of amusement echoing in her ear.

Chapter Seven

Sunrise that morning took place at 6:55. Maddie knew this because she was wide-awake and out on the ship-styled sundeck when the sky began to lighten and the sun's first rays pierced the low-lying clouds.

It was quiet outside. The morning dew clung to the tubular railings and to the leaves of the palms that jutted up around them. She couldn't see the Atlantic Ocean over the tops of the buildings, but she could feel it in the heavy air and the faint scent of salt and the not-so-distant cries of seagulls.

She'd slept badly, every toss and turn reminding her just how much her muscles ached from the week spent cleaning. Kyra's sleep had been equally troubled and even the baby's whimpers had sounded fitful. The settling of the unfamiliar house had woken her on and off through the night. Each time she'd toss and turn some more, wincing at the sharp soreness before willing herself back to sleep.

She'd woken up completely at five, then lay there quietly,

not wanting to wake Kyra, while random thoughts zoomed through her head: Steve's weeklong silence that had begun to feel like a rebuke, Andrew's last weeks at college before the summer break, the network and their intention to turn *Do Over* into something none of them had agreed to, Max Golden's celebrity photos and the wife that he'd lost.

When it became clear that going back to sleep was no longer an option, Madeline got up, pulled on a robe, and made a pot of coffee out on the loggia. Quietly, she had carried a cup of coffee outside to watch the day begin.

Now she did her best to banish the swirl of thoughts from her mind by focusing on the sun's slow but steady ascent into the pale blue sky. When that didn't work, she focused on the day ahead and spent a good thirty minutes thinking about what kind of meals she could cook in Max's kitchen that didn't require a working oven, stove, or uninterrupted electricity.

With a sigh she lifted the cup to her lips. The coffee had cooled but she sipped it anyway, searching for something positive with which to start her day. The best thing she could come up with was that her lips still seemed to move normally. They were the only part of her that she hadn't strained during the relentless days of cleaning.

Inside, Madeline pulled on clothes and brushed her teeth. She was about to head down to the kitchen when she remembered that Troy and Anthony could show up with camera and microphone blazing and she went back into the bathroom to put on makeup.

Madeline found the back kitchen door unlocked and Max sitting at the kitchen banquette freshly shaved and dressed. A copy of *Variety* lay open on the glass tabletop. That day's *Miami Herald* was folded beneath it. A cup of water looked to be boiling in the microwave. A jar of instant coffee and a ceramic mug sat on the counter.

"I like to keep up on what's happening in the business," he said as Maddie entered. "Although I hardly recognize it anymore."

Madeline held up the coffeemaker she had carried downstairs. A bag of ground coffee and filters were tucked under one arm.

"I see you come bearing gifts," Max said.

"Do you mind if I put on a pot?" Madeline asked. "There are people on our crew that aren't safe to be around until they've had at least one cup."

Max smiled. "I appreciate the warning. And the coffee." He folded the paper and pushed it aside. "I never could face a whole pot after I lost Millie. Especially not here in her kitchen. Somebody gave me one of those single-serve ones— you know, as a gift. It just made me feel more alone."

Madeline set up the coffeemaker. She'd rinsed the carafe upstairs and now she measured out the coffee and water. The microwave beeped that Max's water had boiled. "Do you want a cup of the instant or would you like to wait for the pot I'm brewing?"

"I'll wait, thanks."

Madeline opened a cupboard. With Max's permission, she'd emptied the cupboards and drawers yesterday to give everything a good scrubbing. Allowing her to clean was one thing; taking over his Millie's kitchen seemed like a much larger intrusion. Pulling the half-full carafe, she poured Max a cup.

"Would you like something to eat?" she asked as she carried the cup of coffee over and set it in front of him. "I have donuts and granola bars. I know those things don't sound like they go together, but then neither does our crew." She smiled as she remembered how out of sync she, Avery, and Nicole had been when they'd first moved into Bella Flora; three broke strangers in a broken-down house. "We've also got eggs and bread and . . ." Her voice trailed off as she realized she'd bought both sausages and bacon. "Do you keep kosher, Max?" she asked, chastising herself for being so unaware. "I didn't even think to ask yesterday. I should never have assumed that—"

"Madeline, sweetheart," Max said. "Relax. I like the New York Deli and a real bagel as much as the next man, but I've never met a pork product I didn't like. And I learned as a child on the vaudeville circuit and during the Depression to eat whatever I was lucky enough to find in front of me. Don't give it another thought." He took a sip of coffee and sighed with pleasure.

"Are you sure?" Madeline asked. Not that she would have known how to keep kosher if it were required. She knew only that it had something to do with a rabbi's blessing and taking care not to eat or mix certain things. "I don't want to offend you. And I definitely don't want you to feel like I'm taking over your kitchen."

"I'm sure," he said. "And I want you to make yourself at home. *Mi casa es su casa.*" He drank more of the coffee. "It'll be nice to have real food in here. I haven't used anything besides the refrigerator and the microwave since the fire." He nodded toward the smoke-smeared wall behind the stove and the singed cabinets above it.

"What happened?" Maddie asked.

"I don't know," he admitted. "One minute I was making a grilled cheese sandwich and the next thing it was in flames." He looked up at her, his expression hopeful. "Do you make grilled cheese? I love a good grilled cheese sandwich. I think I have a George Foreman Grill around somewhere and maybe an electric skillet."

"Absolutely," Madeline said. "My kids loved them, too. They're one of my specialties. Would you like one now? I saw the skillet in the cupboard yesterday and I could add an egg in to give it a breakfast feel."

He hesitated. Then he grabbed his forearm tightly in one hand, doubling over as if in pain. "Ach, my arm," he groaned. "It hurts."

"From what?" Maddie moved quickly toward Max, all the gruesome possibilities flitting through her mind. Could it be the numbing before a heart attack? The beginning of a stroke? She slapped her pockets looking for her cell phone to dial 911. "What happened? How—"

"It hurts from all that twisting you're doing. I can hardly stand the pain." He grinned at her, his brown eyes twinkling. "Actually, I'd love a grilled-cheese-and-egg sandwich."

Maddie retrieved the electric skillet from the cabinet. When she plugged it in, the lights went out and the refrigerator rattled to a stop. "Yikes," she said. "What do I do now?"

"You could probably unplug the coffeemaker now that the pot is full," he said, holding up his cup of coffee with the arm, now miraculously healed. "Do you think I could have a cup of fresh coffee? The fuse box is in the laundry room. I can change the fuse while you pour." He got slowly to his feet. "You sure do brew a mean cup."

The lights were back on and Max was chewing happily on his breakfast sandwich when the others began to trickle into the kitchen. Kyra arrived with Dustin propped on one shoulder and her camera on the other. The baby broke into a smile when he saw Max. The reaction was mutual.

Kyra pulled the portable high chair up to the table and placed Dustin in it. Maddie slid an omelet onto a plate for Kyra then cut part of it into small pieces, which she put on Dustin's Thomas the Tank Engine plate.

Avery arrived next, Deirdre trailing behind her. Madeline handed Avery a cup of coffee without being asked. Opening the box of donuts, she held it up for her perusal and was rewarded with a half smile, which, given Avery's caffeine-less state, was the equivalent of a standing ovation. Deirdre took a banana from a bowl of fruit and poured a cup of coffee, which she carried over to the table. All of them slid into the large, if tattered, leather banquette.

Maddie unplugged the skillet and carefully replugged the coffeemaker, holding her breath while she waited for the lights to flicker, breathing again when they stayed on.

A few minutes later Nicole appeared, her face flushed and her clothes slick with sweat, her morning run apparently behind her. She, too, went for the fruit bowl before perching on a bar stool. "I'm trying not to think about what full summer's going to feel like." She turned to Avery, who had finished her first cup of coffee and was halfway through a chocolate glazed donut. "You did put central air-conditioning at the top of the list, right?"

"I did," Avery said. "It would definitely be a huge plus to have it in before we're into full summer, but it isn't a fully budgeted item." She finished off her donut before continuing. "In fact almost nothing is. We're going to have to figure out how to get around that."

Max's and Dustin's gazes were glued on each other.

Maddie carried a washcloth over to her grandson and wiped the traces of yolk off his cheeks. She had to stop herself from doing the same for Max.

There was a brief knock on the back door. Troy and Anthony walked in. "Do I smell breakfast?" Troy asked. His hair looked wet from the shower. Anthony gave them a friendly smile that crinkled the corners of his eyes. His beard looked newly trimmed. Which meant, Maddie thought, that they must at least have some form of running water.

"Don't feed them, Mom," Kyra said. "They're *not* a part of the team. Their entire reason for being here is to catch us looking angry or stupid."

"I can do both of those looks on command." Max demonstrated a dazzling array of exaggerated expressions. Dustin giggled.

"It wasn't that long ago that *you* were exposing all our worst faults to the world," Nicole said to Kyra. "I still don't believe my pores could have possibly been that large. Or that we warranted that many hits on YouTube."

"And you all read me the riot act. And I got it," Kyra said. "These guys have a license to make us look bad."

"And running water from the look of them," Avery said. "You two help yourself to coffee and donuts," she said to the Lifetime crew. "There's milk and juice in the fridge."

"Thanks," Troy said.

Maddie looked at the two young men, who were just biting into donuts. "Oh my gosh," she said. "I just realized we forgot all about cleaning the pool house." She studied them for a moment. "It's so swallowed up in that hedge it's practically invisible. How bad is it in there?" She turned to Avery. "Maybe we should take care of that this morning."

"No," Troy said around the bite of donut he was chewing. "Don't worry about us. We're okay." He finished chewing and took a chug of coffee to wash it down. "In fact, we'll, uh, be glad to clean the pool house as partial payment toward our, um, room and board. It's going to take a lot of scrubbing before it's even fit to be assessed."

Anthony looked up from the donut he was holding in his hand, surprise evident on his broad face. "Um, right," he said after a glare from Troy.

"Really," Troy said. "We'll take care of it."

"That's very nice of you," Madeline said. "The cleaning supplies are in the laundry room. I'll get you fixed up with what you need when you're done with your breakfast."

Avery and Kyra looked at the men suspiciously, but Madeline knew that none of her group were about to turn down the offer.

Max made a last funny face for Dustin, stretching his features like so much Silly Putty, then stood, slowly using the table to steady himself. When he reached for his plate and coffee mug, Madeline moved toward him as quickly as she could without breaking into a run. "Here, let me take those for you," she said, not waiting for his agreement.

"Thank you very much for breakfast," he said with a smile. His hands patted his pants pockets as he began to walk. "I'm headed out for my pinochle game and lunch." He moved carefully, not yet fully upright. The straightening process was slow and ongoing. Nicole glanced out the banquette's plate-glass window. "Is someone picking you up?"

"No, no. I'm driving." He patted his pockets again then reached into a breast pocket. "Got 'em," he said, pulling out a set of keys. "My car's in the garage." He paused near the door that led to it. "I may have to ask you to move a couple of vehicles so that I can back out."

"You still drive?" Avery asked.

"Of course," Max said. "Been doing it almost eighty years now. I got my first driver's license in Michigan when I turned twelve."

His hand was on the doorknob now and he seemed to be using it to steady himself. Madeline looked around the kitchen, taking in the assorted looks of disbelief and alarm.

"I'm, um, going to go set up my camera," Troy said, dropping the remains of his donut in the garbage and speed-walking out the other kitchen door. Anthony was right behind him.

The rest of them followed Max down the steps into the garage, ostensibly to see which bay Max was parked in and who would have to go get their keys to let him out. Madeline could tell from their expressions that, like her, they thought he was simply teasing them. That there was no car and that if there were, someone or something would stop him from getting into it.

They piled into one another behind him as he pushed the button on the wall and the old garage door rumbled upward, allowing enough sunlight in so that they could see the outline of a car, draped in a cover, in the far bay. When Max reached it, he grasped a corner of the fabric and pulled it slowly, almost tauntingly, off the vehicle. A gleaming turquoise Cadillac convertible.

"Sweet!" Troy stood in the driveway, both feet planted, his camera on his shoulder. "Look at those fins! That is completely and totally cherry!"

Max stopped the careful stepping around the front of the car, whose vanity plate read LAFFABLE, pulled open the driver's door, and turned to face the camera. "This," he said directly into Troy's camera without the least bit of prompting, "is a 1959 Cadillac convertible. My wife used to tell me it was a babe magnet. And that no woman in her right mind could resist it. Or me."

Chapter Eight

Nicole sat at a table for two on the patio of the News Café overlooking Ocean Drive. The table was round and marble-topped, the chairs wood-slatted. Tree trunks stretched upward between the tables, their leafy canopy providing shade and atmosphere. Gianni Versace had breakfasted here most mornings including the morning that he'd been shot. Nicole glanced around, but she didn't recognize any famous faces.

It was warm and humid outside, but not unpleasantly so. Around her people sat talking over late-afternoon drinks and coffees, others fiddled with their phones, but the main occupation was people-watching and there was no lack of people to watch. They passed in a steady stream, from the costumed and bizarre to the black-socked and sandaled. Beautiful young women, long-legged and professionally thin, also strutted by. Nicole had read somewhere that the number of models per square foot here on South Beach was higher than anywhere else in the world and that commercial and film shoots were common.

The waiter was dark and attractive, his accent vaguely foreign. Nicole treated herself to a second glass of wine and ordered herself to relax. She was not an Art Deco fanatic like Avery, but she had to admit that the run of restored hotels was impressive. The outdoor cafés and restaurants along Ocean Drive had a decidedly European vibe.

She'd partied here on South Beach after her second divorce and had made a point of being seen at the right clubs and private parties while she was building Heart, Incorporated. If she were still in business, this would be a perfect place to troll for wealthy clients, but she hadn't exactly determined whether there was anyone out there who might still want to retain her. Of all the clients she'd found marriageable mates for, only Bitsy Baynard remained willing to invite her to parties or refer her to wealthy friends.

Nicole was careful not to frown at the thought, since she could no longer afford either Botox or the smallest of corrective surgeries. For a time she banished her troubling reality by watching the parade that passed by her and enjoying the waiter's polished flirtation. She'd stashed the Jag at a parking garage off Collins Avenue and had noticed a promising number of boutiques she might walk through. Or she could head up to Lincoln Road. Maybe drive up to the shops at Bal Harbour. She headed off another frown as her grim financial reality struck her once again; window-shopping was only enjoyable if you were only window-shopping by choice.

When her cell phone rang, she was so relieved to have something to divert her from the depressing path her thoughts had taken that she answered without checking the caller ID.

The voice on the line was unfamiliar. And so was the name.

"I'm sorry," Nicole said. "Who's calling?"

"Parker Amherst." The caller paused when Nicole didn't immediately respond. "The Fourth."

"Oh," Nicole said. Once, receiving a call from a Roman-numeraled individual wouldn't have been at all surprising. Today it was the equivalent of a meteor sighting. She sat up straighter and found her voice. "Hello," she said, pleased that the word came out well modulated and professional. "How can I help you?"

His inflections spoke of prep school and privilege. Wasting no time on pleasantries or explanations, Parker Amherst IV got right to the point. "I'm looking for a suitable bride," he said. "And I understand you provide this service. I also understood that you were currently in town."

"Um, yes." Her heart pounded and she was practically stuttering. She felt the tiniest flush of hope. Maybe she wasn't finished after all. Maybe there were wealthy single people out there who had not heard that Malcolm Dyer was her brother and who didn't know that Heart, Incorporated had bitten the dust.

Once she would have screened any potential client very carefully, or gotten her assistant to do it for her. She was afraid to ask or question her good fortune, but knew she couldn't appear too eager. "Who referred you to me?" she asked as professionally as she could.

"Bitsy Baynard," he said, and Nikki's shoulders began to relax. "I was up in Palm Beach at a polo match last year and she mentioned you. I've been in and out of the country so much that I never had the chance to follow up. But I held on to your card."

She was too excited to ask where he'd been traveling. Maybe he *had* hitched a ride on a Soyuz spacecraft. And just returned from another galaxy. One that was far, far away.

"Yes, I'm in Miami Beach, South Beach actually, for the next few months," she said, keeping the time frame intentionally vague. "How about you?"

"I have a house on Star Island." He named the exclusive nearby island, off the MacArthur Causeway, that was known for multimillion-dollar homes and water views. "I'm usually only here in the winter, but I had to come down to see to some renovations." He didn't say where he'd come down from or how many other homes he might own, but Nicole didn't care about the details. All she cared about was that she had a potential client on the line—a client who could put her back in business and her bank balance back into the black.

"Well then," she said, careful to put a smile into her voice. "It seems fortuitous that we're both here at the same time." She pulled up her empty calendar and spent a good deal of time trying to fit him into it. She might be a bit out of practice, but she still remembered how to close a deal. If she were smart, she would close this one as quickly as possible and deposit a retainer before Parker Amherst IV found out that she was no longer *the* A-list matchmaker she used to be. Or much of a matchmaker anymore at all.

• • •

The Millicent was quiet. Every window that could be budged had been thrown or cranked open. The warm breeze that stirred the palms outside reached inside and wrapped its arms around the edgier smell of chemically induced cleanliness. The temperature had peaked in the mid-eighties and the humidity was noticeable but not oppressive, but then this was only early June. The full heat of summer still lay ahead.

For the last couple of hours Madeline had had the house to herself and had spent most of that time puttering happily in the kitchen, wiping the surfaces once again and putting things to rights. Now she sat at the kitchen table nursing a glass of iced tea and staring out at the jungle of yard. A pen, her ever-present yellow pad, and her phone sat on the table in front of her. Tentatively she added the words *lawn mower* to the to-do list. Then she took a sip of iced tea. Her gaze moved to her phone, but no matter how intently she studied it, the instrument refused to ring.

Her last communication from Steve had been a brief but upbeat acknowledgment of her voice mail letting him know that they'd arrived safely. But that had been a week ago. She didn't see how they could right things between them if they didn't actually speak.

Madeline's hand hovered over the phone even as she chided herself for hesitating. She and Steve had been married for more than a quarter of a century. Who called whom when wasn't important. They didn't need to stand on ceremony or jockey for position.

Before she could change her mind, Maddie picked up the phone and hit the speed dial for Steve's office, then stared out the window while she waited for his secretary to put her through.

"Hi, Maddie." His greeting was neutral, not overjoyed to hear from her, but not overtly angry, either.

"Hi." Her own voice sounded tight and small. She couldn't quite let go of the fact that she had had to call him. "How are you?"

"Fine," he said. "How's everything down there?"

"Pretty good," Maddie replied. And then because there was no point in being on the phone if they weren't going to communicate, she said, "Well, except for the state of the electrical system. And the lack of air-conditioning. And the film crew that none of us were expecting." She laughed but he didn't join in or ask for details.

There was a brief but awkward silence before he asked, "How are Kyra and the baby?"

"Good," Madeline said. "Dustin is almost always happy. And the owner of the house, Max, has taken a definite shine to him. Kyra's handling herself really well considering what's going on. I'm really proud of her." Maddie could feel herself beginning to babble, throwing out words like Spider-Man flung webs in an attempt to snare her husband's attention and connect with him completely—something that used to happen automatically. "I think there are going to be a lot of hard lessons on this job. For all of us."

There was another awkward silence and then: "Are you sure you want to do this?" It was the same question he'd asked at their anniversary dinner and again when he'd kissed Maddie, Kyra, and the baby good-bye. "You don't have to."

"There's real opportunity here," she said. "If we can make this work and a series comes out of it . . ." Her voice trailed off. She'd promised herself that she'd never again leave Steve to carry the entire load, and she was not about to break that promise. It was far better to have her own income from Lifetime, tiny though it was at the moment, while they waited to see if *Do Over* would find an audience and whether Bella Flora would sell. Whatever she accomplished here would benefit all of them; surely he understood that.

"You're afraid I can't handle the pressure," he said as if it were just now sinking in. "You think I'm going to snap again if something goes wrong."

"No," she said quickly. This was not the time to admit that she *wanted* to be here. That no matter how hard the work might be, having a job of her own and being with the others were easier than sitting at home surreptitiously watching Steve for signs of cracks like a worried homeowner who'd discovered that her house had a faulty foundation.

The truth was that while she wanted to believe that Steve was once again the strong, almost invincible man she'd thought she'd married, he was right; she was afraid to put him to the test. Because if he broke again, there'd be nothing left to put together.

"When do you think you'll be able to get down for a visit?" she asked. "The Millicent is right in the middle of South Beach and the house is, well, it's a big mess right now, but it's really, really beautiful. And Max Golden, the owner is . . ." She paused for breath hoping he'd go along with the topic change, but Steve cut in so smoothly that she could tell he'd been waiting for the opportunity.

"I'm sorry, Mad," he said, his voice tight with disappointment. "I have a client waiting on the other line. I'm going to have to go."

"But—" Maddie began.

"I'm too new in my position to take time off," he said. "But maybe when Andrew gets home from school for the summer, we can work out a time to come down."

"Okay," Maddie said, knowing that she'd only managed

to make things worse. "Sure." Tears gathered behind her eyelids. "We'll talk later."

"Give Kyra and Dustin hugs from me," he said.

"I will," Madeline said.

But Steve had already hung up.

. . .

Deirdre found Maddie sitting on a neon-striped beach chair next to the cracked and empty pool. A copy of *Easy Gardens for South Florida* sat unopened in her lap, but Deirdre could see no evidence that any mowing, digging, or planting had taken place.

"There's an actual beach for that chair just a few blocks from here. And it has a way better view." She'd been hoping to catch Maddie alone. She looked around, relieved to see no sign of the Lifetime crew.

"Too lazy," Maddie replied. She nodded to the pitcher that sat on a small table beside her. "There's iced tea if you want some."

Deirdre looked more closely at Madeline Singer. Maddie's face was smudged with dirt and her clothes were sweat-stained. Her smile seemed strained.

"How about a glass of wine instead?" Deirdre asked. "You know, to start the mellowing process? I'm not sure I can wait until sunset."

Madeline glanced down at her watch and seemed surprised at the time she saw there.

"It's almost five," Deirdre said. "That's late enough to drink pretty much everywhere."

"Okay," Madeline said, moving as if to rise.

"Stay where you are," Deirdre said even as she tried to figure out how to broach the subject she'd been hoping to discuss. "There's a bottle of white wine in the refrigerator. I'll bring it out. It's just as cool out here as it is inside and the breeze is stronger."

In the kitchen, Deirdre found a tray and assembled the bottle and two wineglasses along with a small bowl of mixed nuts as quickly as she could. Given the sheer number of them living together, any time alone with Madeline was bound to be short. It would be hard enough to ask Maddie for what she wanted; there wasn't time for a slow build.

Back outside, they clinked glasses but neither offered a toast.

"How did things go at the Design District?" Maddie asked politely.

"Good," Deirdre said. "I have an old friend who has a showroom there. We worked together on a project down here a number of years ago. She mentioned a real estate firm that specializes in historic homes on the beach. They might be helpful as we work and could be the right firm for Max to list the house with when we're done."

"Assuming he wants to put the house up for sale," Madeline said.

"It couldn't hurt to have them come over and give Max an idea of the house's value," Deirdre said, noting Maddie's protective tone and the glint of suspicion in her eyes. She and Madeline Singer had come to terms with each other by the end of their stint at Bella Flora, but they weren't exactly BFFs.

"I really don't have an agenda here," Deirdre said. She took a long sip of her wine, gathering her courage. "Well, except for one thing."

The suspicion in Madeline's eyes sharpened; there was

an almost imperceptible tightening of her jaw. "And what one thing is that?"

Deirdre looked down at her already empty glass, embarrassed. But there was no time to dissemble. "I want to mend my relationship with Avery," she said. "No matter how many times I've apologized, she just can't seem to forgive me for leaving. We're sleeping in the same bed, for God's sake, and she's clinging to the edge of her side as if rolling anywhere near me would be some sort of punishment." She looked away, her gaze settling on the citrus trees in the corner of the yard.

Madeline didn't speak, but Deirdre could feel her assessing her. When she turned back, Madeline was appraising her frankly. For someone who was always anticipating the needs of others, the woman sure wasn't rushing to ease the way.

"I want to be a real mother to her." Deirdre set the wineglass aside and leaned toward Maddie. "But I don't really know how." She folded her arms across her chest, feeling chilled despite the balmy weather. "You're really great at being a mother—and grandmother. And I know Avery likes and admires you for it." She glanced down at her empty wineglass. "She barely tolerates me."

Deirdre poured herself another glass and topped off Maddie's without asking, then set the bottle back on the table between them, watching the other woman's face carefully.

"It's not like there's some list of do's and don'ts," Madeline finally said, some decision reached. "At least not outside of the occasional *Good Housekeeping* or *Working Mother* article." She gestured with her wineglass. "I mean, basically you just put your children first. Everything else sorts itself out from there."

She made it sound so simple.

"But how do you do that?" Deirdre pressed. "How do you make sure that you're really always putting them first?" She looked around, checking once again to make sure that no one was watching them. That Troy and Anthony were not hidden behind some tree recording their conversation.

"I guess it's just maternal instinct," Madeline said. "Usually we mother like our own mothers did. Or in some circumstances, we do the exact opposite." She looked up over the deck, her voice thoughtful, and Deirdre could tell that she'd probably never put any of this into words before. "You love unconditionally and you let them know it."

"Yes, well, I didn't have any instruction," Deirdre said. "My mother didn't leave, but she was even less of a mother than I was. When I had Avery, I felt that kind of love, but it was no match for the fear I felt. I was so afraid I'd screw everything up."

"I think she turned out pretty well," Madeline said with a small smile. "A little ornery at times, but very strong and resourceful."

"That was Peter's doing. He was born to be a father; Avery's father," Deirdre admitted. "You should have seen her following him around his construction sites in that little pink hard hat he gave her." Her smile turned lopsided. "I couldn't compete with that. And in the end I bungled everything. But I'm determined to get it right this time." One eyebrow went up. "I guess it's too late for a pony?"

Madeline laughed. "Just a little."

They sipped their wine for a few moments as the shadows

lengthened and the day drew to a close. "Showing love and being a mother is a highly individual thing," Maddie said. "It's not like there's a course with a syllabus and homework assignments."

The bottle was almost gone. Deirdre poured the last of it into their glasses and raised hers to her lips.

A car pulled into the driveway. A door slammed somewhere in the house and Deirdre knew that the time had come to ask for what she wanted. She sincerely hoped Madeline wasn't going to laugh in her face.

"But there could be, couldn't there?" Deirdre asked, setting down her glass. "Some sort of informal syllabus or list of suggestions?"

"I'm sorry?" Madeline said, her brow furrowing.

The garage door rumbled up and Dustin's cry sounded from upstairs.

"I have a feeling that I'm missing something," Maddie said. "What is it that you want?"

Deirdre fingered the stem of her wineglass and looked Maddie square in the eye. "I want to learn to be a real mother." She heard a humiliating note of desperation in her voice, but was powerless to disguise it. "And I want you to teach me how."

Chapter Nine

Their first officially observed sunset in Miami took place a few nights later on The Millicent's stern-shaped deck. Although Avery had already explained that this would be more of a business meeting than their traditional "toasting" whatever good thing they could dredge from their day, she was careful not to mess with the eating-and-drinking portion of the ritual.

Nicole led the way up the gangplank carrying a blender of frozen strawberry daiquiris and was followed by Kyra with a second pitcher of the icy pink concoction. Madeline brought napkins and paper plates, one of which was piled high with the little hot dogs in blankets that had been a sunset staple at Bella Flora, while Avery balanced a tray of glasses and a bag of Cheez Doodles. The women barely nodded to Troy and Anthony, who had planted themselves at the base of the stairs to record their parade up the gangplank.

Nicole poured drinks as they settled into the neon-colored beach chairs that Maddie had salvaged from the previous summer. Deirdre, who was already dressed for dinner with a former client, set a large foil-covered tray on a battered plastic table and dragged it toward Avery.

When she was certain she had Avery's attention, Deirdre unwrapped an artfully displayed assortment of Cheez Doodles, cheese puffs, and Cheez-Its. There wasn't a toast point, a caviar jar, or any foie gras—Deirdre's usual contribution—anywhere in sight.

There was laughter.

"Is this your idea of a joke?" Avery asked, not seeing the humor.

"No, it's my idea of indigestion," Deirdre said, handing Avery a paper plate of Cheez Doodles and a neatly folded napkin. "But I know how much you like artificially colored cheese-food products."

Pinkie up, Deirdre took a small bite of a Cheez Doodle and chewed tentatively. She grimaced as if in pain as she swallowed, then contemplated her orange-stained fingers.

"Thanks," Avery said as Deirdre passed the hors d'oeuvres. And then because she couldn't help herself: "They really taste better out of the bag."

"I think it was very nice of your mother to serve something she knew you'd like," Madeline said.

All of them looked up at Maddie's use of the word *mother*. Deirdre flinched and braced, as if waiting for Avery to object to the term, but Avery wasn't about to debate Deirdre's lack of qualifications or claim to the title. There were things that needed to be accomplished tonight. Slapping down Deirdre wasn't one of them.

"Right," Nicole said, raising her glass. "But I'm voting for something a little more elegant and a lot less orange next time."

"They did have a gourmet, no-artificial-coloring version," Deirdre said.

"Good God, no," Avery replied. "That would suck the pleasure right out of them."

They sipped their drinks for a time with only the low buzz of insects and the sharp slap at the occasional blood-seeking mosquito to break the silence. Maddie had arranged the chairs facing west, and for a few long moments they watched the golden ball of sun shimmer in the sky and reflect off the glass of the condo buildings that lay between them and Biscayne Bay. They were farther removed from the display than they had been at Bella Flora, but the show was well worth watching just the same.

Licking a cheesy finger, Kyra stood and walked to the opposite corner of the deck, where she leaned over the railing and scanned the backyard. The baby monitor was clipped to the waistband of her shorts.

"What are you looking for?" Maddie asked.

"I want to make sure the dastardly duo isn't hiding behind some bush or up a palm tree aiming a parabolic microphone our way," Kyra said. "I wouldn't put anything past Troy Matthews."

When she was satisfied that they were not under covert surveillance, Kyra plopped back into her chair. "I can't believe what a mess everything is," she said. "I was so excited about the opportunity to shoot and produce a series. Karen Crandall seemed to be so on board with our vision for *Do Over* that we didn't spell enough of it out in the contract."

Avery sighed. She had been there, done that, and already

owned the T-shirt. "Don't beat yourself up about it. Even if we had covered everything, there wouldn't have been much we could do if they changed their minds. The only power we ever really have is to walk away. And none of us are in any position to do that."

Kyra stilled.

"How can you be so calm?" Kyra's voice was as tightly clenched as her hands. "I thought we were shooting and producing a television series about redoing really interesting houses for important reasons, but we're really just starring in a reality-TV show. The only thing missing is the professional athlete husbands and the outrageous amounts of money."

Watching Kyra's troubled face, Avery saw herself, shocked and horrified by what her role on the HGTV show *Hammer & Nail* had become. How her then-husband Trent had become the star of the show Avery had conceived and sold, while Avery, a trained architect who had grown up on her father's construction sites, had been reduced to pointing and gesturing and smiling—a role that had caused a whole slew of additional IQ points to be deducted.

"It sucks," Avery said. "But you have to remember that the sole purpose of television programs is to sell products. The more viewers, the more the network can charge for commercial time. And right now reality shows are hot—the more intimate and revealing the better."

"That's what Lisa Hogan said." Kyra wrapped her hands around her now-empty glass. Fading sunlight bathed her in its glow. "Troy and Anthony don't answer to me—or us—in any way," she said. "It was a major coup to get her to agree to any camera-free zones or time frames at all."

Kyra drew a breath and set her glass down. "I may as

well tell you now that the only way I got her to agree was by telling her that we'd walk otherwise."

There was a shocked silence. Avery's heart lurched painfully in her chest. Deirdre swore softly.

"You did what?" Nicole asked. Like the rest of them, her face reflected horror.

"I couldn't get her to agree to anything or give us the slightest concession. And she was so smug about having us at her mercy." Kyra was practically wringing her hands. She looked at her mother, but Maddie appeared as shocked and horrified as the rest of them. "She told me that Dustin's fair game. That his being Daniel Deranian's son is one of the reasons they gave us the show in the first place."

"Jesus," Nicole said. "You had no right to do that."

"I know," Kyra said, clearly miserable. "I know and I'm—"

"We're in this together," Avery said. "No one has the right to put the show at risk like that without discussing it first. No one."

"I know. And I'm sorry." Kyra shook her head. "I just . . ." Her voice trailed off as the first tears fell. "I'm so, so sorry."

Maddie closed her eyes. "Thank God she didn't call you on it."

They sat in silence for a few long moments absorbing what might have happened.

Nicole refilled everyone's glass, but no one suggested a toast.

"Are we clear?" Avery asked when she trusted herself to speak again. "No one, not even me, takes that kind of risk without a vote."

Kyra nodded. Maddie reached out to give her daughter's arm a squeeze, but it was Deirdre who turned the conversation. "Has Deranian seen Dustin? Do you speak to him?"

Kyra shook her head, but quietly, her mind no doubt still on her confession and their reaction. "The only person I've heard from is Daniel's business manager," she said. "Daniel hasn't shirked his financial responsibility, but he hasn't made any effort to see Dustin either." She took a long, glum sip of her daiquiri. "I think I'm pretty much over movie stars."

Maddie lifted her glass. "I'll drink to that."

"Falling for Daniel wasn't the smartest thing I've ever done. That's for sure." Kyra paused, her eyes filled with regret. "I gave him a lot more credit as a human being than he deserved."

"It was like that with Trent," Avery said, going with the conversation. "Everything was great until I got to know him and actually understood him."

Nicole drained her glass. "That's why the 'strong silent type' is so popular," she added. "As long as they keep their mouths shut, we can imbue them with all kinds of intelligent thoughts and attractive personality traits."

Avery looked to Maddie, who'd been married far longer than any of them, expecting an argument, but Maddie busied herself with her drink.

Kyra's laugh was rueful. "I've screwed up all around. With Daniel. With the network. I feel really stupid for showing up here and expecting so much in the first place."

"Kyra, you're twenty-four years old," Maddie said, back in full mother mode. Unlike Avery's "mother," who seemed far more "faux" than full. "You're bound to make mistakes. And if you don't expect a lot, you can't get it. Lowering your expectations isn't the answer."

"Then what is?" Kyra met Avery's gaze.

"I'll have to get back to you on that," Avery said. Her heart was still hammering far faster than she'd like. "But I do have confidence that we can handle the network crew. I mean, if we don't give them the conflict and hysterics and backbiting they're looking for, maybe we can shape this show the way we want it."

"Do you really believe that?" Nicole asked.

"I think so." Avery considered the question and their situation. "Based on their skewed perception of the show, we—*not the house*—are the whole enchilada. But they're going to have to shoot the things we want shot to get us."

"And we've got you," Maddie said to Kyra. "You had no problem documenting the renovation at Bella Flora as well as all the personal issues that nabbed the network."

"And you have our best interests at heart," Deirdre added.

"Most of the time anyway," Nicole threw in.

They considered one another as the sun slid farther down the sky.

"So you just make sure you get all the video you need," Avery said. "And we'll be careful not to give them what they're looking for." She looked around, meeting everyone's eyes, holding on to Deirdre's. "We don't want anyone besides Max performing for the cameras."

"Who me?" Deirdre raised the platter of Cheez products and offered it around, completely overdressed for the ram-shackle deck and the hors d'oeuvres in her hand.

"Got it," Kyra said, reaching for her camera.

"Good." Avery popped a Cheez Doodle in her mouth and chewed, but was careful not to show any sign of appreciation for its greasy, cheesy airiness. "Maddie will be in charge of our next sunset, which I'm sure will be back to our regularly scheduled one-good-thing. But right now there's a last critical item of business."

The sun had disappeared behind the condos and the last bits of color leached from the sky. Avery could feel Madeline, Kyra, Deirdre, and Nicole's expectant gazes.

"Troy and Anthony aren't the only stumbling blocks the network has thrown in our path," Avery continued carefully. "They're just the most visible."

"And annoying," Kyra said from behind her camera.

"Our budget—or rather our lack of budget—is a serious problem. And like the crew, it's intentional. They know there's no way we can do this house justice on the amount they've made available. They can't wait to see us squirm."

"So what do we do?" Madeline asked. "How can they expect us to renovate without money?"

"We're going to have to find sponsors," Avery said. "I may be able to stretch our budget to include at least partial payment for actual goods. But we're going to have to exchange on-air exposure and publicity for a significant part of the labor and installation."

"Will the network go along with that?" Maddie asked.

"They don't really have a choice," Deirdre commented. "This is where not dotting every *i* works to our advantage."

Avery nodded. "We're just going to do it. I have a list of possible vendors for windows and glass and we can call on Deirdre's contacts in the design community.

"I've got an electrical and plumbing company I'd like to go after. They need to be first. After that, I think we've all agreed that air-conditioning is most important. Plus we'll need roofers, painters, and artisans for the tile and plasterwork."

"And don't forget the kitchen," Deirdre interjected. "And furniture refinishing and reupholstering. There's some fabulous stuff here, but almost all of it needs to be repaired or updated."

Dusk deepened to dark as Avery blew a stray bang out of her eyes. She looked at her merry band and saw that they were focused and, she thought, willing to follow her lead. She only hoped that she wouldn't be leading them off a cliff.

"We'll all help with this, just like we're all going to do the unavoidable grunt labor that we can't afford to pay for. But I think Nicole and Deirdre should drive our sponsorship efforts. There aren't a lot of people who can say no to either of them."

Avery handed them the sheets of paper with the company names, addresses, and phone numbers she'd printed out. Deirdre left for her dinner engagement. The rest of them sat beneath the darkening sky drinking the last sips of their daiquiris and licking the final orangey stain of Cheez Doodle from their fingers.

· · ·

Kyra lifted her camera to her shoulder and shot video of Nicole, Maddie, and Avery as they carried the remnants of their sunset down the back stairs and into the kitchen.

Max was there, resplendent in his smoking jacket, which apparently wasn't a costume but a favored part of his "at home" wardrobe. Still trying to regain her equilibrium after the reaction to her confession, Kyra picked up some tight shots of the gnarled fingers of his hands and the unlit cigar that he clenched between them. Slowly she pulled out to include the smiling old man and the just-popped bag of microwaved popcorn that stood open on the counter.

Avery was right. She would shoot her own version of events here at The Millicent and present them in her own way. Troy would focus on the skin and bones of the renovation of The Millicent and the people in it along with whatever eruptions he could capture. She would shoot the heart.

"You're just in time." Clearly happy to see them, Max gave an exaggerated wink into the camera lens. "I'm getting ready to watch *Celebrity Roundup*. Would you like to join me?"

Kyra filmed Madeline, Nicole, and Avery's surprise at the invitation. For her part, Kyra liked celebrity-gossip television even less than she liked celebrity-gossip magazines. But she liked Max Golden quite a lot.

"I've got popcorn," Max added, inviting them to inhale the steamy butter smell that was still escaping from the bag. His tone made it clear that he assumed this would clinch the deal. Maddie put another bag of popcorn in the microwave. It wasn't even nine P.M. and none of them had anything more pressing to do.

Soon they were walking slowly through The Millicent toward Max's bedroom, where the lone television resided. They did their best to allow Max to keep up, but it was surprisingly hard to walk that slowly. In fact, it felt like the absence of movement.

In Max's bedroom the air conditioner managed to do slightly more than stir the hot air around. They followed his directions, pulling the ottoman and the vanity chair over next to his recliner and retrieving the piano bench, which they shoved up against the side of the bed.

Kyra yawned and settled on the bench next to her mother. From there she filmed the women's smiles and their hands dipping into the popcorn. As Max settled into his recliner, she captured his face and his fabulous smile and recorded his deep sigh of contentment.

The theme music began and the celebrity interviews and movie clips flew by. Max knew details about performers that even Kyra had never heard of and had clearly versed himself in the young comedians' styles and careers.

"I love that guy," he said when a brief clip of Jerry Seinfeld doing stand-up came on. "He and Larry David together, they were genius. Larry David by himself?" He shook his head regretfully.

Max kept up a steady stream of patter, and Kyra's attention was split between him, the show, and the faces of the mostly dead celebrities who stared down at them from Max's bedroom wall. The room was warm with the group's body heat and redolent with the smell of popcorn. Her thoughts became unfocused and her eyelids began to grow heavy. A couple of times her eyes closed completely and she only jerked awake when her chin dug into her chest.

"Kyra?" Her mother's voice whispered in her ear. Her fingers rested on her arm. "Honey, I know you were up early with Dustin. And tonight's been . . . well, maybe you should go up to bed."

Despite the piano bench's lack of back, Kyra began to nod off in earnest. She was trying to rouse herself to do as her mother suggested when Maddie's hand clamped down around Kyra's arm and a name pierced her mental fog.

"What?" Kyra jolted upright when she heard Nicole and Avery gasp. The popcorn munching had come to a sudden halt. She followed their gazes to the television.

"Did she just say . . ." Kyra's voice trailed off as a shot of the actor Daniel Deranian filled the television screen. The camera pulled out to reveal his equally famous wife, Tonja Kay, beside him. The shot widened further to include the megastars carrying and herding their four children, who ranged in age from two to seven and who appeared to have been adopted from a wide range of third-world countries, through an airport.

Kyra knew that Maddie, Avery, and Nicole were looking at her, but she couldn't look away from the screen. She actually felt her heart lurch when the host said, "Deranian and Kay arrived in Miami yesterday and are set to star in the already controversial film *Mirage,* which begins shooting Monday on South Beach."

The host flashed her perfectly capped teeth and turned to another camera. "Batten down the hatches, Miami," she said gaily. "Hollywood's most beautiful power couple has arrived!"

"Holy crap," Kyra muttered as the group shot of the famous family dissolved into an extreme close-up of Daniel Deranian's handsome face. Kyra wanted to look away but she was powerless to break the connection. The dark eyes held her spellbound, she remembered how those lips had felt on hers. She stared at the image for what felt like an eternity, wide-awake now, but barely breathing. Until it finally faded away.

Chapter Ten

Avery stood on the upstairs landing, where dust motes floated in what midday light managed to pierce the huge rectangle of glass block and the filthy plate-glass porthole window.

The once white plaster walls were dirty and pockmarked. A low bookcase built into the stair buttress had only half its molding. But at the moment her attention was focused on the wall that had been added at the head of the stairs to separate the first and second floors. She ran a hand up the pockmarked plaster and contemplated the awkward gap between the top of the wall and the domed oval ceiling above it.

She made a mental note of its dimensions and estimated what it would take to remove it. It was neither original nor load bearing. She could hardly wait to bring this sucker down.

The doorbell rang as she was examining the scarred oak flooring. Footsteps sounded down in the foyer and she could hear the front door opening as she turned her attention to the hardware on the bedroom doors, which was original chrome from the 1930s. Every bit of it was dull and scratched.

"Avery?" Nicole's voice rose from downstairs. "Someone's here to see you!"

Since she knew virtually no one in Miami and had no appointments scheduled, she walked quickly through her bedroom and looked out the window to the driveway. Her body stiffened in surprise when she spotted Chase Hardin's truck.

Taking the back stairs two at a time, she practically mowed him down as she rounded the garage.

"Nicole wasn't sure if you heard her or not," he said, drawing her into his arms.

"But what are you doing here?" she asked. "How did—"

His lips were warm and firm on hers. The scent of him filled her nostrils and her arms stole up around his neck. But when he went to deepen the kiss, she stilled.

"What's wrong?" She heard his puzzlement as he nuzzled her neck. "I've been thinking about doing this, and a lot more, for the last hundred miles."

It took all of her will, and a little bit of leverage, to shrug out of his arms. "I don't know where the film crew is," she said with a warning look. She did not want to look up and see them filming her unexpected reunion with Chase. It would take so little for them to spin that into her needing Chase to get the job done. "I can't believe you're here. What happened? Why didn't you tell me you were coming?"

"I wasn't sure until this morning that I'd actually be able to get away." He leaned down and kissed her again, not at all worried about being caught in lip-lock on national television, but then he hadn't been living under constant scrutiny like she had. And no one was going to consider *him* unqualified if they saw him kissing her.

She stepped out of his arms and led him out to the front sidewalk, where they could get a straight-on look at The Millicent without the jungle-that-had-not-yet-been-tamed annihilating their view.

"So, what do you think?" Avery opened her arms wide to encompass The Millicent. "Isn't she fabulous?"

With a crooked smile he took in the overgrown yard, the peeling paint, and the mismatched and broken windows. But Avery also saw his experienced gaze skim over the structure's finely drawn lines and curves, and take in the rounded concrete overhangs called "eyebrows" that shaded the windows. His eyes glowed as they settled on the porthole windows and the observation tower that topped the circular entry.

"She's beautiful all right," he said. "But it's going to take a ton of work and money to bring her back."

"I know." She walked him around the property, pointing out her favorite features, explaining her plans to circumvent the roadblocks the network kept throwing up.

He listened intently. For the most part he smiled and nodded. Just a year ago he'd treated her as if she didn't have two brain cells to rub together. They'd come a long way since then, but he seemed to be having a little trouble with the concept of keeping his suggestions to himself.

They were standing side by side in the living room examining the fireplace. She'd just described the construction schedule and was leading him toward Max's room.

"Have you got a printed copy of that schedule for me?" he asked.

"No."

"I guess you could just e-mail it to me later so I can sign off on it."

"Um." She pretended to think. "No."

"Because?" He looked genuinely baffled.

"Because I've just shared it with you as a courtesy. I'm not submitting it to you for approval." She reached up to knock on Max's door.

Chase wrapped his hand around her fist before she could make contact. "I know you want to prove yourself," he said as her hand dropped to her side. "But I assumed there'd be *some* collaboration."

"We *are* collaborating," she replied. "I've just informed you of my plans and my projected schedule. And you're impressed as hell but for some reason still trying to figure out how to show it."

They stared at each other and she knew that if she didn't address this now, he was going to remind her yet again that it was his license and reputation on the line. And she was going to remind him that she'd grown up on the same construction sites he had and that she had an architectural degree. They'd spend the entire summer locked in their own personal version of *Groundhog Day*.

"Let me clarify my position," she said. "This show is my chance for vindication on national television. I can't afford to have anyone thinking that I'm relying on my looks or leaning on you to get through this job. The network would play that up in a heartbeat. I am not going to risk even the *appearance* of leaning."

She hated that she had to look up at him, but she maintained eye contact so that she could drive her point home. "I really enjoy being with you, Chase, and I'm really glad you're here," she said. She glanced away just to make sure the camera crew hadn't reappeared. "But there can't be any doubt in anyone's mind—including yours—about who's running this project."

Avery knew from the set of his shoulders and the way his blue eyes darkened that Chase was irritated. But when she rapped on Max's door and Max appeared, he shook the old man's hand warmly and seemed unfazed when Troy and Anthony appeared and began to trail after them.

When the doorbell rang sometime later, he turned his back on the Lifetime crew and pulled her aside. "Don't hold this against me," he said. "It was organized with the best of intentions."

Avery had no idea what he was talking about until she pulled open the front door and found herself face-to-face with Enrico Dante, who'd done so much for them and Bella Flora.

She stiffened, ready to give Chase some shit for tracking down Enrico in Tampa and bringing him here without her permission, but then Enrico pulled her into a bear hug and began to introduce the family he'd brought with him.

"They are fine artisans," Enrico said as he pointed out the cousins who—*thank you, God*—lived and worked in north Miami. A large smile bisected his wizened face. "Each of them has his own specialty. And at least some of them are almost as talented as me."

Tall and sparsely built with a thick head of salt-and-pepper hair, Enrico's cousin Mario had an old-world charm and the remnants of an Italian accent. "Ha," he said, cuffing Enrico on the shoulder. "I have been plastering and setting tile in the finest houses on the east coast ever since I came to this country as a child. I will put my skills up against this old man any day." He nodded to a younger version of himself. "Donatello here, he will go up and take a look at the roof with Enrico. And make sure the old man doesn't fall off."

Enrico smiled. "You are, of course, welcome to join us," Enrico said, reminding Avery of her insistence on climbing up to inspect Bella Flora's roof when Chase attempted to leave her out. "This one is much flatter than Bella Flora's angled barrel tile. Even Chase should be able to handle it."

Chase pretended to stagger back from the blow to his ego and Avery bit back a smile, not quite ready to let him off the hook for interfering.

Mario nodded to his other son, who had removed his hat to reveal a head as bald as Enrico's. "Salvatore is an artiste with plaster. He will help me make these walls even finer than they once were." He winked at Avery. "And we will give you the *famiglia* discount. Enrico is very devoted to you. He tells me you are Peter Morgan's daughter and that your father taught you well."

By late afternoon Avery had struck a deal with Mario Dante and was already mentally rearranging her schedule to accommodate the Dantes. After more hugs and many *arrivederci*s, Enrico and his cousins left.

When they were gone, Avery led Chase up the back stairs to the landing to show him the wall she'd targeted for demolition. Her spine was still straight with irritation when she dropped the pad, across which the Dante's had scribbled their contact info, on the floor.

"I'm the contractor of record," he said. "You can't expect me to do nothing."

"I know. But I need you to keep it as close to nothing as possible." She looked away then met his eyes again.

"Thank you for organizing Enrico. For asking him to introduce the local branch of his family." The words were more grudging than she'd intended.

"Boy, that sounded almost painful," he said.

"You have no idea," she replied.

"Arguing is just going to slow things down," he said, taking a step toward her.

"True," she conceded. "We probably could have finished Bella Flora in half the time if you hadn't been such a pain in the ass."

"Ha." His eyes twinkled with amusement. "It was all that chemistry we didn't know what to do with."

"Chemistry, my ass," she said, though she was feeling more than a little of it now. "You were nasty and resentful from the get-go."

"I was pissed off at the way the network and that ridiculous husband of yours had turned you into a bimbette," he said.

"Which is why it needs to be clear that I'm the primary decision maker. It's way too easy for that whole dismissive perception to take hold."

"And I may have been a little bit in lust," he conceded.

They looked at each other. The Lifetime crew had disappeared. Deirdre and Nicole had been gone most of the day. Max had taken Maddie to a gourmet grocery store to pick up some things, and Kyra and Dustin were in their room. At least one of them was probably napping.

Chase reached out. His large hands wrapped around her waist and he pulled her up against the hard expanse of his chest. He bent his head and his warm breath tickled her ear. "Let's go look at your bedroom again and see what it needs."

Avery buried her face in his neck and breathed him in.

Her pulse skittered in her veins as he pulled her even tighter against him. One, or both of them, groaned.

"But Deirdre could come back any minute. Or Nicole." Her voice was breathy. She could feel herself trembling. "We share a bathroom. And I don't think any of the door locks actually work."

"Then I humbly suggest you move locks to the top of the list. You can even pay me to install them if it will make you feel more in charge. But for now, I'm willing to risk it." He lifted her off the ground, holding her up against him as he moved. She could feel how ready his body was for hers.

He backed them into the bedroom and managed to close the door behind them without letting go of her or loosening their connection. But when he set her on the bed and pulled her T-shirt up over her head, she gasped.

"No," she said, unclasping her bra, watching his eyes light up as she shrugged out of it. "Not here. Not on the bed." She couldn't imagine making love to Chase on the same bed she shared with Deirdre.

Chase didn't argue and he didn't take his eyes off her. They were hot and urgent, like his voice. "Take off your clothes," he said, unzipping his jeans and stepping out of them. His boxers followed.

Avery's fingers fumbled with her shorts. When she made no progress, he reached down and slid them and her panties off.

"Jesus," he said, reaching down and lifting her easily. "Hold on."

Avery wrapped her legs around his waist as he locked his lips to hers and carried her over to the wall. The plaster was cold and hard against her back. Chase's body was equally hard but it was far from cold. She lost herself in his heat as he held her in position and joined his body to hers.

There was no place to linger afterward. Avery took a quick shower and was toweling off when they heard a door slam downstairs. Dustin's sharp cry filled the hall.

"I'm looking forward to that hotel room tonight," Chase said as he watched her pull on a pair of jeans and a fresh T-shirt.

"I know what you mean," Avery said. There'd been an appalling lack of time and privacy during the re-renovation of Bella Flora; lovemaking had consisted of stolen moments in less than ideal circumstances. "I'm looking forward to spending a whole night together. In a bed." Not to mention waking up together in the morning; something they'd avoided doing at Chase's place in Tampa for fear of sending the wrong message to his teenage boys. "I think thirty-six is too old for all this makeshift sex."

"Hey." His protest was muffled by the T-shirt he pulled over his head. "Makeshift is the mother of invention."

"True," Avery said. "And you've been very inventive. But I don't want to get caught." And she definitely didn't want Deirdre to know how she felt about Chase; Deirdre had no right to the inner workings of Avery's mind or heart.

They found Kyra in the kitchen warming a bottle. Dustin's head lay on her shoulder; his eyes blinked sleepily.

There was the double *ding* of an incoming text. Avery and Kyra reached for their cell phones at the same time. They burst into laughter.

"What's so funny?" Chase asked.

Kyra's thumbs flew across her phone's keyboard; her forearms held Dustin close. "It's my mother," she said as she typed. "Some people should not be allowed to text."

Avery held her screen out so that Chase could see it. Maddie's text read, *Wud yu lyke sim baby black bugs fr dynr?*

He barked with laughter.

"Oh my God!" Kyra shook her head. "I just don't understand her problem."

"Autocorrect is not your mother's friend," Avery agreed. "And she really doesn't seem to have any control over her thumbs."

Avery typed back rapidly, struggling to control her laughter. *Tempting,* she typed on her iPhone. *But not very filling.*

OMG! Maddie responded a few moments later. *Siree!*

A few long minutes passed, minutes in which Avery assumed Maddie had typed and manually corrected then double-checked the message that arrived with a final *ding* and without a single mistake. It read, *I meant baby back ribs.*

• • •

Nicole sat at an outside table at the Delano Hotel waiting for Parker Amherst IV. The crowd that lounged around the pool and in the canvas-draped cabanas were young and hip, with the kinds of bodies that belonged on billboards and in fashion magazines. Although many of the men were even older than Nicole, the women were far younger. Each and every one of them was beautiful and scantily clad.

She sipped a glass of white wine as she waited, uncomfortably aware that her scantily clad days were behind her. Not that she was over the hill exactly, just over this particular place's hill. She pushed the thought aside and focused on picking Parker Amherst out of the crowd.

She hadn't had the time for a Google search or credit report, and even if she had, she was beyond screening. At the moment a client of any kind was a gift, one to be treasured and held on to. Amherst would have to be the ugliest man in the universe *and* a convicted serial killer to be rejected at this point.

The man who approached her table was none of those things. He was tall and sandy-haired, with patrician features and a decent, if not compelling, build. He wore khakis and a pale pink polo shirt and loafers without socks. His eyes were a pale shade of blue and his handshake was just shy of firm.

"Thank you for meeting with me on such short notice," he said.

Nicole held back her sigh. She'd known she should have put him off until the following week. Her eagerness to deposit a retainer and feel back in the game had caused her to err. "I'm glad I was able to make it work," she said as he took a seat. "Why don't you tell me a bit about yourself and what kind of woman you're looking for."

"Not much to say, I'm afraid," he said. "I grew up here in Miami. Went into the family business." He shrugged. "Never really found a woman I could picture spending my life with. But I'm the last of my branch of Amhersts. My father died last year. And, well, I guess the time has come to produce an heir." He'd struck a casual, almost self-deprecating tone, but his eyes had gone hard at the mention of his father. Nicole was not surprised by this. In her experience the super rich were rarely enamored of the people who'd given birth—and their fortunes—to them. Too often they were raised by staff or family retainers.

Nicole wrote the letters *BM* on her notepad; her shorthand for "broodmare." She was not particularly surprised by this either. She'd found mates for clients based on

IQ—or desired lack thereof—original hair color and breast size—and every possible measurement in between. The wealthier the individual, the more specific the requirements became. Her clients were used to getting what they wanted and were willing to pay for those specifics.

She kept her face and tone neutral as she asked the questions that would help her home in on suitable candidates. She'd learned long ago not to react to the most unusual of requests, and right now she wouldn't have blinked an eye if asked to look for a three-armed woman of twenty-two who knew how to whistle "Dixie" while standing on one leg.

Though she would never admit it, there was a tiny part of her that would have agreed to look for free.

Parker Amherst IV looked her in the eye as he described the future mother of his children, a woman of prime childbearing age with long legs, good teeth, and a "significant" bust, which Nicole finally pinned down to a C cup or better. There was an odd lack of animation on Amherst's face as he asked how long it would take until he could begin to meet candidates and what would happen if none of them met with his approval.

"Once you've paid the initial retainer, I'll start sifting through my current database to pull photos." She did not add that she was no longer sure how many of the women in her database would still return her call. Or that it had been over a year since anyone had retained her.

She held on to her smile while he mulled this over.

"I'll give it some thought," he said finally.

"Great." She continued to hold on to her smile as she called for and then paid the check, being careful not to gasp at the price of their two drinks and knowing that she'd have to tip heavily in case Amherst was looking. She left cash, as if she had an abundance of it and not because she didn't have a credit card that would pass inspection.

Nicole was careful not to think about what it would cost to retrieve the Jag from valet parking. Or what this little fishing expedition could end up costing her. It was important to make as strong an impression now as it had been when she'd arrived. The fish was analyzing the bait, but that didn't mean he was going to bite. Ignoring the noise and laughter around the pool, she kept her eyes on Amherst.

"Here's my card." Nicole slid the creamy embossed rectangle toward him. Like the one she'd given away in Palm Beach, it had only her name and her cell-phone number on it. This brought her supply of them down to eighteen.

She stood when Amherst did and offered him her cheek and smiled again when he left, promising to call soon to let her know what he'd decided. Once, she would have known for sure how this would turn out. Hell, once she wouldn't have cared that much about landing any particular fish. But she couldn't afford to cut her line or throw any fish back no matter how small or uncertain.

A sudden hush fell over the pool area. Heads turned. Free now to consider her surroundings, Nicole followed the collective gazes in time to see Daniel Deranian vault out of the pool and into a sitting position on its edge. She had hoped the closest any of them would come to him was happening across a photo in some publication or on an update of E! or *Celebrity Roundup*.

Nicole edged back behind a nearby umbrella as he stood gracefully, muscles flexing, his suit riding low on slim hips. Like his face, his golden-brown body was perfectly chiseled. He shook water off his dark curls and flashed a white-toothed smile as he accepted a towel from a pool boy. The assembled crowd, Nicole included, watched him move toward the largest and most secluded cabana, where beefy men dressed in black had been posted at each corner. Inside, a woman lay on one of the chaises. She raised herself up on her elbows and lifted her face to receive Deranian's kiss. The hush turned to a buzz as Nicole, and presumably everyone else, recognized his equally famous wife, Tonja Kay.

Shit, Nicole thought, trying to disappear completely behind the umbrella, even though everyone's attention was pinned to the cabana. She didn't know if Deranian would even remember or recognize her, but she didn't want to take a chance.

A flash went off and then another. Neither movie star reacted, but their bodyguards did. One dropped the flaps of the cabana then positioned himself, arms folded across his overly large chest, in front of it. The other strode after the offending photographer presumably to escort him off the premises.

Nicole paid a small fortune to retrieve her car. As she drove south toward The Millicent, she wondered whether Daniel Deranian or his wife had any idea that Kyra and his son were living less than ten minutes away. She hoped not. Wherever the golden couple went, the paparazzi would be sure to follow.

Chapter Eleven

"Gee, Mom, the baby black bugs are really great," Kyra said.

It was early evening and they sat around the dining room table. Racks of the barbecue ribs that Maddie had brought home were piled on a platter in front of them.

Nicole and Deirdre looked up in surprise. Troy, who'd been trying to teach Dustin how to high-five, reached for his video camera. Max smiled, but kept eating.

"I don't know how you got them to stay still long enough to slather on the barbecue sauce, but . . . wow!" Chase added.

"It's true," Avery said, examining the rib she'd been eating. "There's hardly any insect flavor at all."

Maddie wiped her sticky fingers on a wet nap. "You're never going to let me live that text down, are you?"

"Not a chance," Avery said. "Or any of the other gems you've sent."

"Not in this lifetime," Kyra added.

"We're clearly missing something here," Troy said, lifting his camera and aiming it at Maddie.

"It's nothing," Maddie said, looking away from the lens. The last thing she wanted to do was clue the world into her inability to control her thumbs and her phone. "Certainly nothing that anyone who expects to be fed by me needs to discuss on camera."

Kyra laughed and applied a damp washcloth to Dustin's face, which was streaked orange from the pureed carrots that he seemed determined to turn into a finger food. "Let's just say that shortly after my mother texted from the gourmet grocery store to ask if we'd like her to bring baby black bugs for dinner, I posted her text to damnyouautocorrect.com and whenparentstext.com."

"Ah," Nicole said, motioning with a rib. "So *these* are baby black bugs." She aimed a teasing smile at Maddie. "I had no idea how tender they would be."

"I've never seen them on a menu before," Deirdre added. "But then I imagine they're quite a delicacy."

Maddie rolled her eyes. "Can I help it if my thumbs are too big for that tiny keypad?"

"You should have been in Atlanta right after she got her iPhone and texted all of us her plans to 'masterbate penis primavera,'" Kyra said, unsnapping Dustin's bib and scooping him up out of the high chair.

Chase snorted with laughter. Maddie could see the curve of Troy's smile beneath the camera.

"It seems clear that people over forty should not be allowed to text," Kyra said.

"Fine," Maddie said. "Go ahead and make your jokes. You can all yuck it up while you're on KP duty."

Max smiled. "If I were still performing, I might write those down. Millie and I often used to play on words. Not dirty ones, of course," he added. "The audience would never have stood for anything close to profanity from Millie."

Max pushed his plate aside and Maddie passed wet naps around the table.

"Thank you so much for the wonderful dinner," Max said with a look to Troy, who set down his camera and nodded. "I've asked the boys to set up my film projector and screen in the living room. In case you'd like to see just a little bit of Millie and me in action."

"That sounds great," Maddie said, glad for a change of subject and eager to see Max's Millie. She took Dustin from Kyra and hugged him tight against her shoulder. "I'll put the baby to bed," she said. "Kyra, since your young fingers seem to be so much more agile than mine, you can be in charge of cleanup."

. . .

By the time Maddie had changed Dustin's diaper and snapped him into his pajamas, his lids were heavy and his thumb had found its way into his mouth. She laid him gently into the portable crib, tucked his quilt around him, then carried her cell phone out onto the loggia.

For a brief moment she considered texting both Andrew and Steve, but after all the teasing she decided to phone instead. Andrew's phone went immediately to voice mail and Maddie left her son a message promising to try him again soon.

Steve's phone rang for what felt like forever. She sat, listening to the disembodied sound, wanting to share what Chase had said over dinner—that there'd been an inquiry about Bella Flora and that their Realtor, John Franklin, had scheduled a showing.

What she really wanted was to hear the sound of Steve's voice so that she could try to gauge where they stood. When the call went to voice mail, Maddie felt a stirring of unease. Was Steve punishing her for not believing in him? She didn't want to think so. Nor did she want to wonder where he might be on a Saturday night that would prevent him from taking her call.

The living room was dark except for the puddle of light from the foyer and a low-watt table lamp. The ancient sixteen-millimeter projector had been propped up on an end table and aimed at an equally ancient screen. Kyra patted an empty spot beside her on the sofa and took the baby monitor as Maddie sat. Deirdre, Max, and Nicole sat on the opposite sofa while Avery and Chase shared the piano bench.

Anthony threaded a spool of film through the projector, receiving pointers from Max. Troy moved deftly around them, filming the proceedings from a variety of angles. Maddie followed Kyra's gaze as it followed Troy; her daughter's body hummed with tension; her lips were compressed in a thin, tight line. The cameraman had an easy way with Dustin and often spoke to him as if he were a peer; his interactions with Kyra, though, were rarely "easy."

A rectangle of light appeared in the center of the screen and the film began to spool through the projector. At first the rectangle filled with fuzzy gray-and-black shapes that moved and jiggled, but then the images became more focused and a scratchy audio track began to play.

Maddie leaned forward as the couple standing side by side on a brightly lit stage sharpened into focus. One was a young Max Golden, looking much as he had in the celebrity photos that lined his bedroom wall—with a full head of dark hair, expressive dark eyes, and a lit cigar clenched between his fingers. Although of average height, he had several inches on the petite blond woman in the formfitting strapless gown. Even in black and white you could tell she had milky white skin and lively blue eyes and that her blond hair was more honeyed than platinum. Her lips were painted a deep color, most likely some shade of red.

"She's beautiful," Madeline breathed as Millie's lovely face creased into a smile and she laid one hand on her husband's sleeve. "And so are you, Max."

Maddie looked back and forth between Max's face and the screen. The prominent cheekbones had fallen and the angled jaw had gone slack. The once pronounced brow line above the deep-set matinee-idol eyes drooped, the skin beneath them cratered into deep pockets.

"Look at her," Max said. "She had 'no hands.'" He turned to the group, the pride evident in his voice. "That's an old theatrical expression that means a performer's so natural she never even thinks about her hands. The only woman who ever played ditzy better than my Millie was Gracie Allen."

There was a roar of laughter from an unseen audience. On-screen, Millie blinked and looked surprised.

"Now watch," Max said as Millie shrugged and went about her business. Young Max puffed on his cigar. "Me, I had my cigar. I had to puff on it to let people know I'd told a joke. I was the straight man. We didn't start out that way, but the audience didn't want to see anyone, especially me, poke fun at Millie. They were very protective of her. They wanted to see her come out on top."

Millie smiled and folded her arms across her chest.

When she asked Max where he kept his money and he answered "in a bank," she asked him what interest he got. Max said "four percent" and she said, "Ha. I get eight. I keep it in two banks."

"She was different than the other 'Dumb Doras' that were popular then because she played her as if her answers made sense."

"The camera just ate her up, didn't it?" Kyra asked Max.

He nodded and fiddled with his cigar.

"She was a natural," he said quietly. "She barely needed me onstage. I was just there to feed her lines. The best part of my act was her."

They watched the rest of the routine in silence, sitting in their seats long after the last frames of film flickered through the light and flapped to a stop.

"God, I miss her," Max said, almost to himself. "I don't really know what the point is without her." He struggled up off the couch and onto his feet and looked around him as if he'd forgotten they were there.

Maddie's vision blurred at the pain and loss in Max Golden's voice. She'd always thought she and Steve would last a lifetime together like the Goldens had, but she was no longer sure of any of the things she'd believed.

She swallowed thickly as he bid them good night and shuffled toward his bedroom. Troy followed Max's progress with the lens of his video camera. The camera remained on Troy's broad shoulder long after Max's bedroom door clicked shut behind him.

• • •

Avery awoke with her back pressed against something hard. She had a crick in her neck and a heavy arm draped across her chest. She blinked slowly awake as memory returned. She lay in Chase's arms, both of them tucked into the curve of one of Max's living room sofas. Light streamed in through the blinds to dapple the scarred Moroccan tile floor. Max's bedroom door stood open and the scent of freshly brewed coffee wafted from the kitchen.

"Hey." She threw off the blanket someone had draped over them and rubbed sleep from her eyes. "It's time to get up."

"Good God," Chase groaned. "I'm too old to sleep on a couch."

"Tell me about it," she said.

"And way too old to make love in the cab of a truck."

"Ditto." She rubbed the back of her neck and yawned once more, but had to beat back a smile. The act had been one of desperation as well as a physical challenge, but the result had been surprisingly satisfying.

"Next time I buy a truck I'm going with a bench seat," Chase said.

"I can't believe we couldn't find a hotel room." Avery yawned again, reliving the night before when they'd left after Max's movie, assuming they'd just check into the first hotel that looked interesting.

"Or that an arts and foreign film festival could eat up that much hotel room inventory. I know I didn't mean for our first trip up Ocean Drive together to be quite so desperate." He lifted a hand to the nape of her neck then followed it with his lips.

She sighed as he pressed a kiss to the sensitive spot. "Maybe we can walk over and have breakfast at one of the sidewalk cafés and then take our time checking out the Art Deco district."

"Sounds perfect." Though she hadn't even admitted it to herself, she realized that she'd been waiting to see the area for the first time with him.

There was a buzzing sound. Chase's hand left her neck as he felt through his pockets and finally located his cell phone. He looked at the screen before he answered. "Hi, Dad," he said, stifling a yawn. Whatever Jeff Hardin said had him straightening. He threw his legs over the side of the sofa and sat up.

"No," he said, his brow furrowed. "I was planning to stay until tomorrow afternoon, but . . ."

Avery sat where she was as Chase stood and stepped away.

"No, of course. Don't worry about it. It's not a problem." He listened, nodding his head. "I will." He nodded and looked at her. "I'm sure she'll understand."

"What?" Avery asked after he'd ended the call and shoved the phone back into his pocket. "Is everybody okay?"

"The boys are fine. No broken bones or emergency room visits." His smile was apologetic. "But Dad and I were supposed to have drinks with our main investor in Pelican Point," he said, naming the development on which they'd broken ground just before the real estate market crashed and burned. "He called to ask if we could do it today instead. He wants us to meet him at his country club this afternoon at three."

"I hate to leave," he said. "But I don't want Dad to—"

"I know," she said, swallowing her disappointment. "Deep pockets are not easy to come by in this environment. God, I hope that nibble on Bella Flora develops into a serious bite soon."

"That's for sure," Chase said. "It would certainly take a lot of the pressure off." He speared her with another smile. "I'm really sorry to have to cut our time together short."

"You need to be there. Don't worry about it." She stifled a sigh. "And at least you're going home to a bed in a room with a door." She didn't add how much she hated to see him leave. Nor would she ask him how soon he'd be back. The smartest thing would be to keep things light and easy. As soon as things started to get heavy, it became far too easy to abdicate or lean.

"That's true," he said. "I do have a bed and a door."

"And I still get to knock down a wall tomorrow," she said, brightening.

"Most women reserve that look in your eye for designer clothing and major shopping expeditions," Chase said, stretching his arms high above his head.

"Well, all I need is a wall and something to knock it down with." Avery averted her gaze from the taut stomach that was bared as he stretched again. "Demolition is better than a shot of adrenaline or mainlining coffee any day."

"That's incredibly low maintenance of you," he said, pulling her close.

"Speaking of coffee . . ." she said, trying to keep the tone light. "I think I smell breakfast."

They followed the scent of coffee into the kitchen, where they found Maddie, Deirdre, and Max and an electric skillet of scrambled cheese eggs.

Deirdre gave them a once-over. "You wouldn't be looking like you just survived a near-death experience if you'd let me give you two the bedroom like I wanted to," she said reasonably.

"You're too old to sleep on a sofa," Avery said, accepting

a plate of eggs from Maddie, but not feeling the rush of victory she'd hoped for when Deirdre absorbed the blow.

Back from her run, Nicole poured a tall glass of orange juice and sank down next to Max. Kyra appeared with Dustin and strapped him into the high chair. Troy and Anthony showed up next, toting all their gear. Maddie fixed them plates, much to Kyra's obvious distress, then unplugged the skillet so that she could put on another pot of coffee.

"Allowing me to give you something doesn't lessen you," Deirdre said to Avery, her perfectly lipsticked mouth still tight with hurt.

"Right," Avery said, knowing she was taking her disappointment over Chase's departure out on Deirdre, but unwilling or unable to stop herself. She wasn't the only one who noticed that the tone in her voice said, *Of course it does.*

Chapter Twelve

With a loud gnashing of gears and a clatter of metal, the Dumpster landed in position first thing Monday morning. There were shouts and more clattering as the delivery truck left and another arrived. Kyra shot video of Avery standing on the front steps sipping a cup of coffee as a crew unloaded the scaffolding and began to assemble it around The Millicent.

She also documented the spontaneous burst of applause from everyone in the kitchen when Avery led Ted Darnell, the tall gangly electrician from East Coast Electric, past them toward the existing fuse box in the laundry room. Her next shots were of Avery strapping on the worn leather tool belt that had been her father's and reverently poking the prong through the extra hole that had been into it. A smattering of applause accompanied this, too.

Dustin sat in his high chair while his grandmother spooned cereal into his mouth. His chubby palms were full of Cheerios, some of which he occasionally pressed into his mouth. Sometimes the Cheerios actually stayed there when his fist came out. Just watching him made her smile.

Kyra's good mood fled when Troy Matthews backed into the kitchen, camera rolling, with Anthony beside him, their camera and microphone aimed toward Max, who followed in their wake. The old man wore his version of work clothes—crisply pressed jeans, a short-sleeved denim shirt, and a red bandanna tied jauntily around his neck.

Max came to a halt when Troy and Anthony did. He reached for the back of the banquette, his movement casual, his knuckles tightening as he grasped it for support.

"I'm ready to knock that wall down," Max said heartily into the camera, though his legs wobbled a bit beneath him. He held his smile until Troy lowered his camera, then dropped onto the banquette cushion with all the finesse of a stone.

Avery and Maddie exchanged glances and Kyra knew she wasn't the only one questioning Lisa Hogan's directive to put a sledgehammer in the ninety-year-old man's hands. She had no doubt that Troy Matthews would be ready, willing, and even eager to carry out that directive.

Maddie jumped up to get Max breakfast. On her way she shot Kyra a look and nodded toward the film crew.

"Can we talk?" Kyra took Troy by the arm and led him to the far end of the kitchen. Anthony, who had the personality of the teddy bear he resembled, set down his microphone and went over to the counter to study the contents of the donut box.

"So I'm assuming we'll both shoot the wall coming down, but from different angles," she said when they were out of earshot. If she could keep Troy downstairs on the other side of that wall from Max, she could control Max's exposure.

"That's kind of ridiculous. There's no point in shooting everything twice all the time," the cameraman said. "I've been getting everything we need."

"Possibly," Kyra replied. "But I haven't been invited to a screening yet. So I only have your word on that."

Troy's slightly squared jaw jutted. His video camera dangled at his side—an unconcealed weapon. "I don't have permission to share footage at this point in time." He spoke to her in the tone of a parent to a child.

Kyra gritted her teeth. The others' eyes were on them. Not wanting to upset Max, she reined in her irritation and lifted her lips into what she hoped would pass for a smile.

"Well, that seems odd considering we're working on the same show. But then, from what I can see, our goals couldn't be more different. You're sensationalizing whatever you can and trying to pass it off as reality. I'm trying to document what's really happening." She folded her arms across her chest. "I wouldn't want you to be so busy trying to make us look bad that you missed the wall coming down. Given the symbolism of it reuniting the two halves of the house and everything."

His eyes narrowed, but Kyra rushed on before he could interject. "Even if you get permission to share the footage with me at some point—and I can just imagine how hard you're trying—you may not have anywhere near what I want or need." She sniffed as dismissively as she could. "There's no way to *do over* the important parts if you miss them."

"Are you questioning my ability to cover the material?" he asked stiffly.

"You bet," Kyra said. "And I'm also questioning your ability to cover us in a way we can live with. This shoot is your job. But this"——Kyra motioned around her to include the house and all the people in it—"this is our life. We can't really afford to put it in the hands of someone who's only worried about his paycheck."

The tick in the cameraman's cheek grew more pronounced, but Kyra didn't care. Her whole damn body was ticking.

"My mother and Avery and Nicole are here because this series is a way to get back on their feet. And so am I," Kyra said. "You may not have noticed, but I have a child to take care of."

"Oh, I've noticed," Troy said. "I guess sleeping with the star of a movie doesn't get a person as far ahead as it used to."

Kyra felt her mouth drop open as the anger steaming through her searched for an escape.

"On the other hand, what do I know?" Troy continued. "Maybe it helped you get this show. Just like being female and good-looking helped you get on the Daniel Deranian movie in the first place."

"You did *not* just say that," Kyra said, fisting her hands at her side to keep from slapping his smug face.

Troy shrugged and raised his camera to his shoulder. "He does have a reputation for surrounding himself with beautiful women. Brains are often optional." Insolently, he panned his camera from what had to be an extreme close-up of Kyra's angry face, across the banquette, to settle on Dustin, who was waving his arms happily at Max and holding the squishy oversize baseball that Troy had given him.

Avery came over, took Kyra by the shoulder, and led her back to the table. "So much for working this out between yourselves. I'm going to make sure you're the one shooting Max. We don't want him embarrassed or hurt."

Kyra nodded, but she didn't see how this was going to happen.

"Just follow my lead. And try to look angry at what I suggest."

"So . . ." Avery turned to Troy. "I'm thinking that Kyra can shoot all of us getting ready upstairs with our sledgehammers," she said, "while the *real* film crew"—she sent Kyra a warning look—"can be set up below to get the shot of Max breaking through the wall. Does that work for everyone?"

Kyra scowled angrily. No acting was required.

Once Troy was sure she hated the idea, he nodded. "That sounds good," he said. "Max is the money shot. Let's make sure he breaks through first with a big enough hole for the audience to see him clearly."

"So much for documenting what's really happening," Kyra muttered.

"What was that?" Troy asked.

"Nothing." Kyra smiled brightly.

Upstairs, Kyra shot a series of close-ups that could be cut in later: the sledgehammer, bits of the handle, the impact as it crashed repeatedly into the wall. Under her direction, Max huffed and puffed into the wireless microphone on his lapel as if he, and not Avery, were wielding the sledgehammer. On cue, he provided carefully timed grunts and one heartfelt *"oy, vey!"*

When the wall looked like it needed only a final blow, Avery put the sledgehammer in Max's hands. Despite the grin of bravado, he dropped to his knees the moment Avery let go of the tool.

"Here, grab him under the arms," Nicole mouthed as she and Maddie pulled Max quietly to his feet.

"Everything okay up there?" Troy called up the stairs.

"Absolutely!" Kyra framed the shot as Avery wrapped her hands around Max's and dragged the hammer upward.

"Ready, Max?" Avery mouthed.

The old man's forehead glistened with sweat as his grip tightened on the handle. He nodded, and Avery stepped out of the shot and let go.

They all held their breaths as the hammer head fell—more from gravity than force—and pierced a hole large enough for Max to peer through.

"Beautiful!" Troy shouted from below. "Great job, Max!"

The old man beamed down at the camera lens as Maddie took the sledgehammer out of his hands. Avery and Nicole stepped up to the wall and began hammering away at it.

"I hope you're still rolling, Kyra!" Troy shouted. "Wouldn't want to miss a single *sensational* shot!"

"Oh, I'm rolling!" she shouted back, completely satisfied at having beaten the cameraman—and his boss—at their own game.

"Great!" Troy said. "You all can go ahead and bring that sucker down!"

· · ·

John Hendricks escorted Nicole through the lobby of Hendricks Heat & Air. Lunch had been a little longer and more liquid than planned, but Nicole had a signed agreement in her purse and a promise from Hendricks that a crew would be out by the end of the week to draw up schematics and schedule the job.

"Nice car," he said as he escorted Nicole out to the parking lot and noticed the classic XKE, the only luxury from her former life that she'd managed to cling to.

"Thanks." Nicole said good-bye, slid into the driver's seat, and dropped the convertible top. Once she'd adjusted to the flow of traffic, she pulled out her cell phone to check voice mail and felt a mad rush of relief when she heard Parker Amherst's voice. *Please, God,* she thought as she listened to his oddly tentative hello. *Please let me have this one client to build on.*

The message rambled on but was nowhere near as definitive as she'd hoped. "I'd like to sit down again, maybe over drinks or dinner," Amherst said carefully. "And I need to see some of the women you think would be appropriate before I commit. I'm simply not going to pay for what my father used to call a 'pig in a poke.'"

"Damn." Nicole stared out over the causeway, barely noticing the postcard-blue sky or the stately palm trees that whooshed by. She hadn't built Heart, Incorporated into the elite matchmaking service it had become by letting potential clients push her around. Nor had she lured them in by offering cut-rate fees or making exceptions to her stringent standards.

But all that was left of Heart, Incorporated was her; her heart, her moxie. If Parker Amherst IV needed a little extra selling or a peek at a few photos, well, then that's what she'd give him.

Back at The Millicent, Nicole pulled into the open gate and nosed the Jag in behind Maddie's minivan. The electrician's truck was gone, but a battered Jeep Cherokee had taken its place. She heard the whir of a lawn mower and realized that part of the grass had been mowed to normal levels. A section of jungle had been tamed, revealing a low, curved plaster wall with brick trim. Mounds of mown grass lay all around.

Someone had found a lawn guy.

Nikki climbed out of the Jag in time to see a lawn mower round the far corner of the house. A tall hard-bodied male was pushing it. His shoulders were broad and tapered down to a trim waist and hips. He wore only a pair of running shorts; a T-shirt had been tucked into the waistband and hung down one tree-trunk leg.

Nicole sucked in her breath as Special Agent Joe Giraldi pushed the lawn mower toward her.

"Hi," she said, raising her voice to be heard above the mower. "It looks good." She kept her eyes focused on the yard and away from the broad chest. She was especially careful not to look at the patch of hair that arrowed down the taut abdomen.

While he'd been chasing her brother, Giraldi had posed as a sunbather, a cable installer, a plumber's helper, and an old family friend with a childhood crush and a way with power tools, but this was the first time she'd seen him mow a yard. "Why are you doing this?"

"Madeline called and asked me," he said. "And I had a couple of hours free."

"Somehow I didn't picture you doing yards on the side. Contract killings maybe, but trimming hedges?" She smiled. "You're full of surprises."

"I am," he agreed. "And some of them don't even involve inflicting bodily harm or chasing down bad guys."

"That's good to hear," she said, but she wasn't so sure. Did she really want to consider a relationship with the man who had used her to track down her brother?

She'd stayed away from men in general since the failure of her second marriage; a too-many-times-married matchmaker was not a good advertisement. She'd promised herself if she ever took the plunge again, she'd treat the enterprise as scientifically and cold-bloodedly as she did the matches she made for her clients. None of that pitter-pattering of the heart or believing in happily ever after.

Giraldi reached down and turned off the lawn mower. Before Nicole could stop herself, she was watching the ripple of muscle across his back and the flex of his biceps. He straightened and reached for a tall glass of what looked like iced tea. Maddie's work, no doubt. "Would you like a sip?" he asked.

"No thanks."

"Cheers, then." He raised the glass in salute then tilted it to his lips.

She watched him drain the glass.

"There's a box of yard bags in the garage," he said when he'd finished. "I raked the grass into piles, but I'm going to have to get going. Madeline said you all would bag it up."

"Sure," Nicole said. "Thanks for taking care of the yard. I know we all appreciate it."

"My pleasure."

"So, um . . ." She wasn't sure what she intended to say. She was more concerned with not stuttering.

"So, how about dinner one night?" he asked before she could form a sentence. "I don't live all that far from here," he said. "I'm just up off the causeway. There's a nice little place near Lincoln Road that I think you'd enjoy."

"I don't know," she said. "This feels . . . complicated."

"It doesn't have to be. It's just dinner. You know, we go to the restaurant. We order wine and have a nice meal. We talk." Giraldi shrugged. "We take some time to get to know each other in a different way."

"In my experience, nothing's that simple," Nicole replied.

"That doesn't mean it can't be." He handed the empty glass to her; it was cold and slick in her hand.

Nicole shivered.

"I'm going to be out of town on an assignment for a few days. I'll make a reservation for Saturday night."

"You're awfully sure of yourself." She watched more closely than she should have as he lowered the T-shirt over his head. It clung to his sweat-soaked chest.

He shrugged again and smiled. "I prefer to think of it as knowing how to set a goal and go after it. It's just a matter of focus.

"Please thank Maddie for the tea," he said when she didn't respond. "And tell Max it was a pleasure meeting him." He grasped the handle of the mower and tilted it onto its back wheels. "I'll text you when I've made the reservation."

She stood there, empty glass in hand, as he loaded the lawn mower into the Jeep and backed onto the street. She was still standing there, wondering why she hadn't just said no and reassuring herself that she could still cancel long after he'd gone.

. . .

"So let me explain it to you, bubbaleh," Max said, taking a seat at the kitchen table across from Dustin the next day. "There are comics and then there are comedians. And they're not the same thing."

Madeline stood in front of the open refrigerator. It was the coolest spot in the house and she was in no hurry to move. The air-conditioning people were due to start cutting open walls and ceilings for vents and ductwork any day now, but in the meantime the kitchen was hot—too hot—and even with all the windows thrown open, the air barely moved. Upstairs, Avery was supervising the removal of the second-floor kitchenettes—a job that was all about pounding and yanking and the screeching protests of wood and metal, and that left holes in the walls and wires hanging out. Ted, the electrician, was still on the premises working on the wiring, which meant no electricity at all for varying periods of time, often without warning.

"What would you like, Max?" she asked. "We have roast beef and turkey."

"Surprise me," he said. "Do we have any of that good rye bread?"

"We do." Maddie pulled out the spicy brown mustard that Max preferred and a jar of dill pickles.

"Ma-ma-ma-meks," Dustin mouthed happily, waving his hands and feet. And then, "Gax!" He followed Max's unlit cigar with his large dark eyes, his expression intent, as if he were trying to soak up every bit of what the old man was saying.

Maddie set the sandwich makings on the counter and watched the old man and the baby. She wondered if her grandson's first word would be *mama* or *Max*.

"A comic is a guy who depends solely on the joke and how he delivers it," Max explained, looking Dustin in the eye. "A comedian can get a laugh opening a door—if he does it the right way. But a funnyman . . ." He made a face at Dustin. "A funnyman can get a laugh before he even opens his mouth to speak."

Dustin reached for Max's nose and laughed.

"You're a smart boy," Max said. "I knew you'd understand."

Dustin gurgled happily and nodded. Reaching for the

rubber-coated baby spoon on his high-chair tray, he put it in his mouth and gnawed on it. Maddie had seen the first tooth poking through the baby's gums just that morning.

After lunch, Max wiped his mouth carefully with the napkin. "It's time for my volunteer shift at the Jewish home," he said. "I read the newspaper to them. Sometimes I do a little shtick. Or part of a routine. Even though I'm not as funny without Millie."

"Dustin thinks you're pretty entertaining," Maddie pointed out.

"Yes," Max said. "He's very advanced for his age." His smile started as one of his megawatters but faltered midway. "It's good you keep such a close eye on him, Madeline," he said. "Things can happen when you're not paying attention. One minute the people you love are right there and everything's fine. The next minute . . ." He motioned with his cigar. "Poof. They're . . . gone."

Chapter Thirteen

Nikki carried her laptop to the dining room table. It was the heaviest thing she intended to look at for the rest of the day.

Her hands were raw from attempting to pry out countertops and cabinets and the bulky old wall air conditioners. Her arms and back ached from trying to cart them down the frickin' stairs, through the house, and out to the Dumpster. She'd almost wept with relief when Avery had finally accepted the fact that they'd never get the heavier items off the ground and into the Dumpster and spent some of their meager budget on people who could.

With file folders of pictures spread around her, Nikki scrolled through her Heart, Inc. database looking for women who might appeal to Parker Amherst. From where she sat, she had a clear view of the foyer and through to the living room. The electricity had been off for most of the morning and she cursed herself for not charging the laptop overnight.

Stray bits of conversation wafted down from upstairs, as did thumps and curses and the occasional slam of a cabinet door. She heard Deirdre gasp and looked up to see Troy and Anthony walking backward down the stairs, their camera and microphone aimed at the muscled duo with the refrigerator suspended between them.

"Watch the . . . wall." Deirdre winced as the door of the ugly avocado refrigerator fell open and smacked into the plaster. The last refrigerator had landed too heavily on the foyer floor and cracked one of the hexagonal tiles. Deirdre's eyes had gone wide with horror.

At the piano, Max was doing a pretty fair imitation of Jimmy Durante for Dustin, who'd been deposited nearby in the portable playpen. Kyra moved around them, shooting the performance as well as Deirdre and the movers. She and Troy continued to shoot the same things, though not necessarily at the same time.

There was a crash and the sound of wood and metal parting ways. A terse shout from Avery followed.

The lights came back on and Nicole took advantage of the opportunity to plug in the laptop and her portable printer, on which she printed out photos of the women she hoped would induce Amherst to sign on the dotted line.

"Hey, what's going on?"

Nikki looked up to see Maddie standing in the kitchen doorway. Her hair was up in a banana clip and there were smudges of dirt and what might be pollen all over her face and clothes. "You look like you just lost a mud-wrestling match."

"I think I did," Maddie said. "I'm not a gardener. Back in Atlanta I won lawn of the month once due to a technicality. But we sure could use Renée Franklin and her garden ladies. Or someone who's spent time in a tropical rain forest." She rubbed her nose and left another smear of dirt. "Giraldi brought his own lawn mower the other day. Do you think he has gardening tools?"

Nicole frowned. She'd been trying not to picture Joe Giraldi in any environment. She didn't want to imagine him pruning and weeding. Or doing laundry. Or God forbid, making a bed. "I don't know," she said neutrally. She hadn't yet actually agreed to have dinner with the FBI agent, but when he'd texted her the time of their reservation and when he planned to pick her up, she hadn't refused. "If I hear from him, I'll ask."

Nicole closed her laptop and stood to stretch out the kinks. "Maybe we should invite Renée Franklin and her garden ladies down for a visit. Although they'd have to drive. I'm pretty sure chain saws aren't allowed through airport security."

Madeline smiled and rubbed her nose, leaving another smear of dirt. The doorbell rang. Nikki glanced out the window and saw a Volkswagen Beetle angled up into the drive.

"I'll get it," Maddie said, already moving into the foyer. A moment later the screen door squeaked open.

Madeline looked at the woman who stood on the front stoop. She was tall and unusually broad-shouldered. Oversize sunglasses covered much of her face, but it was hard to miss just how badly she could use a facial.

The woman glanced over her shoulder then back at Maddie. She cleared her throat and pursed her lips, which were painted an unforgiving red. "May I come in?"

Her voice was smooth but deep. Straight dark hair fell past her shoulders. She wore a black silk blouse belted over a black print pencil skirt. A designer handbag hung from one broad shoulder. All of the pieces said "woman," but the clothes didn't flatter her figure. And she would have benefited from a session or two of laser hair removal.

Madeline hesitated. She'd been half expecting this since the night they'd watched TV with Max. She suspected Kyra had, too, though they'd both been careful not to talk about it. "What do you want?" Maddie asked, though she already knew.

The woman pulled open the screen door and Madeline noticed that although the stranger's hands were soft, they were large and long-fingered. The nails, while manicured, were cut short and unpainted.

"Is Kyra here?"

"I haven't seen her," Maddie hedged. "Why don't I take a message and then when I do see her I'll give it to her?"

The woman glanced over her shoulder once more then turned back and craned her neck to see over Madeline's shoulder, a not too difficult feat given the woman's height. "Why don't I just come in while you figure out whether she's here or not."

Madeline looked at the line of the stranger's jaw and at the Adam's apple that was roughly the size of Chicago. "I'm sorry," she said again, wishing she could just pretend this was, in fact, some strange woman here to see Kyra. "But I really don't think that's a good idea." She reached for the doorknob. "The house is full of workmen. And if she is here, she's probably shooting."

The piano music stopped and Maddie looked over. Max had both hands on the piano frame and was in the process of straightening. Even as she began to pull the door closed, she knew she was handling the situation poorly. Every instinct told her that allowing this "woman" into the house and their lives would be a colossal mistake, but not a single viable alternative presented itself.

"Sorry." A high-heeled black sandal wedged into the door opening and the voice dropped several octaves as the woman stepped in. "But I can't stand outside anymore. I don't want anyone to see me."

In the foyer the woman pulled off the sunglasses and stepped out of the sandals.

Maddie stood frozen, debating what to do.

The wig came off next and then one large hand plucked off a spidery false eyelash. Daniel Deranian smiled his trademark smile and scrubbed at his famous chin. "I'm in town filming a movie," he said. "I came to meet my son."

. . .

There was a loud crash upstairs as Maddie closed the front door. In the living room, Dustin started to cry.

Deranian turned toward the sound. "Is that Dustin?" He moved into the living room, his steps somewhat mincing due to the tightness of the pencil skirt.

"No. Wait," Maddie said. "I really think we should wait until Kyra . . ."

But Deranian was already halfway across the living room and moving toward the portable playpen as quickly as the pencil skirt would allow. Maddie wasn't sure if he hadn't heard her "no," or perhaps he was so unused to hearing the word that it simply didn't register.

Daniel Deranian didn't have Giraldi's bulk or Chase Hardin's height, but he was broad-shouldered and slim-hipped and the muscles he had were well defined. At forty he easily played mid-thirties heartthrobs. He'd even looked attractive as a woman. Wondering what the chances were of getting him out of the house before Kyra found out he was there, Maddie followed the movie star into the living room. Max stood in front of the playpen, arms crossed, attempting to prevent Deranian from getting too close to Dustin.

"Please step aside," Deranian said. "That's my son you've got there."

"Is that right?" Max lowered his hands to the sides of the playpen. Maddie knew this was less of a protective gesture than it looked; more likely it was Max's attempt to support his body weight. "You're not exactly dressed like anybody's father, are you?"

This was true. But even with Deranian half dressed as a woman, the resemblance between the actor and her grandson was impossible to miss.

Maddie was still debating her next move when Kyra swept into the room with Troy and Anthony close on her heels. "What's wrong, little man?" she cooed. "Did Uncle Max tell you a bad joke?" Kyra reached down to scoop up the baby. "You know he'd do anything for you."

Troy had his camera up on his shoulder and Maddie could tell he was shooting. The cameraman took a step back and swung his camera slowly to include Deranian in the shot. Surprised by the movement, Kyra looked up and spotted the man she'd once believed would come sweep her and their child up into a Hollywood version of happily ever after.

Maddie watched, her heart pounding, as Kyra registered his presence. She couldn't tell if Kyra had been imagining this meeting ever since she'd discovered the actor was in Miami, but Kyra's surprise seemed infused with both tension and satisfaction.

"He looks just like me," the actor said quietly as he stared at his son in Kyra's arms. "I couldn't tell from the photograph you sent, but he has my father's chin."

Troy's fingers moved on the camera. Even Maddie, who knew only what Kyra had shared with her about filmmaking, knew he was probably going in for a close-up. Or was he framing a shot of father and son that would confirm that the baby and the movie star had not only the same chin but the same dark eyes, curly hair, and golden-brown skin?

"No." Deranian put a hand in front of the camera lens. "You can't do that. You'll have all the people I gave the slip to piled up outside."

Troy didn't lower the camera. Maddie suspected the threat of intense coverage didn't sound particularly negative to the young cameraman, who could probably make a fortune with what little he'd already shot. Not to mention how happy he'd make Lisa Hogan with all the extra publicity.

"Put it down, Troy," Kyra said. And when nothing happened. "Please."

Slowly, Troy lowered the camera.

"Please turn it off," Kyra said. "We don't want some shot of Daniel in that skirt being cut together with stray audio and somehow finding its way onto the Internet or anything."

"Who would do that?" Troy asked.

"I've done the equivalent," Kyra said. "To my own mother. And to Avery and Nicole." She looked from Daniel to Troy and back again, her grasp on Dustin tight. "Believe me, I know how tempting this is for you," she said to the cameraman, her animosity temporarily gone.

"I'm wearing a dress," Deranian said. "Not really great for the image."

"Yeah, I noticed that right off," Troy replied. "But I'm not all that worried about your image." His gaze slid over Dustin, who'd slipped a thumb into his mouth. He turned the camera off.

"A lot of the 'he-man' actors in Hollywood in my day were also fagalas," Max said. "That's Yiddish for—"

"We know, Max," Kyra said while Maddie bit back a smile, relieved that disaster had been at least temporarily averted. "But Daniel's not gay. He's in disguise."

"Are you sure?" Max asked. "He fills that skirt out pretty good."

Troy snorted. "I'll say. Did Tonja pick it out for you? Or is it hers? It's not every man who can fit into his wife's clothes."

Deranian put his hands on his skirt-clad hips. Certainly from a distance he would have looked female enough to fool a pack of photographers. If it weren't for the light five o'clock shadow and the erratic shaving job on his legs, he might have passed for Dustin's mother.

"That's enough," Kyra said to Troy. "More than enough."

Maddie read disagreement in the cameraman's eyes. And something that resembled disappointment. The room pulsed with conflicting emotions and flagrant uncertainty. Even Deranian seemed slightly unsure of how to proceed.

"Max," Maddie said. "This is Daniel Deranian, Dustin's father. He's an actor. Daniel, this is Max Golden. He's a comedian."

"No kidding," Deranian said.

"No, she means that literally," Kyra said. "Max is a pretty well-known comedian. He ran with the Rat Pack back in the day."

"So this one's married to someone else, but he's Dustin's father?" Max asked.

"Yep," Troy said. "The guy has a bit of a problem keeping his pants zipped."

"*Oy, gevalt,*" Max said, looking back and forth between father and son. "Did you know about this, Madeline?"

"Yes," Madeline said, unaccountably embarrassed.

"The whole world knows about this, Max," Troy said. "I think you must have missed a couple of episodes of *Entertainment Tonight* and *Celebrity Roundup* along the way."

Daniel Deranian cocked his head to study the cameraman. "What's going on here? Have you got the hots for her too?"

Troy's gaze narrowed and Maddie couldn't help thinking of white and dark knights squaring off to do battle over the damsel, even as they contributed to that damsel's distress. Deranian's taunt had been disturbingly present tense.

"Me-me-me-mex." Now that he was in his mother's arms and the center of attention, Dustin seemed perfectly content.

"What are you *really* doing here, Deranian?" the cameraman asked. "You and your wife have a houseful of children. What do you care about this one?"

"That's definitely enough," Kyra said, staring at Troy. "Could you leave us alone for a few minutes?"

Troy shook his head in disgust. "Please tell me he's not going to show up and snap his fingers and—"

Dustin buried his face in his mother's neck. Kyra jiggled him gently in her arms then began the new-mother sway. Deranian's attention remained fixed on her and the baby.

"That *is* enough," Deranian said, turning to the cameraman, the voice suddenly packed with menace. As if someone had flipped a switch or given a cue on a film set.

"Fine." Troy shrugged as if it didn't matter to him. "I guess some people don't know how to learn from their mistakes." He looked at Max and lowered his voice. "Come on, Max. I want to get some shots of you out front and puttering around the Caddy. I have an idea for a promo."

"Okay." Max turned to Deranian. "You be nice to Kyra and Dustin. They're living in my home and they're under my protection."

"Yes, sir." Deranian stopped just shy of rolling his eyes. They all watched the cameraman and the old man walk slowly away. The actor looked to Maddie.

"Maybe I should go make a, um, grocery list," Maddie said, though she'd done that earlier. It was clear Deranian didn't want her around.

"No, Mom," Kyra said. "I'd like you to stay." She smoothed a hand down over Dustin's cap of dark curls to hold him against her. "Wouldn't you like to know what he's doing here?"

Kyra turned to the actor. "I'm pretty sure the agreement I signed indicated you didn't really want anything to do with Dustin." Her gaze didn't waver from his. "You have other children. And clearly you've had lots of other women before, during and after me. What are you doing here in that getup?"

"Honestly?" he asked, as if he were prepared to answer the question in any number of ways.

"If you have the ability to tell the truth, then yes, that's what I'd like to hear," Kyra replied.

Maddie stood stock-still, barely able to breathe, but neither Kyra nor Deranian seemed concerned about her presence. In fact, they were so focused on each other that Maddie suspected they'd already forgotten she was there.

"Okay then." Deranian dragged a hand through his unruly hair then massaged his stubbled chin thoughtfully. "I'm here because we both happen to be in town at the same time. And . . ." His voice trailed off and Maddie could see from Kyra's face that if that was the best he could do, he was about to be shown to the door. Which would mean Maddie could start breathing again.

Kyra settled Dustin on her other hip. "If this is only about geography, I guess we're done. You've seen Dustin." Her chin jutted out. Maddie could practically feel her holding back tears. "Now you can go back to your wife and your other children."

But Deranian didn't leave. He moved closer to Kyra. Gently, he reached out for the baby. "I do have other children," he said. "And it's true—you're not the only woman I've gotten pregnant." He put out a finger and Dustin grasped it with his tiny hand. "But as far as I know, Dustin is my only biological son."

Chapter Fourteen

Maddie placed the head of lettuce on the cutting board and slashed the knife down through it, hacking it into bits. A green pepper met the same fate. It was only when she reached the tomato, which was too soft to be hacked into anything but a messy pulp, that she found enough control to stop her attack on the helpless vegetables.

She'd stood in shocked silence as Kyra absorbed Deranian's pronouncement, silently cheering when her daughter demanded to know if that meant he would not have wanted to see their child if that child had been a girl. Madeline had slipped out of the room in the middle of Deranian's earnest assurances that this was not the case. But the man was an actor—a good one. Portraying sincerity and deep feeling were hardly a stretch for him; they were part of his stock-in-trade.

She'd been "assembling" a salad since she'd left Kyra and Deranian and her grandson together in Max's living room, hoping that if she kept her hands busy enough she could get the celebrity's visit and its implications out of her mind.

Deranian stayed for thirty minutes. As soon as he left, Kyra had loaded Dustin into his stroller and taken off to the park. She didn't invite Madeline to join her or say when they'd be back. Even more telling, she'd left her video camera behind.

From the refrigerator, Maddie pulled mushrooms and onions and minced them within an inch of their lives. If she'd had any confidence that she could breach their current awkwardness, she would have called Steve to discuss Deranian's reappearance. Instead she kept herself busy. Perhaps when she'd assembled the salad, she'd go up and wipe down the furniture on the deck. Or polish the furniture. She was far too worked up to even consider sitting still.

A car pulled up outside and the kitchen door opened behind her. Deirdre appeared, her arms full of swatches and design books. A sketchbook balanced on top of a large hexagonal tile. She'd tucked the lot of it beneath her chin.

"Good grief," she said as she deposited everything in a heap on the kitchen table. "I miss my assistant." She pulled out a tape measure and a yellow pad and began taking and jotting down measurements. A few minutes later she began to pull wood and tile samples and a variety of catalogs from her bag.

"Do you have a minute to look at these?" Deirdre asked after she'd arranged the samples and several catalogs on the counter.

"Sure," Maddie said, relieved to have something, anything, besides Kyra and Dustin and his movie-star father to think about.

"I'm thinking these cabinets in a sand-colored enamel."

Deirdre pointed to a photo of a bank of contemporary cabinets with an almost patent-leather-look finish. "And these tiles in shades of blue for a wavelike backsplash."

"Cool," Maddie said, meaning it.

"This will go over the sink." She pointed to a light fixture shaped like a beach ball and suspended on a shiny chrome rod. "And this"—she flipped several pages to a rectangle of chrome with a mass of bubble-shaped lights hanging from it—"will go over the banquette."

"I love it," Maddie said.

"And the pièce de résistance . . ." Deirdre held up two blocks of wood. "High-gloss teak for the countertops, like you'd see on the deck of a boat."

"Wow," Maddie said. "The whole nautical thing is perfect for this house. What does Avery think?"

"I don't know." Deirdre looked down at the samples and sketches, her tone glum. "I haven't really had a chance to sit down with her. Frankly, I'm a little worried that she'll automatically reject it just because it's my idea."

Deirdre went to the refrigerator, pulled out an opened bottle of Chardonnay, and without asking poured them each a glass. "Here," she said. "You look like you need this as much as I do."

Maddie took a sip of wine, trying to focus on the feel of the cool liquid sliding down her throat. She had to look pretty freaked out if Deirdre noticed anything but her own concerns. Still, she was glad when Deirdre didn't press for details. She'd thought the threat of Daniel Deranian had been dealt with and resolved when Kyra rejected the "opportunity" to be his mistress, but here he was again. She couldn't seem to push the picture of the actor sitting next to Kyra and holding their baby out of her mind.

"I think I need another lesson," Deirdre said, pulling Maddie back to the present. "I don't feel like I've made any inroads with Avery at all." She took a long drink then pushed the samples away. "I want to do something special for her, but I don't seem to know what that is. I mean, I spent a lot of time finding enough artificial-cheese-snack products to fill a tray and all she said was that Cheez Doodles taste better out of the bag. She won't even accept a snack from me."

Deirdre drew in a breath then expelled it. "And this weekend? She wouldn't even give me the satisfaction of giving her and Chase our room, though Lord knows I think we can all tell they needed one."

Maddie drained her wineglass and held it out for more. So far the alcohol didn't seem to be helping, but she was determined to keep trying. She was not a Deirdre Morgan fan, but it seemed that grown daughters made for strange bedfellows.

"You can't give up after one attempt," Maddie said. "One Cheez Doodle tray is not going to make up for deserting Avery and her father. The important thing is that you keep trying and that you stay as consistent as possible. Like when they're teenagers and hormonal and you are the emotional punching bag. You don't fold up your tent and slink away just because they're suddenly looking at you like you're dumber than dirt. You let them know that it's not okay to treat you that way, but at the same time you don't withdraw your love or your support."

Maddie paused, kind of amazed at all the years of stored-up experience pouring out of her. But Deirdre's look was that of rapt attention. Could she really not know this?

"Your goal is to keep the lines of communication open," Maddie continued. "Over time they come to understand that the people they love aren't going to leave them just because they're not behaving perfectly. If they're secure enough in your love, they'll feel free to treat you like shit. Which is something they can't do with the rest of the world."

"She's already treating me like shit," Deirdre pointed out. "And you're telling me I'm aiming for more of that?" Deirdre didn't look at all happy about this revelation.

"No, that's not what I meant. But frankly, even when you've been there the whole time and done your best to understand, there's only so much you can do. You can't live their lives for them. And you can't force them to see things the way you do." Maddie realized she was speaking to herself as much as to Deirdre.

"So what do you think I should do next?" Deirdre asked.

"You hang in there. You don't cut and run. No matter what. Avery has to come to believe that you're in it for the long haul."

"That's it?" Deirdre asked. She cocked her head in question. "Are you sure?"

"Well, it's not rocket science or brain surgery, though it sometimes feels like it," Maddie said.

"But what can I give her? I want to do something nice for her." Deirdre sighed. "Something a little larger than a menu item."

Maddie looked at Deirdre Morgan. Beneath the perfectly wrapped package was the same morass of uncertainty mothers had felt from the beginning of time. What was too much? What was not enough? Deirdre was not exactly an open book, but her desire to make a good impression on her daughter seemed sincere. "I don't know," Maddie admitted. "I'm kind of confused at the moment myself."

She looked out the kitchen window in an effort to gather her thoughts and saw Kyra pushing the stroller back down the sidewalk toward the house. She had her cell phone up to her ear and was speaking earnestly to someone. Maddie sincerely hoped that someone was not Daniel Deranian.

Madeline turned back to Deirdre. "If Avery and Chase need a room and they won't take yours, maybe the next time he's down here, you should get them one of their own."

. . .

"Rise and shine!"

"Oh, no," Avery groaned. "Not again. What is it with you and morning?"

"You said you wanted to talk to everyone before work started. And I've got some things I'd like to bring up, too."

Avery mumbled and covered her eyes. She attempted to bury her head in the pillow, but Deirdre wrested it away.

"Maddie's already got coffee on. Be grateful we're only going up on the deck. She wanted to have this meeting out on the beach. At sunrise."

With a groan Avery sat up, but it took her a while to commit to opening her eyes. When she did, she saw that Deirdre was fully dressed in something simple yet sophisticated. Her face was flawlessly made up.

Fifteen minutes later they were on the deck facing east, all present and accounted for. Kyra nursed Dustin and sipped a glass of orange juice that Maddie had carried up for her. The rest of them held their stimulant of choice. Most of them were awake.

They sat for a few minutes in the morning quiet, eyes on the sky that was just beginning to lighten. When she felt sufficiently awake to speak, Avery licked the last bits of glazed sugar off her fingers and called the meeting, such as it was, to order.

"Hendricks Heat and Air has had to push back installation a little bit, which gives Ted a little longer to get the electrical completed," she said. "They're going to start cutting vents and running ductwork as soon as possible, though. Which means they're going to have to open the ceiling of Max's closets. I wondered if you might be willing to help him clear them out, Maddie?"

"Sure. I'd be glad to."

"I can help too," Nicole offered.

"Good." Avery checked the item off her list. "Let's get that done as soon as possible so that we're ready the minute Hendricks has a crew free." She looked up from her notes. "How are we coming with a window company?"

"I've been playing phone tag with two of the companies on the list you gave me," Nicole said. "And I know Deirdre's been following up on the glass block."

"Good." Avery sipped her coffee and felt the bonds of sleep starting to loosen. "Once the air-conditioning people are out, we can start removing doors and hardware for refinishing. When the replacement panes I ordered come in, we'll need someone to handle the reglazing." She didn't look directly at Maddie when she said this, but Maddie groaned nonetheless.

"I was doing that in my sleep for months after we finished Bella Flora," she said.

"I'm sorry," Avery replied. "If someone else with the same kind of patience and attention to detail would like to volunteer, I'm good with that."

Avery looked around the group. No one met her eye.

"Right." Maddie took a sip of coffee and sighed.

"After that, the plumber will be coming in." Avery hesitated.

Nicole's head snapped up. "Please tell me we're not going to be down to one bathroom again."

"Just for a little while," Avery said.

"Can you define 'a little while'?" Deirdre asked.

"Not really." Avery winced. She was not looking forward to five women in one bathroom again either, but there was no way around it. Avery speared Maddie with what she hoped was a stern look. "But there should be no feeding of the plumber under any circumstances. We don't want to treat any of our workmen so well that they start dragging out the job."

"Aye, aye." Maddie mock-saluted, but Avery knew that at the first pitiful look or rumble of a stomach, her promise would evaporate. No matter how big the beer belly, the woman couldn't help mothering everyone placed in her path.

Dustin finished nursing and sat with a big smile on his face. Kyra hefted the baby up onto one diaper-draped shoulder. There was a loud belch.

"Am I imagining it or did he do that on cue?" Nicole asked.

"I think Max has been working on it with him," Kyra said. "He wants to incorporate him into his act."

They all shared a smile. "Anything to report, Kyra?" Avery asked.

With the burp out of the way and Dustin still propped against her shoulder, Kyra said, "I've posted a series of 'before' shots to YouTube and we're getting a lot of views and favorable feedback."

"And your commentary?" Avery asked, remembering Kyra's initial scathing posts from Pass-a-Grille.

"I'm keeping it to a minimum right now. Just how excited we are to be starting a new project. Look how cool the house is, look how much it needs, and so on. With maybe a couple of not-so-flattering shots of the Lifetime crew." She mumbled the last before continuing.

"The big thing is building an audience for the *Do Over* pilot on July first. We've got lots of Internet buzz going and we need to keep stoking it. We've got a Facebook page now and we're already up to one thousand 'friends.' I may want you all to come on and post occasionally, you know, make little 'guest appearances.'" Kyra turned Dustin so that he could sit in her lap. A moment later a rubber teething ring was in his mouth.

"Does Facebook have autocorrect?" Maddie asked, her brow knitting in concern.

"No," Kyra said. "So you're safe, Mom. We definitely don't want you sending any potentially scandalous recipes out into cyberspace. I thought we should get Max involved, too. I've also signed up for a Twitter account."

"Could we use Facebook and Twitter to put out a call for local gardeners?" Maddie asked. "Maybe we could host a garden-work day or two."

"Those are both great ideas," Deirdre said.

As much as she hated agreeing with Deirdre, Avery nodded. "Let's do it," she said.

Avery was ready to end the meeting when Deirdre raised her hand.

"What is it, Deirdre?"

"I've got drawings of the kitchen." Deirdre passed around

a board with sketches and finishes, which she explained in enthusiastic detail.

When everyone finished oohing and aahing, she said, "I also have an idea for the downstairs floors."

Avery closed her eyes, not from a desire for sleep but out of irritation.

"The original Moroccan tiles are heavily damaged. I checked with Mario Dante and a couple of local suppliers and we're never going to be able to repair them or find replacement tiles that'll match." She waited for this to sink in before continuing. "I'd like to sand, stain, and seal the entire floor," she said, pulling an enlarged photo and a sample tile from beneath her chair and passing them to Avery. "This is what it would look like in a low gloss."

The tile was a dark, bitter Turkish coffee color. The photo showed a large gleaming expanse of it.

"That looks great," Maddie said. "It'll really unify the space."

Everyone but Avery seemed to be smiling. "What about the cost?" she asked.

"I don't have exact numbers, but it'll be a fraction of what it would cost to rip up that floor and replace it, since it's all over the downstairs except Max's bedroom and bath," Deirdre said.

"Maybe, but it's not exactly a simple process," Avery pointed out.

"True," Deirdre said. "It's not too dissimilar from refinishing the wood floors."

"Which we've already got in the work schedule," Avery said. She was not looking to max out their nonexistent budget. "That wood parquet in the bedrooms is going to be especially time-consuming and labor-intensive. That stuff is really thick."

There was a collective groan. This was the disadvantage of having done a house already. There'd been that horrible learning curve on Bella Flora, but there'd also been the protection of ignorance. They'd had no real idea how onerous many of the tasks would be until they'd done them.

"I'm not dying to do any of this," Nicole said. "But I have to say the color and finish are fabulous."

"Thanks." Deirdre smiled, clearly pleased. "And I've got plans for that moth-eaten area rug in the living room and—"

"We can't just keep adding expense," Avery said, cutting her off.

"I'm well aware of that. I've been out calling on potential sponsors. I think I understand that better than most. But I know you want to do this house justice. And that means the design element is critical."

Avery wanted to argue with her; she hated that Deirdre was right. Absolutely hated that Deirdre did, in fact, know her well enough to know that she'd already won this argument.

Avery studied the photos and the design elements Deirdre was proposing, which included reupholstering the banquette, refinishing the chrome base, and replacing the glass tabletop. Deirdre's designs were more than great; they would bring The Millicent up-to-date without compromising her or the architect's talent and intent. But she couldn't bring herself to say so.

"You can't just go off doing whatever you feel like whenever you feel like it. Not that you haven't done that before." Was that a whine in her voice?

Avery squirmed in the silence that followed. She felt like a perverse child. Or the mean girl in the high school lunchroom who'd gone too far.

"Well, if you don't like my design ideas—despite the fact that this is what I *do* for a living—I'm sure you'll hate my next idea even more," Deirdre said.

Avery reached for the donut box, which was, alas, empty. There were stirrings down in the pool house. And she thought she heard water running beneath them in Max's room. "Then maybe you should save it for another time."

"Unfortunately, I can't do that," Deirdre replied.

Avery would need more coffee to argue effectively. Or at least another donut or two. "Fine," she said. "What is it?"

"You asked Nicole and me to work on signing sponsors."

"Yes, I know. And we all really appreciate that you're doing that," Avery said. "Now—"

"I've come up with a means of approaching companies in a more organized way."

Traffic was starting to pick up on Meridian. Avery heard a bus shuddering to a stop over on Washington. She sighed. "Just tell us what it is already so we can move on."

"I want to invite a handpicked list of potential sponsors to come watch the pilot episode of *Do Over* with us. Actually I'd like to invite the movers and shakers in the design and preservation community along with Realtors who specialize in this area as well as the media. It would be a sort of premiere party."

"You want to give a party?" Avery asked.

"I want us *all* to give a party," Deirdre said with a flash of smile. Her teeth looked especially white against the perfect red of her lipstick. Her blue eyes sparkled with enthusiasm. At this particular moment, anyway, there was no doubting her sincerity. "And you don't need to worry about the budget, because I'm planning to get the network to pick up most of the tab."

"And where would we have this party?" Avery asked, although she was afraid she knew.

"Here, of course," Deirdre replied. "At The Millicent."

"Oh, no," Avery said. "Absolutely not. I'm not going to stop work to get ready for a party. That's completely out of the question."

"But that's the beauty of it," Deirdre said. "You don't have to. This will be the 'before' party. We want things torn apart and gritty. Nobody's been in this house since just after World War Two. People will be dying to get an invitation. I've already started a list and I've put a call in to Chase and Jeff Hardin so that the whole cast can be here." She smiled happily. "I've even got my publicist working on it." Only Deirdre Morgan could be all out of money and still find a way to keep a publicist on retainer.

Maddie looked at Deirdre. "The last time your publicist got involved, the paparazzi descended on Pass-a-Grille." She nodded toward Kyra and the baby. "I'm counting on you to be careful," Maddie said with a warning look. "And no mentioning Dustin's father."

Deirdre made a cross-my-heart motion, but Avery knew how little that really meant.

"You're not going to accept that, are you?" Avery asked Maddie.

Madeline studied Deirdre. Avery could feel her weighing and deciding. "I am because if she uses my child or my grandchild again in any way, I'm going to make her regret it." She narrowed her eyes at Deirdre, whom Maddie had intimidated thoroughly last summer much to everyone's amazement. "And that's a promise."

After that, it was all over. Avery tried her best to stop Deirdre's runaway train, but it seemed everyone had already jumped on board and pulled up the steps.

"We're voting," she huffed, unable to be at all graceful about this defeat. "All opposed?"

No one raised a hand except Avery, who raised two.

"All in favor of this ridiculous idea that I know we're all going to regret?" Avery asked, though it was clear that Deirdre had already lobbied and rallied the troops.

Even Dustin, the traitor, pulled the teething ring out of his mouth long enough to raise his little hand and wave the saliva-covered circle in the air above his head.

Chapter Fifteen

Maddie and Nicole stood in front of Max's bedroom door. They had a rolling garment rack, a stack of boxes, and two large garbage bags with them. After a heated argument with Troy, Kyra positioned herself behind them and to the left. The Lifetime crew stood to the right. As far as Maddie could tell, *everything*—both video cameras and the audio recorder—were rolling.

At their knock Max opened the door, his arms opened wide in welcome. "Come in! Come in!" A smile lit his face as he stepped back to allow them to enter—not an easy task given the number of people, the amount of supplies, and all the equipment. It felt a little like a school of sardines rushing into a can all at once.

Max moved to stand between the closet doors, which flanked the short hall to the bathroom. "This is my closet." He motioned with his unlit cigar to the smaller closet on his left. "And this is . . . was . . . Millie's." He motioned to the other, which had wide double doors.

Maddie pushed the garment rack up against the wall and set the boxes down. "These are for anything you want to put back in the closet once the ceiling's closed up," she said. "We brought the garbage bags in case there's anything you want to donate."

Maddie could feel Kyra and Troy jockeying for position, but shoved the issue out of her mind. "Why don't we start with Millie's closet?" she asked, assuming it would be largely empty.

Max hesitated but then nodded. "Okay."

Nicole pulled both doors open. The closet, which was cedar-lined and far deeper than anyone expected, was packed with brightly colored and sparkly clothing. Equally vivid shoes littered the floor. Boxes of all sizes had been crammed onto the full-width shelf and rose in an almost solid mass to the ceiling.

"Wow." Maddie turned to Max, who'd stepped closer. "I thought . . ."

"I know." Max moved closer then leaned into the closet, his hand grasping a knob. He drew in a breath of the musky perfume scent that wafted out the door. "When we started renting out rooms, Millie began to store things in here."

His shoulders slumped and his voice dropped. For the first time since they'd arrived, he'd turned his back on both cameras. "I just couldn't face going through Millie's things. I couldn't bear the idea of her closet being empty." Max's hand trembled on the doorknob.

"Are you okay with doing this now?" Maddie asked softly. "If you're not, we can find somewhere else to store it all just as it is." She had no idea where that might be, but she was not going to insist Max part with anything he'd rather keep.

"No," he said. "I know this has to happen. And I'd rather do it now. With you."

"Come sit down, Max." Nicole stepped toward him. Grasping his elbow, she led him to the turquoise chaise and helped him settle into it.

"Yes, you sit right there," Maddie said. "We'll take things out one at a time and you can decide what you want to stay, what you might be ready to part with, and what you might want to donate." She put out two boxes—one she labeled KEEP/MILLIE and one she labeled DONATE. Nicole opened a garbage bag and hung its plastic drawstring over the other closet's knob.

"Okay," Maddie said, more cheerily than she thought any of them felt. "Now we're in business."

Max's smile remained in place but there was something uncertain in his eyes. Maddie leaned over in the guise of adjusting a lamp shade on the nightstand and whispered in his ear. "We can stop anytime you want to, Max. We don't have to finish everything today."

Nicole was right beside her, pretending to straighten a picture on the wall. Between them they formed a protective curtain. "If you want or need to stop, just say . . . 'bagel and cream cheese' . . . and we'll be the ones to call a halt." She smoothed the lapel of Max's smoking jacket. "Okay?"

He nodded. "I'm not sure how I'd work that into the conversation," he said, smiling as Nicole had clearly intended. "I don't think I'll have any reason to. But thanks."

They began to work their way through the closet, each pulling out two hangers at a time and holding them up for Max's perusal.

It was possible that they obscured Troy's line of sight just slightly, but the cameraman didn't complain. Maddie understood why when she looked up and saw him swinging his camera lens between Kyra at work and close-ups of Max's face.

The clothes were glamorous and expensive. Maddie was amazed at Max's ability to remember when they'd been purchased and where Millie had worn them.

"She bought that for New Year's Eve at the Fontaine-bleau, 1963," he said of a one-shouldered gold lamé gown. "We opened for Joey Bishop."

The next was black and strapless. "May 1965. It was a roast for Jackie Gleason."

A bright pink sheath had been purchased for dinner out with Meyer and Teddy Lansky.

Max's eyes lit appreciatively over some of them and misted at others. Maddie was struck anew at how close Max and his Millie had been. It had been just the two of them, working and living and loving together. Her own eyes moistened as she thought about Steve and how far apart they were now in so many ways. She'd thought that once he was back on his feet, their relationship would right itself. Instead a chasm had opened between them that she didn't know how to bridge.

"Maddie?"

She looked up to find Nicole looking at her expectantly. "I'm sorry?"

"I was just saying it's too bad Millie was so petite. I'd be offering everything I have for these dresses right now if I thought I had a prayer of squeezing into them. This one's a Chanel." She pointed to a mint-green suit. "And look at this fabulous pillbox hat. It's so Jackie Kennedy."

"Millie loved to dress up and to shop. In fact, R. H. Macy didn't enjoy shopping as much as Millie did."

Maddie and Nicole smiled.

"I used to get a rim shot after that line." Max motioned with his cigar. "And a big laugh."

Maddie would have laughed then, except for the sadness etched on Max's expressive face. Her gaze slid to the portable rack, which bulged and sagged with Millie Golden's clothing. Not a single item had been discarded.

"The thing is, I just can't give her dresses to total strangers who won't appreciate them." Max looked down in his lap. "She would hate that."

"They look like they might fit Avery," Nicole said. "With just a small alteration in the bust." She held a garment up so that Madeline could see it. "Unfortunately, I can just see Avery strapping her father's tool belt on over this Halston," she added with a grimace.

"I don't want Millie turning over in her grave," Max said. "They're beautiful and one of a kind. Just like she was."

There was a silence as they contemplated Millie's wardrobe.

"They should go to someone who can appreciate them and wear them." Maddie reached out to adjust some of the hangers. Opening one of the shoe boxes on the bed, she lifted out a spectacular pair of evening slippers that shimmered gold in the light and had a shiny Plexiglas heel.

"Oh, my goodness," Nikki breathed. "They look like they should belong to Cinderella. They're so tiny. I'm not even sure I could get my big toe in."

Maddie straightened as the idea struck her. Quickly she pulled down the remaining shoe boxes and a large plastic storage container of fabulous hats. "Is there a local theater you could donate them to, Max? Or even a series of regional theaters who might put them onstage where they belong?"

"That's a great idea," Nicole said. "They and Millie would continue on in the theater that way."

Max sat up a bit straighter. "I like it," he said. "I like it a lot."

"Even if they couldn't use an entire outfit, they might be able to use part of one," Maddie said.

There was a clatter on the roof. Troy signaled to Anthony. "Thanks, Max," he said, ignoring Kyra. "They're starting on the roof. We're going to go see what Avery's up to and get some exterior footage."

Kyra kept her camera up in front of her face; it was unclear whether she was still shooting or not. Maddie continued to open boxes as the Lifetime crew left. Each pair of shoes was more gorgeous than the last. "I'd consider having a few toes lopped off to wear some of these," she said, only half joking. "I think we should pull a couple of outfits for Avery and save them for the right occasion."

"I know just the ones," Nicole said, stepping closer to the rack.

Maddie pulled a hard-backed chair up to the closet opening and stepped on it so that she could see all the way to the back of the shelf. Stretching up on her toes, she grasped the edge of another large clear plastic container. Once she'd worked it to the front of the shelf, she got a better grip and handed it down to Nicole, who laid it on the bed and lifted off its lid.

Inside, there were several padded manila envelopes with the word *House* written across them, which she set aside for future inspection. Next came small cardboard boxes of sixteen-millimeter film, each carefully labeled with the date and venue. "Oh my gosh," Maddie said. "This one says 'Us on *The Honeymooners*.' Did you really work with Jackie Gleason?"

"We did," Max said. "And somewhere there's a small clip of Millie on *I Love Lucy*. I think she played Ethel's younger sister."

Kyra moved so that she could kneel at the end of the bed. She braced her elbows on the bedspread to steady the camera.

Nicole pulled the film boxes out so that Max could see the labels. "We should find a way to run these during the premiere party," Nikki said. "I bet Troy or Anthony could transfer them to digital. And we could get the network to provide some big-screen TVs."

Max beamed.

A layer of tissue-paper-wrapped boxes came next. Maddie unwrapped the first one, a delicate bone china with a woman's face painted on the lid. She turned the box over so that she could see the stamp. "It's Limoges," she said. "And look, there's a whole collection of them." She unwrapped the boxes and set them gently on the bed.

Next she unwrapped a sterling-silver dresser set. "Oh my gosh," Maddie said as she held up the hairbrush, comb, and mirror. "These are beautiful. I feel like I've been let loose in a treasure chest."

"Millie used to keep them on her vanity." Max reached for the intricately patterned handle of the brush. "I never really thought about what had happened to them."

At the bottom of the box Maddie found a zippered plasticine bag, like something a sheet set might come in. "Hey, what's this?"

Gently she removed the contents; a stack of baby

clothing that included tiny baby booties and nightgowns in shades of blue. A hand-knit sweater and cap that had taken on the shape of the threadbare stuffed bunny rabbit that had been wrapped inside it. Three small boxes of film had been rubber-banded to two dog-eared photo albums with pale blue covers. One word had been scrawled across the plastic in black Magic Marker in a decidedly feminine hand.

"Max," Madeline said, glancing up at the comedian. "This seems to be full of baby things." She peered more closely at the name, trying to make it out. "I think the name is 'Aaron.'"

Max's face went white as Madeline handed the photo albums to him. He took them carefully and held them almost protectively in his lap.

"I didn't realize," he said. "I didn't know Millie had kept his things." His voice quavered. "Because I couldn't bring myself to talk about him. I made her stop, too."

"Who's Aaron?" Nicole asked.

Max looked up from the albums to meet their eyes. Kyra moved closer, practically lying facedown on the bed as Max caressed them with his gnarled hands.

"Aaron disappeared from our front yard in 1961. When he was three. We were never able to find him." His voice broke and his hands tightened on the albums. "Aaron was . . . he was our son."

. . .

Nicole stood in front of the warped and wavy mirror trying to decide whether she was underdressed or overdressed. Or even whether it mattered.

Deep down she knew that a date, even something as

innocuous as a dinner, with Special Agent Joe Giraldi was a very large mistake. All day she'd promised herself that she would simply text him her apologies, tell him something had come up, that she was sorry but she couldn't make it. Even while she was helping to clean out Max's closets, part of her mind had been worrying about how to handle the invitation, a worry that had been knocked aside briefly by Max's startling revelation.

Maddie had flung her arms around Max, immediately wanting to lavish him with love and make him feel better. Nicole had been unable to stop thinking about the boy Aaron. She and her brother had mostly raised themselves after their father had died and their mother had had to work two and three jobs at a time to keep food on the table. But at least they'd known who their parents were and had some semblance of family. How frightened would a boy of three have been by being picked up by a stranger, if that was what had happened? And what would he have remembered of his parents—assuming he'd survived the abduction?

Nicole drew herself back to the present and told herself to stop dithering. It was too late to cancel now and so she dressed quickly in a vintage Emilio Pucci mini dress with a plunging front and back and inverted Empire waist. The bold geometric graphic in yellow, orange, and white worked perfectly with a pair of ankle-strapped cork wedges that would garner attention without looking like she'd tried too hard.

She chastised herself for the little thrill of anticipation she felt when the doorbell rang precisely at eight. Kyra's voice floated up the stairs to announce Giraldi's arrival a few minutes later, but Nikki made him wait while she applied a second coat of coral lipstick and considered then rejected several pairs of dangly earrings. Plucking a short-sleeved white shrug out of a drawer, she folded it over her arm and scooped up a neon-orange leather clutch.

It was eight-fifteen when she flipped off the light in her room and smoothed her hair back over her shoulders so as not to obscure the plunging V of her neckline. On the stairs she tilted her chin up to smooth out the lines of her neck and felt her lips tilt upward of their own accord. She walked sedately down the stairs reminding herself that this was just a dinner with an attractive man. Of whom she had no expectations and from whom she wanted nothing.

But though she walked carefully in the high wedge sandals, her heart skipped on ahead.

Chapter Sixteen

Giraldi picked Nikki up in a 1960 356 Porsche Speedster, which was just one of what turned out to be many surprises that filled the evening. He opened the door for her with a slight bow and a smile.

"I thought you drove a Jeep," she said as he handed her into the butter-soft leather seat.

"I do." He shrugged as if it were no big deal. "The Jeep's a workhorse. This is for fun." He turned the key in the ignition and the car purred to life. "You're not the only one who likes vintage."

AltaMare was a small and very intimate restaurant on the western end of Lincoln Road. At the front desk the hostess greeted Giraldi enthusiastically and ushered them to a perfectly situated table in a quiet corner. The waiter, who also seemed to know him, nodded approvingly while Giraldi asked Nikki for her input then ordered a bottle of wine he thought she would like along with an appetizer of grilled octopus with *ferro* and saffron aioli. He did both of these things effortlessly, without an ounce of insecurity or a hint of pomposity.

"What?" he asked after she'd taken a first sip of the crisp Chardonnay then considered him closely.

"You're a wine connoisseur *and* a foodie." It wasn't a question but an observation, one she was having trouble coming to terms with. "Did you take James Bond classes at FBI school or something?"

"Hardly." His laughter lit up his eyes and softened the harsh angles of his face. "And I almost never chase down bad guys in a tux or ask for my martinis shaken, not stirred. I just like a good meal and a nice bottle of wine now and then. It's not a calling or anything."

Nikki settled back in her chair and smoothed the cloth napkin the maître d' had placed in her lap. "Fine. Then tell me about your business trip. Who do you have in your crosshairs now?"

He smiled. "No one in particular at the moment. I'm actually part of a new unit working on profiling potential financial criminals." He didn't add "like your brother," but then, he didn't need to. "There are indicators that can be identified if you're looking for them."

It took her a while to realize that that was all he was planning to give her as he smoothly changed the subject and began to ply her with questions about the house and the show. With his attention riveted on her, Nicole found herself telling him things she hadn't even realized she'd been thinking about: the unexpected bond between Max and Dustin; how Kyra and the Lifetime cameraman locked horns at every turn; what it was like to watch Avery hold off Deirdre. Even the way Maddie got quiet when her husband's name was mentioned.

She nattered on all the way through the fabulous appetizer and her second glass of wine, stopping just long enough to listen to the waiter describe the entrées and the day's special. The dining room was tastefully decorated, the atmosphere upscale. The service was impressive but not intrusive.

Giraldi ordered a second bottle of wine, but it was the way he focused on her, how carefully he listened, that kept the words flowing. Over a main course of hogfish with a romesco sauce and baby-arugula-and-artichoke salad, she told him about Parker Amherst IV, relieved as she did so that she was still clearheaded enough to edit out her desperation to land this client who wasn't technically a client yet. "I'd love to relaunch Heart, Inc.," she said as she practically lapped up the meal. "At least to a certain extent."

Giraldi didn't scoff at the idea, nor did he offer false assurances. But his attention remained riveted on her, his dark eyes telegraphing his interest.

"Here, try this." Giraldi placed a forkful of grilled Bûcheron on the edge of her plate. "But save some room for dessert. They serve a deconstructed tiramisu that is completely worth running an extra couple of miles to work off."

Nicole savored each bite of the hogfish, which she was glad was not as large as its name implied. "This is delicious," she said, enjoying the moment almost as much as the food. "But I don't know about dessert. I think the last time I ate this much was Thanksgiving. Maddie invited me to Atlanta and practically force-fed me one great meal after the other the whole time I was there." She looked down at her plate and was shocked to find it empty. Ditto for the wineglass, though it didn't stay that way for long. "I went with them to the hospital that night when Kyra went into labor."

She had been ridiculously grateful to be so welcomed into the Singers' home and included in the holiday that she'd so often spent alone. But it had made her realize just how disconnected she was in the world. Especially with her only living relative in jail. Where, unfortunately, he belonged.

Under Giraldi's warm gaze, Nicole almost told him about Max's missing son and even Deranian's reappearance, neither of which was her story to tell. She stopped talking, appalled at the amount of information she'd divulged and how much more she wanted to share; she whom her first husband had referred to as "the Sphinx." "I can't tell if I've had too much to drink or you're the best interrogator ever," she said, glad that her words remained unslurred.

"I'm thinking it could be a little bit of both," he replied easily in that straightforward manner that had once pissed the hell out of her but that now seemed oddly attractive.

"Are you an interrogator?" Nicole asked.

"I have some training," he replied. "But I try not to use it on the civilian population. And I rarely use it on a date."

"You've got skills all right," she said, intentionally ignoring the word *date* and only realizing after she'd spoken how her observation could be interpreted.

He didn't leer or turn her comment into a double entendre like so many men would have. Nor did he try to rush her through the rest of the meal and out of the restaurant to claim what some men might have thought of as their due after an expensive meal.

But as he joked with the waiter and introduced the chef when he came out of the kitchen to say hello, and even as she gave in and shared the dessert that was every bit as heavenly as he'd promised, Nicole couldn't help thinking about those other skills Giraldi undoubtedly possessed. And if she dared allow herself to experience them. Or whether his pursuit of her could possibly be as straightforward as he professed.

. . .

Maddie brewed a large pot of coffee and pulled a carton of eggs out of the refrigerator. A box of donuts, Mario Dante's contribution, sat on the counter. He had presented them to her with a flourish when he'd arrived to walk through the house with Deirdre and finalize the plans for the tile floors, which he insisted he could either walk them through or handle himself. His son, Donatello, and a nephew were up on the roof with Avery. She could hear them tromping around even down here.

He'd also handed her a carefully wrapped container. "This is the pasta Milanese I told you about," he'd said. "See what you think of it. The recipe has been in my family for a very long time. But if you like it, I would be more than happy to share it with you." His smile had grown warm. "Or perhaps I could make it for you one night."

"Why, thank you, Mario." His admiring gaze had made her feel unaccountably attractive despite this morning's lack of hot water and the humidity that had enlarged her hair so that it floated around her head like a mushroom cloud.

Kyra appeared now with the baby riding on her hip and went into the refrigerator for a glass of orange juice. "When did you have time to go out for donuts?" she asked, helping herself to one.

"Mario brought them," Maddie said. "He's very thoughtful that way."

"Ha," Kyra said, settling Dustin into his high chair. "I

think he's got a crush on you. Dad better watch out." She laughed as if Steve would find this amusing; they'd had so little contact Maddie wasn't sure he'd notice if Mario went down on one knee and sang "O Sole Mio" to her right in front of him.

Max shuffled into the kitchen and took a seat at the banquette within reach of Dustin.

"Good morning," Max said jovially as Maddie brought him a cup of coffee. "Thank you."

He blew a raspberry at Dustin. The baby laughed and reached toward the old man's lips.

"Are you hungry?" Maddie asked as the comedian and the baby communed. "I was thinking I might scramble up some salami and eggs."

"Thank you," Max said, sipping his coffee contentedly. "You're spoiling me," he said. "And I'm enjoying every minute and morsel of it."

"My pleasure," she said as she began to crack the eggs into a bowl. She'd sliced the salami earlier and turned the electric skillet on to warm; Max had not yet refused an offer of food or drink.

"Is it okay if I leave Dustin with you all?" Kyra asked.

"Absolutely," Maddie and Max said in unison.

A few minutes later Maddie plated the salami and eggs, added a piece of buttered rye bread toast and a slice of cantaloupe, and put the dish in front of Max. The old man was shaking a rattle in front of Dustin, much to the baby's delight.

"He's a beautiful boy," Max said. "And he hardly cries at all."

"He is wonderful, isn't he?" Maddie agreed, sliding onto the opposite side of the banquette. She had a small plastic plate of scrambled egg and toast for Dustin. "But then he has no real reason to cry, seeing as there's always someone here ready to feed him, entertain him, or pick him up."

She went back to the pantry for a napkin and brought it to Max, who tucked it into the open collar of his shirt. "I've even seen Troy down on his hands and knees in front of the playpen when he thinks no one's watching."

She fed Dustin tiny bits of egg while Max tucked into his meal. Although the morning paper and that week's *Variety* sat on the table awaiting him, Max kept his gaze on Dustin. His forehead was furrowed in concentration as if he were memorizing the baby's features. Or perhaps remembering another's.

"Tell me about your son," Maddie said softly when Max put down his fork. "If it won't upset you too much to talk about him, I mean."

Max took a long sip of coffee. When he set the cup down, his face was set, his eyes filled with regret. "Millie always wanted to talk about him. But it was so painful that I wouldn't let her." He shook his head then looked up at her. "I can't believe how selfish I was. As if the pain I felt in talking about him somehow trumped the pain she felt in not being able to. I don't know what I was thinking. Or why she let me get away with such awful behavior."

He wiped his mouth again and tucked the napkin under the edge of his plate.

"Losing him was like having my gut ripped out. Everything about it was just . . . I kept thinking I'd wake up and we'd find out it was some awful nightmare and not real at all. But it was real all right. And the pain never goes away."

"What happened?" Maddie asked. "Do you know who took him or why?"

"No," he said. "There was no ransom. No demands. No explanation." He swallowed and looked away. "No body. He was just gone. Forever."

"What did the police say? Did they have any ideas at all?"

"No. I think they tried their best. They brought in the FBI, searched every inch of The Millicent for clues or fingerprints. They interviewed us, our friends, our family, the neighbors, the deliverymen . . ." His voice trailed off.

"But it wasn't like today. There was no such thing as a registered sex offender, no databases to check. For a few days I prayed that he'd just wandered off somehow. But no one ever reported seeing him anywhere. It was like he went up in some puff of smoke.

"And Millie always felt responsible."

"Why?" Maddie asked.

"Because she was out in the front yard with him when she got nauseous. She was pregnant and still had morning sickness. She ran inside into the bathroom. We have a big gate and it was closed. Aaron . . ." His voice broke. "He was playing in the sandbox right near the front steps. Millie was only gone for a few minutes."

"Did anyone ever find anything at all?"

"No. When the police gave up, I hired a private detective. But there were no clues to follow, no leads, no suspects. Nothing to go on. No one saw anything out of the ordinary." He swallowed. "A few days after we lost Aaron, Millie had a miscarriage."

"I'm so sorry," Maddie said, even though the words were completely insufficient. "That must have been so horrible for both of you. I can't even imagine . . ." She looked at her grandchild and couldn't finish the sentence. She'd barely made it through her husband's breakdown and wasn't doing all that well with their current standoff; she didn't know how she would have survived the loss of Kyra or Andrew.

"Have you thought about trying to look now? With all the new technology and the cold-case units, maybe . . ."

"The original detective retired a long time ago. When I contacted the police department, they told me the only way they can reopen a case is if there's something new to justify taking another look." His sad brown eyes grasped hers. "I promised Millie I'd look for him. I promised her on her deathbed. So I hired another private detective. I spent close to everything I had and there's still no trace of Aaron."

"Oh, Max." Maddie put a hand over his and squeezed gently.

"I promised Millie I'd get the house ready for him. That his old room—the one upstairs at the front of the house that you're using—would be waiting for him if someone could find him and bring him home. But he's gone." Max sniffed and swiped at his eyes with the back of one wrinkled hand. "I don't even know if he's dead or alive."

• • •

Maddie couldn't get Max's tortured face or the emotional rasp of his voice out of her mind. All day, while she tended to Dustin, ran to the grocery store, prepared pickup sandwiches, even while she made calls to theater groups around the Southeast to offer Millie Golden's fabulous wardrobe and accessories, she thought about the couple's lost child. Who'd be just a few years older than Maddie right now, assuming he were still alive, but who remained a frightened and vulnerable toddler in his father's eyes. That Millie had also lost the baby she was carrying at the time seemed almost inconceivable.

Haunted by the specter of that kind of loss, she got Dustin up from his afternoon nap, strapped him into the stroller, and set out for the playground at Marjory Stoneman Douglas Ocean Beach Park. There she angled the stroller into the shade of a palm tree and stared down at his beautiful golden face while the warm ocean breeze brushed across his dark curls.

Settling on a stone bench beside him, she pulled out her cell phone and dialed Andrew's number. He was back in Atlanta and she caught him at the neighborhood pool. "I thought you and Dad might come down when the *Do Over* pilot airs on the first of July. Apparently we're having a premiere party." She was still trying to absorb this little tidbit. "Have you seen any of the footage of The Millicent that Kyra has been posting online?"

They chatted for a few minutes as Maddie built up her courage to place her next call, one to Steve. This time, when he tried to put off committing to a trip down to Miami, she refused to let him off the hook.

"The party's on July first," she said. "That's a Saturday. I'm going to expect you and Andrew here for the weekend."

"That's a ridiculously long drive for a weekend, Maddie. And there's no way we can afford to fly." There was a pause. "Besides, you seem to be doing fine on your own."

There it was. The reminder that in his mind she'd chosen Miami over him. That he still hadn't forgiven her for being okay.

"This show is important to our whole family," she said. "And so is spending time with your daughter and your grandson." She left the "even if you don't want to spend time with me" unspoken, but it hurt just the same.

"Is there money in the budget for a party?" Steve asked dubiously. Another jab at how little she was being paid, how uncertain the payoff was.

"I guess so," Maddie replied. "Fortunately, Deirdre's handling the details, so that's not our problem. All you have to do is show up and be charming."

Steve grumbled.

"You *will* be charming, Steve," she said when he complained again, though she was beginning to wonder if he remembered how. She hesitated, not wanting to fight with him over the phone. But she was growing tired of the effort it took to tread so carefully. "I need you to be here." She hesitated again, but knew that backpedaling now would get them nowhere. "Just let me know your ETA and I'll make sure that the welcome mat is out."

Chapter Seventeen

Avery dragged a stepladder into the foyer and climbed onto the top rung so that she could reach and clean the chandelier that dangled from the vaulted ceiling.

It was quiet now in the early afternoon, the scrape of the ladder over the tile a mere whisper in comparison to the morning's pandemonium. Then Donatello Dante and his crew had swarmed over the flat roof above their heads; Ted Darnell, the master electrician, and his young assistant had replaced the last of the knob-and-tube wiring; and the air-conditioning crew had cut into The Millicent's ceilings and walls to accommodate new ductwork, registers, and returns, piercing the plaster like so much Swiss cheese.

In the living room, Maddie knelt in front of the fireplace attempting to sand the last of fifty years' worth of paint off the carved fireplace surround. Kyra sat on the sofa nursing Dustin and talking to her mother. It was just the three of them and the baby in this welcome calm after the morning storm.

The chandelier, which was suspended on a chain from a hammered brass starfish escutcheon, was made of luminescent glass shot through with flecks of gold. Shaped like an upside-down umbrella, its eight glass panels curved up and outward and were held together by upright metal spines. Each panel featured a bas-relief of real or imaginary sea creatures even more fanciful than those that surrounded the front door.

Carefully, Avery sprayed the ammonia-water mixture onto a clean cloth and began to wipe the first panel, a delicately sculpted school of swimming fish, keeping her eye out for the artist's signature or mark that Deirdre seemed certain they would find. As she worked, her thoughts turned to the upcoming premiere party and its ever-expanding invitation list.

Lisa Hogan had come through with large-screen TVs, digital transfers, and all of the other technical things that Troy and Anthony had requested. The network's publicity people were all over the local tie-ins and press. Avery did not plan to come out and say so, but as much as she hated showing The Millicent in its wounded state, she was beginning to believe that the party might not only help build an audience, but provide the underwriting they so badly needed to give the house its due.

From her perch on the ladder, Avery saw a dented car pull into the drive. It stopped with a rattle and a cough of dark smoke. A gaunt white-haired man eased himself out from behind the wheel. He wore a red Hawaiian print shirt, beige Bermuda shorts, and black socks, which he'd paired with sandals that a tire had clearly given up its life to provide.

Leaning on a brass-handled cane, the man moved

carefully toward the entrance. Avery's head bumped hard against the glass chandelier as she bent to hurry down the ladder, worried about how he'd manage the front steps. She reached out to steady it, but she was too late. Several panels of glass slid out of their brackets and beat her to the ground, shattering on the tile floor.

Avery looked down at the shards of glass then back up at the damaged piece of art, appalled.

"Are you all right?" Maddie called from the living room as a surprisingly brisk knock sounded on the door.

"Yes," Avery called out, although she wasn't sure if this would still be true once Deirdre saw what had happened to the fixture she was so in love with. Avery pushed large shards of glass aside with her shoe then pulled open the door, shaking her head to clear it.

The old man was quite tall. Even hunched over his walking stick, he had a good four or five inches on her. He also had a full white mustache and bushy eyebrows of the same color, suspended over Coke-bottle-lens glasses.

"I'm sorry," she said before he could speak, her thoughts on the broken glass. Perhaps if she swept it all up carefully, she could find a way to piece it back together. "Max isn't here right now. I'm not sure when he'll be back."

The man craned his neck to see past her then looked back over his shoulder and she wondered if he was hard of hearing. "I said Max isn't here." She raised her voice and enunciated carefully. "But I'll be glad to give him a message."

He glanced over his shoulder once more then stepped inside. She heard the crunch of glass under his feet. Avery fell back a step and heard the same sound.

Shit.

"Now wait a minute," Avery began as he took another step into the foyer and the last of the shards crunched into pieces too small to ever go back together. Annoyed, she watched the old man close the door behind him. She was just beginning to wonder if there could, in fact, be such a thing as an octogenarian home invasion when the old man said, "I went to a lot of trouble not to draw a crowd and I don't want to give away anything now."

There was one more crunch of glass as Daniel Deranian stepped around the ladder, leaned the cane against the foyer wall, then removed the glasses with hands that were young and firm and unspotted. Without the Coke-bottle lenses to obscure them, his eyes were dark and sharp, in stark contrast to the pasty white makeup that covered his skin.

"Who is it, Avery?" Maddie called out.

"It appears to be Daniel Deranian," Avery replied as she followed the man into the living room. She was so close behind him that she almost plowed into him when he came to a sudden stop in front of the sofa where Kyra held Dustin to her breast, a baby blanket draped strategically over her shoulder. A tiny hand was curled against Kyra's bare skin.

From her vantage point at the fireplace, Maddie could see exactly what it took for Kyra to maintain her aura of calm. All three of them watched the actor's face, or rather the artfully aged face of the white-haired man, as he stood watching mother and child. Maddie didn't feel at all good about the expression on Deranian's face, the way that, despite all of the makeup, it reflected awe and wonder.

"What are you doing here?" Kyra asked, shifting the baby's weight in her arms while being careful not to detach him from her nipple. In the quiet that had fallen, the sound of Dustin suckling seemed as loud as a thunderclap.

The actor didn't answer. His gaze remained fixed on the nursing child. *His* nursing child.

"Good grief," Kyra said, but quietly so as not to disturb the baby. "You act like you've never seen a baby breast-feed before."

Kyra's tone was laced with the same irritation she'd displayed the last time Deranian had arrived in disguise. But Maddie could see that her eyes were drinking in the actor almost as greedily as Dustin was drawing down her milk. Despite the ridiculous disguise and Maddie's and Avery's presence, the tableau of mother and child was extremely intimate.

"I haven't," he said. Without asking, he crossed to the sofa and sat down next to Kyra. "My children are adopted. They've always been bottle-fed." He reached out a finger and traced the baby's cheek. "And usually by a nanny."

Avery excused herself and went into the foyer. Maddie saw her sweeping up something and then saw her climb back up onto the ladder. Maddie knew she should go help her, but hesitated, unsure whether she should leave Kyra and Deranian alone. She wanted to believe that Kyra was immune to the actor's charm—she had, after all, rejected the idea of continuing their relationship once she'd understood he wasn't planning to leave his wife—but those charms were considerable. And he *was* Dustin's father.

Kyra was so focused on Daniel's face that she barely noticed when her mother left the room. He smiled. And despite the white hair and eyebrows and pasty makeup, it was the same smile that had made him one of Hollywood's biggest draws. The same smile that had slain her completely the first time it had been turned on her.

"And here I thought you'd appreciate my disguise," he

said to Kyra. "At least I got to be male this time." He smiled again. "I had to swear my makeup person to secrecy and convince the car wrangler that I needed something that wouldn't call attention to itself. I think I look pretty damned convincing. I drove right by a herd of paparazzi camped out near the set and no one even looked up." His voice rang with delight, like a child who'd pulled off a complicated prank.

Kyra wanted to tell him that he shouldn't have bothered, that she wanted him to leave, but his fingers had moved from Dustin's soft cheek to the baby's fist, which rested on her breast. A shudder rippled through her as the baby's fingers opened briefly then wrapped around his father's.

It took several long seconds to slow her heartbeat and find her voice.

"I don't understand what you want," she said finally. "You're living with your wife and your children and you think it's okay to show up here whenever you feel like it? This isn't a game, Daniel." She paused, trying to swallow the rise of feelings she'd thought she was free of. "You're just making a bad situation harder."

"I don't actually know what I want," Deranian said, a note of surprise in his voice. "I mean, I know what I'm supposed to want, what I've always wanted." He reached out and slipped the baby blanket out of the way. "But I don't see why those things have to be mutually exclusive." The fingers of his free hand trailed across her skin. "I'd like to be more to you and Dustin than a bank account."

The old-man face moved closer to hers and her eyes fluttered shut. She heard the rustle of clothing as he leaned over her. When his lips covered hers, her arm stole up around his neck and the three of them were connected. She said his name, but what she'd meant as a protest came out on a sigh.

Her brain knew and remembered all of the reasons she'd had to give him up. Her heart seemed to have developed a worrisome case of amnesia.

· · ·

Monty's at the Miami Beach Marina was noisy and redolent of boat fumes and fried seafood. Island music played in the background and there was plenty of sun-kissed skin to look at, but it was the view out over Government Cut to the south and the Port of Miami and downtown to the west, where the sun would soon set, that drew the crowds. Well, that and one of the longest happy hours on South Beach, one that Nicole, Avery, Deirdre, and Maddie were currently availing themselves of. Kyra nursed a single glass of wine while Dustin sat in his carrier on the table apparently enjoying the music and the warm breeze off the water.

"Okay," Avery said, settling back in her chair. "This is definitely the life."

Maddie had to agree as she watched yet another expensive-looking speedboat filled with tanned thirty-somethings nudge up to the docks. Out in the channel, powerboats and sailboats of all sizes passed by. Here at Monty's a mix of tourists and locals sipped drinks and ate seafood.

"I can't believe Troy actually thought I'd leave Dustin with him," Kyra said as she handed back the squishy baseball that the baby had almost dropped in the mound of smoked-fish spread. "He seemed to think Dustin belonged there watching baseball with the guys."

Dustin squished the baseball Troy had given him at the

sound of the cameraman's name. A coincidence, no doubt, like early smiles that were actually gas.

"He *is* good with him," Madeline said. "And apparently he has young nieces and nephews he babysits for." She dabbed at a trickle of drool that had slipped out of Dustin's mouth and the baby flashed both of his new teeth at her.

Kyra shot her a look. "Since when are you defending him?"

Since Daniel Deranian showed up, Madeline thought but did not say. An unwanted and argumentative cameraman seemed a far safer choice than an intrusive and potentially irresistible married movie-star father. "I'm not defending him. I just think he could probably be trusted to keep an eye on Dustin for an hour or two in a pinch." She reached for a popcorn shrimp and popped it into her mouth. Beside her, Deirdre squeezed lemon over their order of calamari. Apparently in the grip of a fried-food frenzy, they'd also ordered a loaf of onion rings. Everyone but Kyra was drinking "painkillers," the happy hour specialty, which so far seemed to be delivering on its claim.

"I need you all to give me any final names for the premiere-party guest list," Deirdre said as they munched and drank. "The invitations have started going out, but we have plenty. And I'm also planning to do a phone follow-up." She looked at Nicole. "I invited Giraldi, and I hope he'll feel free to bring along any other good-looking FBI types. And I know Chase and his father are coming down." Now she turned to Avery. "Are they bringing the boys?"

"Unclear," Avery replied. "And I'm also not sure where everyone's going to stay."

It was just a matter of weeks until D-day. Steve had finally texted that he and Andrew were coming. "I know,"

Maddie said. "I'm not sure how Kyra and I are going to fit Steve and Andrew in with us and the baby, either."

"Maybe we should approach one of the local hotels about putting up some of our overflow in exchange for an on-air mention," Nicole said. "Lisa Hogan and a few others are coming from the network, aren't they?"

"They are and I'm on it," Deirdre said.

"Well, if that doesn't work out, maybe we could fit the younger guys into the pool house with Troy and Anthony," Nicole said.

"I don't know," Maddie said. "I keep asking if they're okay in there. And they keep talking about how awful it is. It's easy to forget about, given the way it's been swallowed up by those hedges. But we haven't even set foot inside and there's not really time to deal with it before the party."

"We're going to have to deal with it at some point," Avery said. "From the outside it reminds me of the hollow tree the Keebler elves live in in those commercials. But if we could clean up a bedroom and a bath for Max, we could move him out there when work starts on his room."

The onion-ring loaf arrived and they ordered another round of painkillers. Kyra, who would nurse Dustin before putting him to bed, was still working on her glass of wine.

"Speaking of Max," Maddie said, glad his name had been introduced. "I don't want to betray a confidence, but while Nicole and I were helping him clean out his closets, we discovered that he and Millie had a son."

"Really?" Deirdre asked, surprised. "He's got all those pictures of Millie and the celebrities they worked with. But I don't remember seeing any children."

"Where is he now?" Avery asked. "And why isn't he helping Max? Did they have a falling-out?"

"No," Maddie said, still amazed that this could be true. "Apparently he disappeared from their yard when he was only a toddler. They never found him."

They drank in silence for a few moments as the sun began to sink in the sky. The loaf of onion rings gave off a heavenly aroma, but nobody reached for it.

"Gosh, that's awful," Avery said, stealing a glance at Deirdre. Maddie half expected her to say something about parents abandoning children, but if she was thinking anything of the sort, she kept it to herself.

"Right before Millie died she made him promise that he'd get the house ready for their son and that he'd try once more to find him," Maddie explained. "He disappeared back in 1961 without a trace. Millie had a miscarriage right after."

"Wow." Avery took a long sip of her painkiller, but although the music floated around them and the sunset was proving to be an impressive one, the party atmosphere had fled.

"I've been wondering if we might be able to help in some way," Maddie said.

"It's bad enough to be knowingly separated," Deirdre said. "It's hard to imagine how painful that kind of loss, that not-knowing must be."

Maddie considered the women she'd met only a year ago and with whom she'd been through so much. "I was thinking that tonight, instead of searching for a good thing to toast, we might brainstorm what we could do to help Max try to find out what happened to his son." She took a sip of her drink. "I mean, I know we're all kind of overwhelmed with getting the house ready, and the premiere party, and our own . . . situations. But . . ." Her voice trailed off, suddenly sounding unsure.

"But we can make the time to at least see what we can find out," Nicole said.

"What about Giraldi?" Deirdre asked Nicole. "Do you think he might be able to help or at least give us some direction?"

"I can ask," Nicole said. "I thought about it the other night, but I wasn't sure that Max would appreciate me sharing his private life."

"Do you think we should ask his permission first?" Kyra asked. "I think there are sites where adopted kids looking for their biological parents post."

"But their child wasn't adopted, he just disappeared," Avery pointed out. "And we don't have any idea if he's alive."

"Maybe we could get the story on *Cold Case*," Kyra said. "I saw some chatter online about a *Dr. Phil* episode with a guy who was a 'locator.' "

Maddie pulled out the yellow pad she'd stashed in Kyra's diaper bag and began to jot down notes. "I think putting Kyra on the Internet makes total sense, and asking Giraldi to see if he can talk to anyone about the case file and the original investigation would be good. But I'm not sure we should say anything to Max until there's a reason to. I'd hate to get his hopes up and then come up with nothing."

"I agree," Deirdre said. "Even if we don't find him, even if all we do is find out what really happened, there's value in that, right?"

They raised their glasses and toasted Max and their new mission, but Maddie couldn't help wondering if unearthing information now, assuming they could, was really a good idea. She looked at her daughter and grandson, and thought of Andrew; she could remember all of their births, the instant love and overwhelming connection she'd felt. If one of them had been ripped out of her life, would she want to know if her child were dead? Or would she rather die believing her child was safe somewhere? Anywhere? Was horrible certainty really preferable to even the smallest glimmer of hope?

Chapter Eighteen

Nicole got up early to run before the sun went into what she'd come to think of as "bake" mode. As she jogged eastward toward the beach on that June morning, she scanned the early morning sidewalks. Sometimes the remains of the previous night's partying were still evident: the sequin-clad woman she'd spotted one morning sleeping upright on the bus-stop bench next to a disapproving elderly couple; the pair of designer high heels abandoned on a dirty sidewalk as if someone had simply stepped out of them and kept going.

On more than one occasion she'd spotted young, overdressed women exiting clubs and hotels obviously wearing last night's party clothes, doing what in her day would have been called the walk of shame. Except none of them looked even remotely ashamed.

She'd partied in some of these same hotels and clubs back in the nineties when she was building her business, though, of course, the clubs and whom they attracted had changed. She crossed Ocean Drive and jogged onto the beach, trying not to think about how long ago and far away her prime party days had been.

She tried to vary her run, but still saw plenty of other regulars along the way. She was always slightly braced for Giraldi to appear, and chastised herself regularly for the way her pulse and heartbeat kicked up in anticipation every time someone came up from behind. Ditto for the stab of disappointment she felt when it wasn't him and the jogger passed her.

Each day the temperature and humidity level inched upward and the breezes grew warmer. The air-conditioning installation had proven trickier than expected, but she clung to Hendricks's promise that the system would be functional well before the premiere party, which was now less than two weeks away. Deirdre had smiled and shown Hendricks the sign she intended to plant in the front yard citing his company's commitment and involvement— whether the air-conditioning was working or not. A promise that had had John Hendricks doubling the size of the installation crew and promising to finish the job himself if he had to.

Unlike Deirdre, who seemed able to talk almost anyone—except her daughter—into pretty much anything, Nicole had clearly lost not only her business and her reputation, but her persuasive "touch." She simply couldn't seem to get Parker Amherst to sign on the damned dotted line. Or, more importantly, to write her a check. Oh, he'd smiled over the stack of photos she'd shown him and even picked out a few women whom he agreed he'd like to meet, but the only thing he'd actually committed to was attending the premiere party. During which Nicole intended to get his signature on both contract and check. Or die in the attempt.

Nicole ran north for thirty minutes before turning back. When she reached The Millicent, the driveway was littered with cars, trucks, and vans. The only one missing seemed to be the network crew's. She entered through the kitchen and found Maddie, manning her version of command central, with its gurgling coffeemaker, bagels and cream cheese, and always-filled bowl of fruit.

Deirdre was busy taping renderings and floor plans of the proposed kitchen to the wall so that the premiere guests could see what was planned and had indicated her intention to do this all over the house. Avery had already informed them that the "heavy lifting," as she'd put it, would begin after the premiere; she'd absolutely refused to close up walls or spend time, energy, or money on cosmetic repairs for the party that they'd just have to rip out again.

Max was seated at the banquette near Dustin's high chair. A battered manila envelope sat on the glass tabletop and he was sorting through a large stack of photos as Kyra filmed him.

"Good morning." Nicole greeted the assembled group, then poured a glass of orange juice and rooted around in the pantry for a granola bar. She was sweaty and in serious need of a shower, so she slid all the way into the far end of the banquette nearest the window. "What's going on?"

Maddie brought her cup of coffee to the table. "I asked Max to show us pictures of the house from back in the day—I thought it might be nice to put together a series of them for each room as a sort of counterpoint to Deirdre's 'future' boards. That way people at the party could see the past, the present, and the future."

"That's a great idea," Nicole said.

"Thanks." As always, anything resembling praise brought a blush to Maddie's cheeks. She reached for the envelope. "The house envelopes have some original receipts in them, too. We've been playing around with the idea of posting what decoration used to cost versus now as a sort of incentive for potential sponsors. Deirdre's going through them."

"I'm crossing my fingers there's something in there that will give us a clue about the foyer chandelier," Deirdre said, coming over to join them. "If there's any paperwork and the stars align, I'd like to have it repaired."

Maddie saw Avery brace for an accusatory glare or worse, but Deirdre refrained.

Max spread out the photos and began to sort through them. "This is . . . was . . . Aaron." His hand trembled as he held up a photo for them to see. "Millie always called him her valentine. Because he was born on February fourteenth."

The photo was a black-and-white that had faded to gray-on-gray; the corners were dog-eared. It showed a sturdy, dimple-armed toddler dressed in overalls and a striped T-shirt. He had a head of blond Dennis the Menace hair clearly inherited from his mother and his father's megawatt smile. A 1950s toy fire truck was held up against his chest in a "mine" gesture.

Max laid the photo on the table and began to sort through the others. "Some of these were taken out around the pool three or four months before Aaron disappeared." He positioned them so that Deirdre, Nikki, and Maddie could see.

Nicole looked at the first black-and-white photo. In it, Millie, who wore a sleek maillot, stood in the shallow end of the pool holding on to the canvas ring that Aaron floated in. Max began to set the photo aside, but Maddie stopped him.

"Who's that?" She pointed to a second woman in the photo. She was considerably taller than Millie and had an angular body without an ounce of extra flesh, but her suit was almost identical to Millie's. She sat on the edge of the pool, her legs dipped into the water. Her pixie haircut framed a gamine face.

"Pamela Gentry," Max replied. "She was Millie's interior-designer friend. She and Millie worked on The Millicent together." He hesitated for a moment. "They were good friends for a time."

He began to pass over another pool photo, but Deirdre, who'd perked up noticeably at the mention of the interior designer, asked to see it. It showed Pamela and Millie barefoot and still wet from the pool. They both wore terrycloth cover-ups and similar oversize sunglasses. Aaron stood between them. Each held one of Aaron's chubby hands.

"We had lots of couples we were friendly with both in and out of the entertainment business, but for a while Pamela was Millie's closest friend." He shifted in his seat. "She was single and she sat for Aaron now and then when a babysitter didn't show or we'd have some last-minute booking."

He sighed as he stared down at the photos. They'd faded over the years, but the contrast between the women was still marked; the interior designer's angular features and whip-thin body reflected a tightly leashed intensity that was absent in Millie's warmer, curvier face and form.

"Hmm," Deirdre said. "Maybe we should invite Pamela to the premiere party. The design people would eat it up."

"I don't even know if she's still alive," Max said. "I haven't seen Pamela in fifty years."

"Why not?" Maddie asked.

"Millie and Pamela had a falling-out. I . . . really don't know what happened, Millie wouldn't talk about it. I heard later that she'd moved away—to somewhere in the Midwest. Chicago, I think."

Deirdre picked up another photo. It was of Millie and Pamela again. In this one, they were lounging in chaises by The Millicent's pool. Both of them wore polka-dot bikinis. A concrete wall rose behind them. An old-fashioned life preserver emblazoned with the words SS MILLICENT hung on the wall. "I think we still have that life preserver somewhere."

Avery wandered into the kitchen. Her hair was streaked with plaster dust. She wore a baggy T-shirt with cutoff sleeves. Her tool belt hung low on her hips. She opened the refrigerator and stood in front of it, most likely sucking up the refrigeration as opposed to contemplating its contents.

"It was Pamela who drew up the plans for the pool house and talked us into building it," Max said. "It was far bigger than it needed to be, with a lot of amenities you don't usually see in a pool house." He shrugged. "But we had the property and it came in handy later when we were looking for rental income. It was really ahead of its time."

Kyra lowered the video camera.

The comment snagged Avery's attention and caused her to turn her back on the refrigerator, though she didn't close the door on her temporary personal air conditioner. "What did you say?" she asked Max, hoping she hadn't heard correctly.

"We built the pool house in '56, or '57 maybe. I remember Millie was pregnant with Aaron at the time and the act was doing great. Pamela made sure it looked like it went with the rest of the house, but it was pretty lavish. We first started renting it out to some of the bigger-name comedians who wanted more privacy and space than they could get at one of the big hotels. Later, in the mid-sixties, when Miami Beach took a nosedive, we were able to rent it out pretty steadily. Whatever else we gave up, we made sure to keep it up-to-date and in tiptop shape. It turned out to be a godsend."

Avery closed the refrigerator and walked to the table.

"What kind of shape is the pool house in now?" Kyra asked, which was exactly what Avery was wondering. They'd all heard Troy and Anthony complain about how uncomfortable it was, how much work it needed. They'd been so preoccupied with the main house and grounds that no one had bothered to so much as set foot inside it.

"Well, we did have it completely renovated before Millie got sick. So that we could keep the revenue stream coming. We never had any problem renting it out, that's for sure. It was so much nicer than anything else around."

A heavy silence fell. Max looked at his photos. The women looked at one another.

"I'm thinking we should go check it out," Avery said, trying to process what Max had said.

Kyra removed Dustin's bib and wiped off his mouth. She checked her video camera for battery.

"Max," Maddie said, pulling Dustin out of his high chair. "Will you take us out there and give us a tour?"

"Sure." As always, Max seemed pleased to be the center of attention. He moved slowly and all of them did their best to hang back so that he could lead the way. Part of Avery wanted to charge ahead to see for herself what she might have missed.

Given the snail's pace, it took them a while to get there. When they finally stepped inside the pool house, they were enveloped in marvelously cool air and more than a few unpleasant surprises.

"They have air-conditioning!" Kyra walked over to the wall and reached a hand toward the digital thermostat. It was set at seventy-two degrees.

"But where's the condenser?" Avery asked, still not wanting to believe she'd been so obtuse. "I haven't heard it or seen it. I may not have been inside, but I've walked the property more than once." They were all staring dumbly at the digital readout.

"It's directly behind the pool house and hidden inside a privet hedge. So that it wouldn't create noise or be an eyesore from the main house," Max said.

They turned and sighed as one at the sight of a stainless-steel kitchen with granite countertops.

"Is that a double oven?" Maddie asked.

"Yep," Deirdre said. "And a gas cooktop."

They looked around them in shock. A set of French doors led to a private back garden screened by a U-shaped hedge of hibiscus. A second set opened to another small hidden garden off a beautifully decorated master suite.

"There are three bedrooms!" Avery could hardly absorb it. Troy and Anthony had each claimed a room. The third had been turned into an editing suite with multiple monitors and full-scale audio that had Kyra salivating.

"And two bathrooms," Maddie noted.

They barely breathed as they walked through the space,

while Deirdre cataloged the high-end finishes and amenities. Perhaps like Avery they were simply trying not to hyperventilate as they realized just how well the camera crew had been living.

"Sweet Mother of God," Avery said. "We have been sharing beds, sweating in an un-air-conditioned space, and living with the constant threat of housewide blackouts while—"

"—they have a big-screen TV and some kind of satellite dish!" Kyra added this with a tone of sick fascination. "And a state-of-the-art editing suite."

Max looked around him, taking in their faces, understanding dawning. "I assumed you gave them the best accommodations because they were with the network." He cleared his throat. "I was kind of looking forward to maybe moving out here after the party. Just to get away from the mess and noise."

There were footsteps out on the pool deck and the bark of male laughter. A moment later the front door of the pool house opened and Troy and Anthony walked in, their arms laden with grocery bags.

To put in their stainless-steel refrigerator. And cook in one of their double ovens.

Their laughter died as the twosome spotted their unexpected guests. Troy studied their faces. Anthony shifted uncomfortably from foot to foot.

"We thought we might cook you all a meal in return for . . . everything." Troy held up the grocery bags in his arms as if this was the sole reason for everything they might have bought. "I make a pretty decent arroz con pollo. That's chicken and yellow—"

"We don't care what you know how to cook," Kyra said

angrily. "You . . . you are . . . you should . . ." She seemed to be having trouble finding the right word, but she had no problem raising her camera to her shoulder and aiming it at the network crew.

Avery hoped she was getting a close-up of their guilty faces.

"You should be ashamed of yourselves," Maddie finished, holding Dustin tight against her.

"You intentionally misled us," Nikki added, stating what had become insultingly obvious. "You knew the kind of conditions we've been living in . . ." She looked at Max. "Sorry. And you made us believe that you were even worse off." She shook her head.

"Every time I fed you, you acted as if you were starving out here." Maddie also shook her head in disbelief.

"We were. We do . . . appreciate it," Anthony amended hastily. The round cheeks above his beard flushed red with embarrassment. "Troy's really not that good a cook."

"You've been sitting out here laughing at us," Nikki said. "That sucks."

"We haven't been laughing," Anthony said. "Well, not exactly. We just—"

"Couldn't stay off property. Our job requires us to be here," Troy cut in. "And as I recall, you're the ones who put us out here." His smile was taunting. "Kind of ironic, isn't it?"

"Irony is extremely unattractive when it's being aimed right at you," Deirdre said. "But I must say the layout and design of this space is first rate. I'd definitely like to meet Pamela Gentry."

Max lowered himself into a club chair set into a cozy reading nook. "So. What happens now?" he asked.

Troy ended the standoff by walking past the others to put the groceries on the kitchen counter. Kyra's camera followed and stayed on him as he began to put the groceries away.

"So, our family and friends will be arriving in two days," Avery said. "You two will double up so that they can stay out here. After they leave, Max will move in. I assume he'll be given the master suite, since this is his house."

"Of course," Anthony said. Troy nodded, but less happily.

"We'll discuss what happens after that with Lisa Hogan." Avery turned and saw Kyra moving in for a close-up. "As far as I'm concerned, the network can either put you up nearby or pay Max rent for your accommodations."

"Or maybe we should flip a coin to see who gets to stay out here," Nikki said. "Or we could take turns rotating in and out. They've already been out here for six weeks."

"We can definitely turn this into a communal kitchen. I can't believe I've been cooking in an electric skillet when this place existed all along." Maddie snorted in irritation; a rare thing indeed. "If you'd mentioned this kitchen, we could have all been eating a little better."

"Well, everybody's been keeping things to themselves," Troy said with a jut of his jaw. "And that includes the comings and goings of a major celebrity." He looked right into Kyra's camera lens when he said this. A muscle ticked in his cheek. "That's not really something that a network filming a reality-television show can afford to ignore. In fact, a network might be upset to discover that they're missing out on a huge ratings score because its talent are protecting their privacy. Which they technically gave up when they signed a contract with the network."

Kyra's lips pressed into a thin line. She lowered the camera from her shoulder then glared at the cameraman for a few long moments before turning to her mother and taking the baby out of her arms.

Maddie turned to Max and offered him a hand up. The old man rose slowly then slipped his arm through Maddie's elbow. Nicole came up on his other side.

"I suggest you enjoy your last nights alone," Avery said before turning to join the others. "That ship has sailed."

Chapter Nineteen

Maddie and the others spent the last week before the premiere party in a state of perpetual motion. Anyone who stood still for more than a few seconds was commandeered by Avery or Deirdre for some task then filmed doing it by Troy and/or Kyra, their audio recorded by the small but burly soundman. There was cleaning and straightening and as much strategic "concealment" as the limited closet space allowed.

"Is there really a reason to plump pillows when there's barely a single wall or ceiling intact?" Avery asked Deirdre, who was in the process of frenetic staging. "Who's going to look at your design boards and paint chips when they're staring at exposed ductwork and wiring while standing on gouged tiles and uneven flooring?" She crossed her arms and set her jaw. Her mother did the same.

"They'll love being in on the process," Deirdre insisted for what might have been the hundredth time, though Maddie still wasn't sure whether she was trying to convince them or herself. "I'm sure Michelangelo showed the pope his Sistine Chapel once or twice before it was completed. When we invite our guests back to see our finished masterpiece, they'll feel doubly invested in the project *and* the show."

No one bothered to argue with this. In fact, by the time Lisa Hogan and her entourage swept in the day before the premiere party, they were all too tired to argue and almost too tired to move. The network head was both younger and more attractive than she'd looked in photographs, with a fall of dark hair and mossy-green eyes that seemed to assess everything in their path with all the warmth of an ice cube. Her comments and decisions shot from her mouth at warp speed, rapid and deadly.

From what Maddie could tell, the woman loved Max, thought the house had potential, and had not yet fully committed to the series or them. To the question of her crew living on-site she said simply, "They're here twenty-four/seven. Where they sleep is up to you."

Kyra attempted to avoid her, but Hogan took a look at Dustin then walked right up to Kyra and said into her camera lens, "There will be no secrets or personal agendas." Then she narrowed her laser beams at Avery. "And no budget overruns." As if the budget were more than ample and anything they'd spend above it, frivolous.

To Deirdre and Nicole she said, "Let's sit down with the guest list. I'll want to meet your potential sponsors." As to the running of the party she said, "We'll show Max and Millie performance video on all screens inside and outside the house during cocktails. Then all of you will be introduced via video segments and Max will introduce the pilot, which we'll cut to live at precisely eight P.M." She scanned their faces, though it was clear that she did not anticipate questions or objections. "We'll have a postmortem afterward. I leave first thing the following morning."

With that, she and her people decamped to the Ritz-Carlton, an expense the network apparently deemed more critical than a workable budget for *Do Over*.

Chase Hardin, his father, and his teenage sons arrived later in the afternoon. Avery took Chase and Jeff on a tour of The Millicent, which included everything from the roof to the new breaker box, while Maddie got Josh and Jason settled in the pool-house bedroom they'd be sharing with Andrew.

Nicole had offered to share her room with Kyra and Dustin so that Maddie and Steve could have a room to themselves. Maddie appreciated the gesture, but couldn't help wondering what sort of reunion this would be given how awkward and infrequent her conversations with her husband had become.

As she made dinner in the pool-house kitchen, enjoying both the convenience and the air-conditioning, she peered out windows and stilled at every new sound even though Steve and Andrew weren't due until later in the evening. It seemed incomprehensible that she was this anxious about what she'd say to the man to whom she'd been married for a quarter of a century, but that didn't make the churning in her stomach any less real.

"I've never seen you so squirmy," Nicole said as they sat down to eat at the dining room table, which Deirdre had earmarked for refinishing as soon as the party was over. The windows had all been thrown open without any discernible effect.

"I thought the air-conditioning was going to be up and running," Kyra said.

"Hendricks promised first thing tomorrow morning so that there'll be time to cool down the house for the party," Nicole said. "You should have seen his face when Deirdre escorted him past the sign next to the front steps and showed him the line on the handout and next to the thermostats that read, 'If you're cool and comfortable, thank John Hendricks of Hendricks Heat and Air.'"

"I guess the 'if you're *not* cool and comfortable' part was heavily implied," Chase observed.

"I have fans imprinted with that to hand out just in case," Deirdre said. "I left them in a box right next to the thermostat where John would be sure to see them." She laid a napkin in her lap.

"Sometimes subtle just doesn't cut it," Jeff Hardin agreed.

Maddie and Deirdre exchanged looks. That had been the theme of today's hurried mothering tutorial.

"Deirdre and I were talking about that today," Maddie said with a smile of encouragement aimed at the designer.

"That's as true in comedy as it is in real life," Max said. He seemed to be enjoying the stepped-up activity and the additional people in the house. "Sometimes you need that pratfall. Or a well-placed banana peel."

Maddie passed the antipasto salad she'd made in one direction and the platter of grilled salmon, which she'd marinated in a special mix of ingredients that Mario had suggested, in the other. A loaf of crusty Italian bread followed. With the addition of the Hardins to the table, they were packed tight, but the conversation was lively and the food disappeared quickly. All the way through the meal Maddie kept one ear cocked and an eye out the window to the drive.

They were sitting over their coffee and dessert when a car drove up.

"I bet that's Dad and Andrew." Kyra stood immediately. "Did you hear that, Dustin?" she cooed. "Your grandpa and your uncle are here." For once, she didn't race Troy to reach her camera, but lifted the baby out of his high chair and settled him on her hip.

Maddie felt Deirdre's gaze on her and realized she was still seated. "Are the outside lights on?" she asked as she stood, unable to remember if she'd put them on earlier. Pushing aside a jumble of emotions, Maddie followed Kyra through the kitchen and out the door. Steve and Andrew appeared rumpled from the long drive, but they were here. She hurried out to meet them, reminding herself that Steve had come a long way since last year at this time. He and Andrew had driven all day to get there.

But only because you made him. No, it was time to focus on the positives and not pick apart the things that Steve had and hadn't done or said. But even as she hugged them both and brought them inside to join the others and meet Max, she sensed Steve holding himself back. Oh, he smiled and said all the right things, but there was something beneath the words and in his eyes that she couldn't quite make out. As if he were going through the motions because she'd commanded it, but wasn't going to give her an ounce more than he had to. As she fetched the plates she'd set aside for them, she had an uncomfortable feeling that dwelling only on the positive during this most important of weekends might prove easier said than done.

. . .

"I feel absolutely ridiculous in this outfit," Avery complained the next afternoon as they dressed for the premiere party. "I feel like I'm wearing a costume. I look like a child who raided her mother's closet."

"You used to love to do that when you were little," Deirdre said with a note of nostalgia that set Avery's teeth on edge. "I remember one time when you—"

Avery turned from the mirror to confront Deirdre. "I am not interested in walking down your memory lane. Which is, after all, incredibly short." She sighed at the nasty tone and turned back to consider her image in the still-steamy bathroom-door mirror. At the moment it wasn't Deirdre she was angry with, but herself. "Almost as short as me."

The cocktail dress was low cut and halter-necked and the aquamarine satin bodice clung to her, well, everywhere. A spray of sequins had been sewn into the deep V of the neck and splashed around the hem of the chiffon skirt, which swirled around her knees. A pair of dyed-to-match high-heel sandals studded with rhinestones completed the ensemble that had belonged to Millie Golden.

She remained silent as Nicole slicked her hair into a French twist and affixed large drop earrings to her lobes.

"You look like a fifties movie star. From a distance you could even pass for Marilyn," Deirdre said. Her tone made it clear she was offering the ultimate compliment. She held up a deep red hibiscus blossom. "What do you think of this behind her ear?" she asked Nikki. "It's almost the same shade as her lipstick."

"No flowers," Avery said. "I guess I should be thankful Millie never went for the Carmen Miranda look or you two would be trying to put a banana on my head." But, of course, it wasn't her head that she was worried about.

Although grateful that Troy and Anthony had no upstairs access, Avery couldn't hide from Kyra or her camera. "You look incredible," Kyra said as she widened her shot to include Deirdre, who was not in costume but seemed intent on "acting" like a mother.

"Stop fussing," Avery said to Deirdre. The words *where were you when I went to prom and walked down the aisle?* flitted through her mind, but she clamped her mouth shut to keep from saying them.

"Well, you *do* look fabulous," Nicole said. But then she was the one who'd hidden this outfit of Millie Golden's away, only bringing it out today when it was time to get dressed and too late for Avery to refuse. Especially since the dress she'd planned to wear had somehow ended up in the dirty-clothes hamper.

"Thanks," Avery said. But she suspected what she looked like was Dolly Parton squeezed into a designer dress that emphasized the one thing she did *not* want to define her.

From the bedroom window Avery could see the bartender setting up at one corner of the pool deck and could hear the caterer downstairs in the kitchen. The waitstaff moved like a line of ants between The Millicent's kitchen, which had running water and lots of counter space, and the pool house, where things could be kept warm or reheated. Lights had been strung from deck to deck to create a festive mood. Soon waiters would begin passing hors d'oeuvres.

The air-conditioning was on, thanks primarily to Deirdre's cajoling and threatening. She seemed equally adept with the stick and the carrot, but then the woman's specialty had always been making sure she got what she wanted. It was only a matter of luck, and not love, that what Avery and Deirdre wanted at the moment happened to align.

Avery turned to check herself out one last time, reaching up to retie the halter straps in a vain attempt to lift the V higher. If the others hadn't been all over her, if she'd had a single lick of privacy, she would have simply taken off the dress and put on something more comfortable and less revealing. But Nikki forced her into a chair to dust off and "set" her makeup. Then she told Avery to close her eyes, and sprayed the shit out of her hair.

Deirdre sent her off with a hug that seemed just as awkward to give as it was to receive.

Avery clung to the wall as she made her way down the stairs in the unfamiliar heels, afraid she'd lose her balance and somersault into the foyer. She loved the stepped wall that opened the stairs to the living room, but at the moment she would have loved a handrail even more. Kyra had moved more quickly and had positioned herself at the edge of the foyer. Troy had staked out a spot closer to the stairs. As usual, they were attempting to ignore each other.

Avery spotted Max moving into the foyer at almost the same time as she heard his gasp of surprise and saw his face go pale. "You look so like Millie," he said as she hurried down the last few steps to him as best she could. He gazed at her in wonder. His eyes glistened with what she was afraid might be tears.

"I'm so sorry," Avery began. "I knew this wasn't a good idea." She began to turn, almost relieved to have a legitimate excuse to take off the dress. "I'll go upstairs and change."

Max's age-spotted hand wrapped gently around her wrist. He pulled her back around. "No," he said. "It just surprised me, that's all. You look . . . beautiful. And the memories you're stirring up?" He gave her his biggest smile. "They're all good ones."

"Are you sure?" Avery asked. "Because I can . . ."

"I'm sure." His hand steadied her, or more likely they steadied each other, as they stood together in the foyer. "It's the next best thing to having her here."

He wore a white tux that had probably been the height of sophistication in its day. The black tie was crisply tied and the tux shirt was lined with pearl button covers. Gold cuff links glittered at his wrist.

"She was a lucky woman," Avery said, reaching out to straighten Max's bow tie even though it didn't need it. "You look pretty magnificent yourself."

"Why, thank you." Max performed a shallow bow, which both Troy and Kyra captured on video. "If you'll excuse me, I'm going to see if the bar is set up." He gave her a wink and moved off carefully.

Kyra's lens followed Max as he left, but Troy's camera remained on Avery. Avery looked down and she winced at just how much cleavage was exposed. Since the first day, when she'd been surprised in her Daisy Dukes, she'd been very careful not to show more than the occasional patch of skin.

There was movement nearby and she looked up to see Chase walking toward her. A large smile split his face as he crossed the foyer. "Wow," he said, his eyes glowing. His smile faltered as his gaze dropped lower. He stepped directly between Avery and the camera. "My God," he said quietly. "It's physically impossible to look you in the eye in that dress," he said as he slid an arm around her shoulders and led her away, his body shielding hers. "And believe me, I'm trying." His tone was only half joking. "I hate to give Troy a chance at any *Hammer and Nail*–caliber bust shots."

Avery frowned at the mention of the remodeling show she'd hosted with her now ex-husband and on which most of her close-ups had *not* been of her face.

Chase walked Avery into a corner of the loggia back behind the baby grand piano. It was as out of sight as one could get in a house already teeming with people and about to teem with more. "You look absolutely gorgeous," he said, not sounding at all happy about it. "More than gorgeous. There's not a man here that won't be trying to imagine getting you out of that dress. Including me." He ran a hand through his hair. A crease of worry formed between his brows. "Do you have anything else you could put on?"

Avery wanted to laugh. Or cry. She really couldn't decide which. She actually liked how tortured Chase looked; it made her feel strangely powerful and wonderfully desired. But she hated that the dress would give the network an opportunity to deduct more IQ points, though why people seemed to think large breasts destroyed gray matter, she didn't know. Especially when it was clear that men often thought with their penises and bypassed their brains altogether.

"It's too late for that," Avery said. Besides which she didn't want to hurt Nicole's or even Deirdre's feelings after they'd gone to such trouble to dress her. She drew a breath and saw Chase's eyes grow big.

"No," he said, drawing a breath of his own. "No deep breathing. Promise me at least that." His eyes had turned a darker, almost navy blue. "Shit," he said, a note of panic creeping into his voice. "Now you look like you're . . . cold."

Avery was not about to complain about the air-conditioning now that they finally had it. But under his gaze, or maybe it was the nearby vent and its spill of cool air, she felt her nipples harden. *Good grief.*

"Here." He removed his suit jacket, and before she could protest, he'd helped her into it. It fell to her knees. Her hands disappeared into the sleeves. "At least wear this."

"This is ridiculous," Avery said for the second time that night. "I can't walk around in your coat all night. It'll just draw more attention." She didn't want to flaunt herself, but she was beginning to realize that she didn't want to hide, either.

"No, really," Chase said. "I'll never make it through this party if you . . ."

She leaned forward slightly so that her hands could reach the pockets. Her fingertips brushed against a folded piece of paper. Eager to change the subject, she drew it out. "What's this?"

"Oh, yeah. I almost forgot." He managed to raise his gaze to meet hers. "It's a reservation for two nights at the Clevelander Hotel, it's one of the Deco hotels over on Ocean Drive."

"Are you sure?" Avery asked, his last visit and their inability to find a bed to share still fresh in her mind. "Did you double-confirm it?"

The noise level began to escalate. The front doorbell continued to chime.

"I didn't have to," Chase said. "Deirdre got us the reservation through a contact there."

Surprised, Avery shrugged out of his jacket and handed it back to him, ignoring the strangled groan that left his lips. "That's funny, she didn't mention it to me."

"She was probably afraid you'd turn it down." Chase

slipped the paper back into his coat pocket. "You haven't exactly been receptive to any of her overtures."

"That's true," Avery conceded. But she felt a strange little glow of satisfaction at the gift. "Are you all right now?" she asked Chase in a teasing tone as he put his jacket back on. "Ready to man up?"

"I'll do my best," he said with a glint of his normal humor returning. "But the only thing that's going to get me through the party is this reservation." He leaned down and kissed her. Together they stepped out of their corner and into the party.

Lisa Hogan came up to them in a black cocktail dress that bared one shoulder and skyscraper heels that she didn't need, but that she had no trouble walking in. Her eyes glinted like shards of colored glass. She greeted Chase with what looked like a genuine smile, perhaps because he was a part of the show but not beholden to her. Or maybe just because he was a good-looking man.

"It looks like we're going to have a big turnout," she said, looking Avery up and down. "I'm glad to see you finally dressing in a way that highlights your attributes. This is, after all, a business that relies on ratings."

Avery's jaw set as the network head turned and walked toward the fireplace, where Maddie and her husband stood. Chase growled softly, a low, angry sound.

"Yeah," Avery said. "I'm getting really tired of having to be so careful about how they perceive me. Is one night of cleavage really going to be the end of me?"

"It could definitely be the end of me," Chase said. But he said it with a smile and was looking her straight in the eye. "Just give me the sign and the jacket's yours. I'm going to go check on my dad and the boys."

People poured through the front door and into the circular foyer, oohing and aahing as they came. Through a back living room window she could see others out around the pool, mingling happily. Waiters passed through the rooms with trays of hors d'oeuvres held aloft.

Deirdre practically floated up to her. She wore a sleek white strapless dress that complemented her pale skin and fine blond hair. Her eyes sparkled with excitement. "I do believe it's showtime." She smiled and Avery realized that Deirdre wasn't just fulfilling an obligation, she was enjoying herself. "That's Carl Owen from World of Windows over there." She pointed to a round, darkly tanned man with a blinding smile. "And that's Lori Bakkum and Nate Miller." She motioned toward a friendly-looking blond woman and a young man with a shaved head and an impish grin. "They're 'pillar members' of the Miami Design Preservation League and are also Realtors. Their firm, Retro Home Miami, specializes in important Deco properties." Deirdre waved and sent them a smile of welcome. "I'd like you to give them a personal tour."

"Aye, aye," Avery said with a mock salute.

"And stand up straight," Deirdre added firmly but quietly. "You shouldn't have to be afraid of consulting with Chase or anyone else. And you should never be ashamed of having a figure that others have paid fortunes to imitate. Breasts are not a punishment. They're a gift."

"Yeah, thanks, Moth—" Avery began sarcastically, barely stopping herself before the whole word left her mouth. She looked quickly to see if Deirdre had noticed. Avery hadn't used the word since Deirdre had deserted them; she'd barely let herself think it.

"And, um, thanks for the hotel room. And for not giving

me shit about the chandelier." She looked away to where Maddie and Steve stood, not wanting to give away just how much she appreciated the gesture. She saw Maddie's smile freeze briefly as Mario Dante spotted her and altered his course, heading toward her and Steve.

"You're welcome," Deirdre said. "I hope you enjoy yourselves." She looked up when the room's big-screen TVs flickered to life with images of Max and Millie onstage at the Fontainebleau Hotel.

"Oh, good." Deirdre looked down at her watch. "We're right on schedule. There's a bar right over there." She nodded toward the opposite corner of the living room. "And one out by the pool. I suggest you grab a drink and then introduce yourself to Lori and Nate." She gave Avery another hug. It felt only slightly less awkward than the first. "I'm going to have a quick word with Nicole and Lisa Hogan about the network's stance on screen time. I think I saw Nikki in the dining room with Giraldi a few minutes ago." Her brow furrowed. "I do hope that other man who was looking for her is a potential sponsor."

Chapter Twenty

Nicole was no longer sure what Parker Amherst IV actually wanted or why he had bothered to come to the party. He certainly didn't seem to be enjoying himself, and despite joining a tour she'd given to several potential sponsors, he'd shown little interest in The Millicent and barely glanced at anything but her.

Her attempts to draw him into conversation with Deirdre and the others had garnered a smile that looked more like a grimace. His eyes remained frosty. Even when talking to someone taller than himself, not that he was doing a whole lot of that, he managed to make it appear as if he were looking down his nose at them. She knew from his acquaintance with Bitsy Baynard that he must be used to moving in fairly exalted circles, yet a less socially adept individual would've been hard to find.

Not even Max, at his warmest, smiling best, elicited more than a stiff smile and a grudging nod.

"So what does he want from you?" Giraldi asked when he returned from the bar with drinks in hand and found her watching a nearby group that Deirdre had drawn Amherst into. Despite their less-than-simpatico introduction, Deirdre, too, seemed unwilling to give up on the financial potential of Amherst's Roman numeral.

"I mean, the guy is downright squirrelly," Giraldi said as he contemplated Amherst through the same eyes that had once weighed Nicole's guilt and innocence.

"Well . . ." Nikki hedged, wishing she hadn't noticed the frayed collar of Amherst's tailor-made suit jacket and the lack of shine on his thousand-dollar Edward Greens. "It's been my experience that people from privileged backgrounds often aren't required to develop social skills in the same way the rest of us do. Kind of like how really beautiful women can make it through life without a personality or a sense of humor."

Lord knew she'd had to teach herself everything from basic etiquette to how to dress and make conversation. When your mother worked two jobs to keep even a leaky roof over your head, you appreciated everything she did for you, but you didn't expect her to teach you how to move in the first tiers of society. Both she and Malcolm had turned to magazines and movies as well as the important newspapers' society columns to create their personas—and their fictional backgrounds.

She looked up at the nearby television screen and saw the black-and-white footage of Max and Millie, their backs to each other as each played to the audience. She couldn't hear their audio over the hum of conversation, but you didn't need it to see the completeness of the couple's connection. Nicole had never been that connected to anyone except Malcolm, and that bond had turned out to be excruciatingly one-sided.

Giraldi gave her one of his steely-eyed looks to which she wasn't sure how to respond. Parker Amherst was not the sort of client she would normally have pursued, or even accepted. But there was nothing normal about her current circumstances and she did not want to discuss her desperation with Giraldi. Or admit that she wasn't even sure she could sign a client she didn't really want.

"I'm sorry," she said, meeting Giraldi's gaze. "I need to go thank John Hendricks for our air-conditioning and do my best to talk a few others into signing on."

"Sure." He nodded amiably as they parted. A few moments later she spotted him with Chase and Jeff Hardin over near the pool house. The next time she checked, Maddie's husband Steve had joined them.

The crowd grew and the buzz of voices rose. A group of elderly men Max introduced as his pinochle buddies huddled near the pool bar. Nikki kept an eye out for Amherst and noticed that although he seemed to make no overtures, he ended up in various conversational groups. Every once in a while she'd feel someone's gaze on her and turn, expecting to see Joe, only to find Amherst watching her.

She was standing with John Hendricks when the video of Max and Millie dissolved into a shot of Deirdre, blond hair piled high on her head and resplendent in a white strapless gown, standing in front of a microphone that had been placed near the baby grand piano. Her voice boomed over the televisions that had been mounted throughout The Millicent as she invited everyone to get some food and drink and find a spot near one of the screens. "In the meantime," she continued, "I'd like to introduce you to some of our sponsors." A Hendricks Heat & Air logo appeared and The Millicent's current residents applauded wildly. Next came Dante Fine Artisans, with a family picture of Mario and sons in front of The Millicent and one of Mario and assorted family members waving from The Millicent's roof. Shots of the Randolph Plumbing van and a close-up of the East Coast Electric monogram on Ted Darnell's work-shirt pocket came next.

"There's still time to say yes," Deirdre said on-screen. "You and your company can be a part of this exciting project and be seen on national television weekly." Her smile turned saucy. "Don't make me chase you down and wrestle you to the ground."

There was laughter and then Lisa Hogan stepped forward to take Deirdre's place at the microphone. Showing a warmth she had not yet demonstrated in more personal conversations, she introduced video clips of the cast and crew. As each of their faces loomed larger than Nikki would have liked, a voice-over described their backgrounds and how Malcolm Dyer's Ponzi scheme had rocked their worlds and left them with nothing but co-ownership of the dilapidated Bella Flora.

Nicole kept her chin high and did her best to hide her dismay. If anyone in the house—or on the planet—had been unaware that Malcolm Dyer was her brother, they knew it now. And that included Parker Amherst IV.

The shot of Bella Flora dissolved into an exterior of The Millicent. The angle changed and Max Golden drove into frame in the turquoise Cadillac convertible and pulled into the drive. In the next shot he leaned against it, his arms folded across his chest, his face lit with a smile.

The shot dissolved to a tuxedoed Max Golden standing in front of the microphone, an unlit cigar clutched in one hand.

"I'm Max Golden," he said. "My wife Millie and I moved into this house in 1950."

The audience applauded.

"Millie and I did a comedy act," he said. "Like all smart men, I let my wife do most of the talking." He paused for a beat. "And almost all of the work." Another pause. "*She* was funny. *My* biggest talent was smiling." He flashed his megawatter and bowed at the resulting round of applause. "And puffing on my cigar at the right moment." He winked and mimed a puff of the unlit cigar. "I bet you didn't know a man could make a living smiling and smoking."

There was laughter. Max pointed at a man on the couch. "I see you're surprised to hear this." He leaned forward and struck a confidential tone. "You're probably thinking someone should have told you this before you spent all that money on college."

More laughter.

"Well," Max continued, "I'm an unusually lucky man. Whom women find irresistible." Behind him on the screen, shots of Max with Maddie, Avery, Nicole, Deirdre, and Kyra pulled from their time at The Millicent began to appear. "These special women are here to bring back the home that meant so much to Millie and me."

There were shots of the house as it had looked when they arrived. Jungle-high grass. Missing and mismatched windows. Gouged plaster. Ancient wall air conditioners. And shots of the way it was now followed by close-ups of Deirdre's design boards and several of Pamela Gentry's sketches. The final shots were of Max with his "women." In the babe magnet. On the deck. Together on the couch. The very last shot was one of all of them sitting around the kitchen table having breakfast. Max was dressed in his smoking jacket and ascot.

"I bet you thought Hugh Hefner was the only ninety-year-old man living in a house with this many beautiful women." He puffed out his chest and gestured with his cigar.

There was laughter.

"Me too," he conceded. "But believe me, I'm not complaining."

Like the pro he was, Max waited for the laughter to die down then leaned toward the man he'd singled out in the front. "Try not to hate me too much."

The crowd loved him. And Nikki could tell that the feeling was mutual.

"So," Max said after he'd gotten a few more laughs, "enough about me." He flashed the smile. "It is now my pleasure and privilege to introduce the pilot episode for Lifetime Television's newest hit series, *Do Over!*"

. . .

It was after midnight and The Millicent was finally both dark and quiet. The last guest had been eased out the door at ten, after which Lisa Hogan had conducted a relatively upbeat postmortem. Once she and her entourage had departed, they'd settled around the dining room table, where they'd wolfed down the leftovers and drunk what was left of the opened wine.

They'd toasted Deirdre on the success of the party; the preservation and design communities were excited about The Millicent's renovation, and Superior Pools and Walls of

Windows had committed to sponsorships. Several other companies had promised to get back to them.

Max was still glowing from his turn in the spotlight. Kyra and Troy hadn't killed each other, and as far as Maddie could tell, Daniel Deranian had not shown up in disguise, though she'd come close to challenging one unfortunately mustached woman.

Though they were pleased with the outcome, it was hard to celebrate wholeheartedly when all of them were smarting from the personal revelations and embarrassing moments that had laced the program. Meeting their guests' gazes had been more than a little awkward. But only Steve had resorted to tight-lipped silence.

Maddie turned off the kitchen light. Chase and Avery had left for their hotel. Everyone else had gone to bed. Despite her exhaustion, Maddie was reluctant to go upstairs where she knew Steve was bound to be awake, reliving the most upsetting parts of the program and the light in which he'd been cast.

She moved around the darkened living room checking doors and windows even as she chided herself for stalling. The pilot program had begun exactly as Kyra had said it would, with the opening credits showing them out back at Bella Flora getting the news that they'd been offered a chance to do the show. But the show itself was often gritty; Kyra's footage had shown them exactly as they'd been at the time—bruised and battered but desperate and determined; their bond of friendship had not been immediate but had built slowly.

The audience had hung on every word, every unflattering shot, every groan of exhaustion, every personality clash. When the show ended, there'd been a brief moment of silence. And then a spontaneous roar of applause. If the general public reacted even half as strongly, *Do Over* had a good shot at building a real audience.

But this was not a total victory. Anything that had once been secret had now been exposed to anyone with a television. Including Steve's collapse and his inability to act. If Maddie, Nikki, and Avery were initially the victims and then the heroes of the piece and Malcolm Dyer the villain, Steve Singer was the husband and father who'd collapsed under the strain. Not even his daughter's footage had managed to skirt this ugly truth.

When she couldn't put it off any longer, Madeline climbed the stairs. She hesitated on the landing, looking out through the porthole window over the yard and the sleeping neighborhood. Squaring her shoulders, she turned the doorknob and went into the bedroom. She found Steve sitting on the rattan chair in the loggia, where Kyra often nursed their grandchild.

He watched her as she closed the door, his silence deafening.

"Are you okay?" she asked, though she could see from his face, illuminated in the spill of lamplight, that the answer to this question was no.

"How could I be okay," he asked, "when the whole country has just seen me looking so completely pathetic?"

"I doubt the whole country was watching," Madeline said. "It was just a pilot episode and—"

"Don't," he said wearily. "You know what I mean. Did they really have to make me look so bad? And did I really have to watch it in front of an audience?" He ran a hand over his face, which was dark with stubble. "Didn't you see the pitying looks they were giving me?"

Maddie moved to the other chair and lowered herself into it. The wall the kitchenette had been ripped from was riddled with protruding wires and capped-off pipes. It lay exposed, like the rest of them, its insides spilling out.

"Not even Kyra had any real control over the editing," Maddie said, forcing herself to look at him. "And as I think I told you, *Do Over* is more reality show than how-to show." She swallowed. "I'm sorry you were embarrassed. None of us feel particularly wonderful about how we were portrayed." She forced herself to say what she really thought without the usual dissembling. "But there was nothing on that screen that was untrue."

He snorted quietly. "I think you're secretly glad that everyone saw what a mess I was. How you had to step up and shoulder the responsibility. Because despite all the lip service, you've never forgiven me. Not any more than I've forgiven myself. And I'm starting to wonder if you ever will."

She didn't respond, but the accusation hit its mark. She was guilty of not forgiving him. And she hadn't yet found the faith that would allow her to believe in him again.

"You came off smelling like a rose," Steve continued, his tone accusing. "The poor little housewife who finds out just how strong she is." There was a nasty twist to his voice that she'd never heard before. As if she'd purposely presented him in the worst possible light and now the gloves could come off.

"You were on board with us doing the show," Maddie said, trying to push away the hurt and the anger that nipped at her heels. Her lack of faith did not give him the right to hold her responsible for all of his problems.

"We agreed that it was a break for Kyra and a chance for us to have at least some income until you got back on your feet. Have you forgotten all of that already?" Her heart felt heavy in her chest. She couldn't bear the unfairness of it.

"No, and I'm not likely to with this show on the air, am I? I might not have agreed if I'd known they'd make me look like such a fool."

She stared at him. Easy now to act as if there'd been some other way that they'd refused to consider. Could he possibly have forgotten how desperate things had been even last fall? The fact that he'd finally gotten up off the couch and ultimately found a job had not exactly solved all their financial problems.

"We had no other options, Steve," she said, her hands fisting at her sides. All she wanted was to end this conversation and leave this room and go . . . where? "We've all been put under a microscope and there's not a hell of a lot we can do about it. It's just the nature of this kind of show. It comes with the territory."

There was a small ugly part of her that wanted to shout that no one but he himself had made him appear foolish. Wasn't there some quote about how it was better to remain silent and be thought a fool than to open one's mouth and remove all doubt? At the moment he sounded like a bloody idiot.

"Maybe if you hired a younger more energetic Realtor to try to sell Bella Flora, we'd have enough money to walk away from the show," he said. "Chase said there'd been some interest, but no offers. Franklin must be almost as old as Max."

"Midsummer isn't exactly prime time for Florida real estate," Maddie replied, stung by this additional criticism and Steve's flagrant dismissal of John Franklin, who'd been selling Pass-a-Grille real estate for most of his eighty-plus years. Was there anyone he actually approved of?

He looked at her as if he was waiting for something, but she couldn't imagine what. She'd offered what she could, but she was not going to apologize for things that were beyond her control. Not anymore. She'd been so glad that he and Andrew had come down; now she wished she hadn't forced the issue.

"So," she said, too tired and too hurt to put a complete sentence together.

"So, I think I'll go ahead and drive back to Atlanta tomorrow," Steve said. "It's a long drive. We'll go right after breakfast."

She didn't speak right away because she couldn't summon the right words as an unfamiliar rage built inside her. He would whisk Andrew away, not bother to spend time with Kyra and his grandson—or her—because his feelings were hurt and he felt embarrassed? Because viewers now knew that when their world had crumbled, Steve had fallen apart and she had not?

Neither of them had forgiven or forgotten, and her attempts to pretend otherwise had gotten them nowhere. At least nowhere good.

"You can leave Andrew here," she finally bit out. "He has no reason to rush back to Atlanta and the real work's getting ready to start. We can use an extra pair of hands and some additional muscle."

Too angry to stand still, she wheeled around and went to the dresser to yank out her pajamas. In the bathroom she pulled her robe off its hook. The last place she intended to sleep was anywhere she'd have to look at Steve. She didn't think she could bear to hear his breathing.

"I wouldn't worry about waiting for breakfast," she said when she reached the door. It took serious effort to force herself to turn around and look at him, wrapped up as he was in his injured pride. "If you don't see the kids before you go, I'd at least leave them a note. So they don't think you left because you don't give a crap about anyone but yourself."

He looked surprised at both her words and her tone, but Maddie had already wrapped her hand around the doorknob. She'd tiptoed, she'd cajoled, she'd done everything she could think of to protect his feelings. But all his promises, his insistence that he understood that she had grown strong because she'd had to, even his claims that he respected her for it, were complete and utter bullshit.

"I know you, Steve," she said. "And I see that even now you think you're entitled to an apology. So, how about this: I'm sorry that I've been afraid to put our futures completely in your hands and I'm sorry that I can't pretend none of what happened, happened." She drew a deep breath, but there was nothing cleansing about it. "Frankly, nothing you've said or done tonight inspires me to take that leap. Believe it or not, everything is not always all about you."

Her hand turned on the knob. "And don't forget that note," she said. "I don't want our children to realize that they're nowhere near as important to their father as his ego."

Chapter Twenty-one

It was midnight and still early in South Beach party terms. The strip of Ocean Drive hotels was awash in neon, but their nightclubs and sidewalk cafés were just sputtering to life when Avery and Chase checked into the Clevelander Hotel. The fabulous Art Deco bones of the late-thirties structure stretched over a sleekly remodeled interior and had been joined to newer buildings so that the property anchored a whole block of Ocean Drive.

Avery accepted the welcome package from the desk clerk and laughed when he informed them that they were free to use the contents in any order they deemed fit.

"What's so funny?" Chase asked, pocketing the room key card.

She drew him away from the desk and opened the package to show him their choices.

"Ah . . ." He smiled, contemplating the drink tokens, condoms, earplugs, and aspirin. "Only a partial dilemma." He shot her a wink. "I'm not ready to go to sleep yet and I definitely don't have a headache. Should we flip a coin to decide between the other two?"

"I think not." Avery had been bone tired when they left The Millicent. Her jaw ached from talking and smiling, her back throbbed from standing so long in high heels. But now that the party was behind them, she could feel the exhaustion begin to lift. "We should get a drink. Because we have all night together." A thrill of anticipation shot through her. "And all day tomorrow. And the night after that."

She'd been too preoccupied with the house, getting everyone settled, making it through the party without having a wardrobe malfunction, to even let herself think about having so much time alone. "We'll have lots of opportunities to use the condoms. And I'm pretty sure we're not going to want to come downstairs again for a drink anytime soon."

"There's always room service." Chase's voice went husky.

"True," she said, feeling the warmth in his voice course through her. But let's get a drink first."

Chase handed their bags to the bellman along with a tip. "Can you take these to our room?"

"Absolutely. The pool bar's right through that door." He nodded to the corner of the lobby. "And we have a fourteen-screen sports bar and a nightclub. There's a description of each in your packet."

They stepped outside to the pool area, which dominated the corner of Tenth and Ocean, their gazes drawn by the neon bar and a flying-saucer-shaped structure fashioned out of concrete. The umbrella'd tables along the front sidewalk were almost full, but the music and the party atmosphere at the pool bar were just cranking up. They carried their drinks to a small bar-height table where they could watch the cars and people parade up and down Ocean Drive, their clothes almost as bright as the hotel's neon lights and the stars that shimmered over the Atlantic.

Any one of the people who packed the bar could have easily won a spot on an episode of *America's Next Top Model.* Their bodies were spectacularly formed, their skin smooth and taut. No matter how hard she looked, Avery didn't spot a single muffin top, unintentional hair, or wrinkle. Compared to the bits of shiny fabric that passed for their clothing, Millie's dress and Avery's cleavage appeared downright sedate.

At first she felt old, which was not something that normally occurred to her thirty-six-year-old self. And then she began to feel invisible to everyone but Chase, which was actually incredibly liberating. The way he looked at her—and only her—his blue eyes all smoky, was almost as intoxicating as the drinks of which she'd somehow lost count.

He signed the tab and lifted an eyebrow in question, then led her through the gyrating throng, across the terrazzo'd lobby, and into the elevator, all to a pulsing beat that infused the hallways and echoed in the elevator.

In their room they fell onto the king-size bed with abandon, Avery giggling over the gift condom, both of them eager to put it to use.

Midway through their lovemaking Avery realized that the sound track of music and partying was not in her head, but was seeping through the hotel's hallways, insinuating itself beneath the door.

She and Chase were naked and entwined. His sweat-soaked body melded to hers as he moved inside her. The tension built. She was close, so close she could feel the tiniest of tremors. With a whimper she wrapped her arms and legs more tightly around him. Her nerve endings pulsed with—

There was a shout. The blare of car horns. A curse in a language she didn't recognize.

Her brain stopped speeding through the tunnel and instead began trying to identify the language. She didn't think it was Spanish. Knew it wasn't French. Wondered if it might be something Slavic.

Avery's eyes flew open. Her body slowed. *Damn.*

"What?" Chase asked. "What is it?" He lowered his weight onto his forearms, but his eyes remained shut and his body remained tightly clenched against what had, until a moment ago, seemed like an inevitable orgasm.

"Wait," she said quickly. "Don't move."

Careful not to disengage, Avery ran her hands through the sheets then got a hand onto the nearest nightstand. "It's so loud I can't concentrate. I'm trying to find the earplugs."

Now his eyes opened.

"Hold on," she said.

He blinked as her fingers closed around the welcome packet and fumbled open the cellophane package.

There was a chorus of shrieks outside followed by a thunderous splash. A microphone fed back loudly. Her brain began to picture what was taking place at the pool bar.

She began to move again, slowly and intentionally, holding his gaze with her own, as she managed to jam the rubber stoppers into her ears.

"That's it," she said as his eyes closed, though even her own words were muffled.

Now the sounds that reached her came wrapped in cotton wool. She felt, but couldn't really hear, his breath against her ear, the slap of their bodies moving in tandem, and the faint tremors that began deep inside her and built to a nine or ten on her personal Richter scale.

Sleep did not follow. At three A.M., the bed began to vibrate, not from the heat of their lovemaking but from the throbbing bass of a particularly offensive rap song. To which Avery could have shouted along if she'd had a mind to.

Her fingers went to her ears, but the earplugs were gone. Chase lay on his side facing her. His eyes were open.

"I can hear every single word of that song," she said as the beat throbbed between them. "I think I can even hear what the DJ's *thinking*."

Chase flipped onto his back and pillowed his head in his arms. "I'm thinking about submitting a bid on the sound-proofing they obviously need here," he said, staring up at the ceiling. "Actually, I'd do the work for free if they'd let me start right now."

At four A.M., they split the aspirin.

At four-thirty, Avery located the earplugs—one under each end of the bed. After a brief debate about how best to deploy them, they each stuffed one in an ear and pressed a pillow against their other.

"I thought the welcome packet was a joke," she said at five.

"It should have been labeled 'survival kit,'" Chase agreed. "And they need to up the number of aspirin and earplugs."

At six, the noise evaporated and the sky began to lighten. Palm-tree shadows danced on the curtains. A bird chirped. Avery imagined she could hear the sound of the ocean skimming onto shore. "I thought we'd have brunch out, take a look at the hotels, maybe do a tour if you're up for it." She'd walked up and down Ocean Drive casually once or twice, had been in and out of a few of the hotel lobbies, but she realized now that she'd been waiting for Chase to tour it more thoroughly. "But I can barely keep my eyes open."

"I know the feeling. But we should sleep while we can," Chase said. "Today's Saturday, which makes tonight Saturday night. I don't think things are going to shut down any earlier than they did last night."

"You mean this morning," Avery corrected with a yawn.

Chase reached for his iPhone and flicked his thumb over the screen. "I think the north part of South Beach is a little quieter. We could move up to the Palms, that's up around Thirtieth. I stayed there a couple of years ago. It's very upscale. It might be a little more appropriate for old farts like us."

She rolled onto her side and burrowed up against Chase, burying her nose in his shoulder.

"They've got rooms available," Chase said. "I'm going to make a reservation. Is that okay with you?"

Avery breathed him in. She wanted to sleep all day and never get up. "'S okay," she said groggily as she began to drift off.

His arm wrapped around her and she sighed, exhausted but content. "But don't tell Deirdre." Her thoughts began to blur as her breathing grew more even. ". . . don't want to hurt her feelings."

· · ·

Nikki couldn't wait to get out of bed. It was still dark when she heard footsteps on the landing. A few minutes later there was movement downstairs in the kitchen. A car started up outside. The Maureen McGovern song "There's

Got to Be a Morning After" from *The Poseidon Adventure* had played out in her head for most of the night as she jockeyed for a sliver of the bed she was sharing with Kyra while listening to Dustin's amazing repertoire of snuffles, whimpers, and cries.

Now she lay at the extreme edge of the too-small mattress waiting for some semblance of light as she tried to remember why she'd turned down Giraldi's invitation to stay at his house, where the mattress would have been larger and any lack of sleep consensual. And, she assumed, enjoyable.

She stared up at the pockmarked ceiling as she contemplated her refusal. They were both single adults and the attraction between them was palpable. So . . .

So, Joe Giraldi was different from any man she'd ever dated and light-years from the men she'd married.

Because . . . she prodded when her mind wanted to retreat from the subject.

Because the others had accepted her as she'd presented herself—strong, successful, and polished. After her first marriage, which had been all about what she thought was love while she was actually serving as a doormat, she'd chosen only successful, wealthy type A personalities who saw her as the same.

Giraldi was type A all right. He was also successful in his field and far more sophisticated than she'd expected. But he would be difficult if not impossible to control and not easily fooled. Even now Nikki wasn't sure whether she'd successfully evaded him when she attempted to get Malcolm to turn himself in, or had simply played out some scenario he'd managed to stampede her into.

Morning noises arose from the kitchen. Water ran, the

refrigerator door banged shut. The smell of coffee wafted up, crooked its aromatic finger, and drew her out of bed.

Was she playing games with Giraldi? Simply holding out until she felt she wasn't jumping unthinkingly into bed?

She moved quietly to the bathroom, not wanting to wake Kyra or Dustin. She paused near the portable crib to watch the baby's small chest rise and fall. "Sure, now you're quiet," she whispered, pulling the baby blanket up and tucking it in around him.

She continued to mull over her reticence with Giraldi. It wasn't as if she'd never had a purely sexual relationship before. She was forty-six after all, too old to marry every man she wanted to sleep with. If they could just keep it light, enjoy each other, and move on when it wasn't fun anymore, she might actually consider it. But she sensed Giraldi wanted more from her. And she wasn't sure she had "more" left. Unlike most of the men she'd known, Giraldi would recognize, and probably care about, the difference.

Nicole washed her face, brushed her teeth, and pulled her hair into a low ponytail, then applied a light dusting of powder and lipstick before pulling on her running clothes. Not, she assured herself, because she might run into Giraldi while jogging but because she never left the house without light armor.

On the stairs she looked over the stepped wall to the living room, noting the big-screen TV still affixed to the wall and the stand-up microphone in its place near the piano. She was relieved to see that the room required no additional cleanup, but was surprised to see the pillow and blanket on the sofa. She'd been fairly certain everyone had had a bed—or at least a portion of one.

She found Maddie at the kitchen table staring out the

window. She still wore her pajamas and robe. A cup of coffee sat in front of her. She barely stirred while Nicole poured a cup then joined her at the table.

"What's going on?" Nicole asked when Maddie didn't speak.

Maddie turned her face to Nikki. It was tear-streaked and hollow-eyed.

"What's wrong?" Nicole pressed.

Maddie shook her head, mute.

"Where's Steve? Still sleeping?"

Another head shake. "Gone."

"Gone to pick up bagels? Gone to watch the sunrise? Gone to . . ." Nicole let the question dangle.

"Atlanta," Maddie said. "He went home."

"Seriously?" Nikki asked, trying to take it in.

Maddie nodded, her lips tight, as if she were trying to hold words in, when in fact Nikki was pretty sure they needed to come out. She thought about what Maddie's friendship had come to mean to her, the way Maddie mothered everyone around her, even those who'd thought they were long past needing it. She'd already hung in with Steve far longer and through far more than many women would or could have.

"But why?" Nicole asked.

Maddie turned her gaze back out the window. Her hands wrapped around the coffee mug, which was still full and, Nicole suspected, long cold.

"Because he's embarrassed. Or maybe that's humiliated. I can't remember which." Maddie drew a breath, exhaled it. She looked at Nicole. "He can't bear that he was portrayed in such a negative light on the pilot. As if I had anything to do with that."

"Tell me about it. I'm not exactly doing a happy dance over the fact that now when the headlines about Malcolm have finally begun to disappear, the scandal is being played out all over again to promote *Do Over*." Malcolm had cost her her business; she suspected the pilot had cost her Amherst. Despite her vow to get him to sign, or to die in the attempt, she'd barely had a moment alone with him.

Nikki stood and took Maddie's cup of coffee. Dumping the remnants in the sink, she poured her a fresh cup then creamed and sugared it the way Maddie liked.

"I guess I shouldn't be surprised," Maddie said. "He didn't even want to come. I've had to hunt him down to get him to talk to me on the phone." She clutched the new cup as if trying to warm herself. "Last fall when he came down to Bella Flora, he told me he was proud of me and that he liked that I was strong, that I was able to take charge. But he doesn't really like it. He wants things to go back to the way they were before we lost everything."

She sighed and blew out a breath of air. "But even if we had all our money back and his new job was completely secure, we couldn't go back. *I* couldn't go back. I don't want to be that totally dependent person again."

Nicole heard the pain in her friend's voice, felt the ache of it.

"You're the matchmaker and dating guru," Maddie said. "If I were your client, what would you advise me to do?"

The words *screw Steve* were on the tip of Nicole's tongue. The D-word wanted to push its way out right after them. But Maddie had been married for a long time; she and Steve had two children and a grandchild. It wasn't up to Nicole to rabble-rouse.

"Your daughter once asked me for advice," Nicole said,

choosing her words carefully. "And I explained to her that I was a matchmaker not a therapist or a marriage counselor. And she was smart enough to listen to her mother's advice rather than any I might have offered."

Maddie didn't respond, but she did raise the coffee cup to her lips. Nicole waited while she took a first tentative sip.

"Actually," Nicole said, "I do have an idea."

Maddie looked at her expectantly.

"It's still early and no one needs us here. I'm too tired to run anyway. Let's go for a walk on the beach and then I'll treat you to breakfast at Big Pink." She named the neighborhood restaurant known for its bright pink VW delivery cars and comfort food. Its motto was "Real Food for Real People."

"Oh, I don't know—" Maddie began, but Nicole cut her off.

"Well, I do. I bet Steve's already kicking himself for being such an asshole. And if he isn't, we can suggest it to him later. In the meantime, you've got five minutes to get dressed."

"But—"

"Four minutes and forty-five seconds." She motioned for Maddie to hurry up. "Come on, let's go. We deserve it. And I'd like to get outside while the humidity is under ninety percent."

Chapter Twenty-two

Like a patient on an operating table, The Millicent lay open, her guts spilling out, her innermost self put on display. The kitchen had been stripped down to walls, floors, and windows. They were down to one bathroom for however long it took to replace miles of rusted galvanized iron pipe and reconfigure an equal amount of cast iron. Because they were trying to preserve rather than rip out existing walls, tiles, tubs, showers, and sinks, it often took an excruciating amount of time to move a pipe as little as ten feet. It seemed that for every hole that Mario and Salvatore patched, another was opened up as first electricians and then plumbers reached inside to remove, rearrange, or replace The Millicent's vital organs.

The workday finally over, Avery stood in the shower directly under the stream of frigid water, her eyes closed. Getting shower time wasn't easy and she didn't intend to move until her body temperature lowered to something approaching normal. It was mid-July, which meant temperature and humidity levels that melted your bones and zapped your will. The breeze off the ocean and bay was neither cool nor dry.

"Are you almost done?" Deirdre's voice sounded through the closed bathroom door.

Avery sighed but didn't move. The water was still running. She'd answered what seemed like a million questions today and made even more decisions; she wasn't about to use up the last of her energy to answer Deirdre. Leaning her forehead against the shower wall, letting the cold water sluice down her back, she wondered if people, like horses, could sleep standing up.

The shower door slid open and the water stopped. She straightened and opened her eyes. A towel appeared in her line of vision and was placed in her hands.

"Come on," Deirdre said. "We need to be at Ted's in less than fifteen minutes and we can't all leave together."

Avery wrapped the towel around her body but didn't dry off. She did not want to get dressed. Or move. She'd forgotten that they'd agreed to find ways to leave that wouldn't arouse the Lifetime crew's suspicions and wasn't sure she had an ounce of subterfuge to spare.

"Giraldi picked up Nikki a few minutes ago," Deirdre continued. "They're going to get a table. Maddie and Kyra are going to meet us there; they're pretending they're going to a movie."

"So what are you doing here?" Avery finally asked. "Other than harassing me?"

"I know how hard you've been working and how tired you are." Deirdre stepped aside so that Avery could get out of the shower. "I told them that I was taking you out to dinner."

"Seriously?" Avery asked. "You couldn't come up with anything better than that? They'll never buy it."

Hurt blossomed in Deirdre's eyes, gone as quickly as it appeared. It was nowhere near as satisfying to Avery as it should have been.

"Hurry up," Deirdre said. "I don't want to give them time to think about it or follow us. We don't want them to film us talking about Max's son—not until we have something positive to report anyway."

Avery blew out a breath and walked into the bedroom with its battered walls and scarred floors. At the moment the amount of work that remained to be done seemed endless. She moved toward the dresser.

"Here," Deirdre said, gesturing toward the bed. "I've already laid something out for you."

Avery moved to the bed. A turquoise-and-white-striped sundress with a fitted halter top and a dropped waist had been artfully arranged on the spread. A strappy pair of wedged sandals sat on the floor ready to be stepped into.

"Thanks," Avery said. "But I'm not wearing that."

"Why not?"

"For one thing, because Ted's is not a sundress kind of place. And for another, because it sends out the wrong signals."

"Which ones?" Deirdre asked. " 'I'm young and attractive? I don't buy my clothes at Walmart'?"

Avery moved toward the dresser and pulled out a T-shirt and a pair of baggy khakis. "No," she said, stepping into underpants then turning her back and dropping her towel to shrug into a bra. "My message is actually, 'I have a brain and I'm not afraid to use it.' "

"You looked incredible at the premiere party," Deirdre

replied. "I thought you'd come to terms with things, with your body. There's a happy medium between presenting nothing but cleavage like those morons on *Hammer and Nail* wanted to do and dressing attractively." She grabbed the pants and top from Avery's hands and shook them at her. "These are ugly and boring. And they're two sizes too big."

Avery grabbed them back. She had talked a good game at the premiere and she had enjoyed keeping Chase a bit off balance, but when they'd screened the footage from the party, she'd seen what kinds of shots Troy had gotten. She couldn't really count on the network to be moderate.

"You tried hiding yourself once before," Deirdre pointed out. "Did that work out well for you?"

"How would you know?" Avery snapped, remembering the "camouflage years" after college when she'd been so desperate to be judged on her abilities. "You weren't there."

"I was trying to be," Deirdre said. "The fact that you wouldn't see me doesn't mean I didn't see you. Beige and baggy are not any woman's friend and they're especially brutal for vertically challenged blondes like us. As your mother, I—"

"Oh, please," Avery said, unwilling to listen to another word. "Stop with the mother crap already." She put on the pants and zipped them, then pulled the T-shirt down over her head. "I don't need anyone, especially you, picking out my clothes or dressing me."

Avery expected Deirdre to huff off or at least concede the point, but she refused to back off.

"When you're ready to stop hiding, there are other ways to get respect, you know. Trent wouldn't speak up for you. He liked being top dog on *Hammer and Nail*, but I'm willing to bet that if you make it clear that you won't accept being presented in such a one-dimensional way, everyone here will stand behind you. You don't have to go to such . . . unattractive . . . extremes."

Deirdre kept talking even though Avery was no longer responding. She followed Avery back into the bathroom, yammering on while Avery swiped on mascara and lipstick and ran a comb through her still-wet hair. "No one's going to be looking at your face or hair when the rest of you is so . . ." She finally gave up on trying to find the right word, for which Avery was grateful. "Besides, we're not going to be on camera tonight—or if we are it'll only be whatever Kyra shoots. And while she always showed our 'warts,' she never dwelt on cleavage."

"This conversation is over," Avery said. "You can accept the way I dress and my reasons for it and we can pretend to go out to dinner together. Or you can keep this up and I'll just see you at the bar." With only the slightest glance at the great-looking wedge sandals and not even a tiny peek at the dress, she slid her feet into a pair of flip-flops and grabbed her purse.

With a sniff, Deirdre picked up her own designer handbag and followed her down the stairs.

· · ·

Maddie puttered in the pool-house kitchen while Kyra nursed Dustin in the privacy of what was now Andrew's bedroom and put him down to sleep. Immediately after the premiere party, the pool house had been turned into what Troy liked to refer to as the male bastion and the women referred to as "sweat-sock city." Max now occupied the master bedroom, Troy and Anthony and their editing equipment resided in the second bedroom. Andrew, and an extra bed for guests, filled the third, while the kitchen and living room had been declared gender-free zones, open to all.

With The Millicent's kitchen temporarily obliterated, Maddie had moved command central out to the freestanding building. She kept the refrigerator and pantry stocked, made coffee there each morning, and made sure Max, at least, had breakfast of some kind there every day.

Dinners were often casual pickup affairs eaten in shifts or sometimes carried into the dining room. Maddie also kept Cheez Doodles and other sunset favorites on hand, but with both balcony railings torn out for replacement, sunsets had become more complicated. They'd done a few picnics at the South Pointe Park and even on the jetty, but when they could afford it they went back to Monty's at the Marina. Or took a table outdoors at Smith & Wollensky's on the promenade overlooking Government Cut.

Maddie, who was always up far earlier than she wanted to be in the mornings, continued to lobby for sunrise on the beach, but so far they'd done this exactly twice and there'd been far too much whining and complaining for it to become a regular activity.

Now Max and Andrew sat at the table with plates of reheated lasagna in front of them. Troy and Anthony lounged on the couch watching a Yankees game. Maddie refreshed Max's and Andrew's iced-tea glasses and tried to act like someone whose only concern was getting to a movie on time.

Kyra came out of her brother's bedroom, pulled the door shut behind her, and handed Andrew the baby monitor. "Keep this next to you at all times," she instructed.

Andrew took it. "I don't think we could possibly miss hearing him cry," he said with a nod to the bedroom door that was maybe four steps away.

"Not 'we.' You," Kyra said pointedly. "You and Max are in charge."

Troy didn't say anything, but Maddie knew from the tilt of his head that he was tuned into the conversation. Just as he was tuned into anything Kyra said or did. Although she knew better than to say so to Kyra, Maddie actually hoped the cameraman was going to be there all evening, not just so that the chance of him discovering their subterfuge would be lessened, but because she'd seen how good he was with Dustin.

He turned and asked, "So what movie are you going to see?"

Maddie froze for a moment. Kyra had gone online to look up a movie and a description just in case anyone asked. She looked at Kyra in question, but before she could answer, Troy added, "Is there a Daniel Deranian marathon at the dollar theater?"

"Very funny," Kyra huffed as she slung her purse over her shoulder. "Are you ready, Mom?"

Ted's Hideaway was a small neighborhood bar on Second Avenue just next door to Big Pink and barely a five-minute walk away. Maddie felt silly taking the car, but they wouldn't have walked to the movies and she didn't want to blow their cover story.

"I feel like someone should be playing the *Mission: Impossible* theme in the background," Maddie said as they circled the block looking for ever-elusive parking.

"Maybe Giraldi has an extra trench coat," Kyra cracked when they finally found a spot. "Or a secret handshake."

They climbed out and locked the minivan. Maddie smiled at Kyra as they walked toward the building. "I'll be sure to ask him that first thing," she said.

• • •

Ted's was dark and denlike with deep red walls, a U-shaped bar, and lots of wood, most of it scarred. Jackie Gleason as Minnesota Fats, Paul Newman as *The Hustler*, and W. C. Fields as himself, but with cue in hand, hung near the pool table. The rest of the decor, if it could be called that, was classic dive bar. It was the kind of place where the air smelled of fried food and cigarette smoke, Johnny Cash and ZZ Top duked it out on the jukebox, and sports played on the TV screens.

It wasn't at all the kind of place that Nikki had grown used to and it was a far cry from the quiet intimacy of their dinner at AltaMare, but Giraldi had snagged a table in the back up against a brick wall, which gave them an unimpeded view of the pool table and the front door, a location Nicole assumed came right out of the FBI training manual on seat selection.

Although plenty of people were drinking hard liquor, they'd decided on beer. A half-empty pitcher sat in front of them. Or was it half-full?

Giraldi was big and solid beside her. Even without the brick wall, Nikki couldn't imagine anyone sneaking up behind him or getting the jump on him in any way.

"So how are things going with Amherst?" he asked. "Do you have him fixed up and ready to walk down the aisle?"

Nikki fingered the handle of her beer mug. "Not exactly," she admitted. "He's proven to be a bit elusive. I'm not sure if he simply doesn't know what he's looking for. Or if he's really not ready to settle down."

"I think 'elusive' is way too gentle a word," Giraldi said. "I think the guy smells to high heaven. I'd be happy to run a background check on him for you."

"Is that what you do when you don't like someone?" she asked. "Run their fingerprints and look for criminal activity?" She could feel herself overreacting, but she was embarrassed that she hadn't signed Amherst yet. The fact that he'd so far resisted retaining her and was, in fact, a bit odd didn't mean he deserved to be investigated.

"I didn't mean to offend you," Giraldi said without heat. "It's just that I've learned over the years to trust my instincts. It's one of the reasons I'm still alive."

"Well, he smells okay to me," Nicole said lamely, though in fact it was more a case not of okay, but of okay enough. She'd put up with someone completely unwashed if he'd sign a contract and give her a check. People had short memories and she'd done nothing illegal. Arranging a high-profile marriage could put her back in the headlines in a *good* way. After all, you could choose your friends and your business associates. It was only your family that you were stuck with. "I appreciate your offer," she said stiffly. "But I think we should save your professional services for our search for Max's son. Or some other, actual criminal activity."

Giraldi nodded, unperturbed, and took a sip of beer. His gaze skimmed the bar, ultimately focusing on the front door. A moment later there was a flash of early evening sky and Avery and Deirdre stepped inside.

Nicole raised a hand in greeting and watched the mother and daughter walk back to the table. Deirdre was overdressed for the casual jeans-and-T-shirt atmosphere; she always looked like she belonged somewhere exclusive and expensive, but she didn't seem at all bothered by the smoky air and sticky floors. Avery looked as if she wanted to be anywhere but next to Deirdre. Her small curvy body was lost in the billowing beige-ness of her clothing. They looked like identical Barbie dolls that had been dressed at opposite ends of the style spectrum in some mad fashion comparison gone awry.

Maddie and Kyra arrived a few minutes later. They weren't mirror images in the way that Deirdre and Avery were, but it would be hard to miss the family resemblance.

A waitress appeared to take their drink orders. Kyra, who had apparently left a bottle of expressed breast milk for emergencies, declared she needed a drink. They were still getting settled when another pitcher arrived.

When thirst had been slaked and the chitchat began to die down, Maddie called the meeting, such as it was, to order. "So," she said. "I thought maybe we could ask Kyra and Joe to share what, if anything, they've come up with. And then we can see where we go from there."

"Unfortunately, I've got a lot of nothing," Kyra said. "I made copies of Aaron's baby and toddler photos and posted them along with his full name, and the dates of his birth and disappearance, on the locator sites that looked the most legitimate and didn't charge an arm and a leg." She slid the photos she'd "borrowed" and copied from Max's box. "But it feels a lot like looking for that proverbial needle in a haystack. At least on the adoption sites there's always the chance that both parties have signed up and are looking." She looked at Giraldi. "Do you think that if he was abducted when he was three, he would have any memory of his parents?"

"Unlikely," Joe said.

Their faces fell as they absorbed this.

"And if all we have are those old photos, it wouldn't help to post them elsewhere on missing-person sites, would it? I mean, who would recognize a fifty-four-year-old man from those?" Nikki asked.

"I did see some sites that offer to do age progression," Kyra said. "The sites seem targeted to people who've lost a child and want to know what they might have looked like if they'd lived. It's really heartbreaking. One of them showed the dead child at a prom and in graduation robes."

"People search for and get comfort in different ways." Maddie put a hand on Kyra's. Nikki knew they were both thinking of Dustin.

"Actually, that's something I could help with," Giraldi said. "I have a friend at the Bureau who's a forensic artist. I could have a progression done for use in posting, but the truth is, this *is* like looking for a needle in a haystack."

He lifted the pitcher of beer and topped off their mugs. "I looked over the case files, both the Miami Beach Police Department and the Bureau's. Everybody followed standard operating procedure for the early 1960s. They canvassed and interviewed the family, the neighbors, deliverymen—anyone who might have been in or near the area at the time. They led searches of the area, double-checked Max and Millie's accounts of what happened, broadcast appeals on local television. But there were no signs of a struggle, no ransom demands, no pertinent fingerprints, no anything. And there was never a body."

Giraldi shrugged his broad shoulders. "It was twenty years before Adam Walsh disappeared and changed how these cases were handled forever. There was no Internet, no databases, no DNA testing. And even if there had been, there was no evidence to test and no suspects to do a search on." He took a long pull on his beer and shook his head. "It's just one big dead end."

"You've seen that wrought-iron fence, there's no way a three-year-old could have opened it and just wandered off," Maddie said.

But it had only been latched not locked, Nikki thought. How long would it have taken someone who might have been watching and waiting to push it open, walk over, and scoop up a child—thirty seconds, a minute?

"Millie's statement said she'd been inside for less than five minutes and that she'd left the front door open so that she could hear," Giraldi said. "But by the time she was interviewed, she was hysterical. And none of the neighbors who happened to be home at the time saw or heard anything unusual or suspicious."

Nikki listened to the calm, comprehensive way he presented the facts. There was a strength of purpose there, but compassion, too. Giraldi went by the book, but he wasn't an unfeeling stickler. If there was room to do anything for Max, she had confidence that he would. "What about a cold-case unit?" Nikki asked. "Does Miami have one?"

"Sure," he said. "But after all these years there'd have to be some kind of new information or lead, something that didn't exist when the disappearance was originally investigated, for them to reopen the case."

"And we don't have anything like that," Deirdre said. It was not a question.

"No," Giraldi said. "There's nothing that could legitimately be considered a clue or a lead. If there had even been a suspect, I could take another look at him or her. If anything pointed in any direction, there'd at least be a place to start."

"But doesn't the fact that there was never a body indicate that Aaron might be alive somewhere?" Deirdre asked.

Giraldi shook his head again. His expression and tone were almost apologetic. "I wish I could say yes. But there are lots of ways and places to dispose of a body, especially a small one."

They sat in silence for a moment, absorbing this. Nikki was certain she wasn't the only one trying not to picture what could have happened to Aaron Golden's sturdy little body.

Around them, the country ballads had given way to rock and roll. The bartenders were loud and friendly and fast, which meant the crowd was already well lubricated. There were whoops of victory and shouts of despair from the group around the pool table. Nikki thought their table looked like an island of unhappiness in a sea of good times.

"So there's nothing we can do?" Maddie asked.

"Not at the moment," Giraldi said. "I'll go ahead and get these photos to the artist I mentioned. And if anyone stumbles across anything that gives us somewhere to focus, I'll be happy to help."

They sipped their drinks, looking everywhere but at one another, none of them willing to believe the search could be finished before it had really begun.

"Well, at least once we have the photo of what Aaron would have looked like, we'll have something to give Max," Avery said.

None of them perked up at this. It seemed like such a small thing in comparison to what they'd hoped to give him.

"Remember that our real gift to Max is The Millicent," Maddie said. "That's something significant."

"Of course it is," Kyra agreed, her tone as heavy as their moods. "But unless one of us comes up with something that resembles a clue, he won't have anyone to leave it to."

Chapter Twenty-three

At the moment Maddie could not understand why any house needed this many doors. They'd spent the entire day removing them from their openings and carting them downstairs, where they then spent forever removing and labeling all the hinges and hardware before stacking them out back against The Millicent's exterior walls.

Maddie watched as Avery and Andrew set up the saw-horses in assembly-line fashion, as they'd done at Bella Flora, placing each station in its own patch of shade.

"Okay," Avery said. "Today Nicole and I will strip as many doors as possible. Andrew will handle the sanding at that station." She pointed to a spot near the pool house. "And the third will be for staining. Nikki can move there tomorrow once we have some doors ready and Kyra can help with either stripping or staining in between shooting and Dustin.

"Maddie will start inside at the polishing table," Avery

continued, referring to the long table that had been set up in place of the dining room suite, which had been sent out for refinishing. Polishing hardware was a tedious but much-coveted assignment because of the seated position in which one could do it and the air-conditioned space in which the task would take place. "That's her reward for feeding and taking care of us."

"Max has offered to help too," Avery concluded. "He had plans today, so I told him we'd put him to work tomorrow. Which means we need to find something for him to do that won't be too taxing."

Maddie carried the boxes of hardware into the dining room while the others got to work outside. She found Mario Dante in the foyer patching yet another hole. He greeted her with a smile and an effusive *buongiorno*.

Maddie watched him work for a few moments, impressed anew with his skill and the artful way in which he seamlessly blended the old and new plaster.

"When the wall is repainted, it will be as if this never happened," he said with pleasure. "It will be almost, but not quite, as *bellissima*—as beautiful—as you." His smile was broad and his eyes were admiring. The cheerful flattery was a balm to the barbs of disapproval and criticism that Steve had inflicted.

Madeline looked down at the capris and Big Pink T-shirt she wore. She wasn't exactly "dressed," but with the amount of video being shot, no one was as careless with their appearance as they had been at Bella Flora. All of them had seen what they looked like on the pilot episode just as Kyra had shot them, long before they'd had any inkling that her footage would be seen by strangers. None of them was eager to be beamed into homes across the United States looking quite so much like their *real* selves.

"*Grazie,*" Maddie said as Mario had taught her. "*Grazie, mille.*" Thank you very much.

"I've brought you my recipe for cannoli Siciliani as I promised," he said, gathering up his bucket and his trowel. "And I've put some in the refrigerator in the pool house with your name on it." His brows lowered. "I have told the boys not to touch without your permission."

"Thank you, Mario. Really." He'd been bringing her food and recipes since the day they'd met. "One night I'll make a complete Mario Dante meal for everyone and you can join us and then you can tell me what you think."

He considered her carefully, much as he contemplated The Millicent's walls before he began to work on them. "Better yet, you let Mario make you a Mario Dante meal. I'm ready to do this at any time. It would be my great pleasure to feed you."

"Um, thank you. *Grazie.*" She returned his smile. He had so much positive energy, it was impossible not to. In almost every respect Mario was the "anti-Steve."

Deirdre caught only the tail end of Madeline and Mario's exchange. It was impossible to miss the blush that spread across the other woman's cheeks.

"You'd better be careful," Deirdre said. "The man clearly hopes that the way to your heart is through your stomach." She took a seat at the end of the polishing table and set one of the "House" envelopes in front of her. "The Italian has a crush on you."

"Oh, I'm sure he's just being friendly." Maddie's cheeks went scarlet again.

262 · WENDY WAX

"Well, he hasn't offered to cook for me," Deirdre pointed out, amused. "Or Nicole. Or Avery. Or Kyra." She glanced down at the paper she'd pulled from the envelope then back at Madeline. "I've always thought that a man who wants to feed you is a man who will do anything for you." Unfortunately, this realization had only come to her years after she'd left the man who would have done just that.

Her attention turned briefly to the paper in her hands. "Sorry," she said, after skimming the information in front of her. "I'm still hoping to find something in Pamela Gentry's notes and sketches that might lead me to the artist who created the foyer chandelier, but there are a million bits and pieces of information in no particular order."

She tucked the paper back into the envelope before continuing, "Peter was a good cook, though it doesn't seem he passed any of that talent on to Avery. I can't tell you how many times I was out in some fancy L.A. or New York restaurant that I found myself wishing I was sitting over a home-cooked meal with him and our daughter." Deirdre speared Maddie with a look; after all these years, she was still appalled at all she'd thrown away. "Do you think she's ever going to forgive me?"

"Well, I think you've made great progress," Maddie said.

"But nowhere near what I was hoping for," Deirdre said. "One minute I think we've reached some sort of place we can move on from, and the next she's telling me off and making it clear she wants nothing to do with me." She drew in a shaky breath. "I think I scored a few points for not making a big deal about the damage to the chandelier, but I have no idea what to do next."

Maddie poured polish on one of the cloths and picked up a doorknob, seeming far more comfortable with this subject than with being the object of a possible crush. "I don't know," she said as she began to apply the polish in a smooth circular motion. "I'm not sure there's anything specific to do at this point. But I wouldn't keep giving her things. You don't want her to think you're trying to buy back her love."

"I would if I could," Deirdre said. "Whatever it cost. Hell, I'd give my life for her." The words came out in a rush, surprising both of them with their intensity. Deirdre realized as she looked at Maddie that she'd never said, or felt, anything of which she was more certain.

"So now you just have to stay the course," Maddie said. "The truth is, nothing you say and no number of hotel nights are going to wipe out the fact that you abandoned her. She's been clinging to the hurt and anger attached to your leaving for so long that it's bound to take time for her to let go of it." She smiled gently. "I'm sure there's a part of her that's afraid that just when she lets down her defenses, you'll up and leave again."

"But I wouldn't," Deirdre said. "I won't. I'd never do that again." She said this with a calm resolve that she hoped Madeline would recognize.

"Right," Maddie said. "So you demonstrate that by being here. By being available to her. By continuing to follow through and do what you say you will. No matter what."

"I was kind of hoping for something more specific," Deirdre said. "I'd much rather be proactive than just hang around waiting for Avery to see me in some new light."

Madeline buffed the knob with a cloth and set it aside. "I understand that. But you're not just hanging around. You're working on a project that's important to your daughter. And you're demonstrating that being with her is more important to you than other things."

"She thinks I'm only here to get my design career back on track," Deirdre said.

Maddie reached for a set of hinges. "Are you?"

"No. I've actually heard from several of my former celebrity clients asking me to do projects for them. And another network approached my agent about doing a new design series." She looked Maddie in the eye. It figured this would happen now when she was committed to staying in Miami and trying to repair her relationship with Avery. "Kind of ironic, isn't it?"

"Well, at least someone has options," Maddie muttered.

"I'm not going anywhere," Deirdre said. And then, because she'd heard the envy in Maddie's voice, she added, "At least your daughter shares things with you and wants to be with you. She isn't always trying to wiggle out of being in your company."

• • •

A few hours later, when Kyra stomped in from yet another altercation with Troy Matthews, Maddie had reason to question Deirdre's assessment.

"God, he's insufferable!" Kyra complained. "I never really knew what that word meant before, but I do now."

"What happened?" Maddie's back ached from hunching over the hardware; her fingers felt permanently curled. She glanced at her watch. The workmen had left almost an hour ago. It was definitely time to call it a day.

"He's getting all kinds of tight shots that are completely unnecessary," Kyra said. "I can tell from the way he's setting up and how he approaches the shots, but he absolutely refuses to show me his footage. I haven't seen a single frame since the premiere party."

Kyra stood directly in front of the air-conditioning vent and shoved her hair back off her forehead. There was a cry from upstairs. "Dustin must be up from his nap," she said as her phone rang. She pulled it out of her pocket and looked at the screen, then looked quickly at Maddie.

"What is it?" Maddie asked.

"Nothing. I just have to take this call." Her gaze skittered away. But then she looked back with that "I'm completely innocent" look she'd developed at the age of nine and that she'd typically deployed only when she wasn't. "Would you mind getting Dustin up?"

She looked down at her phone again, but Maddie noticed that Kyra was waiting for her to leave before she answered it.

"Sure." Maddie headed for the stairs, her mother antennae quivering. By the time she'd brought Dustin back down, Kyra had settled on the sofa with a diaper on her shoulder. Madeline handed him into his mother's arms, and Kyra gave him a kiss on the top of his head, unhooked the cup of her nursing bra, and settled him in her lap.

Maddie puttered nearby while the baby nursed. When Dustin had delivered a resounding burp, Kyra stood. "I'm going to put him in the stroller and go for a walk," she said, glancing down at her watch.

"Great," Maddie said. "I'm dying to stretch my legs. I'll be ready in a minute. Let me get my wallet."

"Oh." Kyra looked at her watch again. "I, um, really want to get going. Dustin's eager to get out." They both looked down at the baby, who was so sated from milk he could barely keep his eyes open.

"I'll be right back," Maddie said in the tone that she'd mastered right around the time Kyra had first tried out her

"I'm innocent" look. When she came downstairs, Kyra had already buckled Dustin into his jogging stroller. She didn't protest Maddie's presence but she didn't welcome it either as she set off for Flamingo Park at a pace that had Maddie breaking into a sweat after just a couple of blocks.

When they reached the park, Kyra didn't hesitate, but headed straight for the playground. There she scanned the benches until she spotted whatever, or as it turned out whomever, she'd been looking for.

"What's going on, Kyra?" Madeline asked. But Kyra was smoothing a hand over her hair and adjusting the strap of her tank top.

"Let's go sit over there," she said, pointing toward a shaded bench right near the baby swings, where a dark-skinned man with dreadlocks and baggy neon-colored clothing sat.

"Okay, but . . ." Maddie had barely begun to respond before Kyra had pushed the jogging stroller halfway there.

Once again scurrying to keep up, Madeline could see that the man held an MP3 player in one hand and was swaying and bobbing to an unheard beat. Although he sat in a prime location, the other mothers had given him a wide berth, leaving him alone in the playground equivalent of a no-fly zone.

As they approached the bench, the man stood and stepped forward to greet them, removing one of the ear-buds. "Hallo, mon," he said with the lilt of the islands. "It be good to be sittin' in de shade today, dat's fer sure." He nodded and flashed an instantly recognizable smile, still bobbing to the reggae music that bled out through the earbud in his hand.

Dustin's chubby hands reached out toward the man in the too-colorful clothes and Maddie's heart sank. Because despite the dark makeup, Rasta wig, and island clothing, Daniel Deranian was already slipping an arm around Kyra's shoulder and reaching out to his child.

Chapter Twenty-four

Nikki chose a pale blue 1960s Gigliola Curiel sleeveless linen dress with decorative curved seams and an Empire waist for her appointment at Parker Amherst's home on Star Island. It had three knot buttons centered on the scoop-necked bodice and a narrow skirt that ended just above the knee. She'd bought it in the early days when she'd been building Heart, Inc. both for its cut and its pedigree and because she loved the band-collared, three-quarter-sleeved jacket that made it appropriate for everything from a business lunch to a cocktail party.

She'd lost weight since she'd last worn it, and as she assessed herself in the bathroom's least wavy mirror, she saw that she was not just thinner but tauter and more subtly muscled from the year of hands-on renovation than she'd ever gotten as a result of expensive personal training. Perhaps if things didn't work out with *Do Over* or a return to matchmaking, she'd write an exercise book using renovation as its base. Surely Home Depot or Lowe's or even one of the do-it-yourself networks could get behind that.

Nicole added an Art Nouveau lavaliere necklace, a silver cuff bracelet, and a favorite pair of Maud Frizon high-heel sandals then practiced her sincerest smile in the mirror, pitifully glad that the mirror was too cloudy to reveal the deepening lines around her eyes and across her forehead.

Tonight was do-or-die night for Parker Amherst. She'd do all that she could to convince him to sign the contract she'd tucked into her bag, but if she left empty-handed, her pursuit of him would be over. She might be desperate, but she knew from experience that anyone this difficult to sign would be impossible to please.

The gate at Star Island proved little more than a formality. After a quick look at her and the Jag, and without even asking whom she was visiting, the guard waved her through. The palm-tree-covered island was an interesting combination of old, original, and funky pressed up against spanking new and expensive. The streets were old and narrow and the lots far deeper than they were wide. Just like the houses, whose thick walls, high gates, and tropical foliage blocked all but the smallest slivers of water from view.

Parker Amherst's home ate up every inch of its lot, and from the look of it had tried to gobble up portions of those on either side. The walled gate was so high that only the angles of the barrel-tile roof and some toothpick round palms showed above it.

She parked on the brick driveway, rang the bell on the gate, and when the gate clicked open, she walked into a bricked courtyard, dominated by a gurgling fountain and a lush tropical garden from which the plentiful plant life had gone forth and attempted to conquer.

The house was an impressive Mediterranean Revival that resembled a wedding cake and had all of the style's bells and whistles, including a columned loggia, wrought-iron balconies, and an impressive run of floor-to-ceiling windows. Two bell towers and a chimney poked up above the multigabled roof. The home's fortress-thick walls were an ocher-stained stucco outlined in white icing trim. In square footage it appeared considerably larger than Bella Flora but not so large as Bitsy Baynard's estate in Palm Beach.

Nicole pressed the doorbell beside the massive wooden door and heard it peal melodically inside. Several minutes passed before she heard the echo of footsteps. When the door swung open, Parker Amherst stood framed in the doorway. A marbled foyer stretched out behind him.

"Hello." He studied her for a moment then stepped back and motioned her inside. "Thank you for coming." His manner was stiff and he did not extend his hand; Nicole responded in kind. Parker Amherst was not an air-kiss kind of guy.

The entry was beautifully decorated, with highly polished surfaces that glinted in the stray rays of sunlight that filtered through high clerestory windows. But each sound echoed loudly, all the more noticeable for the vacuum of silence it pierced.

"Come in," Amherst said. "I thought we'd have drinks in the study." He led her down a central hallway past darkened rooms on either side and into a heavily paneled room with a long row of arched windows that overlooked Biscayne Bay. Miami Beach lay in the distance; she could make out several of the high-rises that lined South Beach's western edge.

"Can I fix you something?" Amherst asked, motioning her to a seat as he moved to a drinks cart. "I'm afraid the staff is off tonight, but I make a passable martini."

"Thank you." Nicole took in her surroundings as her would-be client began to assemble the drinks. She was surprised and not at all happy to learn that they were alone. "Your home is beautiful. How long have you lived here?"

"My grandfather built it in the twenties. I was born here." His answers were straightforward, but there was something in his tone that was not.

"It's quite large," she said, striving to stay conversational. "How many people does it take to run it?"

He smiled, his lips turning in a wry twist of amusement. "We used to have a staff of ten. But now that it's just me, I'm down to a skeleton crew. Our housekeeper retired when my father died last year. She wasn't the only one; several of the others were quite old. They'd been with the family since before I was born."

It was an answer, but it wasn't. Nicole felt the hairs prickle on the back of her neck as she contemplated the silence and recalled that no one but the disinterested guard at the front gate even knew she'd come anywhere near this house tonight. If in fact he'd paid attention to anything but the Jag.

"Here you are." Amherst handed her a glass and raised his to it in toast. "Salud," he said, taking a chair across from her. "To happier times."

Nicole took a sip. It was too heavy on the vermouth and far stronger than she liked. She looked up to find him watching her. "It's very good," she said. "Thank you."

"You're welcome." He took a sip of his own then looked at her appraisingly. "I'm sure things were 'happier' for you before your brother's theft was discovered."

Nicole stopped drinking, but took her time swallowing. It was the first time he'd mentioned Malcolm, though after the premiere party pilot she could no longer fool herself that he didn't know all the gory details. "Yes, of course," she said. "What he did was unconscionable."

"At the least," Amherst said, taking a taste of his drink, but continuing to stare at her as if he might glean some bit of information just by looking. "It's always so hard to believe that family members really didn't know in these kinds of situations."

She remained silent under his regard as long as she could. "So why did you ask me here?" Nicole finally asked. "And why did you contact me in the first place? You certainly don't seem in any hurry to find a wife."

"I've been trying to figure out whether you really were duped," he said. "It occurred to me that you might have been in on the whole thing." He paused as if waiting for her protest. "And that you might know where the rest of the money your brother stole is. I mean, it's not like the FBI got all of it back."

She almost laughed at the absurdity of the notion, though the way he was studying her—and the fact that they were completely alone—robbed the situation of humor. "More experienced people than you have tried to figure that out." She thought of Giraldi and wished he were here.

Amherst continued to study her and she wished she'd let Giraldi do a background check on him. She let several long moments go by and still Amherst didn't speak. Which made her wish she'd given up trying to get him to sign a contract as soon as he'd started jerking her around.

The silence became louder and more ominous. Her heart skittered in her chest. The guy and his Roman numeral were really starting to creep her out.

"I did my best to get him to turn himself in," she finally said, fighting the urge to stand and turn and make a break for the front door.

"But he didn't, did he?" Amherst said quietly. Not that he had to speak up to be heard over the mushroom cloud of silence. "And he hasn't admitted where big pockets of money went."

She didn't know what he wanted from her. For the briefest of moments she wondered if maybe this was a bid to get her to find him a wife for free, but when she looked into his eyes, which were definitely not fully focused, she knew this was one more case of wishful thinking.

Leave. The word reverberated in her brain and caused her gut to clench with urgency.

Nicole set the martini aside and stood. "I'm afraid I really have to get going. But I promise you I did not collude with my brother. In fact, he stole everything I had."

"So you say."

"Believe me, if I didn't need the money I wouldn't be sweating on national television over a house that's not my own. And I certainly wouldn't have come here hoping to sign a client who's been so reluctant to pay even a nominal retainer."

She shrugged as if these things happened and stepped out from behind the cocktail table, half anticipating a sudden lunge or move on his part. But although his eyes dilated slightly, he didn't get up or move toward her. His expression remained veiled.

"So I'm going to go ahead and leave," she continued even as she felt around inside her purse for her car keys. When she finally found them, she positioned them in her fist with the sharp ends poking out between her fingers like she'd been taught in self-defense class. "Thank you very much for the drink."

Very careful not to cut and run, though everything inside her was screaming for her to do so, Nicole edged toward the hallway under cover of looking in her purse for the keys that she'd already turned into a potential weapon as she waited for him to speak.

When he didn't, she forced herself to look him in the eye and to keep her shoulders squared and her chin up. She smiled with lips that were practically quivering. "No need to get up. I'll just see myself out."

And then despite the knees that threatened to buckle and the trip-hammer of her heart in her chest, she walked as firmly and as slowly as she could bear back down the central hallway to the front door, listening intently for any hint of him behind her.

At the door, her fingers wrapped around the dead bolt and she uttered one last prayer as she finally managed to unlock it. She didn't breathe again until she'd made it out through the courtyard and into her car, where she hit the autolock, fumbled the key into the ignition, and drove down the street, out past the gate, and off Star Island as fast as the Jag would take her.

Chapter Twenty-five

The sky was dark. Rain pounded on The Millicent's roof, which had—thankfully—already been repaired, and seeped through the crumbling caulk that surrounded the ancient windows, which—unfortunately—had not.

Avery could barely see the pool house through the curtain of rain, and none of them wanted to slosh across the backyard to "command central" more often than absolutely necessary.

Avery held the phone tight to her ear, trying to maximize the reassuring sound of Chase's voice without letting anyone, including him, know that that was what she was doing. He hadn't been able to make it back in the month since the premiere party and he had spent much of this conversation and the ones before it apologizing for not knowing how long it might still be until he returned.

The more time Chase spent apologizing, the less time he had for directives, advice, and suggestions. Who said she couldn't see the silver lining?

"I'm really sorry, Van," he said again. "I'm overwhelmed

at the moment. Dad can't do anywhere near what he used to, although we keep pretending that he can. And the boys are at an age where I don't want to leave them too much to their own devices." He sighed and she could picture him running a hand through his dark hair, distracted. She did not want to be an additional pull on his time or another obligation he needed to find a way to fit in.

"Hey, it's okay," she said. "The rain's causing a few delays." She pushed ahead before he could ask her for an e-mail or fax of her revised schedule. "But it's no big deal. I just hate being cooped up." She didn't like how many early tropical storms had begun to form, either. She'd sworn that she'd never again pour her heart and soul into a house that sat on the tip of a barrier island—not after Mother Nature's assault on Bella Flora last summer. Yet here they were again. Only this time they weren't eyeball to eyeball with the relatively benign Gulf of Mexico, but with the far more aggressive Atlantic Ocean.

"The chances of dealing with another hurricane again so soon are statistically infinitesimal," Chase said. The man might be overwhelmed up in Tampa, but on occasion he seemed alarmingly able to read her mind.

"Can you put that in writing and send a copy to the National Hurricane Center?"

"Gladly," he said, a smile in his voice.

A silence fell between them and she felt what she thought might be an actual ache of longing.

"Why don't you come up to Tampa for a few days?" Chase asked, as if he were once again reading her mind. "From what little I hear"—he paused to let the jab sink in—"you all are making good progress. And we could sit down with John Franklin. He left a message that he'd had another showing of Bella Flora."

If only it were that simple. There was nothing she'd like more than to just pick up and go.

"I can't," she said. "The new windows are ready to go in as soon as the weather breaks. And if I take time off, everyone else will want to, too." Now it was her turn to run a hand through her hair.

Another silence fell. There was really nothing else to be said, but she couldn't quite bring herself to say good-bye. She heard another phone ring in the background. After the second ring, Chase said, "I'm sorry, Avery. I have to take this call."

"That's okay," she said. "Take care."

"You too." The warmth was there in his voice, but it was clear he needed to get off the phone. "I'll take a look at my calendar and see what I can move around."

"Great," she said.

"Okay, then."

Still she couldn't bring herself to hang up. A moment later Chase's voice had been replaced by dead air.

After that, Avery paced The Millicent like a caged animal—through the shell of a kitchen and the dining room, where Maddie had left the polishing station set up and Deirdre had spread out Millie's "House" envelopes, around the ladder in the foyer that Deirdre had set up to photograph the damaged chandelier and not yet put away.

She paused briefly in the living room, where Nicole, who had raced out to retrieve the Sunday paper, was attempting to blow it dry section by section. Kyra and Maddie were on the living room couch. Dustin sat on the floor between them, his hands on the coffee table as he worked to pull himself to his feet. Maddie stared down at her phone screen, shaking her head.

Avery did a circle through Max's room, where newly refinished doors leaned against his newly-patched-but-not-yet-painted walls. His furniture was piled in the center of the room and covered with drop cloths. His bathroom had been stripped of all chrome and mirror.

She plopped down briefly on the piano bench, but stood moments later, too antsy to stay put. She could feel Deirdre's gaze on her and was relieved when she didn't comment.

"I can't believe I texted that," Madeline said with quiet horror.

Kyra rolled her eyes. Avery could see her trying not to laugh.

"I actually texted Mario from the patio store on Friday and asked if he could measure the dick."

"That would explain how eagerly he was waiting for you to get back," Nicole said.

"But he didn't say anything when I got here. He just kept smiling at me." Madeline groaned with embarrassment.

"I think we discussed the importance of double-checking your texts before you hit send," Kyra said even as a snort of laughter escaped. She kept a hand at Dustin's back as he stepped along, holding tightly to the table for balance. Avery was glad to see mother and daughter laughing over anything. Ever since they'd come back from the park earlier in the week, there'd been an unusual distance between them that all of the others had noticed.

"Right, well, what do I do now?" Maddie asked. "I can't exactly text back and tell him I wanted him to measure the deck, not his dick."

"Well, you could." Nicole laughed. "But I suspect he figured that out on his own."

"I'm kind of curious whether he sent you any dimensions," Deirdre said drily.

"Good grief," Maddie said. "I'm never texting again. It's too dangerous. Or maybe I need to have my thumbs shaved." She looked up. "I don't suppose there's a procedure like that?"

There was laughter and the mood in the room lightened.

"Maybe we should go out to a movie this afternoon." Nicole put down the hair dryer and opened the entertainment section of the paper. "I'm starting to go a little stir-crazy."

"Not a bad idea," Maddie said. "We could use a girls' afternoon out."

Deirdre didn't say anything. She looked down at the sheet of paper in her hand.

"What do you think, Deirdre?" Madeline asked.

When Deirdre didn't respond, she repeated the question.

"Sorry," Deirdre said. "You know I've been trying to track down the glass artist who created the chandelier. I finally found this sketch of it in one of Millie's envelopes and I found a notation in what I'm pretty sure is Pamela Gentry's handwriting that indicates it was commissioned in 1958 or '59." She held the paper up to the light and squinted at it in an effort to make out more detail. "The ink's so faded I can't make out the artist's name or much of anything else. I thought if I could track him down, he might be able to create replacement panels. Or failing that, maybe there are other pieces that were produced around the same time in a similar style."

"Any luck?" Maddie asked.

"No. But I'm really tempted to try to find Pamela Gentry. Assuming she's still alive and has her wits about her, she could probably point us in the right direction."

"If you found her, it might be kind of cool to put her back in touch with Max," Kyra said.

"I don't know," Madeline said. "Max didn't seem all that gung ho about her. And there was something weird about Millie dropping her the way she did when they'd been friends for so long."

"It's been fifty years. It's hard to imagine anyone holding a grudge that long. She'd probably like to know that The Millicent is being brought back to life." Kyra sat up straighter, clearly intrigued. "Maybe we could even interview her about her work on the house. That could be a really nice addition to the opening program."

"That's an interesting angle," Avery said. "There could be some real promotional value in that, too, couldn't there?"

"Absolutely," Deirdre said.

"Do you remember where Max said she moved to?" Avery asked.

"Chicago," Maddie said. "Maybe she went to work for a design firm." She turned to Deirdre. "Do you know anybody in the design business there?"

"Yes," Deirdre said thoughtfully. "I do. I have a friend there who's active in the American Society of Interior Designers. I could e-mail or give him a call and see if the name Pamela Gentry rings a bell."

. . .

A few nights later the rain had finally stopped. Dustin was already sound asleep in his crib as Maddie watched Kyra get dressed to go out. Kyra hadn't offered an ounce of information about where she was headed. Which was almost as worrisome as the short black cocktail dress she'd put on, a clingy knit that hugged her newly svelte body and barely covered the breasts that were still abundant from nursing.

"So where are you going?" Maddie asked as Kyra used a compact mirror to apply a bright red lipstick and paint her eyelids in smoky shades of brown.

"To a party," Kyra replied, snapping the compact shut, but not meeting Maddie's eye. "Andrew and Max offered to babysit, so you're off the hook. I expressed two bottles of breast milk and put them in the freezer."

This was an even worse sign than the revealing clothes and overdone makeup. Did she really intend to be out so late that she might miss two feedings? And who did Kyra know well enough to end up on their guest list?

"Where's the party?" Maddie asked.

"At one of the hotels a little bit up the beach."

Madeline noticed the details that sounded like specifics, but weren't—a technique Kyra had added to her innocent routine when she turned sixteen.

"I'd like to know which one," Maddie said, watching Kyra's face. "In case of an emergency."

She could see Kyra mulling over her answer and decided not to back off. "And I'd like to know whose party it is," she added, even though she was afraid she knew.

Kyra drew a breath and it became clear that the dress had not been designed for a nursing mother. "Daniel's giving the party," she said. "Tonja's out of town and he's having a little get-together."

Madeline waited for the rest, but Kyra was looking down at her phone.

"Which hotel, Kyra?"

"It's at the Setai." She named an elegant and expensive hotel on Collins Avenue. "He's taken the penthouse suite." Kyra's voice took on a note of pride.

"Oh, Kyra, honey. This is a bad idea."

"I don't care." Kyra's chin jerked up. "I haven't been to anything resembling a party in more than a year. It's no big deal."

"Kyra . . ."

"And besides, Daniel's gone to such lengths to see Dustin, he really wants to be a part of his life."

"And yours?" Madeline asked. "Does he expect to be a part of yours too?"

"I don't know."

Maddie sighed. "I hate to see you starting something. Especially something we both know is not going to end well."

"I'm not starting anything, Mother. I'm just going to a party, that's all."

"You do remember how he behaved last time, don't you?" Maddie asked. "You know that he's not going to leave Tonja Kay and their 'lifestyles of the rich and famous' to marry you."

Kyra shrugged. "It's okay, Mom. I have no expectations. I'm just going to a party where I hope to have a good time." She said this as if the party couldn't have mattered less and added the innocent look, but her clothes and the excitement in her eyes belied both.

Madeline studied her daughter, who'd spent the last year trying to get her life together just as desperately as Maddie had. And who had become a mother far too early.

Unfortunately, being a mother didn't always ensure making the best personal choices.

Still, it wasn't as if she could forbid Kyra to go out or keep her from attending a party. If she wanted to get involved with Daniel Deranian again despite the man's proven lack of integrity, Maddie couldn't really stop that either. And both of them knew it.

There was a tap of a horn outside and Kyra's face lit up. "No need to wait up," she said as she tucked her cell phone into a tiny evening bag that someone must have loaned her. "You can text if you need to reach me." She laughed, her confidence growing now that she knew Maddie wasn't going to throw herself in front of her to prevent her leaving. "On second thought, maybe you should ask one of the others to do the texting. So that I'll be able to understand it."

Madeline stayed where she was as Kyra's high heels clacked down the stairs and across the tile floor. Then she moved to look out the window and saw Kyra slide into the passenger seat of an expensive-looking sports car. She stood there a few moments after it roared away, thinking.

Then she went to marshal the troops and scout for something appropriate to wear. She might not be able to stop Kyra from going to the party, but that didn't mean she had to roll over and disappear either. Sometimes you had to do whatever it took to protect the people you loved. Even if you were protecting them from themselves.

• • •

"I can't believe that I'm arriving at a private party thrown by a mega–movie star in a beige minivan," Nicole said. "Please don't use the . . . valet."

"We don't have time to look for parking," Maddie said, pulling up to the valet stand in front of the oceanfront hotel.

Nicole tried not to notice the surprised look on the valet's face when the back doors automatically slid open and the four of them spilled out. Nicole, Madeline, Avery, and Deirdre had dressed as rapidly and as splashily as possible, mostly in some version of what they'd worn for the premiere, but none of them looked remotely like the young things in skyscraper heels who were traipsing up the hotel's front steps and being ushered through the front door. No amount of prep time would have made that possible.

Inside, they walked through the Shanghai-paved Art Deco lobby, taking in its Asian influences, breathing in the combined scents of elegance and money. Once Nicole wouldn't have thought twice about that distinctive smell; it had been a part of her everyday life.

"Do you know which room it's in?" Avery asked. "It looks like there's more than one bar here."

"She said he had the penthouse suite," Maddie replied.

Deirdre walked over to the concierge and came back a moment later. "It takes up the whole top floor of the tower building. The elevator's over there."

They rode up in the elevator in silence and walked down the hallway to the suite's entrance, a massive double door guarded by two burly bodyguards. A velvet rope held back a line of truly beautiful people, many of them brandishing invitations.

Nicole bypassed the line and led them up to the least beefy guy. "We're here for the party," she said, gesturing to include them all. "Daniel invited us."

The guy looked them up and down, one at a time and then as a group. It was clear that he found them wanting.

"Seriously?" he said, "Are one of you like his mother or something?"

Nikki's jaw clenched at the insult. Deranian was forty, though he often played midthirties. Deirdre could have been his mother, but Maddie would have had to give birth at ten. Avery looked off over one bare shoulder as if she were not all that interested in being allowed inside, which was how Nikki had felt until this great big buffoon had started with all that attitude.

"No," Madeline said, way too politely for Nicole's liking. "But my daughter is a friend of his."

He shot a look over toward the other bodyguard and called over to him. "Hey, Jeff! Come get a load of this. I think we got a group of, what's the word, geriatric party crashers!"

"Excuse me." Deirdre stepped directly in front of the guy. She was small but elegant. The only tip-off to her irritation was the eyebrow that had practically arched up off her forehead. "But there's no need to be insulting. Our friend told you that we were invited to this party. We all know Daniel. Her daughter is inside."

"Don't get your granny panties in a wad," the beefiest one said as he crossed his ham-size arms across his gorilla chest.

A few of the people waiting behind the velvet rope tittered with amusement.

"What did you say?" Nicole drew herself up to her full height.

"I think you heard me," he said as the door opened and several people tumbled out. None of them looked over twenty-five and there wasn't a less-than-model-caliber face or body among them.

The door stayed open as the rest of the waiting invitation

holders were allowed in, and Nicole, Madeline, Avery, and Deirdre were treated to a view of the massive living room and its sweep of glass and windows overlooking the ocean.

"Oh my God," Avery said. "I think that couple over there is having sex!"

They followed Avery's gaze to a chaise on which a male was stretched out, a drunken smile on his face. The girl was on her knees and had her face buried between his legs.

"Jesus," Madeline said.

Even Nicole, who'd been to more than a few wild Hollywood parties, did a double take.

None of them could take their eyes off the private act being performed in the public place and so they missed the doormen snapping to attention.

Kyra's gasped "Oh my God. What are you doing here?" brought them out of their shocked stupor. They turned to see Kyra and Daniel Deranian, who had a possessive arm around her waist, stepping up behind them.

Kyra didn't look at all glad to see them. But Daniel Deranian's famous smile suffused his famous face and his dark eyes sparkled with fun. "Hello, ladies," he said as if he were thrilled to see them. "You're just in time. It looks like the party's just getting started."

The doormen were slack-jawed with surprise. Nicole couldn't resist reaching out a finger, placing it under the beefiest doorman's chin, and closing his mouth for him. "I guess we'll take our granny panties on inside now," she said as they were swept into the party in Daniel Deranian's wake.

Inside, Maddie leaned toward them, raising her voice to be heard over the music, which had cranked up when

Deranian entered. "I don't care how fancy this place looks. Don't touch anything and try not to sit down," she cautioned, looking pointedly at another couple who were grinding away at each other in a corner. "Did anybody happen to bring Handi Wipes?"

Chapter Twenty-six

As it turned out, Handi Wipes were just one of the things they should have brought to the party with them. Disguises would have been helpful. A little more discretion and a lot less champagne might have also been better. What had started as a mission to keep Kyra out of Daniel Deranian's clutches had turned into something else entirely.

No one jumped out of bed the next morning to work or for anything except to gulp down aspirin and crawl back to bed. Kyra, who'd been too angry the night before to drink anywhere near as much as the rest of them, got up to nurse Dustin and was the first one to spot the photographers camped out on the sidewalk outside.

"Great," Kyra said, not bothering to keep her voice down in the slightest, though this was the first time she'd spoken to Maddie since she'd first spotted her and the others trying to talk their way into Deranian's party. "It looks like we've got company. The paparazzi are knee-deep out there."

Madeline tried to burrow more deeply under the covers. Her head throbbed and the sunlight streaming in through the windows hurt her eyes. The sound of Kyra's fingers on the keyboard of her laptop sounded like claps of thunder.

"And wait until you see the pictures on the Internet," Kyra said. "It's amazing how much better and crisper the shots from camera phones are nowadays than they used to be."

"Shit." Nicole dragged into the room and lowered herself down on the edge of the bed.

Avery and Deirdre trailed in behind her.

"Somebody needs to go to the pool house and get coffee," Deirdre said.

"Don't look at me," Kyra replied. "They've got telephoto lenses aimed all over this place."

Maddie squeezed her eyes tighter. She did not want to wake up and face this day.

"Crap." Avery went into the sunroom and cranked the blind open a few notches. "I think I recognize some of those guys from last night."

Maddie pulled back the covers and sat up, propping her back against the wall.

"They were on the sidewalk outside the hotel when Daniel and his bodyguards helped us into the minivan," Avery continued.

Nikki groaned. "I knew I'd get caught in that beige-mobile sooner or later. Good thing I don't have any clients left to lose."

"Was that your plan all along?" Kyra aimed the question at Maddie, her tone brittle. "To humiliate me and then get so drunk that I'd have to drive you home?"

Maddie wouldn't have called it a plan. It had just sort of worked out that way. Like overprotective parents trying to prevent an overweight child from overeating by scarfing down all the fattening things in the house, they'd gone to the party to make sure that Kyra didn't do anything foolish and then foolishly overindulged themselves. At the moment Maddie's mind was moving far too slowly to understand their behavior, let alone respond to a question composed of multiple parts.

"It was that bartender," Avery said. "The one Daniel assigned to us. The one he told he'd fire if he ever saw our glasses empty."

"Seriously," Nicole added. "I carried my glass into the bathroom one time and he tried to follow me in with the bottle of Taittinger."

Dustin stood in his playpen/crib and peered out over the edge at them while Kyra's fingers pounded on the laptop. An emphatic keystroke and the printer chugged into action.

She waved the page in front of them. "Here you all are dancing on that tabletop together," Kyra said. "The caption reads, '*Do Over* stars attend Deranian private party. Or are they the entertainment?'" She read it carefully, emphasizing each word before handing it to Avery to pass around the room.

"Oh, and this one's really special, too," Kyra continued. "It's a shot of the two doormen/bodyguards looking on with the caption *Deranian bodyguards say reality-TV stars 'partied their asses off!'*"

There was a collective groan. Maddie's eyelids fluttered briefly shut. She was pathetically grateful that the granny panties thought to cover those asses had not been mentioned.

On the nightstand Maddie's cell phone rang. Before she could reach for the mute button to stop the noise, Kyra swooped closer to look at the screen. "It's for you, Mom," she said more loudly than necessary as she lifted the phone to her ear. "Hi, Dad," she said at what might have been the top of her lungs. "Yeah, no kidding. Yeah, hold on a sec."

"Here you go," Kyra said, more cheerful now that the opportunity to torture her mother had presented itself. She handed the phone to Maddie, who slowly raised it to her ear.

She didn't speak, because there was no opportunity to get a word in before Steve began to berate her. "I can't believe you'd put yourself in that sort of position," he huffed. "As if the whole pilot episode wasn't already humiliating enough. What's Kyra doing with that asshole again? And what were you doing there"—he paused, then read the same caption Kyra just had—" 'partying your asses off'?" There was a beat of silence, far too brief for Maddie to formulate a response. "How can you condone her seeing him?"

"I don't condone it. That's why we—" Madeline began, but Steve cut her off.

"You're going to have to do a better job of supervision down there, Maddie. I won't have—"

The blood that had begun to roil in her veins reached her brain and jerked her fully awake. Steve barely responded to her phone calls, but he apparently had time to call and chastise her.

"You're welcome to come down here and supervise her yourself if you're not satisfied with the job I'm doing," Madeline snapped, for once not caring who heard her.

"You know that's not possible," he said. "But you have to—"

"I'm not interested in hearing what you think I have to do." She lowered her voice as everyone else fell silent.

Throwing her legs over the side of the bed, she stood and moved out of the room and onto the upstairs landing, barely listening to his litany of complaints.

Through the porthole window she could make out the crowd of photographers down on the sidewalk. Max, who was wearing his dressing gown and pajamas and held the morning newspaper, appeared to be doing a routine of some kind. Which meant the photographers were getting not only a juicy story but some stand-up comedy as well.

"Look, Maddie," Steve continued to rant. "You're going to have to be more careful. Kyra doesn't need to be around that troublemaker. And neither do you! And I certainly don't see how this is good for Dustin. God knows what Andrew's up to."

Maddie paced the landing, telling herself to calm down, but the unfairness of Steve's attack made it impossible. She'd had more than enough. She was finished taking whatever he felt like dishing out and it was time he understood that.

"*You* look," she cut him off. "I'm doing the best I can here. Kyra's an adult and there's only so far I can intervene. Things would be a hell of a lot better if you were willing to talk things out with me in advance instead of only calling me to criticize later."

Out on the sidewalk, Max took a bow and Maddie imagined she could hear the whir of camera motor drives. Troy and Anthony stepped out onto the driveway and pointed their equipment over Max's shoulder toward the paparazzi. The paparazzi pointed theirs back.

Steve was still on the offensive. Madeline forced herself to tune back in and was immediately sorry that she had.

"Are you actually accusing me of leaving you alone in Atlanta and treating you like a second-class citizen?" she asked in amazement.

"Well, you *are* there taking care of everyone else even though I asked you not to, while I'm—"

"—full of shit."

"What did you say?" The shock in his voice was almost comical.

"I said you're full of shit." Maddie said this slowly, relishing each word.

There was a silence, meant, she knew, to give her a chance to apologize. That was not going to happen. Not this time.

"Listen, Steve," she said, a new resolve building inside her. "I've gotta go. I'm out of time and, frankly, patience."

She did not have to listen to his complaints unless she chose to. In fact, she didn't have to listen to him at all.

"When you're ready to 'sac up'"—she intentionally used one of Andrew's favorite, and grossest, expressions—"and treat me with a little respect and courtesy, I'm all ears. Until then, I don't think we really have all that much to talk about."

She punctuated this last comment with a healthy dose of dial tone.

It was noon by the time they'd dressed and devised a means of crossing the pool deck to the pool house without exposing themselves to the photographers' long lenses any more than was necessary. Avery was glad that it was Sunday, though she had no real hope that the horde outside the gates would be gone by the next morning when they needed to get back to work.

Tension in the pool house was thick. The Lifetime crew had set up just inside the door to film their skulking entrance. Only Andrew, who'd just awoken; Dustin, who was pretty much always happy; and Max, who had apparently gotten a healthy round of applause from his sidewalk audience, seemed unconcerned with the barbarians at the gate.

Troy's camera followed their preparations for what would serve as breakfast, with lots of shots that Avery could tell were far too close up. When he'd shot them in every unflattering way possible, Troy set his camera down.

"Lisa Hogan called me this morning," he said to Kyra. "She's royally pissed off that I didn't have footage of you and Deranian and the rest of the cast at the party last night. She wanted to know why everyone else in the world seemed to have photos and video but me."

He waited for a response, but Kyra looked past him as she busied herself opening a jar of baby food and putting a bib around Dustin's neck.

The rest of them tried to stay out of the conversation, but the space was too small to pretend not to register Kyra's lack of response.

"So what? It's just too bad for me?" Troy demanded, his tone incredulous. "I sit on video of Daniel Deranian dressed up as a woman because you ask me to—video that would have impressed my boss and possibly earned me thousands of dollars on the side—and then you go out and perform for the cameras without any warning whatsoever?"

The cameraman practically quivered with anger as Kyra spooned the baby food into Dustin's mouth.

When no one else spoke, Kyra finally said, "I just went to a party. I'm not the one who put on a camera-worthy show."

Avery glanced at Madeline's face, which was tight. Her gaze was focused on her grandson. Even Max seemed inordinately preoccupied with the baby food Kyra was practically shoveling into Dustin's mouth.

"So your mother and the others would have been at that party even if you hadn't gone?" Troy prodded.

Madeline's mouth opened and then closed as if she'd thought better of whatever she'd been about to say.

"And what are you doing fooling around with that self-centered asshole anyway?" Troy asked. "Don't you have *any* self-respect?"

Avery was kind of glad that someone was giving Kyra the talking-to she needed, but listening in was distinctly uncomfortable.

Kyra's head shot up. She stopped shoveling baby food. "You are so over the line it's not even funny," she said, standing and turning to face him. "Last night was a big screwup from every point of view. But you can take that up with my mother and her merry band, not me."

Troy snorted with derision. "You like to pretend you're an adult, but you sure as hell don't act like one," he chided.

"And you do?" Kyra scoffed right back. "I'm getting really tired of this." She fisted her hands on her hips and glared at him. "You've been in my face since the day we met. What is it with you?"

"Like you don't know," Troy ground out.

"I *don't* know," Kyra snapped. "Maybe it's time you *enlightened* me."

Avery stole a look at Madeline, who was removing the baby's bib and wiping his face with it.

Max speared the baby's attention with a silent disappearing-quarter trick. The baby's laughter struck an oddly normal counterpoint to the words Kyra and Troy were flinging at each other.

"Oh, forget it," Troy said with an angry shake of his head. "But I will tell you one thing. I've looked the other way to try to protect Dustin from the wrong kind of exposure and because you asked me to. But that's over."

"Is that right?" Kyra's tone remained belligerent, but her face was ashen.

"That's right." Troy took another step toward Kyra so that she was forced to look up at him. "You tell your boyfriend that if he shows up here again, he better be wearing a disguise I damned well can't see through. Because Daniel Deranian's free pass is over."

The tick in Troy's cheek grew more pronounced as he struggled visibly to get himself under control. "And so is yours."

. . .

By the end of the week, Nicole felt like a laboratory rat, trapped and surrounded. The slave driver known as Avery Lawford had cracked the whip and put them back to work, but every movement was observed and in many cases reported. Unwilling to jog through the mass of photographers who still littered the sidewalk, Nikki had barely exercised, and her temper, like the others', had frayed. At the moment she was clinging to Giraldi's promise of a sunset boat ride, which would include just the two of them and no audience. She glanced down at her watch. Only eleven hours to go.

Max and Andrew had been posted at the gate to verify the credentials of all workmen and subcontractors, while Troy and Anthony roamed freely shooting inside the house and out. Kyra and her camera moved as well, but she focused primarily on the interiors and kept her face behind the camera when she ventured outside. She didn't respond to the photographers' clamorings to "look this way" and "just give us one clean shot!"

When she passed near Troy, they aimed their cameras at each other, but they didn't speak.

Mario arrived with his nephew, Giuseppe, shaking his head and muttering about the photographer who'd asked to be added to Mario's crew and another who'd offered a camera and a thousand dollars for anything Mario managed to capture on it.

His muttering lapsed in and out of Italian as he presented Madeline with a pan of homemade baked ziti then began to unpack his tools. "Look at my hands," he said. "They're shaking. I don't know how those barbarians could think I would allow them to get anywhere near you. They are *pazzi*—crazy!" He spoke as if to everyone, but his gaze remained on Madeline.

None of them could miss Madeline's blush.

A short time later Mario and Giuseppe were on their hands and knees regrouting and filling in the Moroccan tile. The window people arrived with a sizable crew and Deirdre pressed everyone into service. The only thing Nikki heard more often than Deirdre's voice was the ringing of Deirdre's phone.

Nicole's phone rang too, far more often than she would have liked. Each time she fished it out of her pants pocket and saw Amherst's phone number, she muted her ringer, let the call go to voice mail, and promptly deleted the message without listening. It figured that the man who'd played so hard to get when she'd been pursuing him as a client refused to disappear now that she wanted nothing to do with him. Despite the bright sunlight streaming in through The Millicent's openings and the pandemonium created by the people around her, she shivered at the memory of the empty mansion and its owner's equally empty stare.

Madeline carried the baby into the living room and joined Nicole, turning her back to the windows in an effort to keep Dustin out of camera range. Avery hurried in, her baggy shorts and T-shirt covered in grime. Standing next to the immaculately groomed Deirdre, they looked like a magazine's "before" and "after."

"I can't stand all of those people camped out here," Avery said. "Every time I look up I see some camera lens aimed our way."

"There is an upside," Deirdre said. "My phone's been ringing all morning. Superior Pools saw all the publicity and they're coming out in the next few days to resurface the pool and the pool deck, undoubtedly hoping to end up on camera even before the series airs. Walls of Windows has committed their entire work force to us today, which means they'll be done in half the time."

"Yeah, I noticed those snazzy uniforms they're wearing," Nicole said. "I bet you can read the company logo from all the way across the street."

"Or at least from our sidewalk," Madeline added.

"I also got a huge response to the call for gardeners that

Kyra put out. A whole group of Miami Beach Botanical Garden volunteers are coming. I'm telling you, everybody wants to be a part of this now," Deirdre said. "Honestly, if I'd known we'd get this kind of response, I would have danced on a table at an actor's party sooner."

Nicole noted her expression and knew that Deirdre wasn't joking. Nicole's phone rang; it took her several rings to get a hand on the power slide. She looked down at the screen and frowned.

Madeline followed her gaze. "Oh, it's the Roman numeral. Aren't you going to answer it?" she asked.

"No." Nicole hit the mute button.

"But I thought he was the possible key to getting your business back on track. If you need more time off from the house to pursue things, I'm sure we can work it out."

"No, there's no point," Nikki said, remembering her last meeting with Amherst. "He's not a serious prospect. Rich people can be so strange." A few moments later she deleted the message.

The shadow of movement out on the scaffolding drew her attention and she watched a window guy move into position at the second-floor level. A shaft of light poured through the glass transom and the chandelier glinted, shot through with gold.

"Gosh, I love that chandelier," Maddie said, her eyes drawn by the sparkle of sunlight through the lumines-cent panels. "Did you hear anything from your friend in Chicago?"

"I got an e-mail this morning," Deirdre replied. "He couldn't find a Gentry on the current membership list, but I figure if she was about Millie's age, she'd be what—eighty-five now—and most likely retired. He's only been in Chicago for five or six years. He promised to ask some of the older members. And I thought maybe we should ask Max if he has any other information that might help us locate her. I just hate the thought of having to replace the whole chandelier."

Chapter Twenty-seven

The crowd that surrounded The Millicent did not disperse as the day wore on. In fact, from what Nicole could see out of her bedroom window when she finally went upstairs to shower and change, it had grown and become somewhat rowdier. She'd put on her bathing suit and was slipping shorts and a T-shirt over it when she heard shouts and looked out to see Max escorting Kyra and her stroller through the gate. A number of photographers followed Kyra on what had become a regular late-afternoon trek. Max stayed to entertain those who remained.

It had been a long day and getting out of the gate without running over a photographer proved challenging, but Nicole was so ready to get out on the boat with Giraldi that she'd decided that a certain amount of collateral damage was acceptable. She was almost disappointed when the photographers in her path managed to leap out of the Jag's way.

On the MacArthur Causeway she followed her GPS's prompts past Star Island with its unsettling memories of her meeting with Parker Amherst. Not for the first time she wondered if her disappointment and desperation had fueled her imagination and allowed it to get the better of her.

She was still debating this when she turned onto Palm Island then followed the GPS's prompts across the small bridge to Hibiscus Island. Giraldi's house was one of the smaller homes on the oval-shaped strip of land, an unpretentious one-story with stucco walls and a barrel-tile roof.

"Welcome," he said as he ushered her into a far more contemporary interior than she'd expected.

"Thanks," she said, stepping onto the dark wood floors and taking in the high-ceilinged, open space. The living area was to her right. A beautifully updated kitchen with concrete countertops and stainless-steel appliances bled into an equally large dining area to her left. The back wall, composed of floor-to-ceiling glass and windows provided an unimpeded view over the pool and dock to the gentle swell of Biscayne Bay.

"Wow," Nikki said, her gaze fixed on the water and the glint of cars moving on a causeway beyond. "This is fabulous. How do you make yourself leave?"

"It's not easy," he said. "I was really lucky to stumble on this house when I moved down. The owner had just finished the renovation, but he was upside down on his mortgage. He just wanted out."

She looked at the living room, which was defined by an earth-toned area rug and anchored by a tobacco-colored leather sofa and two tweedy club chairs. A flat-screen TV took up most of the only solid wall, but bookcases had been built around it and they were jam-packed with books, all of which appeared to have been read and not just placed for effect. The decor was sophisticated, with brightly colored modern art on the living- and dining-area walls, but there were cozier touches too: a hand-knit throw draped over one of the club chairs, a stack of well-thumbed magazines teetered on the coffee table.

A collection of framed photos covered the wood-and-glass sofa table and Nicole moved closer to look at them. She saw Giraldi with what she assumed were his parents and siblings at food-laden tables and with arms slung around one another. There were others taken on ski slopes and on beaches. It was the ones of Giraldi with babies cradled in his strong arms and older children smiling beside him or holding on to his pant legs that made her realize for the first time that Special Agent Joe Giraldi had a life outside his work. A life that, unlike her own, was filled with family and friends.

She picked up a photo of Giraldi holding a gap-toothed child upside down by the ankles as if he were about to drop him on his head. "One of my nephews," Giraldi said.

She turned to another of what appeared to be a young Giraldi and an even younger little girl on a boat. He was focused on the fishing line and hook in his hands while she was staring up at him adoringly. An older version of Giraldi looked on.

"Me and my younger sister, Maria, on our dad's boat. To this day she only fishes if someone else will bait her hook."

Nicole thought about her own childhood, or lack thereof.

"Are you okay?" he asked quietly.

"Of course." She turned from the photos and smiled. "Do we have time for a tour?"

"There's not a lot more to see," he said. "But there's a half bath right here off the kitchen." He pointed to a door on the opposite wall then walked her to a bedroom that had a queen-size bed and a sofa sleeper. "I've crammed whole families into this space," he said. "But it doubles as a home office." He gestured to the simple desk, with a laptop open on it. A pair of filing cabinets and a floor-to-ceiling bookcase, this one clearly dedicated to work-related reading, had been built into a corner. The space was completed by a small bathroom and closet.

The other bedroom was the master, a clean, uncluttered space done in shades of gray that were masculine without veering into macho. Like the living area, it commanded a view of the pool and the water. The king-size bed had been positioned to take advantage of that view. For just a moment Nicole allowed herself to imagine falling asleep beside the agent and waking up beside him here.

"Shall we?" he asked.

"I'm sorry?" she said, startled out of her reverie.

"Are you ready to get out on the boat? I can show you Palm, Hibiscus, and Star Island from the water and then I thought we might anchor to watch the sunset. I've got a cooler on board."

"Sounds great," she said, following him out the French doors and past the pool to the dock, where a bright red-and-white cigarette-shaped boat was tied up.

Giraldi handed her onto the boat and started up the motors. Quickly and with no wasted movement, he untied the lines and pulled smoothly away from the dock.

The breeze was warm off the water, and when Giraldi pulled off his T-shirt, Nicole did the same, glad she'd worn her bathing suit underneath. The air and sun caressed her bare skin and teased at the ties of her bikini top. She could see her reflection in Giraldi's sunglasses and saw her hair tossing in the wind and the smile stretched across her face. She'd been on far larger boats, ones so large they needed captains and crews, and had even cruised the Mediterranean on one famous client's yacht. But for once she felt no need to act as if she wasn't impressed. In fact, she felt no need to act at all. Tilting her head back, she closed her eyes so that she could enjoy the weakening rays of the sun and listen to Giraldi's commentary, his voice pitched to be heard above the boat's powerful engines. She only opened them when he slowed to point out some of the larger and more interesting homes on Palm Island, including a Spanish-style estate that had once belonged to Al Capone. A name that he admitted was near and dear to any FBI agent's heart.

It was only when they began their circuit of Star Island that Nikki felt her shoulders tense. "That's your pal Parker Amherst's home." Giraldi gestured toward a dock and a massive expanse of seawall. She could see the tops of palm trees, the ocher-colored stucco, and the gabled roof. "At least for the moment."

"What do you mean?" she asked.

"Amherst's father died a year or so ago, and I understand the son is pretty close to broke," Giraldi replied. "Which may account for his squirrelly behavior."

And his reluctance to pay the expected retainer. "I take it you went ahead with that background check," she said.

He shrugged. "I didn't dig too deep, but information is often the best weapon available. The man's not used to being without money and I'm not sure how readily he's going to adapt."

"About as readily as the dinosaurs, from what I could see," Nikki said. "I went there intending to walk out with a check and a signed contract."

"And did you?" Giraldi was watching her carefully. And she happened to know he had a highly effective bullshit-o-meter.

"No," she admitted. "It was clear we were the only people in that house, which was kind of creepy. When I realized he wasn't going to be a client, I left." This was the truth as far as it went; Giraldi did not need to know that she'd practically knocked the front door down in her haste to get out. Or that she'd already spent far more time than she should have wondering if her imagination had upped the creep factor and caused her to overreact.

She watched Giraldi's face as he turned the boat away from the island and out into the bay. He pushed forward on the throttle and the boat began to pick up speed. After another few turns they were headed directly into the sun, which was turning a reddish gold that glinted off the sky-scrapers in downtown Miami.

"At the risk of forcing you to do just the opposite, I hope you'll keep your distance from Amherst. The guy is under a lot of pressure. Sometimes people under that kind of pressure do really bizarre things."

"Believe me, I'm finished with Parker Amherst the Fourth," Nicole said. Or she would be as soon as he got the message and stopped calling her.

Giraldi studied her face for a moment. She imagined the BS-o-meter clanging loudly.

"Seriously, I'm a big girl," she said, putting the unfocused look in Amherst's eyes out of her mind. "And I'm used to taking care of myself."

"I get that," he said, cutting the engine. "Believe me, I've noticed just how grown up you are." His gaze lingered for a moment on the bikini top she wore. "You're also smart and competent. But not everyone is what they seem to be."

"Duly noted," she said.

"Okay, then." The boat drifted out of the channel. "There's a bottle of white wine in the cooler down below and a corkscrew on the counter. Do you mind pouring us something to drink while I drop anchor?"

She came up on deck with two glasses of wine and joined him on the cushioned back bench, which ran the width of the boat. It was quiet out on the water. They waved to the occasional passing boat and bobbed lazily in each passing wake.

Giraldi slid an arm around her shoulders and she shivered.

"Are you cold?" he asked.

She shook her head, not wanting to admit that it was his touch that had caused her goose bumps.

"Anything new on the search for Max's son?" he asked.

"Not really. We haven't even been able to find Millie's designer friend, Pamela Gentry. Deirdre thought the woman might be able to point her to the artist who created the foyer chandelier. It got broken and needs to be repaired or replaced." She took a sip of wine and sank further into Giraldi's side, enjoying the warmth of him. She breathed in the air and Giraldi's warm, musky scent. "So far we don't look like particularly gifted sleuths."

"You do have a lot of other fine qualities," he said, pulling her closer.

Their gazes remained on the red ball of the sun as it inched toward the water, but they were hyperaware of each other. The sunset was spectacular and the wine first rate, but it was Joe Giraldi who created the warm glow Nicole felt deep in her belly. When he dropped his head to kiss her in the waning light, she gave herself up to it completely and the glow grew warmer. He broke the kiss to look more deeply into her eyes. Whatever he saw there had him pressing her back into the cushion and his mouth moving more insistently on hers.

The boat rocked gently beneath them as he explored her mouth with his. She heard another boat approaching and he went still for a moment as it passed. When the boat's wake had died down, he raised his head and rose up on his elbows.

Nicole felt his absence keenly. He'd be shocked to know just how much. Or how long it had been since she'd been so eager to have sex with someone. Her life had been in shambles for so long that sex was barely a distant memory.

"I want you, Nicole," he said simply. "And unless I'm misreading things, I think the feeling's mutual."

She realized with some surprise that she had no interest in arguing. If that boat hadn't passed, they would probably be making love right now. She wasn't sure when it had happened, but she was no longer thinking "if" but "when." A small purr of desire sounded deep in her throat.

He laughed softly, the sound an even bigger turn-on than the broad chest that had pressed against her and the warmth of his lips moving on hers.

"I'm going to take that as a yes," he said. "But I'm thinking I'd like some time and some privacy. Anything that takes place out here between passing boats won't be either of those things."

"How long will it take us to get back to your place?" she whispered.

"If you keep looking at me like that, we're not going anywhere," he said.

"And if I stop?" she asked, although she wasn't sure she could.

"We'll be there in ten minutes." He'd barely finished speaking before he'd turned the key in the ignition and begun hauling the anchor into the boat. A heartbeat or two later he was standing behind the wheel, jamming the throttle down. When the boat leveled out, he reached for her and drew her up in front of him, bracing her between his body and the steering wheel, tucking the top of her head under his chin as the boat skimmed across the water, following a path of dancing moonbeams.

Chapter Twenty-eight

Maddie paced the house, glancing out each window she passed hoping for some sight of Kyra returning with Dustin from their daily walk—walks on which Maddie was no longer invited and during which she suspected Kyra was taking her son to spend time with his father. What she saw was photographers, though the number had begun to dwindle. She didn't know how many shots of Kyra and Dustin and the rest of them would constitute "enough," but she sincerely hoped they were close to that number.

At the moment the guys were out in the pool house. Avery and Deirdre were down in the kitchen discussing the upcoming installation and Nicole was out. Madeline wished she were out too, but she had nowhere to go and no one to go there with. She had no reason to brave the camera-wielding loiterers alone. How pathetic was that?

She went downstairs and paced the first floor, avoiding the kitchen, where Avery and Deirdre's discussion had taken on an argumentative tone. Maddie sighed at the irony. It was largely because of Avery and Deridre's unique skills and their collaboration that The Millicent was now cleaner, lighter, and healthier, her deadweight removed like unneeded ballast on a ship, and yet their relationship still foundered; the mother-daughter bond could be a lifeline, but sometimes that line was too frayed to hold.

Madeline ran a hand over a living room wall and contemplated Mario Dante's work, noting how skillfully he'd blended the new plaster with the old. Soon a new coat of paint would hide his craftsmanship, but because of all of them, The Millicent would be ready for her next voyage, whatever that might entail.

Her cell phone rang shrill in the quiet and startled Madeline out of her musings. She glanced down at the screen, but the phone number, which had an area code she didn't recognize, was unfamiliar. Caller ID said only "private caller." Eager for a distraction, she answered. And immediately wished she hadn't.

"Are you there or aren't you?" the voice, which Madeline had hoped to never hear again, demanded.

For a long moment she debated whether she could just hang up without speaking and pretend she hadn't really answered.

"I know you're there. I can hear you fucking breathing!"

If there had been any doubt about who was on the other end, the f-bomb eliminated it. Tonja Kay's voice, which was so seductive on a movie screen, tended toward vile and nasty in real life.

"I'm fuckin' pissed off, Maddie," she said. "That *is* what they call you, isn't it?"

Maddie didn't respond. But she was starting to feel a little bit pissed off herself.

"Your daughter is with my husband right now," Tonja Kay said. "Did you know that?"

The answer to this was yes, though Maddie had been hoping she was wrong. Still she didn't speak. She was almost afraid of what might come out.

"I've got a dozen pictures of him in those ridiculous disguises," the movie star said. "As if there's a makeup or wardrobe person in this universe who could keep such a juicy secret to themselves."

Madeline's last phone conversation with the potty-mouthed Tonja Kay had been crude and unpleasant. At the time the movie star had demanded in the foulest possible terms that Kyra leave her husband alone. Her language had not improved.

"The private investigator I've had following him says your bitch of a daughter isn't the only other woman he's seeing." She paused, presumably to let that little tidbit sink in. "But then monogamy has never been Daniel's strong point."

The thought of Kyra and her grandson in the middle of this mockery of a marriage made Maddie sick to her stomach. She would never wish Dustin away, but she'd had more than enough of Daniel Deranian and his wife.

"So why are you calling me, Tonja?" she finally asked.

There was no answer and so Maddie pressed on, her anger gathering steam. "If Kyra's just one of many, why call me? Are you calling all of their mothers?" Though she knew it was childish, she made sure her tone was every bit as snide as the actress's.

She half expected the woman to hang up. When that didn't happen, she braced for a barrage of profanity. She was not at all prepared for Tonja Kay's answer.

"I'm calling because your daughter is one of the few who managed to get pregnant." She said this as if Kyra had achieved this result by herself. "And because she's the only one who's delivered a boy." There was a brief silence. "And Daniel's gone and gotten all sappy about him." The last was spoken so softly Maddie had to strain to hear it.

Unable to stand still, Madeline crossed the living room and stared out a back window at the newly filled swimming pool. No one had been swimming yet because little of the resurfaced deck was out of camera range.

"What is it you want?" Madeline asked when the silence continued. "And why are you calling me? If there's anything to be discussed, and I can't imagine what that might be, the person you should be discussing it with is Kyra."

"Oh, your daughter and I have already had our talk," Tonja Kay said, any hint of softness gone. "But in case the little cunt tries to keep it to herself, I thought you should know that we want joint custody of Daniel's son. In fact, we're thinking he might be better off with us full-time."

The comment carried far more force than any of the expletives the movie star had uttered so far. Madeline had a brief and disturbing mental picture of her grandson being carted around as part of the Deranian-Kay circus. "That will never happen."

"Don't take that fucking tone with me," the movie star snapped.

Madeline straightened her spine and her resolve. She was tired of this woman, tired of Steve, tired of the wall Kyra's involvement with Deranian had built between her and her daughter. She'd vowed when she told Steve off that she was done sitting back and taking whatever others felt like dishing out.

Madeline said, "I doubt any judge would choose a foulmouthed exhibitionist like you or your husband over a normal home and family."

"You've got to be fucking joking. We're fucking moviestar philanthropists!" Tonja shouted. "Last time I checked, fucking 'normal' didn't come close."

"I'm getting kind of tired of lecturing you about your language," Maddie said. "But the last time I checked, 'fuck' was not an adjective." She offered a mental apology to her long-ago charm class instructor, Mrs. Merryweather.

"The fuck it's not. And I don't think I need a fucking judge to make this happen."

"Is that right?" At the moment Madeline might have embraced the comfort of a few hurled profanities.

"Oh, yeah," the movie star said. "I just explained to your fucking—"

"One more 'fuck' "—Maddie put everything she had into the expletive—"and I'm hanging up. Our conversation will be over."

"I told your"—the actress hesitated as if unable to speak without her adjective of choice—". . . daughter that the network—your network—wants me and Daniel and our children to star in a reality show. A show I'm pretty"—there was another pause where the word *fuck* would have been inserted—". . . sure they want a lot more than some"—this time the pause was briefer—". . . remodeling program."

The actress hung up with a last strangled curse. Maddie stared down at the phone. She was still staring at it when

Kyra came in the front door cursing up a storm of her own despite the fact that the baby was sound asleep in her arms.

"I can't believe this," Kyra hissed above Dustin's head. "I fucking can't believe this!"

"Kyra!" Madeline admonished her daughter. "There's no need for profanity." Although she was no longer sure what a couple of unpleasant words meant in comparison to what was going on.

"But there is," Kyra said. "There's every reason for it. Tonja Kay wants custody of Dustin. She's pushing Daniel to go to court to get it."

"But Daniel's not looking for that, is he? If he doesn't want custody, then—"

"But that's the problem, Mom. He thinks it's a good idea. He actually thinks they have more to offer my son than I do. I just listened to thirty minutes of everything he and Tonja can do for him that I can't."

Madeline took Dustin into her arms. "Just take a deep breath and try to calm down, Kyra," she said as the two of them walked upstairs to put the little boy to bed. "We'll figure out something."

"Like what?" Kyra asked, all but wringing her hands. "It's not even just about me. Tonja told me that if I don't agree to hand Dustin over, she's going to go to the network and get *Do Over* canceled before it even airs."

• • •

Faced with the enormity of Tonja Kay's threat, Maddie knew that there was not enough air in the universe to make breathing a reliable relaxation tool. She tried to use the very real anger that simmered inside her to combat the worry that churned in her gut, but the adrenaline turned the emotion into a fireball of panic that burned brightly inside her. Not surprisingly, she slept fitfully and spent the last hours before sunrise staring up at the ceiling listening to Dustin's breathing and Kyra's tossing and turning. Unable to stop thinking about the ramifications of Tonja Kay's threat, she got out of bed bleary-eyed and on edge.

Too many cups of coffee later, Maddie sat on the scaffolding in front of the second-story window she was supposed to repair. Avery sat on one side of her in case Maddie needed any prompting. Andrew, her newly proclaimed assistant/apprentice, sat on her other.

Troy and Anthony stood on the front stoop shooting up at them, so that they could move easily between the exterior and interior, where Deirdre's kitchen cabinets were being installed. Kyra stood on the upstairs landing shooting through the window.

"How many *Do Over* cast and crew members does it take to reglaze a window?" Avery quipped, but Madeline couldn't even find a smile. Her brain scurried through worst-case scenarios at a speed that left her slightly lightheaded. She doubted anyone would be cracking jokes once they found out just how precarious things had become.

Unable to meet Avery's eye, she looked down and noted that the number of photographers on the sidewalk had dwindled further. She attributed this to the headlines she'd seen in Max's paper, and was grateful to the ditzy blond pop singer who had left her husband for one of her female backup singers and was now holed up at the nearby Colony Hotel. And also to the NFL quarterback who had been stopped on a DUI and emerged from his car stark naked. Madeline had never been so glad to see so much bad behavior in others.

"Are you ready?" Avery asked.

Madeline nodded, but without conviction. As she'd discovered the previous summer, when she'd been chosen for the task, reglazing was both torturous and tedious. It required intense concentration and a gentle touch, neither of which she possessed at the moment.

Still, she managed to scrape off the old paint and glazing compound with the putty knife and pull out the first broken pane of glass. She even pried off the paint-caked diamonds of metal that held each corner of the glass in place, and scraped off the rest of the old paint and compound without mishap.

"See, it's just like riding a bike," Avery said. "You just have to get the feel of it back."

Maddie's fingers moved awkwardly in the latex gloves and sweat popped out on her brow as she set the new piece of glass in place.

Avery reached over and mopped Madeline's brow. Mario, who'd claimed he'd just come out for some air but who stood next to Kyra watching Madeline like a worried mother hen, gave her an enthusiastic thumbs-up. Andrew smiled encouragement and said, "Looking good, Mom."

"Thanks," Maddie said, but her thoughts were consumed with a barrage of unanswerable questions: How long would Tonja Kay give them before she went to the network? What possible chance was there of surviving and winning a custody battle against two such public figures? Was there any chance at all that a network would choose an unproven show like *Do Over* over a PG-rated version of Deranian-Kay and Friends?

Her hands shook as she considered Nicole and Avery and Deirdre's circumstances. Unless Bella Flora sold before they got dropped, what would everyone live on without the Lifetime series they'd pinned their hopes on?

She fumbled twice, unable to affix the point to the corner of the new glass as her mind filled with images of Daniel Deranian and Tonja Kay displaying Dustin for the cameras on *their* new reality show. The glass cracked in her hands. "Shit!"

Avery handed her a new piece of glass. "It's okay," she said in a soothing tone. "You can do this. You just need to concentrate."

Andrew took the broken piece of glass and set it out of the way.

"Okay." Madeline drew a steadying breath and reached for the glazing compound, demonstrating for Andrew how to roll it into a thin, snakelike piece and press it around the edges of the glass.

"Cool," Andrew said when she managed this without breakage. "What happens next?"

"We go inside to straighten the seams and seal the pane." She wanted to smile at him, but her lips, like her fingers, felt wobbly and out of control. "And then we move to the next broken pane and go through the whole process again."

She did not want to think about reglazing as a metaphor for her life, but it was hard to miss the similarities.

"How many of these do we have to do?" Andrew asked.

Madeline appreciated the use of the word *we*. Unlike his father, who had once again retreated when she needed him most, Andrew had stepped up to the plate. He performed the tasks he was given to the best of his ability and without complaint.

"A lot," Maddie answered. "But if we split it up between

us—I do the outside portion and you do the finishing steps inside—it'll take half as long." Yet another life truth.

"Good idea," Avery said.

"I'm really glad you're here, sweetie," Madeline said to Andrew as they climbed down the scaffolding and made their way inside. But no matter how hard she tried to focus on the positive, and no matter how deeply she breathed while she was doing it, the worry and panic refused to recede.

• • •

The move into the pool house took a little over an hour if you didn't count the time it took to negotiate who would stay where and why. Kyra had suggested that the Lifetime crew move to a hotel, but in the end Max invited Troy and Anthony to bunk in his room, Andrew took over one of the couches in the living area and Avery, Deirdre, and Nicole took one room while Maddie, Kyra, and Dustin took the other. The bathrooms, now divided by gender, were nicely updated, but like the rest of the building were not designed for nine adults and a baby. Nicole's idea of heaven was rapidly changing from financial security and a once-again-thriving business to a bathroom of her own. Surely that wasn't too much to ask.

"Is it my imagination or are the walls bulging?" Avery asked.

"I don't know, but there's stuff everywhere," Madeline said.

"Well, at least most of us have beds," Deirdre pointed out.

"Which is a lot better than the mattresses on the floor at Bella Flora," Kyra added.

Nicole winced. They were all so damned eager to look for that silver lining.

"It's just for another few weeks," Madeline added. "Right, Avery?"

"Yeah. Pretty much," Avery said.

"Could you be a little more specific?" Nicole asked.

"Well, I'm figuring the reglazing should be done by tomorrow."

Madeline nodded and managed something approximating her usual smile. Nicole knew she wasn't the only one who'd noticed its absence. Andrew sent up a fervent "yahoo!"

"And the kitchen?" Madeline asked.

"The bottom cabinets, the countertops, and the new backsplash are in. The wall-hung cabinets should go up in the morning. The appliances will be delivered in the afternoon," Deirdre said. "I'm just waiting for the banquette to be reupholstered and the light fixtures to be delivered."

"So, after tomorrow I'm figuring somewhere between ten days to two weeks to paint the interior and refinish and reseal the floors." Avery counted it out on her fingers. "Then the exterior gets painted—we'll do the cut-ins and Sunshine Painting will handle the rest, like we're doing inside. Another day or two for the landscaping—a master gardener at the Miami Beach Botanical Garden has taken over the coordination." Avery considered her tally. "Yes, I think we should be done in about three weeks, which will put us right before Labor Day. Assuming Mother Nature cooperates."

Nicole noted Avery's omission of the tropical storms that continued to crop up. And the fact that hurricane season kicked into high gear here in August and September. She wished she could omit last summer's memories of them cowering in a bathroom while a storm named Charlene pummeled the Gulf coast of Florida. She looked from face to face and knew that she wasn't the only one currently stifling fears of a repeat performance.

Chapter Twenty-nine

Max insisted on making dinner that night and he did so on a George Foreman Grill that had fallen out of the back of a kitchen cabinet as it was being tossed into the Dumpster. Nicole's appetite was not stimulated by the ingredients Max layered between the slices of rye bread and was stamped out completely when the smell of hot, pressed sauerkraut began to fill the air.

"Voilà!" Max exclaimed into Kyra and Troy's camera lenses, behind which the two had taken refuge. "Behold the Golden Reuben!" He garnished each plate with potato chips and a dill-pickle spear and, with Madeline's help, handed the plates around before joining the women at the table. Andrew, Troy, and Anthony set their plates on the coffee table and hunkered down to eat on the sofa.

"I offer these sandwiches with thanks for all the meals Madeline has made and served," Max said gallantly. "And to all of you for working so hard to make The Millicent a home again."

Maddie's smile was shaky as she nodded her thanks. But then all of their eyes were kind of misty. Dustin, who was standing upright by steadying himself against his grandmother's chair leg, smiled happily, his new teeth—all three of them—on display, and said, "Gax!" As they watched he moved a hand to Avery's chair and took another careful step to the side.

"Well done, Dustin!" Max said to the little boy. "Before you know it, you'll be ready for your own Reuben."

Everyone but Madeline laughed. Nicole peered at her more closely and noticed that she held her sandwich in a death grip and seemed to be having trouble swallowing. Kyra, too, was chewing extremely slowly and looked more than a little anxious, but Nicole chided herself a few moments later for looking for trouble. For all she knew it was as simple as a dislike of sauerkraut. Or an understandable twinge of claustrophobia.

Dessert was a bag of chocolate chip cookies and a pot of freshly brewed decaf. The guys found a baseball game on the television while Max sat with them at the table. Kyra settled Dustin on the couch next to Andrew and brought her laptop to the table. Nicole knew she'd been tweeting their progress and posting updates to the *Do Over* Facebook page along with occasional blog posts from each of them.

"Are there any loose ends that need to be tied up?" Madeline asked.

"I'm still working on finding Pamela Gentry before I give up and go with something else in the foyer," Deirdre said. "Max, did you ever hear anything about her after she and Millie lost touch?"

Max took a bite of cookie and chewed thoughtfully. "Someone we knew did run into her on a trip to Chicago.

I think she'd gotten married and opened her own design firm." He sipped his coffee, then set down his cup. "Not too surprising that she'd be in business for herself, really. She was quite aggressive for a woman of that time."

"Do you know what her married name was?" Deirdre pressed. "I guess I've gotten a little obsessed about that chandelier, but having such a unique custom piece in the foyer is a hard thing to let go of."

"It was something with an 'M.' Malgrin . . . Martin?" Max's brow creased in concentration. "I'm not sure." He dabbed at his mouth with his napkin as he tried to remember. "Or wait, maybe it was . . . Mitson? No." He rubbed his jaw. "Madsen? Yes, I think that sounds right."

"Can you Google Madsen Design, Chicago, or Pamela Gentry Madsen, Kyra, and see if you come up with anything?" Deirdre asked.

"Sure." Kyra's fingers flew over the keyboard. They watched as her gaze skimmed down the screen. She typed some more.

"Look at this." She turned her screen so the others could see. "This is from an awards ceremony in 1973."

Nicole and the others looked at the photo. Someone was presenting a statuette to Pamela Madsen of Madsen Interiors.

"Love the dress," Nikki said of the evening gown with the jeweled neckline. "Her hair's longer and lighter and she's wearing glasses, but the face is the same."

There was another photo of her accepting the presidency of the Chicago chapter of the American Society of Interior Designers and several more of her heading up various committees and fund-raisers.

"She seems to have been quite a dynamo," Nicole observed.

"Yes," Max said. "She was always a force to be reckoned with. Pamela could be good company and she had a fair sense of humor." He looked slightly uncomfortable. "But sometimes she just wouldn't take no for an answer."

Max's gaze stayed on the screen.

"I'm going to save these photos to print out," Kyra said, and then her fingers tapped quickly across the keys. "Here's the design-firm contact info. I'm sending that to your phone, Deirdre."

"Thanks. Can you tell if she's still active in the business?"

More tapping. Then, "Oh." Kyra looked up from the computer screen then turned to Max. "Here's her . . ." She hesitated. "I just found her obituary."

When Max made no comment, Kyra turned her attention back to the screen. "It looks like she died five years ago."

"Before Millie," Max said quietly. "Can you read what it says?"

"Yes, I'm going to save it to print, too. As soon as I find a place to set up the printer."

There was another keystroke and then Kyra read, "'Pamela Gentry Madsen died yesterday at her home at the age of eighty. She was a former president of the ASID'—then it names those committees and things she chaired. 'Her firm, which carried her name, did many notable commercial and residential interiors in and around the Chicago area. She was especially known for her modern interiors, for mentoring promising artists and artisans, and for her affinity for the Art Deco style.'" Kyra skimmed further. "'She is survived by her son, Ethan, who became the managing partner of Madsen Interiors several years ago, and two grandchildren.' "

They all sat, their eyes on Max.

"Hmm," he said. "Gone all these years already. It never occurred to me." He stood slowly, holding on to the table until his legs steadied beneath him, in much the same way that Dustin clung to chair backs. He looked every one of his ninety years as he excused himself and began to move slowly toward his bedroom.

"So that's it, then," Avery said after the bedroom door had closed behind him. "Do you think you can find another chandelier locally?"

"Possibly," Deirdre said, still staring at Kyra's computer screen. "But the firm seems to be still in business. I don't see any reason not to call and try to speak to her son to see if he knows this artist or his work."

"Seriously?" Nicole asked. She'd been impressed with Deirdre's work, but didn't understand the woman's single-mindedness over this one element.

"Why not?" Deirdre asked. "It's just a phone call. I'll see if I can reach him tomorrow."

. . .

Avery woke the next morning in a foul mood, no doubt caused by being crammed on a roll-away between Deirdre and Nicole and then having to fight for bathroom time for a good twenty minutes. An entire day spent moving the furniture that was going into the POD that had been delivered and carting off the things that Max was donating and selling didn't improve her mood one bit.

She was standing in the living room contemplating the

battered tile floor and trying not to think of what it was going to take to refinish it, when she heard the sound of applause coming from the kitchen. Seconds later Avery stood in the archway between the dining room and kitchen. From there, she watched Deirdre place one hand on a section of the gleaming teak countertop and bend from the waist in an exaggerated bow. Max, Maddie, Nikki, and even Dustin applauded wildly while Troy, Anthony, and Kyra recorded Deirdre's moment of triumph.

Avery's jaw set as she took in the space. Like everything else Deirdre had created or orchestrated, the kitchen was superbly done. It was, in fact, deserving of applause.

The cabinetry was clean-lined and finished in a sand-colored enamel that both complemented and contrasted with the teak and would pop even more strongly once the tobacco-colored stain was applied to the floor.

The gently rolling tile backsplash in shades of blue conjured up the feel of ocean waves. The faucet and the cabinet and drawer pulls were polished chrome fashioned to look like a ship's wheel. The appliances, donated by yet another sponsor that Deirdre had found, were state-of-the-art stainless steel encased in custom cabinetry. The pantry door had been made to look like it led to a cruise-ship stateroom.

When the new light fixtures went in and the banquette was complete, The Millicent kitchen would belong on the cover of *Architectural Digest*.

Avery's gut clenched as she tried to understand how someone so self-absorbed could tune into a space so perfectly. While the rest of them struggled, Deirdre had skated through life letting nothing stand in her way. She'd gotten tired of being a wife and a mother, and so she'd picked up and left. When her career as a Hollywood designer hit a road bump, she'd hotfooted her way to Bella Flora and gotten her face in front of the cameras. Now here she was blowing everybody's socks off on camera while she pretended that all she wanted was Avery's love and forgiveness. Ha!

"What do you think?" Deirdre asked Avery, apparently needing still more adoration despite the fact that everyone else already thought she walked on frickin' water.

Avery took a long look around the space as if she had not already done so. "It's very nice," she said grudgingly. "You did a nice job of capturing The Millicent's vibe."

Silence descended.

"That's it?" Nicole asked. "It's nice?"

"Really?" Kyra added as she lowered her camera.

"You don't like it?" Max asked, looking around the space as if to see if he'd somehow missed something.

Maddie shot her a look of disappointment. Deirdre's face remained impassive, but Avery had seen her eyes widen in surprise before darkening with hurt and she knew she'd scored a direct hit.

"What?" Avery snapped, uncomfortable with the disapproving silence.

"Don't you think it's time to grow up?" Madeline asked.

"It's okay, Maddie," Deirdre said, drawing Madeline's attention. "Please. You don't need to . . ."

"No, it's not okay." Madeline turned back to Avery, her normally soothing tone surprisingly . . . not. "You can't hold a grudge against your mother forever. She screwed up. She left you and your father. She did the wrong thing."

"You've got that right," Avery said, confused. Madeline was generally the most accepting of all of them, but at the moment Avery didn't see a lick of acceptance in her eyes.

"But she's here now," Maddie continued, gesturing toward Deirdre. "And she's apologized and she's trying to make it up to you. The woman has been taking lessons in motherhood, for God's sake."

Avery started in surprise. "What did you say?"

"Really, Maddie," Deirdre said, her discomfort now apparent.

"Yep, she signed up for the first-ever 'Madeline Singer How to Be a Mother' class, though lately I'm not so sure I'm qualified to teach it. I've been coaching her, but she's come up with some interesting attempts on her own: the Cheez Doodle extravaganza. The hotel room. The new clothes. Most importantly, 'the not leaving when the going gets tough.'"

"I don't believe this," Avery said. "This is just more Deirdre Morgan smoke and mirrors. Believe me, she's only here to build back her career. On our backs, I might add."

"Okay," Deirdre said. "I appreciate your defense, Maddie, but it seems pretty clear my daughter has no interest in giving me the benefit of the doubt."

"Good grief," Avery said. "I can't believe this! Now Deirdre's the injured party and I'm the big bad bully?" She wanted to get the hell out of the kitchen, but she felt pinned down, under fire from the most unlikely of directions.

"That may be why she showed up at Bella Flora," Maddie conceded. "But she has other options now and she's still here." She looked pointedly at Avery. "Because of you."

"Right." Avery heard the petulance in her voice, but she wasn't about to concede the point. She wanted to leave but had no idea where she would go. And even if she went somewhere, she'd have to come back.

"It's true," Deirdre said. "I'd give anything to prove it. But I don't know what else to do."

"Seriously, Avery," Madeline said. "It's time to get over it. Your mother's here and she's trying. She's not without flaws. But then who of us is?"

For a few long agonizing moments no one spoke. The whole thing felt somewhat surreal. And then Madeline's face crumpled.

"I'm sorry," she began. "I didn't mean to jump on you. I just . . . Being a mother, a good mother, isn't all that easy. I just couldn't help thinking you could at least give her a chance."

Avery opened her mouth, though she had no idea what to say. She did the mouth-open-like-a-fish-out-of-water-and-gasping-for-air thing, then managed to close it. She didn't know what had loosened Maddie's normal reticence, but it was clear that the floodgates were now open and she seemed unable, or unwilling, to censor what came out of her mouth.

"God, I'm sorry I started all of this," Madeline said in yet another rush. "But since I have, I might as well add that I wish you would stop hiding yourself in those baggy clothes."

She paused while everyone's mouths gaped open, but that pause was brief.

"I mean, everybody knows you've got a body under there," Maddie concluded. "You're doing yourself a disservice."

Avery's vision blurred with tears as she absorbed this attack from the last place she'd ever expected one. She might have cried right there except for the horrified look spreading over Maddie's face. And the unexpected movement she caught out of the corner of her eye, movement that turned out to be Troy moving in for a closer shot.

Now even Maddie fell silent as everyone looked at one another and then at the camera.

Crap! Avery's mouth opened again in horror as she realized that she had set into motion the very thing she'd reassured Kyra they could avoid. She'd allowed her hurt and anger to get the better of her, and as a result they'd handed the Lifetime crew exactly what they'd been waiting for: a great big boatload of backbiting and discord.

• • •

Reeling in shock, they retreated to their separate corners as much as people living in a fishbowl with a whole lot of other fish can. Avery jumped into the Mini Cooper and drove off. With no destination in mind, she ended up on Collins Avenue heading north. For a while she simply drove and breathed, her only objective to get as far away as possible.

The hotels of South Beach had given way to high-rise condo buildings and then sprawling waterfront estates when she picked up her cell phone and called Chase. She continued to breathe in and exhale the salt-tinged air as she waited for him to pick up.

"Hey," he said just when she was afraid she was going to be routed to voice mail. "What's going on?"

Avery spilled it all, replaying every last word and look, spewing out her hurt and her sense of betrayal.

"I just don't understand how Maddie could take Deirdre's side," she said for what might have been the third or fourth time. "And all of it happened on camera."

"Something must be going on," Chase said reasonably. "Maddie is a good friend of yours. And maybe she just put things in the wrong way."

"Humph." She wasn't sure where she was at the moment, but she figured she couldn't get completely lost as long as she kept heading north. "She said that Deirdre had been taking mothering lessons from her."

"Really?"

"That's what she said."

"So Deirdre's trying," Chase said. "That's a good thing, right?"

Another "humph." No one was going to accuse her of being overly articulate tonight.

"She ran out on us. She ran out on *me*."

"I know," he said soothingly. "But she's back. And she doesn't seem to be going anywhere."

"That's what Maddie said."

"Maybe it's time to give her a chance," Chase said gently.

"Maddie said that, too."

He hesitated, but there was no judgment in the silence or in his voice when he finally spoke. "It may be time to let go of the anger, Avery," he said.

"But I can't," she said automatically. And then, "How do you even do that?"

"You just do," Chase said. "It's a choice you make." He paused. "It's like when Dawn died. I was so angry with her for leaving us. And so scared. I had no idea how I was going to raise the boys without her." She heard him swallow, could picture him running a hand through his dark hair. "I couldn't imagine that we could have a life, just the three of us. I held on to the anger and fear for a long time. But at some point you have to just let go of it and move on. It's damaging to you and everyone around you."

Avery continued to drive, the wind whipping her hair. As annoying as Chase Hardin could be, right now the sound of his voice in her ear was as comforting as NASA control must have been to the Apollo 13 astronauts, stranded in space with a crippled spacecraft.

"I don't know if I can do that," she said.

"You can," Chase said. "If you want to. I know you can."

He fell silent and she drove for another mile just listening to the reassuring rhythm of his breathing. She made a U-turn and headed south.

"Where are you, Van?" he asked as the neon lights of South Beach came into view.

"I'm on my way back," she said. "But I'm not sure how I'm going to handle the thing with Maddie."

"It'll work itself out," he said. "But it sounds like maybe you need to find out what's going on with her first."

"Thanks," she said as she pulled the Mini Cooper into the drive.

"Anytime, Van," he said softly. "I know you'll do the right thing. Sleep tight and hang in there. I'll see you soon."

Minutes later Avery raised the convertible top and sat staring at the dark house in front of her, trying to process all that had happened, replaying Chase's words of advice. She appreciated his confidence in her, but it was hard to do the right thing when you had no idea what that thing was.

She walked past the silent house and around the pool still trying to come to terms with what she should do. Troy and Anthony were in the pool-house living room playing a video game while Andrew snored softly on the couch. She passed them without comment.

In the bedroom, Deirdre and Nicole appeared to be asleep. Careful not to wake them, Avery washed her face and brushed her teeth, staring at herself in the mirror as she played back Maddie's comments. This time, rather than the hurtful words, she focused on the total "un-Maddie-ness" of what had been said.

It was only then that she knew what she had to do. Pull-ing on her pajamas, Avery crawled into bed, plugged in her phone, and set her alarm for O-dark-thirty.

Chapter Thirty

It was still dark when the bedroom door creaked open and a hand grasped Maddie's shoulder and shook it none too gently.

"What?" She sat up, eyes wide open.

"Get up." It was Avery, which made no sense at all. Avery was anti-morning and relied on heavy doses of caffeine to get herself going each day.

"We've got about thirty minutes until sunrise. And we're going to the beach to watch it. But be quiet. I don't want to wake Troy and Anthony."

"Look, I'm sorry about yesterday," Maddie began, disoriented but eager to apologize. She'd lain awake a good part of the night kicking herself for the things she'd said and the way she'd said them. "I didn't hear you come in last night or I would have apologized then."

"Not now." Avery shushed her. "Nicole and Deirdre are getting dressed. Can you get Kyra and Dustin organized? We'll pick up coffee on the way."

Ten minutes later they tiptoed out of the pool house and across the dew-draped lawn like thieves in the night. The air was already heavy with humidity and the morning breeze was warm and salty. There was little traffic and even less conversation as they walked over to Ocean, Kyra pushing a sleepy-eyed Dustin in the jogging stroller.

At an open café they stopped at the counter for *café con leche*—Avery bought two—then carried them out to the beach, where they settled on the blankets they'd brought.

They faced the Atlantic and drank their coffees in silence for a few minutes. The jetty and Government Cut were visible to the south. The white sand beach angled northward. A few hearty souls were already out walking, and they'd passed a few joggers, but for the most part they were alone.

Madeline watched as the sky began to lighten and the first glow of morning sun appeared on the horizon. She breathed deeply, drawing the beginning of the new day into her lungs and holding on to it like a talisman. There were so many things unraveling in her life, and all of them seemed beyond her control. How could she help Kyra navigate the mine-strewn waters of her relationship with Daniel Deranian when her own relationship with Steve seemed to be detonating around her? And what would happen to *Do Over* when they'd finished The Millicent? Where would they go and what would they do if Tonja Kay made good on her threat?

She stole a look at Dustin, asleep in his stroller. Beside him, Kyra leaned back on her hands, arms straight, long legs crossed in the sand. She too stared out at the ocean. The jiggle of her bare feet belied the placid expression on her face.

"So," Avery said when she'd finished the first coffee and planted the empty cup into the sand. "You may be wondering why I called this meeting. Especially since this isn't my favorite part of the day."

"No kidding." Nicole pulled her knees up to her chest and wrapped her arms around them. "I don't remember the last time I saw you awake before the sun. Thank God that café was open."

"I'm glad we're here," Maddie said, relieved to have a chance to unburden herself. "I want to apologize for my behavior yesterday. I had no right to give Avery all that unasked-for advice in public. And I definitely shouldn't have done it in front of Troy and Anthony."

"No," Avery said. "I called this meeting, I hauled your asses out of bed, and I get to apologize first." She took a long drag on her second coffee. Madeline wouldn't have been surprised to hear the caffeine zinging through Avery's veins.

"So first I want to apologize to Deirdre for being so stingy with my praise." Avery turned to face her mother. "The kitchen looks great. Everything you've done in the house has been first rate. Given our . . . history, sometimes I have a hard time acknowledging your achievements."

Avery nodded curtly to signal that the apology was over. Clearly she wasn't planning to throw herself into Deirdre's arms and tell her that she loved her.

Deirdre looked more than satisfied with the apology. Who knew, perhaps there was a place for motherhood tutoring after all. The way things were going, maybe Maddie herself needed to take a refresher course.

"I also want to apologize to everyone for starting all that in front of Troy and Anthony," Avery continued. "I hate that they got us arguing on video. I know how easy it is to twist things around and make it look like we're at each other's throats all the time."

She took another sip and the second cup joined the first in its sand cup holder.

"That wasn't your fault," Maddie said. "I was really out of line. I know you felt attacked, which was so not my intent. I mean, I did want you to think a little bit more about Deirdre's efforts to establish a relationship, but I shouldn't have put you on the spot like that in front of everyone. And especially not in front of the film crew." She could feel herself blathering on now, twisting her coffee cup in her hands, unable to stop. She ended the apology in a rush and fell silent.

"Great," Avery said. "Now that the apologies are over, maybe you can tell us what's going on." She was looking directly at Maddie, as were Nicole and Deirdre. Kyra was still looking out over the ocean and jiggling her feet.

The sun inched upward. Its glow reflected off the water and bounced back to singe the sky.

"I don't know what you mean," Maddie replied, not quite meeting their eyes.

Dustin woke and reached for his bare toes. His gaze was pinned on the emerging ball of sun.

"We're not buying it," Avery said. "If ever anyone was not acting like herself, it's you, Maddie. Give it up."

"No, really," Maddie began. She was not remotely ready for this conversation. "Everything's . . ."

· · ·

"Oh, Mom," Kyra said, unable to bear watching her mother continue to try to protect her. "Everything's not fine and there's no point in trying to keep it from them. It impacts them, too." She turned the stroller and reached inside to retrieve Dustin. He windmilled his arms and kicked his legs happily as she pulled his sturdy warm body out of the stroller and sat him on the blanket next to her.

Now that all eyes were on her, Kyra had a brief thought that this meeting might have gone down easier at the end of the day when everyone was bone tired and there was alcohol to cushion the blow. The relentless clarity of morning left no room for minimizing the seriousness of the situation.

Dustin put one hand on her shoulder and another on Nicole's. With total concentration and some fairly impressive upper-body strength, he used them to pull himself to his feet. Kyra wrapped one hand around his calf to steady him. And herself. It took everything she had to look everyone in the eye.

"Tonja Kay and Daniel Deranian want custody of Dustin." Kyra said it straight out, as if a quick announcement might somehow lessen the pain. It didn't.

"What?" Avery said.

"But why?" Nicole asked.

"They say they can do more for him than I can—that they can give him more." Kyra looked away briefly, her gaze drawn by a windsurfer hauling up his sail.

"That's ridiculous," Nicole said with an angry shake of her head.

"Believe me," Avery said. "No one's better off without their mother." She said this without the usual accusatory tone.

Kyra watched Deirdre dart a hopeful look at her daughter. She couldn't bring herself to look at her own mother.

"There are things they could afford to do for him that I can't," Kyra said, thinking of the way Daniel had positioned his world against hers. "Opportunities I could never provide."

"What, get him his own personal nanny?" Nicole asked. "Drag his little ass all over the world? Pose him for the cameras?"

"Do you know of any famous children who are especially well adjusted?" Deirdre asked. "I did a ton of celebrity homes while I was working in Hollywood and I didn't run into too many of them."

A silence fell as all of them contemplated the idea of Dustin as a part of the Deranian-Kay entourage, something Kyra had been trying her hardest not to do.

"I've heard Tonja's got really strange eating habits," Avery said. "There's been a lot of leaks from the household staff lately. That woman's not just foulmouthed, she's crazy."

"She's also powerful," Madeline said. "Much as I'd like to, we can't just dismiss her. The two of them have serious clout."

The sun cut through a bank of low-lying clouds. Rays of golden light shot through the pale blue sky and skidded across the green-blue surface of the ocean.

Kyra looked at her mother. She did not want to have to explain how serious that clout was. How easily it could destroy them all. Once again she'd managed to put everyone's livelihood at risk.

"Tonja's threatened to get the network to cancel *Do Over* if I refuse." Kyra looked away again, then forced herself to meet their eyes. "She says that Lifetime wants a Deranian-Kay family reality show and that the network wants them more than they want us."

A seagull wheeled overhead, cawing loudly. Dustin

looked up, clapped his hands in delight, and went down hard on his bottom. Kyra reached for her son, gathering him in her arms and putting him back on his feet before he could cry. He smelled of sleep and baby shampoo. Less than thirty minutes ago he'd been at her breast, nursing, looking up at her like she was his everything. "Neither Mom or I wants you all to be hurt by this. It's not fair for you to be penalized because of me and Dustin." Maintaining eye contact with them at that moment was one of the hardest things she'd ever had to do. "I'm so, so sorry."

No one spoke as everyone tried to absorb the shock waves from the depth charge that had just gone off beneath them.

Kyra felt her mother's gaze on her in the silence. Maddie had tried to warn her not to give in to wishful thinking, and Kyra had ignored her. If she'd refused to see Daniel, if she'd discouraged him from spending time with Dustin, none of this might have happened.

"Christ," Nicole said. "We've spent more than a year sweating our guts out for this opportunity, and they're using it as a bargaining chip?"

Kyra watched their faces as they weighed what they knew was the right thing to say with the consequences that were attached to saying it. She felt like shit for putting them in this position, but she was scared, too. There was no way she could give up Dustin.

"Well, obviously none of us would ever ask you to give up custody so that we can do a television show," Avery finally said.

"No, of course, not," Deirdre agreed, her tone nowhere near as adamant as the nod of her head.

Nicole looked like she wanted to cry. Or beat someone to a pulp. She nodded glumly.

"You shouldn't have to ask me to do anything," Kyra said. "I . . . maybe if I leave the show, if Dustin and I are gone, they'll have no reason to go after *Do Over.*" She wasn't sure what was worse—the fear of losing Dustin or the guilt she felt for what she'd brought down on everyone. "It's not fair for me to jeopardize the series."

"Except that it's because of you we even have the show," Avery said, not at all happily.

"No, we need to come up with some way to solve this," Maddie said. "There must be something we could do."

"Maybe we could go to Lisa Hogan and try to head them off?" Avery asked.

"No," Deirdre said. "Not now when we and the show are so vulnerable. If *Do Over* were already established, it might be different. But—"

"Besides, it might just be a threat," Nicole said. "Maybe Tonja doesn't really plan to discuss it with the network. If that's the case, we don't want to be the ones to bring it up."

"I'm so sorry," Kyra said again. "This shouldn't be your problem. I'll think of something. I will."

Dustin wrapped his arm around Kyra's neck and blew a raspberry on her cheek just like Troy had taught him. He pulled back and offered his cheek for a return raspberry, but Kyra's eyes blurred with tears and the raspberry sounded more like air quietly leaving a balloon, lame in the extreme.

"We'll all think," Deirdre said. "There has to be a way to get them to back off."

"In the meantime, maybe you should tell Deranian that you're willing to consider giving them custody," Nicole suggested. "You know, just to buy some time until we figure out what to do."

Kyra nodded slowly, but she didn't believe that all they

needed in order to come up with a winning plan was time. What were the chances of going up against two major celebrities with more money than God and coming out ahead?

The sun continued its ascent. The breeze grew warmer and the clouds began to burn off as the women gathered up their things. They left the beach and walked back to The Millicent in silence. No one mentioned Tonja Kay and Daniel Deranian or the threat they posed. But Kyra could practically hear all of them thinking about it.

• • •

Nikki couldn't stop thinking about Kyra's sunrise revelation. As she wielded her paintbrush along the corners and edges of the living room walls and later on the upstairs landing, she tried to push the worry aside, tried to tell herself that after all they'd been through they were not going to end up out on the street, but the worry had taken on heft and shape and it refused to budge. She could tell from the lack of jokes and smack talk that typically accompanied the most onerous or boring renovation chores that everyone else's mind was similarly occupied.

The number of paparazzi on the sidewalk was down to single digits, and by late afternoon she'd managed to convince herself that a dip in the swimming pool with drink in hand would go a long way toward soothing frayed nerves. She stared at the water through an upstairs bedroom window as her arm grew weary from painting, and she imagined the feel of it on her skin, anticipating the buoyant weight of it ebbing around her. She began to imbue it with cleansing properties well beyond the realm of possibility. This kidney-shaped concrete container was not going to wash all their troubles away.

When Avery finally released them for the day, Nikki sprinted to the pool house, put on her bathing suit, and popped open the admittedly cheap bottle of vodka she'd purchased during their lunch break. After assembling the alcohol, orange juice, and glasses on a tray, she carried it to the pool, set it and her cell phone on one of the new wrought-iron tables, and took the first of what she hoped would be many screwdrivers into the pool with her.

Avery was right behind her, a long T-shirt over her bikini and an industrial-size bag of Cheez Doodles in her hands. Deirdre carried a plate of more dignified appetizers from Epicure while Kyra carried Dustin and a swim ring with a seat built into it; her camera hung over her shoulder.

Maddie came more slowly, her elbow crooked through Max's, a pile of towels balanced against her chest. Max, who wore what might be the world's oldest bathing trunks and his captain's hat, smiled jauntily into the camera lens that remained in front of them as Troy and Anthony walked backward in order to record their tortoiselike progress.

In two long steps Andrew passed them and cannonballed into the deep end of the pool, much to Dustin's delight.

"I suppose it's pointless to hope they just keep backing up all the way into the pool," Kyra said as she carried Dustin into the shallow end and fit him into the swim ring.

Max exchanged Maddie's arm for the shallow-end hand-rail. Setting his towel on the side of the pool, he inched his way down the steps and into the water, an unlit cigar in his free hand. "Ahhh." He sighed blissfully as he bent his knees and dunked his upper body, careful to hold the cigar aloft. "This is the life." He inserted the cigar into his mouth, reached into the towel on the edge of the pool, and pulled out a tiny replica of his own captain's hat. With a flourish he placed it on Dustin's head, tilting it at a jaunty angle. "Here you go." He smiled around the unlit cigar. "Now you're officially my second in command."

"Gax! Gax!" Dustin clapped his hands and laughed when he saw the splash that resulted. Kyra and the Lifetime crew filmed the scene. Even Nikki joined in the collective "awww."

"Despite the fact that it's still hours until sunset, I'd like to propose a toast," Nicole said, raising her glass. "To Avery and Deirdre, for their organization and splendid taste."

They raised their glasses and drank.

"To Maddie, for feeding and mothering us," Avery added.

They drank again.

Maddie and Kyra exchanged glances and raised their glasses to the others. "For being there," Maddie said.

Nicole was grateful that Madeline didn't bring up the subject they'd discussed on the beach now that she herself was so intent on numbing her brain enough to stop dwelling on it.

"You all are my 'one good thing.'" Maddie continued looking at each of them in turn. "For that reason—and because it's nowhere near sunset—I give you special dispensation not to have to come up with a good thing to share today."

"That's a good thing right there," Nicole said fervently, and getting a laugh.

Her phone rang and she beat back a surge of excitement as she moved toward the side of the pool to retrieve it. Giraldi had been out of town for almost three weeks and was due back today or tomorrow. "Can you reach my phone?" she called to Deirdre, who'd gotten out to retrieve the plate of hors d'oeuvres.

"Sure." Deirdre handed the still-ringing phone to her.

Nicole's finger was already poised to answer when she saw Amherst's name on the caller ID. She placed the phone back on the edge of the pool. The calls had tapered off and Amherst had finally stopped leaving messages, but she would be glad when the job at The Millicent was over and she could be completely rid of him. "Sales call," she said in answer to Deirdre's raised eyebrow.

Dustin and the guys splashed happily while the women talked. Once Troy and Anthony stopped filming and joined Andrew in the deep end, Avery got rid of the now-sodden T-shirt she'd been hiding behind. The alcohol began to flow more freely.

Nicole, whose thoughts kept straying to Joe Giraldi, felt a definite shiver of anticipation when the phone rang again. Until she realized that it wasn't hers, but Deirdre's.

"Hello?" Deirdre pressed the phone close to her ear, listening intently. "Oh."

She covered the mouthpiece and signaled Nicole, Maddie, and Avery closer. "It's Madsen Interiors in Chicago," she said. "They're calling about the chandelier. I'm going to put them on speakerphone."

"Ms. Morgan?" The voice was that of a young man, Nikki thought somewhere in his twenties, with a decidedly midwestern accent. "This is Jacob Madsen. I got a message that you called for our father."

"Yes," Deirdre said. "Thank you for returning my call."

"No problem." He paused before continuing. "Unfortunately, my father's no longer alive. My sister and I are the only family left in the business."

"I'm sorry to hear that," Deirdre said.

"Thank you. We're still getting used to being without him. He died a little over a year ago. A car accident."

Deirdre murmured additional condolences.

"Thank you," he said again. "I should be used to talking about it, but it's still such a shock. Our grandmother, the founder of the firm, was eighty, it was expected. But he was so young—only in his fifties."

The women looked at one another. It was slightly surreal to be standing in a swimming pool talking to a stranger about an unknown family loss halfway across the country.

"Anyway," Madsen said, "I understand you were looking for the name of a particular glass artist."

"Yes," Deirdre said clearly, relieved to discuss something less personal. "We're redoing a fabulous house down here in Miami; it's an Art Deco Streamline that your grandmother worked on back in the late fifties, early sixties. Does that ring a bell?"

"Not really," he said. "I mean, we all knew Grandmother lived in Miami before she came to Chicago, but she rarely talked about it."

"Oh." Deirdre's disappointment showed on her face. "We're actually looking for the artist that she commissioned to create a chandelier for the foyer. It's umbrella-shaped, made of Sabino glass, hangs from a starfish escutcheon and has eight panels—"

"—of sculpted sea creatures?" Madsen finished.

"Yes." Nicole could see Deirdre's excitement that Jacob

Madsen seemed familiar with The Millicent's chandelier, but was trying not to get her hopes up. "We've got our fingers crossed that the artist is still alive and might be able to re-create two panels that were damaged. Or that he might have something similar that we could hang in its place."

"It's a Jonathan Civelli," Jacob Madsen said without hesitation. "My grandmother was a great admirer and patron of his. His pieces have become very valuable."

"Oh, then—" Deirdre began.

"But I'm afraid he retired a long time ago. Last I heard he was in a nursing home somewhere in north Florida."

Deirdre's face wasn't the only one that fell. The chandelier had begun to feel like a symbol of The Millicent's glory days to all of them. "I know the subject matter and style are a little tropical for the Midwest, but do you know if your grandmother might have placed anything similar in another client's home?"

There was a pause and then the designer said, "Oddly enough, she placed one almost exactly like the one you described in hers."

Nicole noticed that Max had moved closer to Deirdre and was listening intently.

"It hung in the foyer of her home until the day she died. I never understood why she had this fanciful nautical piece in the entry of a suburban Chicago Prairie-style home. Especially given how *not* a fan of Miami she was.

"But no matter how many times she redecorated, she would never take it down. It was beautiful, but not of a piece with the whole, you know?"

"Yes," Deirdre said. "I do. But it obviously meant

something to her." She aimed a small smile at Max. "So where is it now?"

"I don't know," he said. "I haven't thought about it in years. But I can check with my sister to see if she knows what happened to it. She's the one who dismantled our grandmother's house after she died. I have no idea whether she sold it or put it in one of our warehouses."

Deirdre thanked the designer and hung up, her expression far more optimistic than Nicole would have expected. Given the way their luck seemed to be running at the moment, she estimated the chances that this particular chandelier was simply sitting in a convenient place waiting to be shipped off to them at zero-point-zero-zero-zero.

Chapter Thirty-one

"I can't feel my fingers anymore." Nicole held up her hands, which were bent like claws, as they staggered out of The Millicent to collapse around the pool. "I have to keep looking to make sure they're still there."

Their breathing masks hung down around their necks. Their knee pads were dark from the days spent kneeling and crawling from spot to spot as they hand-sanded the hard-to-reach areas of The Millicent's wood floors.

"I'd go for a swim, but I don't think I could get my clothes off or put on a bathing suit without the use of my fingers." Like the rest of them, Nicole's face was streaked with fine wood dust and dirt. "Actually, it's not just my fingers. I don't think I can move at all. Could someone please roll me into the pool?"

Maddie would have smiled except she didn't have the strength. Her shoulders and back ached from days spent hunched over as they'd hand-sanded around the upstairs baseboards, down the edges of the stairs, under cabinets and toe kicks, wherever the belt sander had been unable to reach. The physical exhaustion was made even worse by their inability to come up with a counter to Tonja Kay's threat. "We could probably get you in, but I'm not sure any of us have enough muscle left to get you back out."

Avery just grunted. When Chase had been unable to come down to Miami with the belt sander as planned, she'd rented one; then she and one of the younger Dantes had used it on the large expanses, while the rest of them—and their hand-numbing, sandpaper-wrapped blocks of wood— had tackled the rest.

"I must have blanked out how horrible hand-sanding actually is," Kyra said. "It was just last summer that we were doing the same thing at Bella Flora. But it all came back to me about fifteen minutes after we started."

"Yes," Madeline said. "It's like giving birth. If the brain didn't blot out the worst of it, we'd all be only children."

"Tomorrow we apply the stain and let it sit overnight," Avery said. "Then we'll do the first coat of polyurethane— I'm thinking Maddie and I can handle the upstairs and Nicole can do Max's room."

One, or possibly all, of them groaned. Funny how their mouths were moving while their bodies were so "not."

"That muriatic acid before sanding really got rid of the stains on the parquet," Deirdre said.

"You looked like an astronaut in the rubber gloves and boots and mask," Kyra said to Avery. "But the footage is really cool. I posted it on YouTube with the sound track from *2001: A Space Odyssey*." She laughed, something that had become rare of late. "It got a ton of hits."

Madeline stole a glance at Kyra. The furtive afternoon walks had ceased and Daniel Deranian hadn't shown up in

352 · WENDY WAX

or out of disguise since Tonja's threatening phone call, but all of them had been uneasy, waiting for the actress to make her next move.

Maddie had begun hoping that they'd be finished with the house and out of Miami before the woman began to throw her considerable weight around at the network. Maddie was not a religious person, but she'd taken to praying for some sort of miracle, one that would convince the Deranian-Kays that they didn't need another child in their menagerie.

"Mario said he'll have the Morrocan tile ready for staining and sealing by the end of the day tomorrow," Deirdre said. "I can work with him while you all finish the wood floors. That way we'll be ready to start on exterior painting at least a day sooner."

Maddie half expected Avery to take exception to Deirdre's interfering with her "schedule" or for her to point out that Deirdre didn't typically "do" manual labor, but Avery just said, "Thanks."

Deirdre's smile of surprise was quickly squelched, but Maddie knew she wasn't the only one who'd noticed Avery becoming less combative.

"Well, I'm taking a sleeping pill or something tonight," Nicole said, still eyeing the pool but not making a move. "Refinishing floors is bad enough. Dreaming about refinishing floors is cruel and unusual punishment. I swear I've been inhaling the dust and hearing that damned belt sander in my sleep. I say on the next house we hold out for a budget big enough to hire professionals to redo the floors."

"*We'll* be professionals by then," Avery said.

"If there *is* another house once Tonja Kay's finished with us," Kyra said, her tone doleful. "I keep trying to think what we could do that would stop her in her tracks, some secret or something that we could hold against her."

"Maybe she'll fold up her tent and go away if you make it clear she can't push you around," Maddie said.

"I don't think she's a folding-up-her-tent kind of person," Nicole said.

"Me neither," Deirdre said. "But there's no point worrying about things that haven't happened yet."

It sounded like something that should be stitched on a pillow. Or hung on the wall. But like most hand-stitched sayings, it was easier said than done.

Moving was no easier the following morning when Maddie awoke. Dustin was still sound asleep, but Kyra's bed was empty. Once she'd levered herself out of bed and through her morning toilette, she walked into the pool-house living area, where she found Kyra checking her camera and a pot of coffee already made.

They both looked up when Troy walked into the pool house with Max's morning paper. An odd smile twisted his face.

"I guess some things never change," he said, dropping the paper on the table in front of Kyra. "It looks like your boyfriend sees his movie sets as one big pickup opportunity." He went into the kitchen to pour himself a cup of coffee while he let the comment sink in.

Kyra took the paper and skimmed the headline. Her face went white.

"What is it?" Maddie asked.

" 'Daniel Deranian Caught on His Dressing Room Couch with a Young Production Assistant,' " Troy said. "A real shocker, huh?"

Kyra set the paper on the table and turned to him. Her

mouth was tight and her eyes welled with tears but her tone was combative. "What did I ever do to you that would make you feel so good about this?"

The question hung there for a long moment, filling the space between them, while Maddie skimmed the article.

"If you want to keep pretending like you don't know, I'll tell you," the cameraman said. "You got your job on Deranian's movie just like this assistant probably got hers." He gestured to the photo of the dark-haired girl, which had been positioned next to a publicity head shot of Daniel Deranian. "A good friend of mine was supposed to be the production assistant on *Halfway Home*." His eyes blazed with anger. "This was supposed to be her big break. She gave up other work. She was *on* that shoot. Until Deranian saw you come in to apply and decided he wanted *you* on the picture." His lips twisted into a sneer. "I'm sure he insisted they hire you because of your *obvious* talent."

Kyra's chin jerked up at the blow. Her eyes squeezed shut. When she opened them, the first tears oozed out. "I guess I'm as stupid as you seem to think I am," she said. "Because I actually thought they hired me because of my demo reel."

Maddie watched the tears slither down Kyra's cheek. She ached to wipe them away, but kept her hands occupied stirring sweetener into her coffee.

Troy's sneer faltered.

"You want to know what else?" Kyra asked him. "You'll really like this part. I thought Daniel wanted to sleep with me because he cared about me." She looked down at the newspaper before forcing herself to look back up into the cameraman's eyes. "And when he told me that he loved me?" Kyra continued. "I believed that, too."

The tears were in free fall now. Maddie felt her own eyes tearing up in sympathy.

"Stupid, huh?" Kyra sniffed but made no move to wipe away the tears that dampened her face. "I'm a frickin' moron."

Troy shifted his weight. The sneer had disappeared completely. It was clear this confrontation was not playing out the way he'd envisioned.

Kyra began to sob full-out.

Troy watched her helplessly for a few minutes and then he looked at Maddie as if for guidance. Maddie put her arms around her sobbing daughter and rocked her in her arms, trying her best to soothe her. But in the end, heartache, just like reality, was something you had to accept and somehow get through. Maddie had learned that one the hard way.

• • •

Nikki sat on the scaffolding, her legs dangling in front of her, her paint tray and brush at her side. It was ninety-eight degrees wrapped in a wet blanket of humidity. She was supposed to be painting around the porthole on the upstairs landing, but she was tired and sunburned to the point of crispy-critterdom. The only places she wanted to be were in front of an air-conditioning duct or in the pool, preferably both. If this hadn't been the last day of painting, she would have already jumped ship and never looked back.

In an effort to cool down, she poured the last of her bottled water on the bandanna she'd used to tie her hair back and tied it around her neck instead, but it was practically useless by the time she finished and offered little in the way of relief. It didn't smell all that great, either. For a minute she contemplated standing, tiptoeing to the edge of the scaffold, and threatening to jump. But she suspected Avery would just tell her to be careful not to hit The Millicent on the way down so as not to dent her newly smoothed plaster or mar any of her fresh white paint.

Her phone dinged and she reached for it. It was Amherst again. He'd taken to texting, which was far harder to ignore than the recorded messages. She refused to respond, but the texts were impossible not to read. This one said, *Sorry for awkward last meeting. Can we talk?* His cell-phone number followed. As if he actually thought there was some small chance in hell that she might call him back.

She dabbed the paintbrush in the tray and began to cut in around the edge of the circular opening. She'd finished the opening and was contemplating whether to move to the next assigned space or simply blow her brains out to escape the heat and boredom, when her phone rang. She perked up appreciably—and decided to continue living—when she recognized Giraldi's number. He'd been out of town far too much for her to pass up an opportunity to talk to him.

"All Girl Painting," she answered. "How can I help you?"

"Hi," Giraldi said. "How's it going?"

"Good," she said automatically. Which was mostly true if you didn't count the fact that they were all waiting for Tonja Kay to drop the other stiletto, that Amherst refused to disappear, and that she had no idea where she would go or live once The Millicent was done.

"You don't sound so good," Giraldi said.

"Well, we're painting the exterior and it's a wee bit on the warm side out here," Nicole said. "But we're really close to done. The paint company comes in behind us tomorrow. After that, all that's really left is placing the furniture and artwork, which is really Deirdre's thing. Apparently a small volunteer army has been raised to do the landscaping."

"Congratulations," he said. "That's quite an accomplishment. Why don't we take the boat out for dinner somewhere to celebrate?"

"Sure," she said, already imagining the feel of the breeze in her face and the wind in her hair. Giraldi's hands on her . . . "Oh, I almost forgot. You're invited to a celebration here, too. Maddie wants to break in the new kitchen. And we thought we might give Max the age progression of Aaron then if you can bring it."

"Absolutely," Giraldi said. "I left a message for the artist yesterday. I've been in and out of town so much that it's taken a lot longer than I anticipated. I didn't want to rush him since the work wasn't tied to a case."

There was the rumble of a truck out on the street. Nicole looked down to see a UPS truck angle onto the drive. Two guys climbed out and walked around to the back.

"Shall I come to your place?" Nicole asked, glancing down at her watch.

"Yes," Giraldi said. "I've got to run over to the Bureau to take care of a few things, then I'll come back and get the boat in the water."

They agreed to a time and Nicole hung up as the two UPS guys carried a crate up to the front door. They set it down carefully then rang the doorbell. She read the word stenciled across the top of the crate in big black letters: FRAGILE.

Nicole pulled her sweat-soaked tank top away from her body and stuffed her cell phone into her shorts pocket so that she could carry her paint tray to her next porthole. She got one last glimpse at the crate before the door opened and it disappeared inside. As she lifted her paintbrush and used the thick white paint to blot out The Millicent's pockmarks and age spots, she reflected on the black stenciled letters on the top of the crate and wondered how just hearing Giraldi's voice could make her feel so much less fragile than she'd felt before he called.

Chapter Thirty-two

"Rise and shine!"

"Oh my God!" Avery's eyes flew open and she stared up into Deirdre's face. She closed them again. "I'm sleeping," she mumbled, feeling around for the covers so that she could pull them up over her face. The painters had finished and The Millicent was in the process of drying. The gardeners wouldn't arrive until tomorrow. For the first time since they'd arrived in May, there was no rush to be up. If it weren't for the weight of Tonja Kay's threat hanging over them, she would have been savoring all that they'd accomplished instead of worrying that it was about to be snatched away. "Leave me alone."

It was quiet for a few moments, no footsteps retreating, no doors opening and closing, leaving her in peace. But she could feel Deirdre looming over her.

The smell of coffee, warm and full-bodied, teased her nostrils. She breathed in the scent and her eyelids fluttered open. Deirdre was fully dressed and completely made up.

Her eyes were that of a child eager for permission to go downstairs on Christmas morning to see what Santa had brought. Afraid she might be told no.

"What?" Avery snapped. She didn't know where Deirdre had gotten this ability to be so upbeat in the face of possible ruin. Unlike the oversize bust and lack of height, Avery had apparently not inherited Deirdre's positivity gene.

Deirdre waited for her to sit up then handed her the cup of coffee, already creamed and sugared just the way she liked it.

"Now I'm not only irritated, I'm suspicious. What do you want?" Avery sipped the coffee, barely resisting the urge to sigh over its wonderfulness.

"I've got Pamela Madsen's chandelier uncrated—Andrew helped me—and I just spoke with East Coast Electric," Deirdre said. "Ted's on his way over to help hang it." Her blue eyes glowed with excitement like that of an expectant child. "I'm so glad Max gave me permission to trade Millie's sterling-silver dresser set and the Limoges boxes for it. I can't wait to see it up. Kyra and Troy and Anthony are going to come shoot it being put in place."

Avery groaned. "You don't really need me for this."

"Come on," Deirdre said. "This is the crowning touch. I want you to be a part of it."

Avery gave an exaggerated yawn.

"Then he can install the kitchen light fixtures and we can start to position some of the furniture. There might even be time to hang some artwork in the dining room before tonight's dinner."

Avery took another sip of coffee while Deirdre whipped around the room, throwing open the blinds and pulling clothes out of the closet.

"And why don't you wear these?" Deirdre laid a pair of

capri jeans and a Miami Design Preservation League T-shirt on the edge of the bed. "There's absolutely nothing risqué or revealing about them, they just happen to be your size instead of two sizes too big."

Avery opened her mouth to object, but really, what was the point? She was tired of all the baggy beige; wearing it had begun to feel less like making a point and more like abject cowardice. The same was true of her reactions to Deirdre. Even a week ago she would have automatically refused to get out of bed; now she looked at the excited eyes, which were the exact same shade of blue as her own, and knew that refusing this too would be cowardly.

Deirdre must have read the decision in Avery's face, because she smiled and said, "Thanks. I'll give you a few minutes to get dressed, but I want you to come meet us in the foyer as soon as you can."

• • •

Maddie was alone in the foyer when Max came in to inspect the chandelier. It had been uncrated and rested on a furniture pad on the floor. The glass panels had been arranged on a card table beside it. Max studied the panels solemnly for several minutes then picked one up and, holding on to the wall with his free hand, carefully lowered himself to a seat on the stair. Maddie sat down next to him.

The panel was the one of two mermaids sunning on a rock—one tall and thin, one short and curvy—the figures sculpted in remembrance of a friendship that had been over for more than half a century.

Max rubbed a finger over the sculpted rock beneath the mermaids. Although he looked right at the panel, Maddie sensed that his thoughts were far away.

"Pamela came on to me once," he said without preamble, his gaze still on the luminescent rectangle of glass. "I'd realized for a while that she was noticing me in that way. Strange as it sounds, I don't think I meant all that much to her. I'm not even sure how much she liked me. But Pamela always seemed to want whatever Millie wanted. Sometimes I had the feeling she actually wanted to *be* Millie. Not that anyone ever could be."

He looked up to the hole in the center of the domed ceiling where the chandelier would soon hang, then at Maddie. "I turned her down and she didn't like it. She was a determined woman and she was used to getting what she wanted."

Maddie listened intently in the way she imagined a priest might listen to the confession of a long-held, and possibly damning, secret. Was there a Jewish equivalent to "say five Hail Marys and call me in the morning"?

"She persisted for a while," Max continued. "Just when I thought I was going to have to say something to Millie, she fired Pamela and that was that." He looked down at his gnarled hands, their misshapenness magnified behind the gold-flecked glass. "I told myself that Millie didn't know, that her getting rid of Pamela had nothing to do with me. And I was relieved that we never had to talk about it."

Maddie thought about Max's regret at not having allowed Millie to talk about their missing son. And his relief at not having to talk about Millie's best friend coming on to her husband. It seemed even the best-intentioned men shied away from the difficult conversations.

He turned to face Maddie. "I was so glad when I heard that Pamela had left town and so grateful that she went quietly. Pamela Gentry wasn't a leave-quietly-with-her-tail-tucked-between-her-legs kind of person."

Maddie reached out and squeezed Max's arm. "The more I hear about Millie, the more I wish I'd known her."

"She was something," he said wistfully. "Me, I don't care about Moroccan tile or bas-relief, or Sabino glass, but Millie did. I know she'd be glad to see this chandelier that she inspired sparkling and whole in its rightful place. Just like she'd be thrilled to see everything else you've done for the house she loved.

"Here." He handed her the panel and watched as she set it gently back on the table. Then he smiled and she knew the subject was closed. "I'm planning to stay right here for the chandelier raising if you want to sit with me. I think it's definitely the best seat in the house."

· · ·

By the time Avery arrived, a small crowd had gathered in the foyer. Troy and Anthony stood on the dining room side of the foyer opening. Kyra was positioned midway up the stairs, while Max and Maddie sat companionably on the bottom step. Andrew stood nearby waiting for instruction.

There were two ladders in position, one directly beneath the electrical juncture and another next to the first. A pulley had been rigged to hoist the new chandelier.

Deirdre nodded and motioned Avery closer as Kyra and Troy moved in for close-ups of the panels and their sculpted figures. There was no jockeying for position, no blocking the other.

Avery looked closely at the fixture. "The detail is exquisite. And Pamela had already replated hers," she said. "It's in far better shape than the original that hung here. But it is hard to picture this in a Prairie-style home in the suburbs of Chicago."

"We were lucky to find it," Deirdre said. "I can't wait to see it hanging and lit."

For the first time Deirdre's modesty didn't strike Avery as false. Deirdre had not allowed anything to stand in the way of finding and acquiring the chandelier and she seemed genuinely glad to have the piece for The Millicent, not to make herself look good, but because the project—and The Millicent—deserved it.

"It wouldn't have happened without you." Avery was surprised at the compliment as it left her lips. "You were like a dog with a bone. No one else would have gone to the trouble you did over one design element."

"I think that was a compliment?" Madeline sounded unsure.

Nicole pretended to look out the window. "Oh my God," she said. "It's been pushing a hundred for days, but I think hell is about to freeze over!"

"Very funny," Avery said. "She did a good job and I'm saying so. You don't have to make a federal case of it."

Madeline wore a strange look of satisfaction, but Deirdre's eyes glowed with . . . Avery didn't want to think a simple compliment could create all that happiness.

Max smiled and leaned on Madeline's arm as Deirdre began to direct the installation. "Okay, Ted's going to go up his ladder and handle the pulley. Andrew and Avery are going to each go up a ladder and steady the chandelier as it's raised."

Avery nodded at the efficiency of the plan, more than a little impressed by Deirdre's attention to detail. She could find no fault with Deirdre's approach and ability to orchestrate the installation. Even more surprisingly, she wasn't looking for one.

· · ·

Maddie spent the rest of the day cooking in The Millicent's new kitchen while Dustin played happily on the floor and everyone else flitted in and out in no discernible order to lend a hand or keep her company.

Giraldi was bringing the wine for that night's celebratory dinner and Mario had dropped off homemade tiramisu for dessert. He'd stayed for more than an hour to help Madeline with some of the intricacies of his recipe for veal scaloppine.

"It's not right for you to cook half the meal and not stay for dinner," Maddie told him when he bowed over her hand and told her what a pleasure it had been to work with and get to know her.

"It's completely right," he said in his heavily accented English. "I do not think workmen, not even the best of the best like me, are meant to be a part of the celebration tonight. It's for *famiglia*, family, and . . . what is it called . . . significant others like Giraldi." He looked into her eyes, a question in his. "Your husband, he is not coming?"

She looked down at her hand. "No, he couldn't make it," she lied, withdrawing her hand. The truth was, she hadn't heard from Steve since the phone call in which she'd told him off and she hadn't had the heart to call him. She knew the kids had spoken to him, but she had no idea whether he thought she'd simply come home when they were done here or had given her no thought at all. Resolutely, she pushed thoughts of their relationship aside to be dealt with after The Millicent was finished. She wished she could do the same with Tonja Kay's threat, but the actress was like a loose cannon that might ignite and blow a hole in them and their future at any time.

"Well then," he said with a smile. "I will say *arrivederci*. But I will count on us meeting again." A moment later he was gone.

Madeline went into the dining room to check on Kyra's progress.

The dining room credenza, table, and skyscraper-back chairs had been beautifully refinished. Ten place settings of Millie's Minton china and Reed & Barton silver gleamed atop a cutwork tablecloth. An arrangement of birds of paradise and white spider lilies plucked fresh from the yard sat at the table's center.

Maddie set out wineglasses and an ice bucket on the kitchen table and then began to toss the Caesar salad while Kyra pulled salad plates from the cupboard.

"This kitchen rocks," Kyra said. "I love the teak countertops and the wavy backsplash. The whole nautical thing is so cool."

Looking up, Maddie took in the beach-ball-shaped light fixture now hanging above the sink and the mass of clear bubbles floating on clear thread that dangled from the ceiling above the banquette, which had been re-covered in a sunshine-yellow leather. "I know, I'm not sure how Deirdre managed to make it fun and sophisticated at the same time," she said even as she tried to picture Max alone in here making his instant coffee and eating his meager meals.

She refused to try even to picture where the rest of them would be if Tonja Kay convinced the network to cancel the show.

"Have you heard from Daniel?" Maddie asked Kyra tentatively. Not long ago she'd wished that the celebrity would disappear. Now she wasn't sure how such a disappearance might impact them.

"No," Kyra said. "I haven't seen him since Tonja's phone call. And ever since the headlines about him and that production assistant, he's stopped answering my calls. I don't know if someone else is screening them or he's just not bothering to listen to my messages." She stopped looking at her hands and met Maddie's eye. "There was an article on one of the blog sites that said he and Tonja and the children were taking a vacation together.

"It's just like last summer when I was trying to reach him to tell him I was pregnant. Only now it's not just me and my future on the line."

And far too similar to Steve's behavior, minus the exotic vacation, Maddie thought, wondering for the second time that day why men so often opted for avoidance. She wanted so much more for Kyra and Dustin.

"I keep waiting for something to happen with the network," Kyra said. "I'd almost feel better if Lisa Hogan called and told us she'd heard from Tonja Kay and they wanted to cancel us so I could try to talk her out of it. Anything would be better than having the threat of cancellation hanging over us."

Maddie nodded. Like an invisible elephant in the room, Tonja's threat continued to infuse everything.

"Maybe she was just trying to scare us," Kyra said.

"Then she succeeded," Maddie said.

"Yeah." Kyra hesitated. "Do you think Daniel's new . . . affair . . . distracted her enough to lose interest in Dustin?"

"I don't know. I imagine they've left town to let things

blow over a bit, and put on a united front," Maddie said carefully. "But I wouldn't count on Tonja having a change of heart. The woman is not exactly rational or predictable."

"I know." Kyra shivered. "I can't stomach the thought of Tonja Kay having a hand of any kind in Dustin's upbringing. There has to be some way to stop her."

• • •

The scaloppine di Vitello alla Senese was a culinary success. There were actual moans of pleasure when the first bites of it were taken.

Giraldi kissed his fingers in a classic Italian gesture of approval. "This veal scaloppine is wonderful. Almost as good as my mother's," he said with a smile. "And that's saying a lot."

Madeline glowed at the praise and everyone's enjoyment of the meal. Max ate appreciatively. Dustin's face was smeared with the bits of pasta and veal that had been put on his plastic plate and that he'd been happily cramming into his mouth.

"I hope Millie's watching," Max said as he reached for a glass of the Borolo that Giraldi had paired with the main course. "She would love to see the house looking like this and her things being used by people who appreciate them."

"You know, Max, there are a lot of people who would love to see this house," Deirdre said. "I had a call from a Miami Design Preservation League tour volunteer who's interested in adding The Millicent to his tour of the Ocean Beach Historic District. And Lori Bakkum and Nate Miller are interested in hosting a mixer here to showcase the house now that it's complete."

Max listened but didn't comment.

"Then, if a time ever came when you wanted to put it on the market, it would already have a high profile. People would know its name."

"But I don't want to sell," Max said. "I promised Millie I'd leave it for Aaron. Now that it's ready, I feel even more strongly about saving it for him—or his offspring."

Maddie felt a tug of sadness. She looked around the table and knew they were all thinking the same thing. They had no reason to believe Aaron Golden was alive or had remained alive long enough to have children. Could they all simply walk away a week from now and leave Max sitting here alone waiting for a child that had most likely been dead for over fifty years?

Dustin began to fuss to get down from his high chair. The more mobile he became, the less he liked to be confined for long periods of time. Dustin held on to chair legs as he worked his way around the table toward Max. As they all watched, he flung his arms wide, shouted "Gax!," and took a long step toward the old man before plopping down on his diapered behind.

Max applauded and threw a big kiss to the little boy. "He's so close," he said. "Any day now he'll be walking." He fell silent and Maddie knew he was seeing his own child taking those first steps. "Aaron means 'strong' in Hebrew, you know," Max said. "And he was." He swallowed. "Maybe he still is."

There was a silence and then Giraldi got up and brought a large envelope over to Max. He removed a photograph and placed it in Max's hand. "An artist at the FBI did this from Aaron's last photos. This is what he would look like as an adult."

Max studied the photograph. His shoulders shook. Tears seeped out from beneath his lashes.

"We know it's not the same as having him back," Maddie said. "Or knowing what happened. But we wanted you to have at least something of him."

All of them were fighting to hold back tears, some more successfully than others. Maddie could barely see through the blur. Troy kept his camera pressed to his face. Even Anthony had buried his face in his equipment bag.

Max passed the photo around so that they could each see it. "He looks like me, doesn't he? I always thought he had Millie's nose, but it grew into mine." He smiled at that.

Maddie looked at the photograph when it came to her. The artist was skillful, the face complete and very real-looking. Her brow furrowed as she considered it. There was something about it . . . something familiar. She handed it back to Max and dismissed the thought. It was probably just how closely he resembled Max.

Max stood and said, "You've done such an incredible job on the house. I can never thank you all enough. Or tell you how much it means to me. And to Millie. You appeared in my life when I was feeling the most alone, and as far as I'm concerned, you're family now.

"I know what you're thinking about me holding on to the house," he continued quietly and with no sign of the comedian that he was. "I would probably think the same thing if I were you. But The Millicent has become my field of dreams. I just feel certain that now that the house is ready, Aaron—or at least some word of him—will come."

Chapter Thirty-three

Nikki woke naked and cocooned in the warmth of Giraldi's arms. It was early, the morning light just beginning to pierce the dark of his bedroom, and she sighed in quiet contentment. The first time he'd cradled her to him after lovemaking, pulling her bottom tight against him, tucking her head under his chin, and wrapping his arms loosely around her, she'd been so stunned that she'd lain awake all night afraid to move, afraid that she'd disturb him, afraid to believe that he'd wanted that closeness even after sex, when, so often in her experience, a man's tenderness ended with orgasm and reappeared only when he was ready for another.

Over the last months Giraldi had blown so many of her long-held beliefs about men that it was hard to keep her bearings around him. For a man whose career often called for subterfuge, he was amazingly direct. He enjoyed being with her and he told her so. He thought she was smart and appreciated her dry wit and he told her that, too. When they were together, his eyes didn't stray to younger, firmer women, though there were an infinite supply of them all over South Beach and she could tell from the looks they sent him that Giraldi could have had any or all of them that he chose. For all of the reasons he continued to spell out for her, but that she still couldn't quite grasp, he continued to choose her.

He pressed a kiss to the nape of her neck and she felt him come awake behind her.

"Mmm." The sound rumbled in his chest and vibrated against the bare skin of her back. His hands tightened across her abdomen.

She sighed and turned in his arms. Dark stubble covered his jaw. His eyes were warm and liquid. She felt a tug of desire as he pulled her closer. She kept her eyes open as he kissed her, intent on memorizing his face and the way he looked at her, refusing to think about how much she'd miss him and this surprising intimacy when it was time to leave Miami.

"How long do we have until you have to report for garden duty?" he asked, skimming a hand down the curve of her hip.

"Long enough," Nicole murmured, slipping her arms around his neck and pulling his face down to hers. "I'm hoping Maddie and Avery will be so busy organizing the volunteers that they won't even notice what time I get there."

"Perfect." He brushed his lips against hers and skimmed his hand up to her breast. "That's exactly how long I was planning to take."

• • •

By the time Nikki got to The Millicent, the street and grounds were already swimming in a sea of gardeners. After some aggressive circling, she pulled the Jag into a spot several blocks away and walked through the open gates. Madeline and a tall, thin woman with coffee-colored skin and a pith helmet of a sun hat stood at the top of the front steps preparing to address their volunteer workforce. The *Millicent* in all her freshly painted glory soared and curved behind them. Her windows and portholes sparkled in the sunlight. Her smokestacks seemed to signal "full speed ahead."

With a small wave to Maddie, Nikki wended her way through the crowd and back to the pool house, where she drank a glass of orange juice, ate a banana, and went inside the main house, hoping she was going to get to stay there. She found Avery and Deirdre in the living room contemplating paintings and artwork that leaned against the walls. A rolled-up carpet sat beside a sofa. Dustin stood in his playpen near the piano bending and straightening his knees, an exercise he seemed to be finding very amusing.

The sound of chain saws and lawn mowers wafted inside and the view through every window was of people at work. Unlike the gardeners that Renée Franklin had assembled to tame Bella Flora's jungle, these volunteers were not uniformly white-haired, and their style of dress, though utilitarian, was hipper and brighter. Every now and again, she caught a glimpse of Troy and Anthony moving around outside, filming the gardeners in action.

"Oh, good," Deirdre said when she spotted her. "The rug just got back from being repaired and I want to put it in place. But we need help moving the furniture."

Nicole, who would have agreed to anything that would keep her inside today, smiled. Her phone dinged and she glanced down. Her smile faded when she read Amherst's text, which was yet another, *I just need a few minutes of your time.* Putting her ringer on silent, she jammed the phone deep into her pocket.

Deirdre unrolled the carpet with the same excitement she'd displayed over every step of the renovation of The Millicent. "Just look at these colors," she exclaimed as the full pattern of the area rug was revealed. The geometric design on the cream background was done in vibrant jewel tones with a thread of black running through them.

"This looks great against the tobacco-color stain on the tiles," Avery said. "I didn't realize it had so much color in it."

"I know," Deirdre said happily. "I knew when I first saw it that it was spectacular, but rug repair can be dicey."

There was a knock on the back door. It opened and a woman, one of the gardeners, popped her head in. "Is there a bathroom I can use?"

"There's a guest bath off the kitchen." Deirdre directed her around the back of the house to the other entrance.

"Good thing the plumbing's been updated," she said when she came back. "But I wonder if we should have brought in a portalet for the gardeners. I had no idea we'd have this many people turn up."

"Maddie's out there with pitchers of lemonade and iced tea," Avery said. "Maybe we should tell her not to push the liquids quite so hard."

"It's almost one hundred degrees out there," Nicole said. "We don't want people passing out on the lawn."

"True," Avery said. "And I guess it's okay if the floors get a little dirty. The dark stain will camouflage a lot of it and I've got cleaners coming in before we leave next week."

Next week.

They all looked at one another.

They'd been so focused on finishing that no one had really talked about the future and their plans for it. Nikki had no life, no family, and no home to go back to. Unless you counted Bella Flora, which, at least until it sold, was still one-third hers. She caught herself thinking of Giraldi and chided herself for her wistful imaginings.

Following Deirdre's direction, they pushed the sofas and cocktail table out of the way and carried the two swivel chairs over near Dustin so that there was room to position the pad and then the area rug. Kyra showed up and shot footage of them at work as Deirdre had them move and reposition the furnishings far more times than seemed necessary.

When Deirdre finally seemed satisfied, Nicole plopped down on one of the sofas. Her phone buzzed and she pulled it out of her pocket, but instead of Giraldi, as she'd hoped, it was Amherst again. She swore under her breath and hit the decline button.

Avery shot her a questioning look and Nicole shrugged it off. "Time-share offer," she said. She turned to Deirdre. "What's next?"

"Well, I thought we'd go ahead and hang the artwork in here. Then if we have time we can start on Max's room. I bought new linens and towels for him and had his area rug cleaned. It was in a lot better shape than this one."

"Where *is* Max?" Nicole asked.

"I sent him out with Andrew," Avery said. "We have plenty of gardeners and I knew if Max was here he'd feel like he needed to be outside helping. He's ninety. I don't think spending the day working outside is a particularly good idea."

Maddie rushed in the front door, her hair sticking up at

odd angles and her clothes dirt-stained and sweat-soaked. "We're taking a break," she said. "I've got sack lunches for the volunteers to eat out around the pool. Can you all help me pass them out?"

They distributed lunches and drinks and left Maddie outside strategizing with the pith-helmeted master gardener while the volunteers sat in every available patch of shade and chatted quietly among themselves. Kyra retreated to the pool house to feed Dustin, then brought him back to the playpen. "If you're okay with it, I'm going to leave him here while I shoot a bit more outside," she said. "Call me if he gets fussy, and I'll take him and put him down for a nap."

After she left, Avery handed Nicole a hammer.

Deirdre held up an abstract of sinuous curves that hinted at a nude draped across a bed. "I'd like to hang this over the fireplace," she said. "What do you think?"

Nicole lost track of time as they followed Deirdre's instructions. They hung artwork and placed and re-placed lamps and accessories as Dustin watched from his playpen. For a while the hammering and rearranging held his attention, but then he began to whimper. Nicole looked over and saw him grinding a fist against one eye. "I'm no expert," she said, "but I think Dustin's getting tired."

Nicole texted Kyra, and when she got no response, she sent a text to Maddie, although she doubted Maddie would hear or feel a message coming in. And who knew what would happen if she decided to text back?

Troy came in and got some shots of them at work, then set his camera on the piano. He exchanged high fives with Dustin, which perked the little boy up for a while. "I'll be back in a bit," he said, preparing to leave.

"If you see Kyra, will you let her know we think Dustin may be ready for his nap?" Avery asked.

"Sure," Troy said as he headed outside, leaving his camera behind. "But somebody might want to check his diaper. I think I got a whiff of eau de poop."

Nicole crossed to the playpen and looked down at Dustin.

"I think you have to get a little closer than that to check his diaper," Deirdre said.

Nicole looked back at them helplessly.

Avery just shrugged. "Don't look at me. I have no experience whatsoever."

That made them statistically even, so Nicole leaned down over the edge of the playpen, pulled the waistband of Dustin's shorts away as she'd seen Kyra do, and gagged.

"Oh my God!" She clamped a hand over her nose and backed away.

"Don't be such a wuss," Avery said.

"You come here and deal with it, then."

"I can't, my hands are full."

Holding her breath and keeping her arms straight, Nicole reached out and grasped Dustin at the waist, intent on keeping the source of the smell as far away as possible. The back door opened and she turned around with relief, assuming it must be either Kyra or Maddie responding to her text.

Her relief fled when she saw that it was not a potential diaper changer but one of the gardeners. The man stepped into the room and closed the door behind him. He wore loose khakis and a nondescript, but grimy T-shirt. A baseball cap, pulled low on his head, shadowed his face.

"There you are," the man said as he moved into the room.

Nicole's head jerked up as she recognized the voice. Parker Amherst moved toward her.

"Watch out for the rug," Deirdre began. "We just had it cleaned and . . ." She stopped speaking when she, too, recognized Amherst.

"You haven't been answering my calls or returning my texts," Parker Amherst said to Nicole. He stopped in front of her. His voice was conversational. His eyes were dead.

Nicole's mouth went dry. She could think of nothing to say. Had he come for an apology?

"It's proven surprisingly difficult to get your attention." Amherst pulled a gun from his pocket as casually as he might a bunch of keys. "I thought this might help."

Deirdre and Avery gasped in shock.

"What's going on?" Deirdre demanded.

Amherst didn't answer. He pointed the gun at Deirdre and used it to motion her and Avery closer to Nicole.

"I'm sorry." Nicole tried to match Amherst's casual tone as she bent to put the baby down and hopefully out of harm's way. Her breath caught in panic when Dustin wrapped his chubby hands around her leg and used it to remain standing. "I've been . . ." She swallowed hard. "I've been busy. We're trying to get the house done."

"I had a house," Amherst said. "At least I did until your brother stole it." The matter-of-fact tone raised the hairs on the back of Nicole's neck.

Avery and Deirdre pressed closer to each other. She could feel their fear, as palpable as her own.

"The bank took it today," Amherst continued. "They kicked me out of the house my grandfather built, the house I was born in. The house my father blew his brains out in."

He let that one sink in. "I lost my fiancée because of Dyer, too."

The surprise must have shown on Nicole's face. He gave a harsh bark of laughter. "You really didn't do your homework, did you?"

"No." Nicole shook her head, but she did it slowly and without moving any other part of her body. Despite the calm tone, Amherst's eyes remained vacant. She did not want to spook him.

"After my father killed himself and word got out that he'd lost everything, she decided she didn't love me quite as much as she'd thought."

"I'm sorry to hear that," Nicole said, trying to sound sincere.

"I bet you are."

Dustin let go of Nicole's leg and stood there, getting his balance. She needed to get him out of the line of fire, but she was afraid that if she moved she'd set Amherst off.

Her phone began to vibrate in her pocket. She hurried to speak over the sound, afraid her only connection to the outside world would be taken away.

"I *am* sorry," Nicole said. "For what you've been through." Her heart was beating so frantically that she wondered if she might die of cardiac arrest before he pulled the trigger. "But I don't know what you want from me. I don't have anything you can take."

She felt Avery and Deirdre beside her, but was afraid to look at them. Her mind raced, searching for something that might resemble a plan, but the gun was too big and too close. Her palms were clammy. Her knees had gone weak.

"I'm here to give you one last chance to hand over the unrecovered money," Amherst said.

Nicole's brain raced but went nowhere. Should she pretend she knew how to get her hands on some money? Try to trick him into leaving with her so that the others would be safe? But where would she take him and how would she get away with it? And what guarantee did she have that Amherst wouldn't simply shoot everybody before he went with her?

From the corner of her eye, she saw movement outside. The yard was full of people. A broken window, a scream, could summon help. But anyone who came running would be easy to pick off.

"Well?" he asked, as if he were asking her to choose an item from a menu. He stood directly across from her, barely a foot away. The gun was aimed directly at her chest.

"I'm really sorry," she said in what had to be the understatement of the century. "But I have no idea where any of the missing money is. Believe me, I wish I did. Do you think I'd be working like a sweat hog if I had any money?"

She watched his face as he processed this. Dustin's hands on her leg loosened and she could feel him swaying next to her.

"Your brother stole my life. I'm not leaving until I take something that matters to him," Amherst said. "As far as I can tell, you're it."

Talk about not doing your homework. She would have laughed except for the way Amherst's eyes had dilated and the matter-of-fact tone he was still using to discuss his plans to end her life. She sensed Avery and Deirdre inching closer to each other. Dustin fell on his butt. Nicole held her breath while she waited for him to cry, but he simply put his hands around her leg and started to pull himself up again.

"I hate to break it to you," she said, trying to keep her

voice even. "But my brother really doesn't give a shit about me." This was the first time that admitting this came as a relief rather than an embarrassment.

"That's true." Avery spoke for the first time. "Her brother bankrupted her just like he did everybody else. And she practically raised him."

"It's a good thing you won't be having children, then," Amherst said in that spooky conversational tone. "Given what a crappy job you did with Dyer."

Nicole's mouth was so dry with fear that she could barely form words. Her life wasn't exactly full of Hallmark moments, but she wasn't ready to die. Nor was she about to let Dustin, Avery, and Deirdre die with her. "I can promise you he won't lose a second of sleep over my death."

"So you say," Amherst replied, waving the gun menacingly.

"No, it's the truth," Nicole said. "You don't want to commit murder for nothing, do you?"

Before Amherst could answer, the back door flew open and Kyra barreled into the living room, her attention completely focused on Dustin, who was teetering next to Nicole's leg. "Troy said you need to go night-night, little man," she cooed, already bending down and reaching toward her child.

"Hold it right there." Amherst brought her up short with a wave of the gun. "Step away from that baby."

Kyra straightened and took in the frightening tableau. Nicole's phone buzzed loudly from her pocket.

"Whose phone is that?" Amherst asked, his air of calm disintegrating.

No one answered and he waved the gun around again, growing more agitated. Kyra raised her hands in a sign of surrender and took a step back, but her eyes remained on Dustin. Her face was white with fear.

There was another loud buzz. This time Amherst looked right at Nicole. "Show me that phone."

She pulled it out of her pocket, stealing a glance at the screen as she did so. It was Giraldi.

"Throw it away from you," Amherst said.

Nicole tried to push the answer button as she tossed the phone toward the closest sofa. She missed the sofa and it skidded across the tile floor. She had no idea if she'd succeeded in answering or whether Giraldi would be able to hear and understand what was going on, if she had.

Dustin took a step toward his mother and fell. Kyra moved to pick him up.

"No," Amherst said. "Don't move."

Nicole was still trying to come up with a plan that didn't involve all of them dying, but she couldn't get her thoughts under control.

"It's me you want," she finally said. "Just let everybody else go. They're all Malcolm's victims, too. They haven't done anything to you." If her eyes hadn't been so glued to the gun and so dry from fright, she might have rolled them. She sounded like a character in one of those television police dramas. Except there was no guarantee of a happy ending before the closing credits.

Nikki was pretty certain that things couldn't get any worse when she heard footsteps in the foyer. Careful not to move her head, she cut her eyes in that direction and saw Madeline, with Max holding on to her arm for support, shuffling into the living room.

Nikki couldn't believe how long it took Maddie to grasp what was going on. She watched her take in the assembled group, saw her notice the presence of one of the volunteer gardeners, and then take in Dustin's excitement at Max's arrival. It was only then that she noticed the gun. Her eyes grew wide.

"Well," Amherst said, the creepy monotone replaced by a snide sort of glee. "It looks like the gang's all here."

"What's going on?" Max asked, letting go of Madeline's arm and taking a step toward Dustin.

The little boy said, "Gax!" and clapped his hands.

"Stop right there," Amherst said. "Nobody moves." His eyes darted between Nicole and the baby and Max.

"What's going on here?" Max asked again.

"He's trying to decide who to shoot!" Nicole raised her voice in hopes that Giraldi was listening. "He came here to shoot *me,* but now he has so many potential targets he's not sure how many of us he wants to kill!"

"Stop shouting," Amherst said, raising his own voice for the first time.

Nicole could practically feel all of their brains racing, but it seemed she wasn't the only one who had no idea what to do. This was when the cavalry was supposed to rush in. Or someone created a diversion so that the gun could be wrestled away from the madman. But they all just stood there frozen, waiting for him to decide whom to kill first.

All of them except Dustin.

"Gax! Gax!" He windmilled his arms like he always did to build momentum and took a drunken step forward. Then he took another one. He waved his arms again and took two more steps. Nicole could not believe the child had chosen this time and place to start walking.

Amherst's gaze was drawn to the baby. His gun arm followed.

Nicole felt Avery move next to her and the gun swung her way. "Stop!" Amherst shouted, swinging the gun between Avery and Dustin. "Don't move!"

Too many things happened then for Nicole to register them or the order in which they took place. Amherst squeezed the trigger at the same moment that Deirdre shoved Avery out of the way.

The smoking gun swung back toward the baby.

Nicole closed her eyes and launched herself at Amherst as Max moved and yelled, "Dustin! No!"

The gun went off again.

Nikki kicked and clawed at Amherst, operating on instinct and adrenaline as she tried to knock the gun out of Amherst's hands.

A body landed on top of Nicole, knocking the air out of her. There was a deafening crack and a flash of heat as the gun fired a third time. Amherst went limp beneath her.

Chapter Thirty-four

When she regained her senses, Maddie heard the wail of sirens in the distance and the sound of her own harsh breathing in her ears. Panic got her up off Nicole and onto her feet. She had to find Kyra and Dustin.

The front door burst open and Giraldi and Troy raced in.

"Don't let anybody else in until the police or the ambulance get here!" Giraldi barked over his shoulder as he moved quickly into the living room, his gun drawn. He strode toward Kyra, who was kneeling in the pool of blood that surrounded Max.

"Help me!" Kyra shouted. "I can't tell if Max is breathing or not. Dustin's trapped underneath him."

Maddie's heart seized up as Giraldi lifted Max's limp body off the little boy so that Kyra could reach her son. Maddie's heart began to beat again when Dustin's chubby arms reached for his mother and he began to wail. Breathing in a ragged sigh of relief, she took in the rest of the scene.

"Max has a pulse, but it's faint," Giraldi said as the sirens drew closer.

Deirdre sat up, clutching her arm, her face twisted in pain. Avery knelt protectively beside her. "Deirdre's shot," Avery said. Then, almost to herself, "She stepped in front of a bullet for me."

Giraldi crossed the room and knelt down next to Nikki, who lay crumpled on the floor. His manner was cool and professional, but his eyes flashed with relief when she raised her head and opened her eyes.

"Don't move," he said to her. "I can't tell if that's your blood or Amherst's. Just stay still until the paramedics get here."

"But I'm right on top of him," Nicole said, a note of hysteria in her voice.

Giraldi took Amherst's wrist between his fingers and felt for a pulse. "Doesn't matter," he said. "He's not feeling a thing."

Nicole scrambled up off the floor like someone shot from a cannon. "I'm not lying here on top of a dead guy."

The sirens sounded outside then cut off in midscreech. Two paramedics and a policeman rushed in through the front door. Giraldi flashed his badge.

"We've got one confirmed dead," he said, pointing to Amherst. "The lady took a bullet in the arm." He nodded toward Deirdre. "This is Max," he continued. "He's ninety. And he's lost a lot of blood."

The paramedics knelt around Max. Gently they turned him onto his back. His shirt was saturated with blood. His eyes remained closed.

"Is he breathing?" Maddie asked, praying that he was.

"Barely," Giraldi said as one paramedic worked to stabilize the old man. The other checked Dustin for injury, finally determining that the blood on the child belonged to Max, then moved to examine Deirdre.

"Gax!" The little boy shrieked as Max was carried out on the stretcher and placed in the ambulance. Deirdre was strapped in beside him.

Maddie's throat clogged with fear as Giraldi piled them into the minivan and followed the ambulance to the hospital. Troy and Anthony followed behind them.

Maddie looked back at The Millicent as they turned off Meridian onto Third and she wondered whether Max would be back. Or whether he'd even make it to the hospital.

. . .

They huddled together in the hospital waiting room for what felt like an eternity while the surgeons struggled to remove the bullet that had lodged in Max's chest.

They spoke little, staring at one another blankly as they waited for word. When the doctor finally came out to look for Max's family, it took all of their persuasive powers and Giraldi's badge to convince him that they were the closest thing to family that Max had.

"He lost a lot of blood and we think one of his lungs may have been compromised. He hasn't regained consciousness." The young doctor's eyes were weary. "It's possible he never will."

The hours passed slowly while they waited for Max to come out of recovery. Still numb, they tried to piece together what had happened.

"I don't understand where Amherst came from. Or why he would bring a gun and go after Nicole," Kyra said, cradling Dustin in her arms.

Nicole swallowed thickly. Her hands shook as she thought of how close they'd all come to death. How completely her fault it was. "Joe tried to tell me how squirrelly Amherst was, but I . . . I was so desperate to believe he was a potential matchmaking client that I refused to listen." She looked at the others whose lives she'd put at risk. "I had this weird encounter with him at his house where he tried to pick my brain about where the unrecovered money Malcolm stole was, but I didn't know that his family had lost everything to Malcolm.

"I wrote him off as a client after that, but when he kept calling and texting and wanting to get together, I figured if I didn't answer he'd just give up and disappear."

Giraldi's arm was strong and solid around her, but he didn't interrupt. He hadn't yet said "I told you so," and she didn't think he ever would.

"I hate to say it, but your visit to the Land of Denial almost got people killed," Avery said with a glance at Deirdre and Dustin.

"I lived there for a while myself," Maddie said. "And it's not a good place."

"I'm so sorry," Nicole said, though she knew the words were nowhere near enough. "Losing his family home today must have pushed him over the edge. I . . ." She felt the tears well in her eyes. Her voice broke. "I never meant to put you all in danger. I didn't realize . . ."

Giraldi pulled her tighter to him while she cried.

"So how did Deirdre get shot?" Andrew asked.

"She pushed me out of the way," Avery said. "I still can't believe she took a bullet for me."

"And then Dustin started walking toward Max," Maddie continued. "And Amherst pointed the gun at Dustin." She closed her eyes tightly for a moment. "Max threw himself on top of Dustin. He saved his life. Oh God, I hope Max isn't going to die."

Kyra slipped an arm around her mother's shoulders.

"I suspect he'd consider it a worthwhile exchange," Giraldi said quietly. "He loves that boy. And he never had a chance to save his own son."

There was a long silence.

"It's unclear whether the shot that killed Amherst was accidental or an attempt at suicide," Giraldi said.

Nicole grimaced. "All I could think about was trying to get the gun out of his hand. But I don't know what triggered that last shot. I thought I was dead when the gun went off. And I don't know how Maddie ended up on top of me, either." She expelled a shaky breath of air.

"That was pretty quick thinking keeping the phone line open when he made you toss it," Giraldi said. "I was able to call it in, but I was too far away to get there in time. When I heard those shots—"

"You're all lucky to be alive," Troy said.

Nicole knew they were all praying that Max would be lucky, too.

"It's almost too bad there was no camera rolling," Deirdre said. "Lisa Hogan would be eating all of this with a spoon."

There was a beat of silence.

"Who says there was no camera rolling?" Troy asked.

They all turned to the cameraman.

"Remember when I left my camera on the piano and said I'd be back?" Troy asked.

Nikki nodded along with the others, though she didn't seem to be thinking any more clearly now than she had been then.

"I've been doing that on occasion over the last few weeks," Troy went on, looking everywhere but at Kyra. "You know, leaving it sitting around." He paused. "Set to record." There was another hesitation. "It was the only way I could think of to get around the way you all clammed up when you knew I was shooting."

Kyra shook her head, but she seemed too dazed to engage in debate over the cameraman's tactics.

"We're not going to have to look at the footage right now, are we?" Maddie asked. "I'm already feeling sick to my stomach. I don't think I could take it."

"No, actually, the police took it," Troy said. "It's evidence."

Which made Max's living room a crime scene.

· · ·

It was dark out by the time Max had stabilized enough to be moved to ICU. Through the plate-glass window he appeared shrunken and far too small for the number of machines he'd been connected to. One of them forced his chest up and down. Another blipped with each heartbeat. Maddie watched for some sign of the Max that they'd come to love, but his eyes remained closed. Not even a finger moved.

Giraldi was still there when Chase arrived at the hospital that evening. The local news played on the waiting room television. They all went still when a shot of a reporter in front of The Millicent, cordoned off with crime-scene tape, appeared on the screen. None of them could look away as the details of Amherst's attack were relayed, including Nicole's relationship to Malcolm Dyer, the demise of the Amherst family fortune, and the fact that Daniel Deranian's son was almost killed by the madman.

A shot of the actor and his wife and their brood stranded in a Scandinavian airport because of the ash cloud from an Icelandic volcano followed along with a sound bite from Deranian, who was anxious to get back to Miami to see to the welfare of his son.

The report concluded with a shot of the *Do Over* cast and crew members taken at the premiere party, which faded into a final shot of the paparazzi out in front of Mount Sinai Hospital at that very moment jockeying for position.

They were still sitting in the hospital late that night when Steve finally called. "Are you all right?" he asked Maddie after he'd spoken to Kyra and Andrew. "I'm sorry, I didn't pick up your messages until just a few minutes ago and I haven't had the television on."

Maddie stepped away from the group and carried her cell phone out into the hallway. "You were a lot quicker to call when you wanted to criticize me for my lack of supervision," she said. "But then I guess that's what happens when you get used to taking your time returning your family's calls. You miss a few near-death experiences now and then."

She heard the bitterness in her voice and sighed. In the waiting room, Chase held Avery's hand while Deirdre, her arm in a sling, sat beside them. Giraldi and Nicole huddled close together. His arm was slung across her shoulders. Maddie had never felt so alone.

"Andrew can pick you up at the airport," Maddie said

in a less combative tone. "What time does your flight get in?" She began to work out the logistics in her head.

"Actually, I'm not going to be able to come right now," Steve said. "I have important meetings that I just can't miss or reschedule. Not now when I'm working so hard to build a client base."

"Steve, we just barely survived an attack by a crazed gunman. Dustin and Kyra and I could have died. Max may never wake up. I really can't believe—"

"But everyone's okay. You all are fine. And Max is ninety; every time he goes to sleep, chances are he won't wake up."

She listened in silence, unable to believe he wasn't already on his way to the airport, that he wasn't planning to come.

"And you're so strong, Mad. You're practically the Rock of Gibraltar." The words were offered as a compliment, but she heard what lay beneath them. He still had not forgiven her for keeping it together when he had fallen apart. He hated that she was strong in ways he was not.

She hung up and walked slowly back to the others. They all looked at her expectantly.

"When's Dad coming down?" Andrew asked when Maddie had returned to her seat.

"He's not."

Kyra held tighter to Dustin, who'd fallen asleep on her shoulder. Her lips pursed in disapproval.

"What an asshole," Andrew said.

Maddie couldn't have agreed more. She said only, "He's your father and he loves you."

"Well, he has a strange way of showing it," Kyra said.

Maddie had no answer for this. She was not inclined to defend Steve, but she also knew this was not the moment to grapple with her husband's place within their family. But deep in her heart she wondered whether there was enough of "them" left to hang on to.

Kyra's cell phone was the next to ring.

"It's Lisa Hogan," she mouthed as she answered.

All of them watched as an odd sequence of expressions flitted across Kyra's face.

"We were fighting for our lives," Kyra said curtly. "My child was almost killed right in front of me."

Madeline watched her daughter struggle to hold on to her temper.

"No," Kyra bit out. "I wasn't shooting at the time. You'll have to check with Troy about that."

Kyra's look turned incredulous. "No," she said. "I don't have my camera with me right now." She shook her head in disbelief. "And I'm fairly certain they don't allow cameras, lights, or audio in ICU."

Kyra hung up. "Lisa Hogan and the network are extremely worried about all of us and wanted to know how we are." She snorted. "I have this really disturbing feeling that she would have been okay with at least one of us biting the dust. As long as we did it on camera. I'm glad I won't have to watch her happy dance when she finds out about Troy's footage."

The next call was also for Kyra, and from what Maddie could see, it was even more disturbing.

"He's fine," Kyra said. "Dustin is absolutely fine." And then, "I would have called, but I've had such a hard time getting through lately I thought maybe you'd changed your number."

Kyra listened, her shoulders tightening and her face growing dark. Once again Madeline saw her struggle to hold on to her temper. Maddie looked around the waiting room; they were all straining to listen while trying to pretend not to.

"No, this is not a perfect example of why Dustin would be safer with you," Kyra said. "This is a perfect example of a crazy person with a grudge and a gun."

There was more listening and face scrunching.

"No. I'm not okay with that. No. Really, that's not a good idea. I . . ." Kyra closed her eyes and fell silent.

The waiting room had emptied except for their group. They exchanged nervous glances, but no one seemed worried about being caught listening. Maddie was watching Kyra's face when she saw a speculative gleam come into her daughter's eyes.

"You know," she said now, "the more I think about it, the more I guess maybe that would be okay." A small smile stole onto her face, but her voice remained tentative, as if she were being talked into something against her will. "All right," she said. "Okay. I'll see you then."

She hung up and slipped her cell phone into her pocket then folded her arms across her chest.

"Well?" Maddie, Nicole, Avery, and Deirdre demanded as one.

"Well," Kyra said. "That was Daniel calling from Norway. He and Tonja are waiting for the ash cloud to pass. As soon as he can get here, he intends to come and see for himself that Dustin is okay."

. . .

Two days later Max opened his eyes for the first time. They were cloudy and uncertain and stayed open for only a matter of seconds. Nicole couldn't tell what, if anything, they'd registered, but she texted the achievement to the others and promised to let them know if anything more happened. Though she stayed in the hospital the rest of the day until Maddie came to take over, there wasn't so much as a flutter of his eyelashes.

Occasionally, she stood up and paced the tiny space, wishing she could wake Max up so that she could apologize for being Malcolm's sister and for bringing Parker Amherst into everyone's life. Most of all she wanted to tell him that he was a hero and that his heroic act had saved Dustin's life.

The machines hissed and beeped and his chest continued to rise and fall, but Nikki thought he looked smaller and less substantial by the hour. As if the machines were sucking the life out of him a little at a time rather than restoring it.

. . .

The crime-scene tape had been removed and most of the blood in the living room cleaned up. The Millicent looked more beautiful than it ever had, but it was a hollow beauty without Max there to fill it up. They sat around the kitchen table picking at the remains of breakfast, a meal Maddie had cooked halfheartedly and that they'd consumed in the same spirit. Other than taking turns sitting at the hospital waiting for the brief intervals during which they were allowed to sit in Max's room, trying to will him into consciousness, none of them were sure what to do next.

"Well, I'm going to have to replace that living room rug and I want to rehang Max's wall of fame and get his bedroom ready for when he comes home," Deirdre said when the dishes had been cleared away. "I had all the photos rematted and his chair and ottoman reupholstered. They just have to be set in place."

Everyone looked at her for a long moment, but it was Maddie who gave voice to their fear. "What if he never comes home? What's the point when he may never even see the house again and has no one to leave it to?"

"We'll get it ready for Aaron because he promised Millie he would," Deirdre said. "Everything is just a leap of faith now. It wouldn't hurt us to try to have some."

They exchanged glances. No one disagreed with the sentiment, but it was hard to dig down that deep underneath the worry and sadness.

"I liked the movie *Field of Dreams* as much as the next person," Nicole said. "But I don't think it's a philosophy to live by."

"Well, right now it's all we've got," Deirdre said. "I'd do his room myself, but I only have one good arm at the moment. And I know Maddie's planning to spend the morning at the hospital." She looked pointedly at Avery.

"Jeez," Avery said. "The woman saves my life and now she thinks I'm supposed to be her slave or something."

"Damn straight," Chase said. "She did take a bullet for you."

"I'd settle for temporary slave." Deirdre paused then added tentatively, "And maybe full-time daughter?"

Avery looked away for a moment, the hope in Deirdre's eyes impossible to ignore. Chase and Andrew excused themselves. Displaying a heretofore unsuspected degree of tact, Troy and Anthony went with them.

Avery faced her mother and finally said, "I'll be your

slave for the day. Maybe we could just let the rest play out."
She cleared her throat. "You know, see how it goes."

Deirdre nodded, her eyes brimming with tears.

"Oh, man," Avery said. "Don't go getting all weepy on
me. It's not like I'm offering you a kidney or anything."

Maddie smiled at both of them, looking kind of weepy
herself. "I'm proud of you two," she said.

Deirdre swiped at the tears and smiled. "If I'd known
how effective a crazy guy with a grudge could be at the
beginning of the summer, I might not have needed the
classes."

They laughed as they left the table, but the laughter was
uneasy and short-lived. They were still too close to the
nightmare they'd shared. All of them were aware of just
how much damage that crazy guy had done. And they had
no idea how far the Deranian-Kays would go to make
Dustin their own.

· · ·

Later that morning Maddie sat next to the hospital bed
watching Max's chest go up and down, trying not to look at
the tubes, monitors, and machines, but deep down inside the
man who lay there. The ICU nurse came in to replace a bag
of fluids, her manner professional but kind. Her name tag
read NANCY. "His vitals are up a bit," she said. "He opened
his eyes again this morning when the doctor came through."

"Thanks," Maddie replied. She would have liked to cling
to this little bit of positive, but the doctors had been frank.
They were doing everything they could to ward off infection
and keep Max comfortable, but they didn't hold out much
hope.

"Max," she said when the nurse had gone. "We wanted to make sure you know that Dustin is okay because of you. You saved his life." She waited for him to respond, holding her breath so that she could hear even the faintest sound. But if she'd convinced herself that this news would wake him up like the prince kissing Sleeping Beauty, she'd been mistaken. Max didn't move or blink. His chest continued to rise and fall only because a machine had taken over the chore.

Madeline stared down at the photos that she'd put in frames and brought for him. There was a favorite shot of Millie, several of Aaron as a baby and toddler, and one of the three of them. She studied the age progression Giraldi had had done and traced a finger over the face that was so like Max's. She arranged the photographs on the nightstand next to his bed so he wouldn't feel alone if he finally woke up and none of them were there.

Sensing movement, she stopped arranging the photos and looked up to see Max watching her. His eyes fluttered shut then opened again.

"Hi, Max," she said, sinking back down into the chair. "Did you hear what I said?" She spoke quietly and clearly, trying not to rush in her excitement to communicate before he disappeared again. She had been fantasizing that this news would wake him up completely. Heal him. Send him home to The Millicent. "Dustin is okay because of you. He keeps asking for his 'Gax.' You saved his life. *You* did. Everyone else is okay. The Millicent is ready." She was rushing now, trying to cram in every positive thing she could think of while he was still present.

"We're all just waiting for you to come home," she finished as his eyes fluttered shut.

She waited for some time, sitting on the edge of the chair, preparing what she'd say at her next opportunity, but his eyes remained shut. She texted everyone the good news and tried to do what Deirdre had suggested. But locating the faith underneath all the dire things that loomed proved even harder than she'd expected.

. . .

Back in the waiting room, Madeline woke to a hand on her shoulder. She opened her eyes to see Kyra peering down at her.

"Did he wake up again?" Kyra asked.

"No." Maddie rubbed the sleep out of her eyes then looked at the clock on the wall, unsure how long ago she'd nodded off. "I kept hoping he would, but that was it."

"It took us a while to figure out what 'Mix geys pipen' meant." Kyra smiled. "But we were all pretty excited once we understood your text."

Maddie groaned. "Seriously. They need to make keyboards for the clumsy like they make touch-tone phones for the elderly—great big backlit squares with glowing letters would be really helpful."

"Or you could just take a quick look before you hit send."

"Yeah," Maddie said, "but where's the fun in that?"

Kyra sat down next to her. Their smiles faltered.

"I don't know, Mom," Kyra said. "Do you think he's going to get better? Everything's such a mess. And I feel like there's no good end in sight."

"I know," Maddie said.

Kyra hesitated a moment before continuing. "All I could think about when Dustin was in danger was how I would never be able to live without him. I don't know how Max and Millie did that for all those years." She worried a loose thread on the hem of her shirt. "I just can't put Dustin in Tonja's hands. I don't think she's said anything to Lisa Hogan yet, do you?"

"No," Maddie said. "I suspect she's hoping that the threat of losing the show will be enough to get you to go along with whatever they want." She brushed a stray bit of bang off Kyra's forehead. "Despite the number of children in their household, I'm not sure Tonja Kay really understands the strength of the maternal bond."

"Frankly, I'd just tell her to go ahead and give it her best shot. Dustin and I could live without the show if we had to, but I don't feel like I have the right to play around with everybody else's future."

Madeline looked around her at all the people sitting in the hospital waiting room hoping and praying for the ones they loved. Some things—the trajectory of a bullet, the ferocity of a disease, the skill of a surgeon—were beyond your control. All the more reason to act when you could.

"Last year when your dad lost everything to Malcolm Dyer and our life fell apart, I learned that it's almost always better to take action than be acted upon. Even if the outcome of that action is less than perfect."

She smiled and reached a finger under her daughter's chin, tilting it up, like she had when Kyra was small and Madeline wanted to see the understanding dawn in her eyes. "We're all a lot stronger than you think," Maddie said. "And that includes you."

Kyra looked away, her gaze drawn to a television set airing what looked like a re-run of *Biography*. Scratchy black-and-white film of a young William Randolph Hearst filled the screen. The audio was low, but the voice-over seemed to be describing the visuals as recently unearthed footage shot without the mogul's knowledge.

Maddie saw the gleam that lit Kyra's eyes. It was followed by a pensive look. "You know," Kyra said, straightening, "I think I'm going to talk to Troy." She smiled. "He's not quite as big a pain in the ass as I thought—and I have an idea that I think might help convince Daniel and Tonja to back off."

Now Kyra was searching Maddie's eyes. "But I have to ask you a favor. For once, you have to try not to be my mother. You have to just trust me. Even if what I'm doing seems weird, I need you to have faith and follow my lead."

Chapter Thirty-five

The paparazzi who once again littered the sidewalk in front of The Millicent buzzed with happiness when Daniel Deranian arrived. When they saw who was with him, they went berserk with joy.

Maddie heard the shouts from outside and drew what was intended to be a calming breath. "I guess he didn't come in disguise," she said as camera flashes went off outside, turning the Miami sky even brighter.

"No," Kyra said as they walked to the door. "And he didn't come alone."

Maddie glanced over her shoulder to make sure that Nicole, Avery, and Deirdre couldn't be seen from the foyer and ran sweaty palms down the sides of her best capris.

With her hand on the knob, Kyra said, "Remember, I have a plan. No matter what happens, no matter what gets said, just follow my lead. Okay?"

Maddie nodded warily. But she was grateful for the warning when Kyra pulled open the door and Maddie saw

Daniel Deranian and Tonja Kay standing side by side on the welcome mat. Two bodyguards stood directly behind them, blocking out the sun.

If she'd been Catholic, Maddie might have crossed herself. Or perhaps held up a crucifix to ward off the almost otherworldly beauty that stood in front of them. Daniel Deranian was dark-haired and golden-skinned, while Tonja Kay was shades of blond and alabaster. Together they were the yin and yang of gorgeousness, the male and female embodiments of physical perfection.

Daniel Deranian wore expensive jeans and a plain white T-shirt that clung to his well-defined chest and abs. His dark hair looked intentionally unruly and his angled cheekbones carried a hint of five o'clock shadow. He carried a gaily wrapped box for Dustin, and when he treated them to a flash of his famous smile, it carried a warmth that didn't quite stand up to Tonja Kay's icy perfection.

The actor nodded his hellos, but there were no hugs or air kisses as the power couple posted the bodyguards on the front stoop and stepped inside.

Kyra gritted her teeth but didn't speak as Tonja Kay looked right through her.

"I'm Maddie, Dustin's grandmother," Maddie said to the actress. "We've spoken on the phone."

A raised eyebrow and a sniff served as Tonja Kay's reply. The only real reaction from either of the celebrities took place in the living room when Daniel swept Dustin off the floor and up into his arms.

The child chortled happily as the movie star swung him around and then presented him with the gift.

Tonja watched them cavort with a tight little smile that in a less attractive person might have been attributed to gas. Then she took in her surroundings. Madeline followed her gaze and saw her surprise before she schooled her features. A flicker of movement behind Max's partially opened bedroom door drew Maddie's attention, but she shrugged it off to nerves.

The only truly comfortable person in the room seemed to be Dustin, who was tugging on the ribbon of his gift. Kyra took a seat on the sofa closest to the fireplace and motioned the two celebrities to the sofa opposite. Daniel sat Dustin beside him and helped him unwrap the gift.

The room practically pulsed with tension and Maddie hoped Kyra actually had a plan of some kind and was not merely hoping to persuade these two, who were used to getting whatever they wanted whenever they wanted it, to see reason.

"Mom," Kyra said, "would you mind making a pot of coffee for all of us?"

"Um, sure." Maddie looked at Kyra, but her daughter was watching Tonja Kay watch Dustin and Daniel.

"Their faces are almost identical, aren't they?" Kyra observed. "I'm sure girls will be crazy about him when he's older just like they are for his dad." She paused briefly. "Of course, as his mother, I plan to make sure he has a little more sensitivity and a lot more restraint than his father does."

There was a sharp intake of breath. Maddie wasn't sure if it was hers or Tonja's or possibly the room itself gasping in surprise. She shot her daughter a look of warning, but Kyra's attention was fixed on Tonja Kay.

"Honestly," Kyra said. "I don't know how you put up with Daniel's . . . indiscretions. I know I never could."

Madeline hotfooted it to the kitchen. Nicole, Avery, and

Deirdre sat around the banquette, where Deirdre had spread out the contents of the "House" envelopes. Photos, sketches, and drawings were strewn across the table.

"Come sit down," Nicole said. "We're dying to hear what's going on out there."

"We tried the glass against the dining-room-wall thing, but the walls are too thick," Avery said.

"And Deirdre threatened to maim us if we messed up the paint," Nikki added. "Did you know Tonja was coming?"

"No! I don't really understand what Kyra's up to. When I left, she was baiting the woman, which seems like a really poor idea."

Maddie went to the coffeemaker and attempted to still her shaking hands with the familiar tasks of fitting a filter into the basket, scooping coffee into it, and pouring water into the reservoir. She looked at the others. "I hope she knows what she's doing."

"Everything will be okay," Deirdre said. "And if it's not, we're here to help."

"What's Tonja Kay like?" Nikki asked.

"Cold," Maddie said automatically. "Almost angelic-looking, which is really weird given the phone conversations I've had with her." She flipped the brew button and took an empty seat at the kitchen table. "I need to think about something else right now. Tell me what's going on here."

"I'm cataloging The Millicent's art and furnishings," Deirdre said. "I thought I'd use it for the basis of an article about Hohauser's design from the perspective of someone living in one of his homes today. I also want to write about Millie and Pamela Gentry's additions to the house. Pamela was extremely talented and she and Millie created an incredible space together. The article would draw attention to the house and could be a very positive promotional tool for *Do Over.*"

Maddie glanced at Avery, who would normally have already pointed out that it would be a promotional tool for Deirdre, too. Even Deirdre paused, eyebrow raised, but Avery just stirred more milk into her coffee.

"And of course, the Realtors could use the catalog to help market the property," Deirdre concluded.

"You were the one who told us we should have some faith that Max would recover and that there'd be someone he could leave the house to," Madeline said, trying to focus on the conversation here rather than straining to hear the one taking place in the living room.

"I know and I meant it," Deirdre replied. "But that doesn't mean we shouldn't be as prepared as possible. Just in case."

They fell silent as they all contemplated what "just in case" was a euphemism for. Madeline couldn't bear thinking about this house—and them—without Max. Once again she caught herself straining to hear what might be happening in the living room. All she could hear was the low murmur of voices and the occasional exclamation from Dustin.

Maddie looked down at the closest pile of photos and papers and picked up a photo of Pamela's chandelier. Which had hung in her home in Chicago, where she would see it every day. As a reminder of . . . what? A friendship she still treasured? A house she'd put so much into but had never, in fifty years, mentioned to her family? Or a double rejection?

Why would a designer of her caliber cling to a piece that would be so out of place in her own home?

"Doesn't it seem odd that Pamela Gentry had an identical chandelier made for herself? Have you ever done that, Deirdre? Copied something you had made for a client?" Maddie asked.

Deirdre shrugged. "The more custom and personalized the item, the less likely a designer would be to do that. But it's certainly not unheard of. All things considered, I'm glad she did."

Madeline slid the sheet to the back and studied the shot of Pamela Gentry receiving her design award, which shared a page with her obituary. On another sheet of paper was a printout of the Madsen Interiors home page, which included a grainy black-and-white publicity photo of Pamela Gentry Madsen and her son, Ethan, when he was named managing partner of the firm. She peered more closely at the mother and son. From what she could see, Ethan must have resembled his father; his features didn't run to the gamine like Pamela's did and he had none of her lean ranginess.

"Mom?" Kyra's voice was easily heard from the living room. "I think we're ready for that coffee now!"

"Yikes." Madeline set the photos aside. With nervous fingers, she set mugs of coffee on a tray, added a small pitcher of cream, a bowl of sugar, napkins, and a couple of spoons, then picked up the tray and carried it as far as the dining room. Nicole, Avery, and Deirdre gave up all pretense of working on the catalog and followed her. She drew a deep breath of air and expelled it slowly. The spoons stopped rattling.

"We'll be right here if you need us," Avery said.

Nicole gave her a smile. "Everything will work out."

"It'll be fine," Deirdre said.

Madeline left them huddled in the dining room, their ears, rather than water glasses, pressed to the wall. "Here we go," she said far too gaily as she sailed into the living room and put the tray on the cocktail table just out of Dustin's reach.

Kyra and the Deranian-Kays sat right where she'd left them, beautiful bookends with irritated looks on their faces. Dustin played with a new car on the carpet near his father's feet.

Out of the corner of her eye, Maddie thought she saw a flash of something in Max's bedroom. When she looked more closely, it was gone.

"Coffee?" Kyra asked.

Tonja and Daniel declined. Kyra shrugged and served herself a cup. "Mom?"

"Um, sure," Maddie replied, though she couldn't imagine drinking a drop.

She watched her daughter pour and stir in cream and sugar. Kyra handed one of the mugs to Maddie then took a long sip of her own. Maddie had the impression that Kyra was playacting, trying to set some sort of scene or mood. She hoped her daughter remembered that the people she was facing were professionals.

"Daniel and Tonja have been laying out all of the things they can do for Dustin," Kyra said. "You know, like A-list birthday parties with other celebrity children, world travel, mind-broadening experiences, his own room in each of their five homes, and his own personal nanny. Each of their kids has one."

"Yes," Daniel said, eager to capitalize on this selling point. "Tonja interviews and hires them all personally. Each of them has to speak the language of the individual child's country of origin."

Kyra shot him a look.

"Of course, in Dustin's case that would be English," he added hastily.

Kyra said brightly, "That should broaden the pool of applicants. And keep at least one job from going 'offshore.'"

"Yes," Daniel said. "Most importantly, we want what's best for our children and for Dustin."

Maddie bristled at the implication that Kyra and her family did not. Kyra did the same.

"And that includes keeping him safe." He looked and sounded impressively sincere.

"Which is something *you* have failed to do," Tonja said with a certain amount of heat beneath the icy exterior. The two had a certain "good movie star, bad movie star" thing going. "Our bodyguards would have never allowed that weirdo to get within a mile of any of our children."

"Except Dustin's not yours, is he?" Kyra asked.

Tonja's lips pursed. Her eyes flashed with irritation.

Kyra smiled at her and then at Daniel.

Maddie could barely drink her coffee without sloshing it, but Kyra actually seemed to be enjoying herself.

She leaned forward and said, "What I've really been wanting to ask is where you all went on vacation after Tonja found out Daniel was sleeping with me."

The room went still. Tonja Kay and Daniel Deranian's surprise shone in their eyes. Neither of them moved.

Maddie shifted uncomfortably in her seat. She thought she heard shushing sounds from the dining room.

"I mean, I was thinking about how I saw that photo of you

two on vacation on some beach somewhere while we were still at Bella Flora, but it really never said where. This time, after the assistant on the Miami film, you took the whole family to Scandinavia." Kyra paused as if waiting for an answer.

"What the fuck?" Tonja said, more in amazement than anything else.

Daniel put a hand on his wife's arm. "Women come on to me all the time," he said. "I haven't always resisted like I should." He smiled like a child admitting he'd had one too many sweets. Or who'd been caught with a hand in the cookie jar.

"Yes," Kyra added, in a conversational tone that did not match the tilt of her chin. "I saw an article recently in which you described celebrity of a certain magnitude as a kind of sexual all-you-can-eat buffet."

Maddie did not want to think about where her daughter had fit in all of this; was she a small but tasty appetizer? A chocolate dessert? She remained silent, telling herself Kyra was going somewhere with this, though she couldn't imagine where.

Tonja shrugged off her husband's arm.

"Would you agree with that, Tonja?" Kyra asked. "That celebrity entitles a person to sleep with whoever they want whenever they feel like it?"

The blonde's jaw clenched. Her overplumped lip curled. It seemed the ice maiden had begun to melt from within.

"I may not be the greatest husband fidelity-wise," Deranian admitted. "But Tonja has been very understanding and . . . supportive." He offered this as if it were a glowing testimonial to his wife.

Kyra kept her gaze fixed on Tonja's face. Two angry spots of color dotted her pale cheeks.

Maddie looked at the husband and wife. They were both very talented actors, but they had very different styles. Daniel always seemed to be playing "everyman" and wanted to be universally liked; Tonja seemed far less inclined to perform at all. Especially not for people lower down the food chain than herself. Which was, of course, pretty much everyone else.

Kyra leaned toward Tonja, still acting as if they were having a friendly conversation. "You must be running low on exotic places to trot out your family for the press," she said. "Given how often he screws around on you."

"Fuck this shit!" Tonja exclaimed, moving to stand. Her husband put a hand on her arm.

"I think we're getting a little bit off topic here," Daniel said, cutting his eyes to Tonja.

"I don't know," Kyra said. "I would think your relationship would be kind of key to what sort of home environment you provide for your children." She shrugged. "I mean, what sort of example are you setting?" Her tone turned less friendly. "I think you're the ones who aren't fit parents."

"Goddamn it," Tonja shrieked. "This cunt has no right to talk to me this way. Fuck that!"

Dustin stopped playing with the truck. He looked up at Tonja Kay's reddening face and blazing eyes and started to cry.

"I told you this was fucking ridiculous!" Tonja Kay shouted. "I do not need to convince this cunt that your little bastard would be better off with us. I fucking knew Mother Teresa!"

Kyra got up and retrieved her crying child. Sitting him in her lap, she rocked him against her, covering his ears as she did so.

"This bitch will be begging to give him to us when I

get the network to cancel this bullshit *Do Over* excuse for a show!"

Tonja Kay jumped up and let loose a string of profanities that had even Daniel blanching.

Kyra's eyes narrowed, but she wore an oddly satisfied smile on her face. "I don't know if you talk like that in front of your children, Tonja, but you're not going to talk like that in front of mine ever again."

She stood, still cradling Dustin close. Maddie and Daniel also rose to their feet, although Maddie couldn't quite imagine what was coming next.

"But I'll be happy to play this conversation back for anyone who wants to hear it, including the network," Kyra continued. "I'm not sure either of you will be all that attractive to them once the world finds out you were trying to blackmail me into giving up my child." She looked toward Max's bedroom door and nodded.

Daniel looked nonplussed. Tonja just looked pissed. Maddie couldn't even imagine what her own face looked like.

All of them turned when Max's bedroom door opened and Troy and Anthony emerged.

"Got it! That's a keeper!" Troy had his camera on his shoulder. He gave Kyra a thumbs-up as they moved across the living room, stopping briefly for Anthony to remove wireless microphones from the mantel and the lamp next to where Tonja Kay had been sitting. "Anybody interested in a playback?"

"What the fuck?" Tonja Kay whispered at a much lower volume.

"Hey!" Daniel Deranian said, knitting his brows. "What's going on here, man?"

"We're shooting a reality-TV show here, *man*," Troy

replied. "I shot what just took place. It's my job. And at the moment I'm lovin' it."

Daniel Deranian and Tonja Kay turned to Kyra, their faces painted with shock. This time Maddie didn't think either of them was acting.

"Oh my gosh," Kyra said, her eyes wide in mock surprise. "You mean you didn't realize you'd be on camera?"

She let that hang for a long moment. "I didn't think to warn you." She looked at Daniel over Dustin's head and her tone turned steely. "Any more than you warned me that you and your wife were going to try to take my child away."

Maddie felt her shock begin to give way to relief and amazement. She couldn't believe how cleanly Kyra had managed to turn the tables on the celebrity couple.

"If you ever make a complaint to the network—any network—threaten our livelihoods, or even hint that you want custody, I'll go public with this video. It'll be all over the airwaves and the Internet. I'll send it out by carrier pigeon if I have to."

Kyra locked gazes with Daniel Deranian. "You're Dustin's father and you should be a part of his life," she said. "But Tonja's not welcome, and any relationship will have to be on terms that I'm comfortable with and that will be good for Dustin."

Avery, Deirdre, and Nicole spilled out of the dining room smiling and high-fiving as the movie stars strode into the foyer.

"Well done, Kyra!" Nicole called. Deirdre nodded her agreement. Avery opened the door and ushered the couple out.

There were shouts and the pop of flashbulbs outside. The bodyguards snapped to attention.

From the window they watched the two movie stars pull themselves up, put smiles on their faces, and walk arm in arm down the front steps toward the photographers.

• • •

They came home from the hospital late the next evening far more subdued than they'd been after the Deranian-Kays' departure. The ventilator had been removed and Max had been transferred to a regular room. They took turns sitting with him and trying to snag his attention, but he was weak and only awake for short periods. Maddie had the distinct impression that everyone at the hospital, including Max, was waiting for him to die.

Maddie had fallen into a stupor of her own, staring at the photos she'd placed next to Max's bed. Something about them kept drawing her attention, something that wasn't quite right. Or maybe it was just that she couldn't bear to watch Max slipping away.

"I'm glad Dustin . . . 'kay." His voice was raspy, most likely from the ventilator and lack of use. "Wish Aaron . . . 'kay."

Maddie scooted forward on the chair and leaned closer to Max. "Are you thirsty?" She held the cup of water and the straw up to his lips. He took a few sips, but she could tell from the look in his eyes that he only did it to please her. She held on to his papery-skinned hand, careful not to squeeze it too hard as she tried to entreat him to hang on.

• • •

Back at The Millicent, there was little left to do but worry. The house was finished, the transformation documented. Theoretically, the show was complete and it was time to move on. Yet all of them lingered. Visiting with Max each day, spending their sunsets at the hospital. The only "good thing" any of them could come up with was the possibility of Max recovering and coming home to take possession of The Millicent.

Madeline fell asleep early and slept deeply; her dreams were unusually vivid. At first they were filled with Daniel Deranian and Dustin on an amusement-park roller coaster, their faces side by side, their smiles and shrieks of joy identical. And then she was with Max and Millie in the days after Aaron disappeared. She felt Millie's pain and panic; she felt the desolation. Felt the sharp splintering when the new life she was carrying detached itself from her womb and seeped out of her along with the flood of tears. A barrage of faces floated in a briny bubble of what Maddie somehow knew was amniotic fluid.

She heard Max shout and then Pamela Gentry's face was there, sharp and angry as it shimmered in the light of the chandelier. With a menacing snarl, she landed on The Millicent's Moroccan tile floor and reached behind her polkadot bikini to rip the tail from between her legs so that she could throw it at Max and Millie.

Max's voice sounded in Maddie's ear. *Pamela Gentry wasn't a leave-quietly-with-her-tail-tucked-between-her-legs kind of person.* The words reverberated in her head. They were filled with a desperate despair.

At four A.M., she sat straight up in bed, her sweaty pajamas stuck to her body despite the air-conditioning, the sheets twisted around her. Frantic, she raced downstairs to the dining room table, where Deirdre had left the "House" envelope materials and began to paw through the papers and photos. She needed to be careful and not jump to any conclusions. She tiptoed back upstairs to retrieve Kyra's laptop, her fingers shaking too badly to even attempt to search for confirmation on her phone's tiny screen. But even as she told herself to calm down and not get carried away, deep in her heart she knew that the unbelievable had happened. She'd figured out what had happened to Aaron Golden.

Chapter Thirty-six

A hand shook Avery's shoulder. She kept her eyes closed and resisted, hoping against hope that whoever it was would give up and go away. She did *not* want to hear the words *rise and shine!*

The hand went away and was replaced by the smell of coffee. "Boy, Deirdre, you really play dirty," she said as her eyes flew open. But when they focused on the coffee cup, the hand holding it belonged to Maddie.

"What's going on?" Avery asked, taking in the look of excitement on Maddie's face.

"I need you to wake up!" Maddie said in a rush. "I've been waving this cup under your nose forever. I need to talk to you."

Avery yawned and sat up against the pillows, reaching for the coffee. She took a long, wonderful sip. "Now this is how I'd like to wake up every morning," she said. "If I ever sign another talent contract, I'm writing in 'coffee in bed' every morning."

"There's no time for rhapsodizing," Maddie said quickly, barely taking a moment for a roll of her eyes. "Deirdre's in the bathroom and Nikki's awake. Hurry up and come downstairs. But remind Deirdre to bring her phone. I need her to place a call."

"Isn't it kind of early for all this?" Avery stared down into her now-empty coffee cup.

"You're lucky I didn't wake you up like I wanted to at four A.M.," Maddie replied. "Hurry up and get downstairs." She'd already turned and headed for the door, the cup in her hand. "I'll have another cup waiting for you," she said, holding out the irresistible caffeine carrot.

Avery threw her legs over the side of the bed and sat for a moment yawning. Deirdre came out of the bathroom fully dressed and made up. "We need to head downstairs before Madeline explodes," she said.

Footsteps sounded out in the hallway, followed by a knock on the door. It opened and Nicole poked her head in. "Come on," she said. "Maddie's started sending texts and it isn't pretty." She squinted down at her phone. "Any idea what 'Wnpin chicnw' means?"

"No." Avery moved to the dresser. "But tell her I'll be down in a minute." She pulled on the first clothes she came across then went into the bathroom to wash her face, brush her teeth, and pull a comb through her hair.

In the kitchen she found them all assembled around the kitchen table. As promised, a steaming mug of coffee sat at the empty place. A granola bar sat beside it.

Maddie handed Deirdre her cell phone. "I want you to call Chicago. I have a question I want to ask Jacob Madsen."

"What?" Deirdre looked at her phone and then at

Maddie. "I think you need to explain what's got you all worked up before we call anyone. Besides, it's only, what, seven A.M. in Chicago. I only have his office number. I seriously doubt anyone's there yet."

"What's going on, Mom?" Kyra asked.

Avery looked at Madeline, who was practically levitating with excitement. "Just take a deep breath," she said. "We don't want you hyperventilating. Tell us why you're so worked up."

Madeline nodded. "Yes, yes, of course. Sorry. It's just . . . well, I woke up at four this morning and all of a sudden I just knew . . ." She slowed herself down. "I mean, I thought I knew." She paused, drew a deep breath, then said, "Let me lay it all out for you and you tell me if I'm crazy or not."

When they'd all agreed, Maddie picked up the sheet with Pamela Gentry Madsen's obituary and the photo of her son, Ethan Madsen. "When I first saw this photo of Ethan Madsen, all I thought was that he didn't look much like his mother. But then I spent all those days sitting with Max at the hospital and looking at the age progression of Aaron Golden—who looked so much like his father—and something just kept kind of niggling at the back of my mind. About four o'clock this morning I realized that the person Ethan Madsen looked most like was Aaron Golden's age-progressed picture."

There was a silence.

"But that's . . ." Avery's voice trailed off, as if she was unable to find the right word.

"I know," Maddie said. "It seemed ridiculous. I mean, how could that happen? Unless Max and Pamela had something going on. But Max told me the day the chandelier went up that Pamela had come on to him and that he'd said no. And that before he had to say anything about it, Millie fired Pamela."

"Because the wife isn't always the last to know," Nicole said thoughtfully.

"Max also told me that Pamela Gentry was not a leave-quietly-with-her-tail-tucked-between-her-legs kind of person," Maddie said. "And I don't think she did."

Maddie paused for breath and, Avery thought, to let them catch up. Maddie had been stewing over this since four A.M.; some of them were still waiting for the caffeine to kick in.

"I don't think Pamela left town until she'd gotten her revenge by taking the thing that mattered most to Max and Millie."

"Jesus," Deirdre said.

"Yeah," Maddie replied. "I pulled up the computer copy of the age progression Giraldi had done. And I found a better shot of Ethan Madsen on the design firm's website, and, well, it took me a while, but I finally managed to put them side by side on the screen and they looked uncannily alike." She passed Kyra's laptop, with the split screen around the table.

Avery peered closely. The resemblance was marked.

Madeline clicked the mouse a few times. "This is a photo of Martin Madsen, Pamela's husband." She set the screen in the middle of the table and turned it so that everyone could see. "Ethan doesn't look any more like his father than he looks like his mother."

She paused and let that one sink in. Then she pulled up a shot of Max and Millie. A few more keystrokes and there was a split screen of them next to Ethan.

Avery looked carefully at Ethan Madsen and then at Max and Millie.

"Ethan Madsen looks like Max," Deirdre said.

"With Millie's eyes and coloring," Nicole added.

"Yes," Maddie agreed. "That's exactly what I thought."

"I don't know what's more amazing," Avery said, trying to lighten the moment. "All of this information or the fact that someone who can't text was able to figure all of this out on a computer."

There were a few smiles but no laughter as everyone focused on taking it all in.

"So after I finished freaking out and pacing and barely stopping myself from waking you all up, I Googled a couple of baby-name websites," Maddie continued. "And look at this."

She showed them the two sites she'd bookmarked. "You remember how Max told us that Aaron meant 'strong'? Well, so does Ethan. And both names have Hebrew origins."

"Wow," Avery said.

"And Pamela would have had total access to Max and Millie's house, not only as their friend but as their designer," Deirdre said. "I mean, I always have copies of my client's house keys because you're in and out all the time to take care of things. And she would have known their schedule. It would have just been a matter of watching and waiting for the right time."

"And she'd been here so much over the years, none of the neighbors would have thought anything at all of seeing her car here," Kyra said. "They certainly wouldn't have mentioned it to the police."

"It all fits," Maddie said. "The puzzle pieces started slamming together in a way I never imagined." She looked at them, unable to contain her excitement. "I guess I just need you to tell me that I haven't gone completely around the bend and started jumping to bizarre conclusions."

"This is all way too coincidental to be a coincidence," Kyra said.

"It *is* pretty compelling but everything's circumstantial," Avery felt the need to point out.

"It's not like we have to prove anything in a court of law," Nicole said. "And there's always DNA testing if anyone needs that."

"So who do you want me to call in Chicago?" Deirdre asked.

"I was thinking about how Jacob Madsen said that his father was only in his fifties when he died a year ago," Madeline said.

"Aaron Golden would have been fifty-four," Avery said, her excitement beginning to match Maddie's. "And we know he was a Valentine's Day baby."

"Exactly," Maddie said. "Aaron was born in 1958. He was three when he disappeared in 1961. Even if Pamela had been pregnant when she left and gave birth in Chicago, her biological son would have been at least four years younger than Aaron."

Deirdre pulled out her phone. "So we're calling Jacob Madsen?"

"Yes," Maddie said. "All we want to know is when his father was born. Let's just ask. I guess there's always the chance I've got this all wrong."

They practically held their breaths while Deirdre placed the call and asked for the interior designer. They forced themselves to breathe normally when Deirdre covered the phone and said, "He just arrived. The receptionist is putting the call through to his office."

A few moments later Deirdre was saying hello. "Yes," she said. "The chandelier arrived safe and sound. It looks absolutely fabulous. Yes." A pause. "Yes, I will." She listened intently for a few moments while the rest of them leaned forward, trying to follow the one-sided conversation.

Avery got Deirdre's attention and pointed to all of them and then her ear.

"Oh!" Deirdre said. "We're all here together, Jacob, would you mind if I put you on speakerphone? . . . Thanks," she said, and then they were all hearing Jacob Madsen ask, "You're not all in the pool again, are you?"

"No," Deirdre replied. "And we just have one, kind of odd question for you."

"Okay," he said tentatively.

"You said your father was in his fifties when he died," Deirdre said.

"Yes." They could hear the surprise in Madsen's voice.

"Do you mind telling us his birth date?"

There was no hesitation this time. "February fourteenth, 1958. He was a Valentine's baby."

There was a silence in The Millicent kitchen as they all heard Aaron Golden's birth date echo in the room.

"But didn't your parents meet in Chicago?" Deirdre asked carefully.

"Yes," Jacob Madsen said, "they met here in 1963 and married in 1965."

All of them sat there doing the math.

"But that was my grandmother's second marriage. My father was three when he and my grandmother moved here.

My biological grandfather died down in Miami not too long after my father was born."

. . .

They all crowded into the hospital room wanting to share the news with Max, all of them imagining, Maddie knew, that finally knowing what had happened to Aaron would prove to be that magic elixir that would revive the old man and have him sitting up and telling jokes again. But Max didn't rouse enough for them to tell him anything.

For two days the nurses walked in and out with worried looks on their faces. The doctor shook his head as he read Max's vital signs and moved a stethoscope over his chest. They didn't need a medical person to tell them what they could all see: Max was tethered to life by the slimmest of threads. No one knew when he might let go.

"Max?" Maddie said when the others had gone to the hospital cafeteria. "Max, can you hear me?"

With what looked like great effort, he opened his eyes, then expended considerable energy attempting to focus them. He blinked and Maddie was afraid that his eyes wouldn't open again.

She watched his chest rise and then fall. His breathing seemed shallow, not enough to keep anything going. The beep of the heart monitor seemed hesitant, the sounds as weak as the man whose heart produced them.

She needed to tell him the news. Even if it didn't revive him, he had to know before he died. She glanced up at the clock and then back down at Max. They were running out of time in every possible way.

"We know what happened, Max," she said. "We know what happened to Aaron."

She held her breath at the sight of movement beneath his eyelids. The hand she held in hers curled slightly. "Pamela Gentry took him to Chicago to get back at you and Millie," she said. "She changed his name to Ethan and she raised him as her own."

His hand was dry and cold, the papery skin bruised from the IVs. His lips were cracked and peeling. When he opened his eyes, they were weary, but interested. She felt him present in a way he hadn't been since he'd arrived in the hospital.

His eyes cut to the cup of water on the tray table and she lifted it and positioned the straw between his lips, then watched his Adam's apple move in the thin column of his throat as he drank.

"Yur shure?" His words were slightly slurred and she had to lean close to hear them.

"Yes," Maddie said. She held up the photo of Ethan Madsen so that Max could see it. With great effort he opened his hand and she placed the photo between his fingers.

"Looks like me." He drew a breath to continue. "And Millie."

"Yes."

"But . . . how . . ." He wasn't able to finish the sentence.

"She arrived in Chicago as a widow with a small son. It wouldn't have been all that difficult to get a birth certificate for him back then. Everyone assumed he was hers."

He closed his eyes tightly and a tear seeped out from the corner of one eye.

"I know it doesn't make up for the loss in any way, but he does seem to have been raised in a loving home."

"So wrong," he said. "Never thought . . ."

She saw the effort it took for Max to open his eyes again.

But when he did, some of the old Max burned inside. "Want to see him."

Maddie squeezed his hand gently, wondering why she'd thought this was a good idea. "He died, Max. A year ago, in a car accident."

He closed his eyes again and his lips pulled tight in a grimace of pain. He let go of her hand.

"But he had children. Two of them. Twins. And they're on their way to see you."

He didn't open his eyes but he nodded slightly.

When she thought he'd gone back to sleep, he said, "Want . . . see." And then after another long breath, "Hurry."

· · ·

Avery, Nicole, Madeline, Kyra, and Deirdre rotated in and out of Max's room and the waiting room, each of them taking a turn to tell him just how much he meant to them and whispering to him to hold on as the time, Max's time, ticked away. Andrew brought Dustin in for a few minutes and Max shuddered awake when the little boy cried "Gax!" and put his arms around the old man and buried his face in his neck.

Kyra shot video of their good-bye, and not even the video camera could hide the tears that streamed down her cheeks.

It was late and Maddie was once again sitting with Max when Giraldi and Nicole got back from the airport. The old man had been sleeping. Several times she'd leaned her head against his chest to make sure he was still breathing. Now she leaned forward to rouse him, shaking him gently by the shoulder when the two young people appeared in the doorway.

"Wake up, Max. They're here."

She watched as the two walked into the hospital room and moved toward the bed. When she looked down at Max, he too was watching their approach. If there'd been any doubt at all about their blood connection, it disappeared when the twins drew closer. Max's eyes widened in wonder; his smile was filled with happiness.

His grandson leaned over and took Max's hand in his. "I'm Jacob," he said. "I'm almost thirty and I always wondered where I got this nose." His face split in a fair facsimile of Max's megawatt smile. "And this is my sister," he said as his twin stepped out from behind him.

"Hello," she said in the warm, breathy voice they'd all heard on Max's movies. Her blue eyes shone with intelligence, and although she was petite and fine-boned like her grandmother, there was something larger than life about her. "I'm Pamela Millicent Madsen," she said, leaning forward to place a kiss on Max's cheek. "But everyone calls me Millie."

Epilogue

Max Golden's funeral played to a packed house. The rabbi who had married Max and Millie came out of retirement to officiate and did an impressive stand-up routine of his own, a performance that elicited both tears and laughter. Max's grandchildren sat with Avery, Nicole, Maddie, Kyra, and Deirdre in the front row.

At the cemetery, Max was finally laid to rest next to his Millie, but Maddie had no doubt that Millie had been there the day that their grandchildren arrived and that she'd been waiting for her husband when he'd finally smiled and let go. She imagined them on some heavenly version of a backstage, Millie in one of her fabulous gowns and Max fiddling with his cigar, eager to go on.

She could feel their essence in The Millicent as they showed Jake and Millie the home that now belonged to them. She and Nicole smiled at the twins' enthusiasm while Deirdre and Avery basked in their praise. If ever there had been perfect recipients for this particular gift, it was these two interior designers. Max had "built it" and they had, indeed, come.

Before the twins left for the airport, Kyra presented them with a videotape of their grandparents' favorite performances, which she'd labeled simply *The Best of M&M*.

"Not to be confused with Eminem," Avery quipped as she presented them with a key to The Millicent and promised to drop the second in the mail the following morning on her way out of town.

The farewell with the network crew was less emotionally fraught. In the foyer Troy pulled out a videotape and handed it to Kyra. "These are the outtakes," he said gruffly. "The footage I don't think Lisa Hogan or the network really need to see."

Kyra looked down at the list of video cuts. " 'Avery's Chest'?" she read aloud.

"It's mostly from the premiere party," Troy explained at Avery's strangled gasp. "Lisa Hogan made me shoot it, but I don't really see how it's germane to the series."

Avery blew out a sigh of relief along with a kiss.

" 'Deranian in Drag and Custody Conversation'?" Kyra read, looking at the cameraman in surprise. "You're not giving them footage of Daniel?"

Troy shrugged. "I thought you might want to hold on to it. You know, just in case he or Potty Mouth forgets what they agreed to."

"But won't the network be upset that you don't have anything of him?" Deirdre asked.

"I'm not worried about it," Troy said. "The footage I got of the Amherst thing makes me pretty much golden as far as the network is concerned. I've already been offered some primo projects to choose from." He looked down for a moment before looking into Kyra's eyes again. "If you want, you could sit in with me when we do the final editing of the shows. I think that would help us create a better balance between our footage and yours."

Kyra smiled with pleasure. "I'd like that," she said. "I still can't believe I didn't realize why you'd left the camera sitting on the piano. Or notice that it was recording. I must have been off my game."

"Well, there was a madman with a gun threatening your child," Troy said. "It's understandable."

Madeline looked over Kyra's shoulder at the list as Kyra read the last entry aloud. It was "Kitchen Catfight."

Maddie sighed in relief. "You're good boys," she said, giving Troy and Anthony a hug. "Thank you for everything."

"Ditto," said Avery, going up on tiptoe to give both crew members a hug.

"Yes, it's very reassuring to know that we'll only look marginally ridiculous," Nicole said drily.

"Your tackle of Amherst was pretty impressive," Anthony said.

"I agree," Deirdre teased. "You're a natural."

"Great," Nicole said. "If *Do Over* doesn't get picked up, maybe I'll give the NFL a go."

• • •

"Rise and shine!" It was still dark the next morning when Avery felt a hand on her shoulder and heard Deirdre's too-cheery voice.

"No. Not yet. I—"

"Come on, sleepyhead." Maddie's voice joined Deirdre's.

The smell of freshly brewed coffee tickled her nostrils. Her eyes, the traitors, sprang open and she was staring into the lens of Kyra's video camera.

"Jeez, really?" Avery groaned. "I thought the shooting was over." She sat up and Madeline placed the cup of coffee in her hands. Dustin, who stood with one arm wrapped around his mother's leg, offered her a sunny smile and watched her raise the cup to her lips.

"It's not over until we lock the front door behind us," Kyra said. "I'm not prepared to witness what may be my last sunrise on Miami Beach without a camera in my hand."

"Just a few more sips," Maddie said in her best mother voice. "I'll add whatever's left to a to-go cup. We've only got about twenty minutes before the sun comes up."

"Have I mentioned that I think sunsets are far more civilized than sunrises?" Avery asked as she put a hand up to block the camera lens and climbed out of bed.

"Yes, I think you've made that clear," Deirdre said. "And you'll see plenty of them when we get to Bella Flora. I believe Chase already had a case of Cheez Doodles delivered. In a way it's lucky that offer on Bella Flora fell through. It's good to have a place to stay while we wait to hear what's happening with the show. Seeing as how some of us are somewhat . . . homeless . . . at the moment."

They left Andrew sleeping for one last hour and walked to the beach, where they settled on a blanket just in time to see the first exploratory rays of the sun ease up out of the ocean. Dustin toddled happily on the sand, plopping down occasionally before clambering back up again.

"There is something life affirming about witnessing the very beginnings of a new day," Madeline said, her gaze fixed on the golden ball rising in front of them. "It makes almost anything seem possible." Although she spoke of hope, they could all hear the sadness in her voice.

"Maybe we should stop at Bella Flora for a while before we go home," Kyra said. "How long will you and Deirdre be there, Avery?"

"I don't know," Avery said. "Chase and Jeff have invited us to work on the new development they're building. I can help design the spec homes and Deirdre's offered to handle the interior design. I'm not sure where Chase and I are really headed—he's got so many other commitments—but it'll be nice to be in the same place at least for a while. And there's something kind of comforting about the idea of working with him in the business our fathers built."

She looked at Deirdre. The fact that she was actually looking forward to being there with her mother was the oddest part of all.

"It'll be great," Deirdre said. "There's a certain symmetry to being involved in the company that Peter started. I did my first design work on his starter homes."

Avery suppressed the automatic remark about how easily Deirdre had left that with a long sip of coffee, and was rewarded with a smile of approval from Maddie. Maybe it was time to sign up for a course in daughter-hood.

"Why don't you stop over in Pass-a-Grille for a while?" Avery asked Maddie, noting the resignation in her eyes and the resolute set of her mouth.

"No, we need to get back. I'll have to get Andrew ready to go back to college. And there are things that need to be settled."

They all knew she was referring to the absent Steve, but her tone made it clear that she was not ready to discuss it.

"Fine," Nicole said, never one to be stopped by something as insubstantial as a tone of voice. "But once you kick his butt, I say you should take at least a vacation at Bella Flora while it still belongs to us." She looked up at the sky, which had lightened to a pale watercolor blue. The ocean glittered with golden bits of sun. "Giraldi invited me to stay with him for a while."

Avery saw her blush and had to bite back a laugh.

"But then I thought I'd head up to Bella Flora," Nikki continued. "Maybe if it hasn't sold yet, we could do Thanksgiving or Christmas there. I wouldn't mind some moral support when we hear whether *Do Over* is going to continue."

"I didn't think the west coast of Florida was your style," Kyra said.

"I'm not sure I *have* a style anymore," Nicole replied.

Avery smiled again. Maybe this whole sunrise thing wasn't so bad after all. "I must say, for a group of people who need money as badly as we all do, no one seems in any big hurry to see Bella Flora sell."

There was laughter and the mood lightened. Together they'd helped Max fulfill his Millie's dying wish, brought another spectacular house back to life, and in the process once again shored up their own lives. They sipped their coffees and turned their attention to the sky, watching it turn bright with promise. Like their friendship, the glowing sun warmed them.

Together they breathed in the new day.

OCEAN BEACH

by Wendy Wax

DISCUSSION QUESTIONS

1. During Madeline and Steve's twenty-six-year wedding anniversary celebration, Madeline recalls how the past year and a half had been difficult and that "it had reframed an entire lifetime of memories." Do you think that difficult moments in life can completely change how you remember the past? Are the difficulties something you work to forget or are they something that affects your future as well?

2. What do you think about Max and Millie's relationship? How did the emotional prologue set the tone of the novel?

3. When Avery, Nicole, Kyra, and Deirdre arrive at The Millicent to tape *Do Over*, they find themselves as part of a reality show instead of a show about a renovation. What are your opinions about reality shows? Do you think they have value in our society? Should those featured have the right to have "off-limits" areas?

4. Do you think Nicole made the right decision when she turned her brother in to Special Agent Joe Giraldi? Could you have done that? Do you think it was a conflict of interest that Joe romantically pursued Nicole after her brother went to jail?

5. How did you feel when Daniel Deranian was introduced? Do you feel like his feelings were genuine regarding Dustin and Kyra? Do you sympathize with Tonja at all?

6. Why did Deirdre ask Madeline to teach her how to be a real mother? Can someone be taught how to be a parent? How can one better prepare to become a parent?

7. Is there a correlation between renovating The Millicent and the characters' personal lives? What role does Max's character play in regard to their development?

8. Describe the changes in Avery and Deirdre's relationship throughout the novel. Was the shooting the turning point or were there signs of change before that incident?

9. Prior to reading this novel, what did you know about cold-case investigations? How long would you continue to search for someone you loved?

10. How did Aaron's disappearance shape Max and Millie's lives? How would their lives have been different if he had never disappeared?

11. Were you surprised when Steve said he wasn't going to see his family after the shooting? What do you think his actual motivations were for not doing this? Was it because he never wanted Madeline to do the show to begin with?

12. When Aaron's true identity was revealed, what was your reaction?

13. Imagine the lives of the characters after the novel. How do they unfold? Do Madeline and Steve stay married? Will Daniel come back into Kyra's life? Do Avery and Deirdre continue to stay close? What happens with Nicole's business?

Chapter One

As a child, Samantha Jackson Davis loved fairy tales as much as the next girl. She just hadn't expected to end up in one.

Every morning when her eyes fluttered open and every night before she closed them to go to sleep, Samantha marveled at her good fortune. In a Disney version of the airline passenger held up in security just long enough to miss the plane that goes down, or the driver who runs back for a forgotten cell phone and barely avoids a deadly ten-car pileup, Samantha averted disaster in the once-upon-a-time way: she married the prince.

Over the past twenty-five years Samantha had sometimes wished she'd spent a little more time and energy considering alternatives. But when your world comes crashing down around you at the age of twenty-one, deep thinking and soul-searching are rarely your first response.

There was plenty of precedent for prince-marrying in the fairy-tale world. Sleeping Beauty had not ignored the prince's kiss in favor of a few more years of shut-eye. Cinderella never considered refusing to try on the glass slipper. And Snow White didn't bat an eyelash at moving in with those seven little men.

It wasn't as if Samantha had gone out searching for a man to rescue her and her siblings when their world fell apart. She hadn't feigned a poisoned apple, induced sleep, or gotten herself locked in a tower with only her hair as a means of escape. She hadn't attempted to hide how desperate her situation was. But the fact remained that when the handsome prince (in the form of an old family friend who had even older family money) rode up on his white horse (which had been cleverly disguised as a Mercedes convertible), she had not turned down the ride.

The fact that she hadn't loved the prince at the time he carried her over the threshold of their starter castle was something she tried not to think about. She'd been trying not to think about it pretty much every day for the last twenty-five years.

• • •

Samantha smiled sleepily that early September morning when her husband's lips brushed her forehead before he left for the office, but she didn't get up. Instead she lay in bed watching beams of sunlight dance across the wooden floors of the master bedroom, breathing in the scent of freshly brewed coffee that wafted from the kitchen, and listening to the muted sound of traffic twelve floors below on Peachtree Street as she pushed aside all traces of regret and guilt and renewed her vow to make Jonathan Davis happy, his life smooth, and his confidence in his choice of her unshaken.

This, of course, required a great deal of organization and focus, many hours of volunteer work, and now that she was on the downhill slide toward fifty, ever greater amounts of "maintenance." Today's efforts would begin with an hour of targeted torture courtesy of her trainer Michael and would be followed by laser, nail, and hair appointments. Since it was Wednesday, her morning maintenance and afternoon committee meetings would be punctuated by a much-dreaded-but-never-complained-about weekly lunch with her mother-in-law. Which would last exactly one hour but would feel more like three.

Samantha padded into the kitchen of their current "castle," which took up the entire top floor of the Alexander, a beautifully renovated Beaux Arts and Renaissance Revival–styled apartment building in the center of Midtown Atlanta.

When it opened in 1913, the Alexander, with its hot and cold running water, steam heat, elevators, and electric lights, had been billed as one of the South's most luxurious apartments. Like much of mid- and downtown Atlanta, it had fallen on hard times but had been "saved" in the eighties when a bottom-fishing developer bought it, converted it to condos, and began the first of an ongoing round of renovations.

A little over ten years ago Samantha and her prince spent a year turning the high-ceilinged, light-filled, and architecturally detailed twelfth-floor units into a four-bedroom, five-bath, amenity-filled home with three-hundred-sixty-degree views and north- and south-facing terraces.

For Samantha its most prized feature was its location in

the midst of trendy shops, galleries, and restaurants as well as its comfortable, but not offensive, distance from Belle-wood, Jonathan's ancestral home in Buckhead, one of Atlanta's toniest and oldest suburbs, where both of them had grown up and where his often-outspoken mother still reigned.

The doorbell rang. As Samantha went to answer it she pushed aside thoughts of Cynthia Davis and gave herself a silent but spirited pep talk. She'd married into Atlanta royalty. Her prince was attractive and generous. A difficult mother-in-law and a life built around pleasing others was a small price to pay for the fairy-tale life she led. As Sheryl Crow so aptly put it, the secret wasn't having what you wanted but wanting what you got.

. . .

Shortly after the morning's training session ended, Samantha rode a mahogany-paneled elevator down to the Alexander's marbled lobby. The gurgle of the atrium fountain muffled the click of her heels on the polished surface as she took in the surprisingly contemporary high-backed banquette that encircled the deliciously carved fountain. Conversation groups of club chairs and sofas, separated by large potted palms, softened the elegant space. A burled walnut security desk, manned twenty-four-seven, sat just inside the en-trance. The concierge desk sat in the opposite corner and commanded a view of the lobby as well as the short hall that accessed the parking garage and the elevators.

"Good morning, madam." Edward Parker's British accent was clipped, his suit perfectly tailored, his starched shirt crisp. His manner was deferential but friendly. A relatively recent addition to the Alexander, the concierge was tall and dark with rugged good looks that seemed at odds with his dignified air. "Shall I have your car brought around?"

"Thank you." She was of course capable of simply going into the Alexander's parking garage to retrieve her own car, but the last time she'd insisted on doing this Edward had looked genuinely disappointed, and the minutes saved would come in handy if she ran behind or hit traffic between appointments or on the way to lunch with her mother-in-law. Punctuality was a virtue that Cynthia Davis prized; tardiness a vice to be stamped out at all cost.

"Very good," he said, his brown eyes warm, his whitetoothed smile decidedly un-British. When he lost some of the stiff upper lip that seemed welded to his accent and his occupation, there was a rakish George Clooney–ness about him. Although Parker was in his early fifties, Samantha's younger sister Meredith had pronounced him both "hot" and "dishy."

Samantha arrived at the Piedmont Driving Club—where the Davises had belonged since its inception as a gentleman's club in the late 1880s—ten minutes before noon, buffed, coifed, and polished. Though she was early, her mother-in-law was already seated at a favored table with her back to the window, the better to keep an eye on the room's comings and goings. Samantha smiled and leaned down to kiss her mother-in-law's rouged cheek. Cynthia Davis might be seventy-five, but she was still formidable. Like her son and the husband she'd already outlived for a decade, she could drive a golf ball straight down a fairway and had a tennis backhand that was almost as sharp as her tongue. Born into one of Atlanta's oldest and most revered families and married into another, she remained a snob at heart; one who liked to remind anyone who would listen that "you can't make a silk purse out of a sow's ear" and the vaguer but more ominous "breeding will out." Samantha had heard these summations applied to everything from a disappointing fund-raiser to the scandal that had ensued when Samantha's father, Davis & Davis's managing partner, had dipped into client trust accounts, almost ruining the firm that had been in the Davis family since shortly after the Civil War. He'd been under investigation when his car had run off the road just a few miles from home, killing both him and Samantha's mother instantly.

Cynthia Davis had been horrified when her only son chose to marry the daughter of onetime friends who had disgraced themselves publicly before dying spectacularly. Samantha's failure to produce a grandchild had made her even less desirable in her mother-in-law's eyes.

Samantha had barely settled into her seat when Cynthia leveled her steeliest look at her and asked, "What do you intend to do about Hunter and Meredith?"

"Do?" Samantha ordered a glass of Chardonnay. Hearing her brother and sister's names on her mother-in-law's lips made her regret she could have only one glass. As she considered possible replies, she made a mental note not to schedule anything after their weekly lunch in the future so that she could drink as much as the meal required.

"I don't believe either of them are employed at the moment, are they?" Cynthia asked, as if there might be some doubt. For Cynthia Davis, idleness was an even greater personality defect than lack of income.

"Not exactly, no."

"Then perhaps we need to put our heads together to come up with something for them to do." This was not a question. "After all, Hunter's last venture did show some . . . promise." Cynthia was referring to her brother's recent attempt to launch a chain of soul food/sushi restaurants in the Midwest, which had ended badly. Hunter could make a better first impression than almost anyone she knew and could sell almost anything while in the first flush of enthusiasm. Unfortunately, follow-through was not his forte.

Samantha smiled and nodded as if Cynthia's comment had been meant as a compliment, and perhaps it had been. Her mother-in-law did not approve of Hunter Jackson, or the money Jonathan spent on Hunter's upkeep, but she was not immune to Hunter's charm.

The basket of corn bread and rolls that neither of them would touch arrived. A group of women stopped by the table to pay their respects on their way out.

"Don't you think it's time we find Meredith an opportunity here in Atlanta where she can make use of her degree? She did spend quite a lot of time in school acquiring it." Cynthia had been furious when she'd realized the size of the tuition Jonathan had paid for Samantha's younger sister to receive a master's degree in Historic Preservation from the College of Charleston. But while Jonathan loved his mother and preferred her happy—or at least satisfied— he didn't ask her input on his decisions or bow to her wishes unless they happened to coincide with his.

"I don't imagine the Atlanta Preservation Board has heard about her little contretemps in Charleston yet. Maybe I could put a word in." This was so Cynthia—first the slap down, then the oddly magnanimous gesture. Samantha allowed herself another measured sip of wine. At least Cynthia hadn't brought up her sister's taste in men.

"And that last boy she brought to the Labor Day party at the club?" Cynthia shook her head sadly. "Really, dear.

Meredith is quite presentable when she tries. I'd think she might aim a little higher."

Samantha swallowed slowly, bracing for the "bless her heart" that Cynthia all too often tacked on to the end of Meredith's name; the final condemnation of her sister and the job Samantha had done raising her. A job for which she'd been unprepared and which had led her to marry the first prince who had galloped to her aid.

Chapter Two

Claire Walker had barely placed one dyed-to-match silk pump on the church aisle when she realized she was making a big mistake. Unable to find the courage to call off the ceremony, she'd walked as slowly as she could down the aisle to Daniel Walker's side. When she got there, she smiled and said "I do" even though she didn't.

That was nineteen years ago, and to this day she could still remember the lightning bolt of revelation, the bitter taste of the words she couldn't speak, and her fear that she might gag on them as she struggled to swallow them. For a crazed moment she'd imagined them bubbling up and spewing all over the minister, Daniel, and the two-thousand-dollar dress that her mother, who had eloped with Claire's father and deeply regretted not having a church wedding, had insisted on buying her.

She still wasn't sure how she made it through the ceremony and reception, but by the time the limo arrived to whisk them to the airport, she could hardly refuse to go on the island honeymoon that Daniel's parents had given them. Nor could she maintain the fiction of a weeklong headache, which was how she'd come home from Belize pregnant with Hailey.

She'd tried to convince herself that love and respect weren't absolute requirements for a successful marriage, but three years later, holding her two-year-old daughter in her arms, she'd done what she should have done that day at church; she apologized for the screwup and with equal parts fear, regret, and relief sundered what should have never been joined together.

Sixteen years of single parenthood on a shoestring had followed.

Today her life had changed again. Tonight she stood on the small balcony of the Midtown Atlanta condo she'd spent the Labor Day weekend moving into, trying to come to terms with that change.

She took an exploratory breath of the night air. It was thick with humidity, redolent with the aroma of marinara from a nearby Italian restaurant, car exhaust, and possibility. Bits of music arrived on the warm breeze, carried from one of the bars over on Crescent Avenue. Below on Peachtree, horns sounded. A siren blared. Voices rose from the sidewalk where despite the late hour a steady stream of people walked alone, in pairs, in groups; all of them going somewhere to do something.

Here, dark and quiet were not synonymous.

"You are so not in suburbia anymore," she whispered on another breath of night air. Here, people were living the kind of life that she'd barely allowed herself to imagine. A frisson of excitement ran through her and she leaned farther out over the railing, not wanting to miss a thing. She'd have to be very careful not to accidentally click her heels together three times and end up back where she'd come from.

Her cell phone rang and she hurried inside. As she hunted for the instrument, a part of her brain reveled in the fresh-paint smell of her new home, the sparkle of the tall windows that overlooked Peachtree, the gleam of the polished wood floor.

She stepped around the new gray flannel sofa and area rug from West Elm, scanned the Crate & Barrel dining room table that would double as her office, and checked the nightstand next to the brand-new never-before-slept-on-by-anyone queen bed, which she'd tucked into a corner behind a tri-fold screen.

Sidestepping half-opened boxes, she searched the stand on which her new flat-screen TV perched and the bookcases that bracketed the Murphy bed that would be her daughter Hailey's, when she came home from college. *College.*

Claire exhaled heavily. Breathed in shakily. Out with the old life. In with the new.

She found the phone hidden behind a box on the kitchen counter—a lovely dappled granite that she'd fallen in love with the first time she'd entered the studio apartment—and managed to answer it before it went to voicemail.

"Hi, Mom." Her daughter's voice was achingly familiar and surprisingly grown-up after only two weeks in Chicago at Northwestern University.

Claire reached for a framed photo that lay on the counter and was intended for the nightstand. It was from Hailey's high school graduation and showed the two of them with their arms slung around one another's shoulder staring happily into the camera. They were both of average height and had the same even features and wide smiles above pointed, some might say determined, chins. Their heads were bent together in a tangle of hair—Hailey's long and smooth, the blond tinged with honey overtones, Claire's a shade that resembled dishwater and which she kept cut in short, low-maintenance layers.

Claire listened to the hum of happiness that infused Hailey's voice. It made her happy just to hear it. It also made her aware of just how alone she was.

No. Claire silently rejected the word and all its synonyms. She refused to be lonely. No new beginning was without its bumps.

"How was the move?" Hailey asked.

"Good," Claire replied. When you'd sold or given away 95 percent of your former life and arranged to have most of your new life delivered, moving wasn't particularly onerous. She'd been able to fit the few things she couldn't part with in her SUV.

"Have you met any of your neighbors?" Hailey asked. She had helped her search for a rental unit before she'd left for Chicago, tramping in and out of every unit in the geographical area Claire had outlined on her map. They'd made the choice together over cardboard containers of pad Thai and panang chicken, just as they'd made so many other decisions over their years of dynamic duo–dom.

"Not really. The concierge has been helpful and the other residents seem nice enough." There seemed to be a diverse group of owners and tenants, which was part of what had attracted her to the building. And while Claire hadn't seen anyone who looked like they were counting their pennies quite as carefully as she was—no one had turned up a nose or been unfriendly.

"Edward Parker is way hot," Hailey said, turning the conversation back to the concierge. "That British accent is fabulous." She giggled. "I could probably be okay with him for a stepdad." She said this as if it were only a matter of time before she had one; just as she had since she turned five and began trying to picture pretty much every man they ran into—including her soccer coach, the mailman, and her favorite elementary school janitor—as potential husband material for her mother.

"I've talked to him exactly twice for about five minutes each time," Claire pointed out.

"But he's cute, right?" Hailey said.

"So are puppies, but I don't have the time or energy to housebreak one." Even Claire had to smile as she pictured leading the elegant Englishman to a pile of newspaper or out to a strip of green between buildings and ordering him to "piddle." "I'm not here to get married, I'm here to write," Claire reminded her daughter. Somehow in the years filled with work and single parenting that added up to too much stress and too little sleep, Claire had managed to write two historical romance novels and see them published. Writing *Highland Kiss* and *Highland Hellion* had been her great escape from the often overwhelming responsibilities of her real life; a chance to live in another time and place and to experience the kind of romantic love and devotion that people like her could only dream about; the kind of love that led to happily-ever-after.

"You're there to have a life, too," Hailey added.

"I already have a life."

"No, you had Grandmom and Grandpop to take care of all those years before they died. And you've had me and everything you had to do to take care of me," Hailey corrected. "That's not a life. Now it's your turn to just take care of you." There was a brief pause. "Or find someone else who will."

"I'm going to ignore just how chauvinistic that statement was to say that raising you has been a privilege and an honor. And I'm still here to take care of you when you need it," Claire said.

"I'd rather you write your breakout bestseller and find some hot men to go out with," Hailey replied. "And FYI, I don't think those things are mutually exclusive."

"God," Claire said, feigning displeasure. "How did you turn into such a relentless optimist?"

"I learned it from the same woman I learned everything else from," Hailey said quietly. "You deserve the best, Mom. I hope you're going to go for it."

A silence fell, reminding Claire just how far away her daughter was and how completely their life had changed. She'd sold their home, bought what she needed to start fresh, and had exactly enough money left over to pay the rent on this condo for one year. That meant she had three hundred and sixty-five days to plot and write a new and hopefully bestselling novel.

"One thing at a time," she said, falling back on the adage turned mantra that she'd used to get over each new hurdle. To put one foot in front of the other. To take care of increasingly infirm parents and raise her daughter alone. To keep going no matter how tired she was or how short of cash.

Claire plugged in her earbuds and tucked her cell phone in the pocket of her jeans. "Tell me about your classes while I make up the bed," she said as she located the box marked *sheets* and ripped off the packing tape. "Did you finish that paper for sociology?"

Hailey chattered happily while Claire smoothed on the bottom and top sheets, slipped pillowcases over the pillows, and arranged the comforter, turning one corner down invitingly. The bed might be new, but the sheets were well worn and familiar.

Moving into the bathroom, she laid out a towel and stacked the others in the linen closet, then arranged her toiletries on the bathroom counter. She'd do just what she had to tonight and tackle the rest in the morning. As they talked, Claire focused on Hailey's voice and her obvious happiness and knew that Hailey was hearing the same in hers. Both of them were poised to add a new and exciting chapter to their lives.

Hailey yawned midsentence and Claire glanced at the closest clock. It was getting late.

"I think it's time for both of us to turn in," she said when Hailey yawned a second time.

"Okay." The word was followed by another yawn. "G'night, Mom. I'll text you tomorrow."

"Night-night, sweetheart," she said automatically as she had so many times over the years. And then despite the fact that her daughter was eighteen and too grown-up and too far away to be tucked in, she finished with the same non-sensical cliché she'd uttered when the bedtime story was over and the lamp turned off. "Sleep tight. Don't let the bedbugs bite."

The line disconnected and Claire stood alone in the center of the cluttered condo. *Hers, all hers.* A thrill of anticipation coursed through her. How in the world would she ever calm down enough to fall asleep?

"Don't be a goon," she said aloud as she plugged in the Snoopy night-light that had always glowed in a corner of Hailey's room and that Claire had not been able to throw away. "You wanted a new life and you've got one."

Now all she had to do was hurry up and go to sleep so

that she could wake up tomorrow morning and start making the most of it.

· · ·

Claire gave herself two full days to unpack, hang her artwork and photos, and organize the kitchen. She slept fitfully both nights, thrown off by each unfamiliar noise that reached her from within the building and the streets below. Each time she woke she had to remind herself where she was. Then she would look around the apartment and consciously think the word "home," but as excited as she was to be here, her brain was not fooled. Home was the house on Juniper Lane with the fenced backyard and the cul-de-sac out front that filled with kids each evening after dinner.

In between bouts of unpacking she explored the Alexander, trying to make it familiar and vowing to use the fitness room, the pool, and the clubroom with its big-screen TV, kitchen, and bar, which was available for entertaining. Even though she didn't know enough people in this part of town to fill her tiny bathroom.

Late on the second afternoon she stood in the center of her new home and pronounced it "done." Her laptop and a yellow pad of character notes and ideas sat on the dining room table/desk right next to the brocade-covered journal that Hailey had given her to record her new life.

Other than her brief conversations with Hailey, a food-and-drink order on a quick stroll up Peachtree, and a deep Dumpster discussion with Edward Parker, she hadn't really communicated with anyone. She cleared her throat just to make sure her vocal cords still worked.

"Okay," she said aloud just to confirm that everything was operational, "you're going to walk to Piedmont Park and find a nice shady spot where you can prime your pump by writing in your journal." Eager to get outside, she put on her sneakers, tucked the journal and a pen into her cross-body bag, and left the condo. In the lobby, she strode purposefully with her chin up and her eyes on the front door; a woman on a mission. Which may have been why she didn't see whatever it was that got tangled in her feet. Or understand how she ended up on the hard marble floor with something small and heavy on top of her and an unfamiliar woman's voice yelling in the distance.

On the brink of ruin, three very different women
discover themselves where they least expect…
at Ten Beach Road.

FROM BESTSELLING AUTHOR
WENDY WAX

TEN BEACH ROAD

Madeline, Avery, and Nicole are strangers to one another, but they have one thing in common. They each
wake up one morning to discover that their life savings
have vanished, along with their trusted financial manager…leaving them with nothing but co-ownership of a
dilapidated beachfront house.

No one is going to save them but themselves. Determined to fight back, they throw their lots in together
and take on the challenge of restoring the historic mansion to its former glory. But just as they begin to rein-
vent themselves and discover the power of friendship,
their secrets threaten to tear down their trust and destroy their lives a second time.

PRAISE FOR *TEN BEACH ROAD*

"[A] warm, wry novel."   —*St. Petersburg Times*

"Fun…heartwarming…A loving tribute to friendship and the
power of the female spirit."   —*Las Vegas Review-Journal*

AuthorWendyWax.com
facebook.com/AuthorWendyWax

penguin.com

M1256T0213